The Undergrou

Producer & International Distributor
eBookPro Publishing
www.ebook-pro.com

The Underground Engineer
Ruth Eshel

Translation: Shira Carmen Aji
Contact: eshel.ruth@gmail.com
ISBN 9798370813467

I would like to thank my husband and good friend, Reuven. Without his support, the remarkable advice he gave me, and the financial support he provided me, this book would not have been published. I would also like to thank Nava Zuckerman, Gaby Aldor, and Yosi Zaider, who read my drafts, gave me crucial comments, and encouraged me. Likewise, I want to thank Shai Amit and the "Notsa Vakeset" (Feather and Inkwell) prose writing course, which opened up the prose writing world to me.

The book is a novel based on a combination of my imagination and my memories of my father, Jenka, his archive, and professional advice from my husband, Reuven Eshel, primarily regarding the technical side of things. I was aided in describing Jenka's travels by the rich documentation of his voyages to Northern Africa and Europe and by the article that he wrote for Geographical Magazine about his incredible journey to India. The chapter about my father's activities in the British Admiralty during World War II is based on original documents and photographs. His activities in the Haganah, the Science Corps, and Rafael rely on audio interviews and films about him, and on information from Avraham Levi, Moshe Ritterband, Aharonchik Donagi, Elyashiv Shacham, David Barak, Moshe Zarhy, Uzi Sharon, Shlomo Gur, and Mordechai Sharoni. I drew further details from the books of Munya Mardor ("On an Unknown Mission" and "Rafael") and from newspaper articles. The Ilioff family's experiences are based on photographs, letters, newspaper articles, and an interview I conducted with Bosa (Hannah) Ilioff.

Ruth Eshel

Contents

Chapter 1: Love Story

A young woman walked down the avenue in broad, determined steps, wearing a long dark winter coat with a beaver-fur collar and a wide-brimmed hat. Despite the early morning hour, the workers had already shoveled the snow that had fallen that night and piled it into mounds. Anna raised her head up toward the tall trees, which towered like a guard of honor along the path. From the corner of her eye, she could see little clumps of snow accumulated on the treetops like birds' nests. Soon, she would see Ben-Zion, and the little bird within her began to sing.

A black blot appeared between the branches of the white trees, coming in and out of sight, its size changing as the road twisted and turned. She picked up her pace. The weather was truly freezing. Now she could see the immense Kharkiv prison building. In her mind's eye, she could see Ben-Zion: short, thin, nimble, clever, resourceful. David, who could handle the Russian Goliaths. She'd brought him pastries, meat, fruit, and warm clothes in the large bag on her shoulder.

Thoughts ran through her mind, and she let them flow. The year 1905 was coming to an end. Two years ago, thousands of proud Russian soldiers had marched through the city streets heading toward Manchuria. Uniforms ironed, polished boots shining, rifles with protruding bayonets slung over their shoulders, they'd smiled at the cheering girls who flung flowers to them. Who would have believed that the Russian military, the largest army in the world, would be defeated by the little Japanese with their slanted eyes? If the streets could talk, they would tell stories of hundreds of carts laden with wounded young men making their way back to Russia.

She'd met him two months ago while accompanying her friends to visit Jewish political prisoners. It was the first time she had met any young people who did not belong to her social circle. He was the son of a poor family of Jewish immigrants who came from eastern Russia. He had a serious look and rarely smiled. His black eyes were set above high cheekbones, like those of the Tatar people. "And perhaps Genghis Khan made a nightly visit to one of his ancestors?" she'd asked, laughing as she'd brushed his black hair from his temples. He'd raised his right eyebrow, opened his eyes in astonishment, shook his head slightly from side to side, and maybe even smiled slightly. He spoke only when he had something to say and was straightforward. With her, everything was instinctive and impulsive.

The accelerated walk had tired her. She took off her hat, revealing her face; she had a delicate, somewhat fanciful countenance framed by brown hair gathered lightly into a bun at the back of her neck. The bag was heavy. She sat down. It was a pity that she hadn't taken her mother's carriage, but to pull up in a carriage to visit a prisoner? She grinned to herself and closed her eyes. There wasn't much further to walk, yet she decided to continue sitting. Her thoughts wouldn't let her alone; they stacked up inside her mind in layers. No matter how much she attempted to shake them off, they came crawling back, stuffing her brain. She just hoped she wouldn't develop anxiety and shortness of breath like her mother. Anna was concerned about the political situation in Russia. The people were divided, and hatred was bubbling. The intelligentsia and many of the aristocracy believed in enlightened communism, which would promote equal rights for all citizens. They supported the liberal communist faction led by Julius Martov. While they were busy philosophizing about what should be permitted and what forbidden, Ilyich Lenin managed to successfully unite the communist extremists – the Bolsheviks. Her Ben-Zion was also a Bolshevik. He often explained enthusiastically that the workers would lead to a dictatorship of the proletariat, and a classless society would rise.

She patted her coat lightly, removing the snowflakes that clung to it. She opened the bag, reached in with her hand, and felt that moisture had started to seep inside. She had to hurry up. Ideas and words without actions were worthless, Ben-Zion always told her. She idolized him for this. She was all talk, but he was a man of action. He took to the streets to protest against the Czar; he was prepared to be beaten up and thrown in jail. He dreamed of becoming a doctor. "Who will finance your studies?" she had questioned him with the practicality of a woman. He had bowed his head and took a deep breath. "When the revolution succeeds, there will be civic equality, and higher education will be available to everyone," he had whispered and looked her straight in the eyes with the devotion of a true believer. She hadn't told him that she'd applied to study at a women's medical school that had opened in St. Petersburg. She hadn't received an answer yet and feared she would be rejected because the quota for Jewish students had been limited at all universities. But she wasn't worried. Her family could afford to send her to a university in Germany or Switzerland.

As she approached the building, she saw women wearing layers of clothing. It was hard to tell who was old and who was young; they carried large bags of provisions. The guards recognized her. She walked down the corridors quickly; she knew her way. There is no time to waste. Ben-Zion sat before her, upright and focused. She sat down before him, upright, her heart beating fast. There were so many things to say.

*

The home of Clara and Professor Alexander Ilioff was located in a prestigious district in Kharkiv. The front door was adorned with Baroque-style moldings. There was a large iron gate on the side of the building and behind it, a square for the carriage and horses. At the back of the house was an entrance for the servants and a staircase leading to the basement kitchen. A spacious living room, dining room, and library were on the ground floor. A large staircase, its railing decorated with moldings, led to the second floor, which had six rooms – the master bedroom, Anna's room, Daniel's, Yasha's, Ilioff's study, and another room for guests. On the top floor were the servants' quarters.

Clara climbed the stairs to Ilioff's study. Since the closure of the Polytechnic University, due to student demonstrations supporting the communists, the home study had been turned into an experimental laboratory. The room was located at the end of the left corridor, and Ilioff had chosen it because of the light, which shone through the two large windows from two sides. She knocked on the door but did not wait for him to respond, "Come in, Clarushka," or "Not now, please." Concentrated and relaxed, wearing a white robe, he held a glass test tube full of liquid. She took a deep breath as if trying to control herself, but the words erupted from her impulsively: "Anna has fallen in love with a Bolshevik prisoner."

He continued to examine the fluid. Maybe he hadn't heard her, she thought. His hearing was no longer what it used to be. He swirled the test tube gently and exclaimed, "She's at an age where people fall in love, is she not, Clarushka?"

"A Bolshevik! Did you not hear me, Ilioff?" She approached him to make sure he heard her words. "A Bolshevik! Penniless. His family is from the east. He's uneducated, a nobody."

"Is he Jewish?" The question came out of his mouth almost subconsciously. Clara was surprised. Since when had the issue of Judaism been important to him? After all, he believed in equality and assimilation, no matter who a person was. It had always seemed to him a reasonable price to pay in order to integrate into society.

"Yes, he's a Jew," she replied, shaking her head in ridicule. That was her Ilioff: he always found the good in everything. He saw the entire world through optimistic glasses. Calm. Logical.

Ilioff slowly closed the test tube and carefully placed it on a stand beside its fellows. He then sat down in his armchair, ready to listen. She spoke quickly, as if fearful that he would interrupt her before she could voice everything on her mind. She'd heard him say so many times, "Clarushka, why are you assailing me? Can't you see that I am in the middle of an experiment? Can't we discuss this later?"

He wasn't perturbed. "You know that young people are extremists. They are passionate about ideologies. I was like that too. We grow up and relax later on. We know our daughter. If our Anna has fallen in love with him, he is more than just a Bolshevik bully." He saw his wife's body harden at his words, her lips twitched, and he knew tears would soon fall from her eyes. "Clarushka, do not think for a moment that I'm happy about this, but it will pass. Anna will not agree to break up with him if we demand it. We can try to separate them if we speed things up and send her to study in Switzerland. There will be more suitable than Germany, which is full of communists. Switzerland is beautiful, and she will enjoy studying there."

He stood up slowly, approached her, and held her hands. "Chaim Weizmann is a lecturer at the University of Geneva. I received a letter from him in which he shared that he's met a young Jewish girl named Vera, who is studying medicine in Geneva, and they intend to marry. I can write to him and ask about the admissions requirements, but first, we need to get Anna's consent." A small smile spread across his face. "At least we can be sure that as long as the Bolshevik is in jail, Anna won't bring home a little bastard."

*

Clara went downstairs to the entrance floor, entered the living room, and quietly closed the door behind her. She leaned against the sofa's frame, her hand sliding along the smooth artistry of the carved wood. Her eyes wandered with pleasure over the furniture, the porcelain bowls, the candlesticks, the dining table, the Persian rugs, and the original paintings. Everything was arranged according to her design, special ordered from Paris. The house had been purchased with her dowry money. Ilioff did not intervene.

Her father, Isaac Moses Stanislavski, had founded his company in Ekaterinoslav, on the banks of the Dnieper River and north of the Black Sea. The company carried agricultural produce from Ukraine across the river and, from there, marketed it around the world. Her parents had sent her to Switzerland, to a boarding school for upper-class girls, in order to prepare her for the life of a socialite. Her fair hair and gray eyes didn't disclose her Judaism. She'd returned home to Ekaterinoslav when she was seventeen and proceeded to demonstrate the knowledge she had acquired by hosting balls and evenings of culture. Light-footed, she'd danced among her guests, conversing in fluent French and wearing expensive jewelry and pastel-colored dresses she'd ordered from Paris. She sighed with longing.

Then she'd met Ilioff. She fell in love with the handsome, humble, brilliant scientist. Although he had no money of his own, her family welcomed him with open arms. She was the youngest daughter, her brothers were college graduates, and her sisters were married to a railway engineer and a lawyer. A scientist was welcome. Her friends muttered that he was marrying her because of her money. What nonsense. Her Ilioff was so modest. He didn't buy new shoes until his old ones fell apart. She tried to entice him to buy fashionable new clothes, but he said, "I have enough. What do I need more for?" She admitted that she was ashamed that he always showed up to meet her friends wearing the same clothes, and he dismissed her embarrassment with a wave of his hand.

He did not like to dance; he stood on the side leisurely and watched her dance with other men. He was a man with a strong backbone, knew his own value, and wanted her to be happy. He allowed her freedom, and she was grateful. The only thing he loved more than her was his work. In Ekaterinoslav, he participated in studies for the Land Inspection Institute of the region, examined the Dnieper River, and processed a detailed proposal for the electrification of southern Russia. He engaged in geological searches for copper-lead, researched coal, and handled the plans for a writing-paper factory. Her Ilioff was also among the founders of the People's University.

Clara went to the window. Snow was still falling. The sky was full of heavy, dark gray clouds. She sat down by the fireplace, resting her head on the raised back of the armchair. She closed her eyes. Their children, Anna, Daniel, and Yasha, were born in Ekaterinoslav. They had nannies, and she was happy. She thought it would go on like that forever. She never forgot the day, during a family picnic, when Ilioff suggested to her that they take a walk in the woods. She flirtatiously hung on to his arm, waiting for him to notice her new dress. But instead, he told her excitedly that Professor Pilchikov from the Kharkiv Polytechnic University had invited him to become Physics assistant. "I plan to return to academia," he informed her decisively. For the first time, she realized that the limits of her freedom depended on his will. He gave her the illusion of freedom. Yes, he was a progressive man in his views regarding women's rights. He was a kind man by nature and a gentleman. And yes, he loved her very much until it came to his work.

Tears welled up in her eyes. What did she have in common with all the scientists' wives who complained about their academic husbands' modest salaries? When they first came to Kharkiv, they would go to the opera, exhibitions, and concerts, but recently they'd been staying home due to the political unrest. Her wardrobe was crammed with stunning fashions that remained on their hangers.

The Bolshevik's rise in power was depriving her of sleep. In the past, she had been proud that her father had lent the Czar large sums of money to help finance the war against the Japanese. As a Jew, he had wanted to show patriotism. But what if the Bolsheviks found out?

*

Ilioff rang the bell and heard the click-clacking of the maid's footsteps. He asked that she add another log to the fireplace and bring him a cup of tea. He stood up and looked out the window of his room. In amazement, he watched the heavy metallic clouds as they miraculously generated endless snowflakes, which glided down elegantly, gradually painting the ground white. He marveled again at what a great painter nature was. Clara was right. He was an optimistic type while she darkened life for herself. He loved music. When Chaim Weizmann visited their home with his sister Dunia, who had demonstrated extraordinary abilities while playing their old-fashioned piano, he'd suggested that she stay with them for a few days. But Clara had erupted in a rage: "No way! They talk about Zionism all the time. What will I discuss with Dunia? Benjamin Ze'ev Herzl? The World Jewish Congress? The Dreyfus trial in France?"

He knew that she was worried. As Jewish men rose to higher positions within Russian academia, the relative number of Jews increased, and they became prominent representatives in education, secularism, and modernism. They became targets of jealousy and hatred. When Czar Alexander II was assassinated, people rushed to blame the Jews. Terrible pogroms broke out all across Russia that lasted almost two years. Now radical Bolshevism was taking over, and yet again, the Jews were among its leaders. Lenin's mother had a Jewish father and the surname Blank. Leon Trotsky was also a Jew, born Lev Davidovich Bronstein. One of the men who organized the march of thousands of demonstrators in St. Petersburg towards the Czar's palace was a Jew named Pinhas Rutenberg. Where did they acquire the courage to ignore the soldiers' warnings and approach the palace? The soldiers fired at them. How many people were killed? The official report stood at 150, but the Bolshevik leader, Vladimir Ilyich Lenin, claimed that a booming 4,600 were dead or wounded. He must have been exaggerating. Could Lenin be believed? The hospitals and doctors supported the official casualty count. The fake news industry was prospering.

And now it had arrived at their door. Anna had fallen in love with a young Bolshevik. Daniel dreamed of owning an agricultural farm in a liberal communist spirit, and the young Yasha was a Zionist. He wanted to join a group of young people and board a ship in Odessa that was set to sail to the Land of Israel. He declared that a "Herzliya Hebrew Gymnasium," a Hebrew High School, had opened on the sands of the new city of Tel Aviv. With no other choice, he agreed to finish his studies in Russia. Ilioff and Clara hoped that by the time he finished, his Zionist fervor would wane.

*

When Anna got home, her mother opened the door. Since when did mother do so and not the maid?

"Your father wants to talk to you. Come to the library."

The wind blew snowflakes inside. Anna hurried to close the door and took off her coat and hat. She'd been dreading this moment for weeks, memorizing sentences to say to her parents. But now, her body was betraying her. She felt short of breath; the air was stuck in her diaphragm. Father would try to persuade her to part from Ben-Zion, and mother would list all of the compromises she made for the sake of the family's integrity. Tones would rise, and the conversation would proceed to a bad place.

Anna entered the living room. Her father was sitting in the armchair. She stood in front of him. She knew he was waiting for her to sit down. When he saw that she did not sit, he didn't press.

"Anushka," he said. She expected him to address her affectionately. This was how he always behaved before he intended to say things that were not to her liking. It was a kind of softening before the blow so that she would know he understood and that he loved her. "I talked to your mother, and we've decided that it's time for you to start medical school. There is no point in continuing to wait for an answer from the St. Petersburg Women's Medical School. There are too many Jew-haters there who adhere to the admission quotas. What do you think about studying in Switzerland, in Geneva? There is a good school there, where I have connections, and it's a beautiful city."

The offer did not surprise her. They were playing with her, sidestepping her relationship with Ben-Zion. She sat down slowly, her feet glued to the floor and her back straight as a tree waiting for a strong gust of wind. But the silence thawed the stiffness inside her, and she felt herself become thin as a reed. Words burst out of her, some fragmented, as she struggled against the weakness that gripped her. Her father listened, his intelligent brown eyes understanding.

"Anushka, he must be a serious man if you fell in love with him." She knew his technique – he always began gently, but soon his reservations would come. "But you are young; romance and physical attraction are one thing. But marriage is something else. You want to study to be a doctor to fulfill yourself. All that your mother and I ask is that you refrain from making any rash decisions that you may regret."

"I have not yet decided whether I will marry him."

Clara sat down beside her, "Anna, heed me. He has no profession. How will he support you? You are blinded. He's caught a naive girl from a wealthy family and intends to live off her dowry. He will only bring trouble." Faced with these accusations, Anna had a list of retorts that she'd prepared in advance, but before she could answer, her mother asked a question that surprised her, "Are you sure that this is the man you want to spend your entire life with?"

Anna had never thought about it. Is he the man I want to live my whole life with? How do I know? Does anyone know for sure what will happen in ten, twenty, and thirty years? The now is so strong, so powerful, and I love Ben-Zion so much. What do I know beyond that? Mother had been happy with Father in Ekaterinoslav. Had she known she would be so unhappy now? Would she have married Father if she'd known? Perhaps Mother was actually asking herself this question?

Anna got up, walked out of the living room, quickly climbed the stairs, entered her room, slammed the door, took off her shoes, threw her clothes on the floor, covered herself with a blanket, and shrank like a fetus inside a secret lair. She felt protected in the dark. She whispered a mantra to herself, "We will find a solution, we will find a solution. Relax. Relax." A pleasant warmth spread over her organs; it will be fine, everything will be fine. And with that, she fell asleep.

*

The next day, she took broad, determined steps toward the prison. An icy and robust wind slowed her progress. When she arrived, the gate was closed, and dozens of women crowded along the wall seeking protection from the wind. Some sat, and others stood with their scarves fluttering in the wind.

"What happened?" Anna asked a young woman with a baby in her arms.

"The political prisoners are being transferred to Siberia for forced labor. Do you have connections with the prison administration?" she asked hopefully as she stared at the beaver fur hat on Anna's head.

"Why did they close the gate?"

"The prisoners revolted. The leaders of the uprising will be hung."

Anna was horrified, "Did they release their names?"

"No."

"We won't leave until they open the gate."

They made room for Anna to sit along the wall. Time moved at a glacial pace. The women began losing their patience. They stood up, shouted, approached the gate, hit it, and cursed.

"Join us," the women called out to her. She was embarrassed. She hadn't been raised to push and to shout, perhaps because she'd never needed to.

"Shame, shame, shame!" the women yelled as they raised their fists in anger.

"Black Sunday. Black Sunday," said a hoarse-voiced old woman, her face wrinkled like a witch's.

"St. Petersburg is here," shouted the others.

"Kharkiv is St. Petersburg," shouted the old woman, her eyes burning with a vengeance.

"The Bolsheviks will slaughter you all," they cried as they crowded forward, shouting, advancing together as a mass.

Anna sat mesmerized. For a moment, it all seemed to her like a scene from an opera. Camille Saint-Saën's "Samson and Delilah," in which the Philistine mob gathers, demanding to execute Samson. She shook her head quickly, waving away such thoughts. How could she daydream when Ben-Zion's life was at stake? She knew she must join the women and shake the prison's foundations.

The guards started beating the women with batons. The warden of the prison stepped outside. Silence fell, and they made room for him.

"I will not allow anarchy. If you quietly disperse, visits will be permitted tomorrow."

"Not Siberia!" shouted the women over and over.

"There will be a trial, and the court will decide. Return tomorrow, and the gates will be open."

"Why should we believe you?"

"If you do not disperse, I will order the guards to shoot."

Anna returned home exhausted. She didn't say a word to her parents. Her mother would probably be happy that the prisoners were being sent to Siberia.

*

No report of the uprising reached the press. Anna went back to the prison the following day, and the gate was open. She walked quickly down the long corridor to the visitors' hall. She saw Ben-Zion with his eyes fixed on her. They sat facing one another with a divider between them. She wanted to tell him about the conversation with her parents and how worried she was about him, but he interrupted her.

"I have to escape from this prison." Ben Zion lowered his voice and looked into her eyes earnestly.

Her body shrank sharply at the words coming out of his mouth.

"I have a plan, but I need your help."

"You can trust me," she replied quickly without considering what may be required of her.

"I need money to bribe the guards, counterfeit documents, and an apartment to hide out in." He studied her face to see if she had comprehended what he was requesting. "I'll also need warm clothes."

She didn't move. She looked worried.

Suddenly he began to chuckle, "When Joseph Stalin escaped from prison, he found himself in the freezing cold with no warm clothes. So he went back to prison, sat in the dungeon, ran away again, and ensured in advance that he'd be given warm clothes that time. Then he arrived in Georgia, where he joined the resistance."

"Are you planning on escaping to Georgia?"

"I haven't decided yet."

"Where do I fit into this whole escape plan?"

"You'll come with me. We'll be married. And together, we'll fight for the revolution."

"No. I don't want that. If that's what you want, then we should forget about one another. I want us both to flee to Switzerland, study medicine, and start a family together."

He leaned back as if taking a punch. He opened his eyes in astonishment.

"I plan to flee to Georgia."

"But I have another plan."

He didn't know how to respond.

"You have to choose between me and the revolution. You have to decide if you want to remain a revolutionary who ends up being hung or if you want to fulfill your dream of becoming a doctor. I love you, I will do anything, I am willing to risk everything, but these are my conditions."

She spoke softly, decisively, in a clear, precise voice. He did not know whether to be angry with her or to hug her in amazement.

After all, the man is the one who should make the decisions. He recalled telling her offhandedly that he dreamed of studying medicine. It was just a dream, unlikely to come true. It surprised him that she'd remembered and hadn't told him that she, too, wanted to study medicine. Looking at her, he knew that he couldn't give her up. The Bolshevik ideology seemed insignificant compared to the possibility of living alongside her and studying medicine. "Wherever you go, I will go."

*

Anna went up to her room, emptied her jewelry box, and put the contents in a small cloth bag. She then discreetly entered her parent's bedroom and opened her mother's jewelry cabinet, which contained dozens of boxes – each box and its designated piece of jewelry. As always, she was mesmerized by the spectacular creations made for her mother by the greatest jewelry designers in Russia. Every so often, her mother would take the jewels out of their boxes, put them on, and tell Anna the story behind each one. Anna put a platinum necklace set with diamonds that her mother promised to give her as a gift when she got married in the bag. She also picked two gold rings, a pair of earrings, and a gold bracelet adorned with diamonds. Anna hoped that her mother would only notice they were missing in a few months, and by then, she would have already told her and apologized. She tried not to think of the maid's fate if her mother discovered they were missing sooner. But she had more fateful and meaningful things to deal with. After that, she left the house. She did not take her carriage, so they wouldn't find out where she'd gone. Ben-Zion had told her where she could sell the jewelry and acquire forged documents.

In the evening, she spoke with her parents.

"I've decided I wanted to study in Switzerland. I want to leave next week to strengthen my proficiency in German and French and to take the entrance examinations." Her mother hugged her.

"You've made the right decision, Anushka." Her father stood up and joined in the hug. "I will transfer money to the bank in Switzerland to finance your studies, rent, and living expenses. I will write to Chaim Weizmann that you are coming and ask him to take care of you."

A maid entered the living room and announced that dinner was ready. They proceeded to the dining room, and Daniel and Yasha joined them. "Bring us a bottle of fine wine," Ilioff instructed the maid, and he felt his body get lighter as if a weight had dropped from his shoulders.

They took their seats around the table, sitting in their assigned places, each with their own personal napkin embroidered with their monogram. Ilioff opened the bottle and poured wine for everyone, "Our Anushka is going off to Switzerland next week to study medicine. Let's wish her good luck."

Thoughts raced through Ilioff's mind as he lay in bed waiting for Clara to finish brushing her hair before bed. "Isn't it strange that Anna wants to leave next week with such haste?"

"The most important thing is that she forgets the Bolshevik."

After brushing her hair, she got into bed and turned off the gas lamp.

"We've saved our daughter from making a terrible mistake," Clara said. "And it's all thanks to you, Ilioff. I wouldn't have known how to handle things with Anna," she said and stroked his hair.

Ilioff grabbed her hand and kissed it.

"We are so lucky," Ilioff whispered.

"Yes," she smiled and kept her hand in his.

They escorted Anna to the platform at the train station. Anna climbed the train's steps, sat down in her compartment, and waved to them.

*

The moon went in and out from behind the clouds, shining spontaneous beams of light at the dozens of prisoners crammed together in the grand square. In the past, prisoners used to be marched through the city streets at noon towards the central train station, where they boarded the train to Siberia. The city's residents would gather to see the procession of criminals, shower them with curses, and throw stones at them while boys laughed. But since the prisons had been filled with political prisoners, these processions started provoking riots and demonstrations of support.

They silently climbed onto the carts with their hands cuffed behind their backs. They sat in two rows, their backs glued to the sides of the carts, their knees rubbing against one another's. The guards crammed them in to make room for the two guards who sat at the cart's entrance. Ben-Zion felt pain in his temples. He'd never felt a pain quite like it. He calmed himself down; the plan was progressing as planned. He and his friends boarded the last wagon in the procession.

The procession of carts left the prison yard, moaning under the weight of the prisoners. Ben-Zion pushed his fingers down his back, shoved them between his belt and back, and felt the touch of the small stone that had absorbed the heat of his body. He'd recalled a book that his parents had bought him when he was ten about cavemen; inside were drawings of small, sharp, jagged stones used to skin animals of their furs. Many small rocks were scattered around the square, and it hadn't been difficult to chisel one. He began to chafe the rope against the rock, adjusting his movements to the bumping cart. When he finished, he passed the chiseled stone to the man sitting next to him. His friends had wanted to stock up on such stones, but he'd rejected the idea, fearing that it would increase the chance that the guards would discover the sharpened stone.

The packed carts maneuvered slowly through the city streets. The moon illuminated the dark buildings and cast shadows on the procession. When the cart that Ben-Zion was sitting in arrived at the Damankov Alley junction, the crowded buildings obscured the light of the moon. Complaining to the guards that he felt unwell, Ben-Zion dropped his body forward. The jailer stood up, made his way between the prisoners' knees, approached him, bent down, pulled his face up by his hair, and slapped him on the cheek. The arms of the two prisoners on Ben-Zion's either side clung to the guard's temples and turned his head rapidly, breaking his neck. Additional prisoners flew at the other guard, who hadn't noticed what was happening yet. The monotonous creaking of the wooden wheels continued the same as before. One by one, they jumped out of the cart and were engulfed by darkness, every man for himself.

Ben-Zion hid in the yard of a house. His heart was pounding; he tried to regulate the rhythm of his breathing. Where was Anna? Had she gotten off the train at the first stop? Had she come back to Kharkiv? The guards would soon discover they had escaped. Then, he saw a woman with braids carrying a large bag on her shoulder. She advanced towards him quickly, grabbed onto his hand, and pulled him into the darkness of a nearby public park. They hid under a large bush, holding hands, clinging to each other, smiling, like children who had outwitted their parents. A group of drunks entered the park. The couple crouched down. The drunks walked towards a gazebo at the park's center, which was overgrown with leaves and flowers in the summer, but currently, bare branches curled around it like bewitched twisted bars. With rapid and precise movements, Anna opened the bag and took out clothing, a warm winter coat and high boots. Ben-Zion dressed while she held and pushed the bush's branches away from him for fear that any rustling might expose them. Ben-Zion put on a wig and a hat. She looked at him, and her eyes and lips narrowed as she tried to keep from laughing.

Holding hands, they marched through the dark streets. Ben-Zion patted Anna lightly on the arm, whispering to her to slow down. They should try and look like a casual couple. When they arrived at the Opera Theater Square, they saw a handful of policemen chatting. As people began to leave the show, they crossed the square, reached the row of carriages', and hastened to hire one. Anna gave the coachman the address. They didn't utter a syllable the entire ride. The darkness of the alleyway swallowed them up as they stepped down from the carriage.

"This is the building. The apartment is on the third floor," Anna whispered.

They quickly climbed the creaking wooden stairs that threatened to wake the building's residents. She took the key out of her purse; her hands trembled so much that she couldn't put the key in the lock. Ben-Zion took the key and slipped it gently into the keyhole, turning it slowly and noiselessly. When the door opened, they dove inside. For many minutes, they remained locked in a tight embrace, as if afraid that they would be separated. As if cops would emerge out of the darkness and drag them each separately off to jail. They listened to the quiet. To every whisper and murmur. Then, they burst into tears. They cried out of happiness mixed with intractable pain over the reality that had been forced upon them.

The room was cold. A damp smell rose from the bed and the curtains. Anna wanted to turn on the gas lamp, but Ben-Zion stopped her. It's better to stay in the dark, safer. He started to shake, so she sat him on the bed, took off his coat, took off his boots, and took off his hat and wig. Without taking her eyes off him, she quickly took off her coat, her shoes, and her glasses. She placed them on their suitcase that was hiding near the wall. She went back to Ben-Zion and hugged him. His trembling stopped. They kept their clothes on, got under the blankets, and fell asleep, locked in an embrace, shivering with cold.

Ben-Zion woke up first. He was restless. "They have surely discovered the escape and are looking for us by now."

There wasn't much food in the suitcase. They ate toast with sausage, drank tea, and went down to get their pictures taken. They introduced themselves as Natalie and Boris Plushenko.

"The photos will be ready by noon," said the photographer who was leaving for the darkroom to develop them.

Back at the apartment, they turned on the gas heater, drank hot tea, and got into bed. They cuddled, smiling happily in anticipation of what was to come. Ben-Zion looked into his beloved's eyes and said, "Anushka, I want you so badly, but we must be careful. We're in Kharkiv, and Switzerland is still far off. So many things can go wrong along the way. We are in great danger. The last thing we need right now is for you to get pregnant," and then he added with a grin, "but we can still make love."

She stroked his thin chest, unable to decide if she was disappointed or if she admired his logic and self-control. He pressed his lips to hers, stroking her hair, her breasts, gently pinching her nipples, and she felt palpitations in her lower abdomen. She'd never felt anything like it before. Her pelvis began to move frantically, curling and arching, her entire body hardening. She couldn't control what was happening to her. Her breathing became deep and rapid. Her chest rose, serving up her breasts as an offering to his lips, which she longed for. Her thoughts clouded; she was exhausted; her entire body went slack, yearning for him.

He stopped his hand. "My beloved Anushka," he waited for her to calm down. "My love, I cannot describe how much I would like to continue, but we mustn't."

At noon, Anna quickly got dressed and let Ben-Zion sleep. She picked up the photographs from the photographer and, from there, went to the forger who pasted on the pictures and stamped the documents he'd prepared for them. She heard a newspaper vendor on the street call out about the escaped prisoners who had murdered two guards. She bought a newspaper, saw the photos of the prisoners, and read a report about the great escape and a monetary reward to anyone who had information that would help capture them.

When she arrived at the apartment, she showed Ben-Zion the newspaper. His face became solemn. "We must leave the city immediately."

"Wouldn't it be better to stay and hide in the apartment? I paid for the next two weeks."

"They'll search everywhere. We need to be on the move. The police will get to the photographer or the landlady. Who knows who saw us and will rat us out," he said as he hurried to get dressed and pack his suitcase.

"Maybe we should eat something before we set off?" I bought fresh bread, fruit, and vegetables."

"We can eat on the way. Let's go."

When they reached the outskirts of the city, darkness had fallen. Police officers looked at the young couple, peeked inside a suitcase, checked the IDs, and let the carriage pass. By the time they arrived at the hostel, it was night. Ben-Zion locked the door and peered through the curtains, checking to see that no one had followed them. Anna fell asleep, and he sat alert at the door, holding a knife.

The next day, they boarded a public carriage that would take them to the border of the Austro-Hungarian Empire. A week of travel awaited them. Every day they changed carriages and rarely spoke in the presence of other people. Every night they slept in a different hostel and made love. On the way, they discovered the infinite stretches of Ukraine. They knew they were parting from their homeland. When they reached the Austro-Hungarian border, the carriage passengers were required to get off and show their documents. An army officer circled around Ben-Zion, sniffing him like a hunting dog. Then, he circled around Anna, stopped, looked at her picture, looked at both of them, stood in front of her, brought his face close to hers, and ordered her to accompany him to the nearby building. Ben-Zion wanted to join, but the soldier pushed him away. So, she looked at Ben-Zion and said in a calm and decisive voice that there was no need. In the office, the officer sat down at a table, and she stood in front of him. He didn't ask her to sit. He looked at her and then at her documentation; he took a magnifying glass out of the drawer.

"It's fake," he ruled. He threw it on the table and looked her straight in the eyes.

"So, what's your story? Who are you running away from? Are you thieves or vile communists?"

She was relieved that he hadn't linked them to the escaped prisoners.

She was afraid of getting caught in a lie. "We are a couple who has fallen in love, but our parents have forbidden us from getting married. We are running away from them to start a new life elsewhere."

"I see" he narrowed his eyes. "You are among the young folk poisoned by the ideas of Western capitalism. You're sticking it to tradition, to Mother Russia," he recited what his superiors had taught him.

"No. We love Mother Russia. We are just a couple who fell in love."

He came close to her, "I don't believe you, little girl," and began stroking her cheeks, and from there, his fingers slid down her neck to her chest, where he started to open the buttons of her blouse. She took a large sum of money out of her bag and shoved it into his hand, "I beg of you. Let us go."

He looked at the money and put it in his pocket, "This will suffice for you to cross the border, but your husband looks like a communist to me, so he will have to stay here."

"We're together," she said and took a deep breath. "You are our age. You know what love is."

"Yes, I do know, and if you love him so much and want him to fuck you so badly, then be a nice girl and show me some love, too."

"No. No. Please. I'm begging you. If you rape me, I will be damaged in my husband's eyes. He won't want me. He comes from a conservative home."

"He'll want you. Yes, he will," he said as he stared at her beautiful, full, shapely breasts. She burst into tears, "When I get pregnant, my husband won't know if the newborn is his or yours. My life and my child's life will be ruined. I beg of you to let me be."

"I feel fantastic about ruining the life of a communist bitch," he said and walked over to the table, poured himself a glass of vodka, drank one sip, and continued watching her, smiling, like a hunter admiring his prey. He poured her a glass as well and pushed it into her hand, but she pushed back, vodka splashed all over him, and the glass fell on the floor and broke.

His face flushed angrily. "I'll teach you a lesson on how to treat a gentleman, you damn bitch." He opened his belt buckle in a quick, decisive motion, picked up her skirt, and she didn't have the strength to resist.

When he finished, he opened the door and pushed her out. Discarded like a bottle emptied of its beverage, like worthless junk. Ben-Zion saw her, ran towards her, and a soldier hit him with the butt of a rifle. He dropped to the ground, and the soldier kicked him in the stomach. When Anna saw this, she couldn't control her bladder, and hot liquid ran down her legs. She pulled her hips together, but the flow continued, leaving a small puddle on the ground. Anna leaned against the wall, tears welling up in her eyes, she covered them with her hands, trying to escape into the darkness, and felt a hand touch her softly on the shoulder. She opened her eyes and saw the old woman from the carriage. Her soft, wise old eyes expressed the compassion and understanding of a woman who had seen a thing or two in her life. She gave Anna her hand, and they walked towards the carriage. Ben-Zion helped them get inside. The rest of the passengers watched them in silence, their faces shocked. The carriage began to move. The silence continued. Anna burrowed her head in Ben-Zion's neck and felt a comforting warmth, the safety of home. She raised her head and saw in his loving eyes that he understood the intensity of her pain. He pinned her to his body, and they both cried in silence.

*

In the Austro-Hungarian Empire, they boarded a train. This time, they paid for their own compartment. The train crossed the border. At the next stop, they transferred to a train headed to Geneva. They rented a small apartment with the money her parents had put into her account in the Swiss bank and settled their status as political refugees. She could write on the forms that needed to be filled out that she had a considerable amount of money in the bank. She knew that the Swiss were sensitive regarding the subject of money and feared refugees who would pose a financial burden on the Swiss taxpayer. She had never been keen on money, but now she was learning to recognize its importance. Money can save lives. She was grateful that her parents' solid financial status could fund her studies. The Rabbi of Geneva's Jewish community married them. Equipped with residence permits, they proceeded to enroll in medical school.

Anna began her studies in a preparatory class to strengthen her proficiency in French. Meanwhile, Ben-Zion had to learn German and French. They tore into their studies as if possessed by a *dybbuk*.[1] After a while, the tensions dissipated, and they finally realized that

1 In Jewish mysticism, an evil spirit that wanders the earth, seeking to possess the body of a living human.

they were free, fulfilling their dream. And they were in love. Two months after the escape, Anna sat down to write to her parents.

*

Clara and Ilioff were overwhelmed with concern for Anna. No letters from her arrived. Ilioff wrote to Chiam Weizmann, and their concern only increased when they heard that he had not met with her. He knew nothing. In the same letter, he shared that he'd married Vera, and they were moving to the University of Manchester in England, where he'd gotten a teaching job. Ilioff called the bank in Switzerland and was told that large sums were being withdrawn from the account. At first, he was relieved, but then he began to fear that maybe something terrible had happened and someone was blackmailing Anna out of her money. Clara urged Ilioff to go to Switzerland and look for the girl. Daniel joked that maybe the Bolshevik prisoner had kidnapped her, and they gave him an angry look and said that it wasn't a laughing matter.

When the maid burst into the sitting room waving a letter, Daniel and Yasha jumped up, snatched it, and handed it to their father.

"There's a photograph in the letter," he said and pulled it out. He saw Anna and, next to her, a slender young man; they were both smiling. She was wearing a fancy wide-brimmed hat, and he was in a black suit. Ilioff turned the photo over, and on its back, the words "Anna and Ben-Zion Ratner on their wedding day" were written.

"Ilioff. What did Anna write?" Clara shouted.

"Anna got married. Anna got married," he whispered in disbelief.

Clara snatched the photo and held it closer to her eyes; her head spun; she almost fell down. "What kind of a girl have I raised? She tricked us, married the Bolshevik, and we believed her that she'd left him." Tears of anger and humiliation made it difficult for her to breathe, and she began to whimper, "She got married without her mother and father, like an orphan. How could she do this to us?"

Ilioff took the letter out of the envelope and began reading:

Dear Mother and Father,

I ask for your forgiveness for hiding my plan from you and for the great concern I have caused you. If I had told you, you would have prevented me from following through with it. Likewise, I didn't want to involve you in Ben-Zion's escape from prison. After all, something may have gone wrong, and therefore it was better that you didn't know anything. The responsibility is mine and Ben-Zion's alone. I won't get into details, but we managed to get safely to Switzerland. We were married by a Rabbi in the Jewish community.

I will start my medical studies next semester after I complete the preparatory course. Ben-Zion must pass German and French tests to be admitted to the medical preparatory program. He wants to be a surgeon. He is so talented and eager to learn and I am sure he will succeed. We lead a modest and very happy life.

I also have a small request: there is little money left in the bank account. I had to spend extremely large sums to get us to Switzerland and for us both to enroll in school. We are not allowed to work, and I do not want us to engage in illegal work.

And there is one more matter concerning Mother. I took the necklace you promised to give me when I got married, as well as two rings, a pair of earrings, and a bracelet. I sold them so I could save Ben-Zion and get us safely to Switzerland. I hope you didn't accuse the maid. I never imagined that I would have to steal jewelry, but I had no other choice.

I love you. Hugs and kisses to you and to my beloved brothers Daniel and Yasha.

Yours, Anna

In the envelope was another letter.

To the Honorable and Esteemed Alexander and Clara Ilioff,

I ask for your forgiveness that I did not ask for your consent to marry Anna. As you know, our unique circumstances did not allow for this. I know that Anna took significant risks when she helped me, and we did not want to endanger you. We will not be able to return to Russia, but perhaps you can come to Switzerland to meet me and learn to believe in me. I promise to be worthy of Anna and to do anything to make her happy.

Sincerely,

Ben-Zion Ratner

The room was silent. You could hear the crackling sounds of the wood burning in the fireplace. A few minutes later, Ilioff got up and said, "I'm heading to the bank to transfer them some money. Before that, let's raise a glass to Anna and Ben-Zion."

*

They were both admitted into medical school. Their lives lit up. Ilioff was right in always saying that Anna had the excellent combination of a scientist's analytical mind and a poet's spirit. She filled the bookcase in their modest apartment with art books and insisted on saving money for them to travel to Paris, which was renowned for its abundance of cultural attractions, and to see the Eiffel Tower. They hiked in the mountains, visited museums, attended theater productions, and listened to concerts. For Ben-Zion, Anna opened up a whole new world. At first, he went to performances with her to please her, but later, he accompanied her willingly. Anna had changed his life and saved him from prison, and he knew how to appreciate it.

Ilioff and Clara came to visit. They met Ben-Zion for the first time. They were impressed by his academic success and his love for their daughter. They invited the young couple to spend a week at a hotel in the mountains, a classy place that the young couple couldn't afford. Their table in the dining hall was under a massive window with a view of the Alps, out of which the tip of Mt. Matterhorn protruded. After their meals, they went into an adjoining hall with a large table, the center of which was laden with desserts and a pile of bright red strawberries and clotted cream. Then the guests continued to another hall where they danced to the music of a live orchestra. Most of the guests were elderly, and Anna and Ben-Zion's presence added a young and refreshing touch. They spoke to Anna's parents about school and their plans for the future, and they avoided the subject of the escape. Ben-Zion was interested in Ilioff's recent studies, and Ilioff was impressed by his son-in-law's in-depth questions and distinctions. They took short walks together in nature and refrained from talking about politics, whether the Czar or the communists.

*

Four years after they were married, Anna became pregnant, and in 1909, Evgeni, whom his parents affectionately called Jenka, was born. Clara and Ilioff came to Switzerland to see their grandson and determined that he was not only beautiful but also had wise eyes like his grandfather. Ilioff needed to return to teach his classes at the Polytechnic, which had since reopened. But before he left, he deposited a considerable amount of money into the young couple's bank account so that they could continue their studies without financial concern. Clara stayed for several weeks and chose an excellent nanny for the baby so that her grandson would receive the best possible care. The couple moved into a more spacious apartment with a room where the nanny could sleep so that she could take care of all the housework and be available at all times.

They were both busy with their studies during the day, and they only got home in the evenings. Anna would put Jenka to sleep and read him poems by Pushkin in Russian and Heinrich Heine in German.

"When you grow up, you will board a ship and discover new places like the great explorers," she would say, stroking his head. "You will lead a life rich with adventure."

Ben-Zion would look on as Jenka lay calmly, beaming happily at his mother.

"What can a toddler possibly understand from the poems of Pushkin and Heine?" Ben-Zion stood with his hands tucked in his pants pockets, his head tilted toward the small bed, and grinned forgivingly at his wife.

"He understands. Not the lyrics, but the heart and soul of the song," she tickled Jenka's belly, and he burst out laughing.

When Jenka turned four, they went to a photographer who created a series of photos of the boy – Jenka in sailors clothing, Jenka in a judge's costume with a giant wig of curly white hair flowing behind him, and a joint photo of Jenka and Anna with tenderness and love emanating from their eyes. In 1912, Anna and Ben-Zion finished their studies and received their medical licenses. They were both eager to travel the world, perhaps to Paris, where culture was flourishing, or to England, where Chaim Weizmann was making a living in Rochester, and perhaps to America. They began exploring their options.

*

At first, her fever rose, then the coughing and the battle over every breath of air began. Her diagnosis was advanced pneumonia. Anna was transferred to the hospital where Ben-Zion worked. The medical staff did their best to provide her what relief they could. Ben-Zion did not leave her bedside. He watched as Anna faded before his eyes, and he, the doctor, could do nothing to save her. Between harrowed breaths, she mentioned the name of Jenka, the lovely child born to them; how could she not be there to see him grow up, and who would be the stepmother that raised him? Ben-Zion squeezed her hand as a deep pain pierced his chest, incapable of speaking a word.

Jenka was five years old, old enough to realize something was wrong. His mother wasn't home, his father stopped coming home from the hospital, and the nanny wasn't giving him straight answers. She took him for walks in nature and kept him busy so that he stayed tired and distracted.

"Mother wants to see you." Ben-Zion hugged Jenka and carried him in his arms. "She is sick and very weak. You won't be allowed to get on her bed to hug her. Don't ask her questions because it's difficult for her to speak." Jenka nodded his head in understanding. When he got to the ward, he was startled to see how pale she was and wanted to run to her, but his father stopped him. He made tiny fists and began beating his father, hitting him again and again. Jenka's skin turned red from the punching. The little boy sat down on the floor, crawled towards the bed, and grabbed his mother's hand. Ben-Zion went over, gently removed Jenka's little hand, pulled up a chair, sat down next to his son, and took his hand. They sat like that for hours; Jenka refused to move, eat or talk. He understood that this may be the last time he would see his mother.

Ben-Zion sent a telegraph to Clara and Ilioff briefly describing their daughter's medical condition. They hurried to arrive, he met them at the train station, and they drove to the hospital. His expression revealed everything. Anna could no longer recognize them. Two days later, she was buried in the Jewish cemetery in Switzerland. The young woman, who had been only 26 years old, left behind a child, broken parents, and a husband in which every drop of optimism had dried up, and who'd shrunken inward like a hardened black stone. Ilioff and Clara wanted to take Jenka with them to Russia, but Ben-Zion refused to part from his son.

Without Anna, the curiosity to travel, to discover the world seemed meaningless to him. As an escaped prisoner, he could not return to Russia, so he stayed in Switzerland to complete his internship.

Chapter 2: Pistols Drawn in the Parlor

World War I broke out a year after Anna's death. Russia, France, and Britain fought against Germany, the Austro-Hungarian Empire, and the Ottoman Empire. It was unclear with whom Switzerland would unite. The uncertainty filled Ben-Zion with grave concern. If Switzerland joined Russia, he would be extradited to the Czarist regime and executed, and if Switzerland joined Germany, he would be imprisoned as a possible Russian spy. But thankfully, Switzerland remained neutral. He labored with devotion at the hospital, which helped to ease the pain over Anna's death, albeit slightly.

Unlike Anna, he thought the child should be raised tough to prepare him for real life. So, he hired a new nanny, a Swiss woman of German descent. One evening, when Ben-Zion put Jenka to bed and asked him what he had learned recently, Jenka proudly recited, "Germany is above all." He knew Anna would be shocked to hear these words and that she would have fired the nanny. But, instead, Ben-Zion chastised the nanny and didn't fire her.

*

Ben-Zion returned to the living room and sat down to read the newspapers, which were filled with reports of the heavy losses the

Russian army had sustained. According to one of the papers, by January 1917, there were about six million wounded, captive, and missing persons in the Russian army.

Letters from Ilioff had continued to arrive from Russia. He had been officially appointed a professor at the Polytechnic University, and the military had approached him, asking for his expertise to help build a factory for dry electric batteries. He also advised on the implementation of a medical thermometer factory. Daniel had enlisted in the military and received a Medal of Heroism, a Cross of St. George from the Czar.

Ben-Zion opened the last letter, which announced that Ilioff had managed to transfer a large sum of money to a bank in Switzerland before all of his remaining funds were confiscated. The money was Anna's inheritance and was meant for Jenka when he turned eighteen.

Ben-Zion flung the newspapers and the letter on the floor. He opened the door to Jenka's room, saw that the boy was asleep, and notified the nanny that he was going for a short walk to freshen up. He knew that Lenin was in Switzerland and was holding a conference that night where he would call on workers in every country in the world to rise up for an international revolution. Ben-Zion wandered back and forth through the streets. Yes, he had promised Anna to cut all his ties with the Bolsheviks when she had refused to help him escape from prison if he didn't. But Anna was gone. Tears flowed from his eyes and became loud cries, he was angry at the cruelty of fate, and his feet carried him to the conference.

*

In the doctors' lounge, his colleagues greeted him, excitedly reporting the news that on March 7th, a strike had broken out at Putilov

Mill in Petrograd, and the military had refused to use force to suppress it. Members of the Parliament had joined the uprising. And eventually, the army had joined with the protesters and opened the gates to the weapons depots for the workers.

"What does the Russian doctor have to say about the Bolshevik criminals?" They expected Ben-Zion to join them in condemning the protesters. But he remained silent.

The newspapers reported that on March 15th, the Provisional Government of the Russian Republic was formed under the leadership of Alexander Kerensky, and Czar Nikolai II announced his abdication. The political winds blew, and the medical staff, as well as the patients, talked of anarchy and declared that the communist offenders should be stopped."

Lenin returned to Russia. He begrudged the socialist-democratic government that had formed in Russia, which included liberal communists, intelligentsia, priests, aristocrats, and human rights advocates. He called on the workers to take over industrial production, the banks, and the agricultural lands, thus overthrowing Kerensky's provisional government. Lenin began by eliminating the old social classes – nobles, officers, and ministers of the monarchy.

Ben-Zion wrote to Ilioff, explaining that he wanted to return to Russia with Jenka. Ilioff begged him to stay in Switzerland. He wrote that Lenin was also eliminating the bourgeoisie and intelligentsia associated with the liberal socialists who had supported the revolution. Communist Jews were being persecuted and imprisoned and were looking for any way to reach the Land of Israel. Even Yosef Trumpeldor, the Jewish hero from the Russian Japanese War, and Pinhas Rutenberg, one of the former communist leaders, had fled there. In July 1918, the Bolsheviks murdered Czar Nikolai II and his family. A civil war broke out between the White Army and the Red Bolshevik Army.

In the end, Ben-Zion decided to return to Russia and join his

Bolshevik comrades. He went to visit Anna's grave one last time, laid flowers on it, and told her he was returning to Russia with Jenka. She would have stopped him from doing so if she were alive so that they could start a new life in another country across the sea, and he would have followed her. But he was alive, and she was dead.

*

Ben-Zion and eight-year-old Jenka arrived in Kharkiv and searched for the Ilioff house. It was not the Kharkiv he remembered. Entire streets of buildings were destroyed. Wooden fences were uprooted from front yards, and trees were cut down and used to warm the homes in the cold Russian winter. People were terrified of gossip and scared of their own shadows.

He knocked on the door, and a dour-looking woman appeared in the doorway.

"We are looking for the home of Clara and Alexander Ilioff."

"You mean the professor?" She giggled. Ben-Zion did not like her laugh. She eyed him with a sneer. "And who are you?"

"I am a doctor and am married to Professor Ilioff's daughter, and the boy is his grandson."

"Shame on you. Do you know how many rooms this family lives in? This home belongs to the Soviet now. They're teaching these bourgeoises a lesson."

She yelled Clara's name, "You have visitors!"

A door opened, and Clara peeked out, glanced at them, ran over, grabbed Jenka's hand, and quickly whispered, "Come with me."

They entered a room loaded with furniture, like a warehouse. Crying with excitement, Clara and Ilioff hugged and kissed their grandson.

"We've become strangers in our own home. Two families have moved into the second floor by order of the Soviet, and we're left with the downstairs living room," said Ilioff as his hand unconsciously stroked Jenka's hair.

"They showed consideration towards us because we are older, and it's difficult for us to climb stairs," Clara said sarcastically. "We use the living room as a bedroom, a library, and for what is left of Ilioff's chemistry laboratory. The kitchen and the bathroom are shared by all the families."

Ben-Zion's heart broke at the sight of the elderly couple getting their first taste of a life more similar to what his family had experienced. Although their property had been taken from them, they remained aristocratic in their speech and body language. It was impossible to take away the fine education they had received.

"Ben-Zion, why did you return to this hellhole?"

"I want to join the Red Army. They need doctors."

The elderly couple almost had a heart attack. "Then Jenka must stay with us. We will take care of him, and whenever you can, come and visit him," they said as they hugged Jenka tightly.

*

As a military doctor of the Red Army, Ben-Zion traveled throughout Russia's battlegrounds. After about six months, he managed to receive leave to journey to Kharkiv and visit his son. He did not like to see the boy cuddling up in the arms of his elderly grandparents, who hugged and kissed him like a baby. On his next visit, he met with Daniel and two of his friends from the White Army. And during another visit, he met Yasha, who was also a soldier in the White Army. This time guns were drawn by both sides while the dreadful screams of the old couple and Jenka filled the room. The next day Ben-Zion came back and declared that he was taking Jenka. He proceeded to grab the boy's hand and drag him outside. The old couple ran after him, begging him to leave their grandson with them. Jenka went berserk, and Ben-Zion ordered him to stop crying like a baby. The boy then became hysterical, and his father struck him twice across the face. Jenka stopped crying but continued to moan.

"Quiet. Control yourself!" Ben-Zion shouted at him. Jenka froze. Ben-Zion proclaimed to the grandfather and grandmother, "No son of mine will grow up spoiled in a family of traitorous Whites."

*

Ben-Zion couldn't find anyone to whom he could entrust the child. There was chaos; residents wandered frightened from district to district, whether from fear of the armies or because of the famine. Out of options, he decided that Jenka, who was eight years old, would come with him. He requested permission from his commander and received a negative response. There was a war, families were being torn apart, but Ben-Zion insisted. He had special rank, as he was among those who had sat in the Czar's prison following the First Revolution in 1905. He was also a doctor, and his expertise was needed. So, he turned to the party, and they approved his request.

Ben-Zion and the boy moved around following the battles. The makeshift hospitals were full of wounded soldiers, and the conditions were awful. Ben-Zion would come back to their tent exhausted every night and fall right to sleep. During the day, the boy walked around bored. He wandered about alone. Jenka learned about superstitions and he liked to cover his head with a sheet, jump out at people and make spooky sounds. He learned that any Friday that falls on the 13th of the month is a day of misfortune. That it's better to shut oneself in the house and by no means should one do anything important, for the day is cursed. He learned that a black cat is a bad omen, and when encountering one, he should spit and knock on wood. Despite his father's repeated warnings, Jenka would jump onto frozen rivers to check the thickness of the ice. When his father learned of this, Jenka was severely beaten. In Caucasia, he joined the youngsters who would run after Jewish children and shout "pig, pig" at them. He was friends with the guard soldiers. They were ordinary, working-class soldiers who taught him to curse in Russian. They would have competitions to see who could swear the most. Cursing became part of his rhetoric, and his father beat him for every swear word. Jenka learned to suppress his discomfort and not cry. He got stronger.

A town near the hospital where Ben-Zion was serving was attacked by the White Army. Attempts to repel them were unsuccessful, so a mass escape from the town began. The military hospital was evacuated as well. Thousands of civilians, women, children, elderly people, and even soldiers crowded the train station's platform. When the train arrived, they bombarded it, pushing each other and trampling the weak. Amidst the anarchy, Ben-Zion gripped Jenka's hand tightly, and the two managed to climb onto the train's roof, carving out a seat for themselves amongst the hundreds of refugees huddled atop the locomotive. With no food and no toilets, they could see the burnt-down villages from the roof of the train. They saw women, children, old people, and wounded soldiers begging for a slice of bread. Every field they passed was untilled, and the trees everywhere had been cut down to use as firewood for heating. There was a commotion at every station where the train stopped as more people tried to board the train. When the train reached the mountains, it sped into a tunnel. The hundreds of people standing on the rooftop were thrown up in the air, their decapitated heads and amputated bodies flying in every direction. Thankfully, Jenka and Ben-Zion were sitting, and their lives were spared.

Daniel and Yasha, who served in the White Army, were captured. The Bolsheviks drowned Yasha in a river with a rope attached to a large stone tied around his neck. Ilioff and Clara were notified of Yasha's death but hadn't heard from Daniel in months. They were distraught that they hadn't allowed Yasha to immigrate to the Land of Israel. Occasionally, an officer of the Soviet secret police would come to interrogate the families living in their house, asking whether Daniel had come home or contacted his family. They were required to report anything they knew.

"If they're searching for him, it means that he escaped." Ilioff tried to cheer Clara up. "He is alive. We can keep up hope."

He was worried about Clara's mental state; she would sit for hours in the armchair in their room staring into space. They had lost their daughter and their youngest son, the fate of their eldest son was unknown, and their only grandson had been taken from them. She had heard nothing from her family in Ekaterinoslav and was worried about their fate. "I no longer have any reason to live," she murmured to herself repeatedly.

*

It was a lovely spring day. Ilioff thought it would be good to go outside and breathe some fresh air. He wore a warm coat and wrapped a scarf around his neck. At his age, he had to be careful about his health; he mustn't catch cold. He sat down on a bench in the public park, and a young man approached him.

"Are you Professor Ilioff?"

"Yes."

"You are Daniel's father?"

Ilioff's heart skipped a beat. "Daniel is alive?"

"He's alive and well, a Hebrew worker in the Land of Israel."

Ilioff clutched the young man's hands as if it were Daniel he was holding.

"I've come back to Russia for just a few days. I am looking for my younger sister and brother to bring them to the Land of Israel. I promised Daniel I would give you this letter." He got up and disappeared.

Ilioff opened the envelope and took out the stationary. Yes, it was Daniel's penmanship – large, rounded, and clear.

Dear Father and Mother,

I can imagine how hard the news about Yasha was on you. I know that you believed I was missing in action, too. I dared not contact you, and, in fact, I didn't have a way to. I lived every day like my last, like an animal fleeing from the Bolshevik hunters. I knew that if they couldn't find me, they would interrogate you and accuse you of aiding me.

I managed to get to Constantinople, and the good Jewish community there cared for me. I was sick, and when I recovered, I was given money to get to Israel by way of Syria. I am now with a group of Russian men who work guarding Jewish settlements. We are finally working for our own people. Every drop of Jewish blood that is shed in the wars of others is a waste. Yasha was right; we were blind. We believed the world was a global village where a brotherhood of nations would govern together in the enlightened spirit of socialism.

The Ottoman Empire that ruled the Land of Israel for 400 years has fallen, and currently, the land, now called Palestine, is under a British mandate. The land is waiting for a scientist like you. In Haifa, a building that will house a Polytechnic University called the "Technion" has been erected. They have not yet begun classes because they haven't finished recruiting the entire teaching staff. Next door, a high school called "The Reali" has been up and running for several years, and I've heard that the studies there are at a high level. You will have a job and Jenka a school. The ocean line from Odessa to the Land of Israel has been renewed. Let me know when you plan to arrive, and I will wait for you at the Jaffa port.

Kisses and hugs,

Your son, Daniel

He hurried home to tell Clara. She got up from her chair, stood upright, and said decisively, "Go get Jenka."

*

After a lengthy investigation, Ilioff learned that Ben-Zion had been stationed at a civilian hospital in a small town, four days' drive from Kharkiv, for the last two months. He didn't want to send a telegraph; the postal service could not be trusted. More than anything, he feared receiving a short decisive answer like, "Jenka will stay in Russia with me." The carriage ride was challenging for Ilioff. People sat crowded together, their eyes blank. There was a shortage of food, and they slept in makeshift campsites at night.

He arrived at the hospital yard physically drained.

"How may I help you, grandfather?" asked one of the soldiers, whose heart ached to see the old man dragging his feet.

"I'm looking for Dr. Ben-Zion Ratner. Can you assist me, please?"

"Grisha," the soldier shouted at his friend. "*Deda* here is looking for Jenka's father."

"You know Jenka?" Ilioff was unsure whether he'd actually heard his grandson's name or imagined it out of sheer longing for him.

"We all know Jenka," the soldier chuckled and shouted, "who here knows Jenka?" A group of soldiers hurried to gather around them.

"You all know my grandson?" Ilioff marveled. "So, where is he?" he asked, feeling his hands begin to tremble.

"His father beat him with a belt and forbade him to leave the room."

"He punished Jenka? That sweet boy?" Ilioff felt anxiety rising in his chest.

"Jenka? Sweet?" the soldiers burst out laughing. "Jenka is one of us; he's a brave boy. He does what he wants. He gets in a lot of trouble."

"Did his father beat him with a belt?" Ilioff whispered worriedly.

"Jenka went too far this time," Grisha said, and they all nodded in agreement. "Last night, he put kittens in the boots the officers' left outside for us to shine. When the officers put on the boots in the morning, a commotion broke out. There was screaming and yelling. So, the doctor took a belt and beat Jenka so hard that the entire hospital heard him shouting. He only stopped when his fellow doctors intervened."

"I'm feeling unwell. Can you direct me to Dr. Ratner's office?"

Grisha straightened up and began to show him the way, "Lean on me, *Deda*. I'm the son of a sturdy Russian farmer."

He knocked on the door, which had a sign that read "Dr. Ben-Zion Ratner – Chief of Surgery." A nurse opened the door, he explained his request to her, and she called the doctor over.

When Ben-Zion saw Ilioff's face, he sat down beside him, grabbed his wrist, and checked the old man's pulse.

"We'll go to my apartment. It's very close." He called over the nurse and informed her that he would be absent for the next two hours.

Jenka opened the door, now a tall, thin twelve-year-old boy with a serious look and something angry about him, similar to Ben-Zion. His sweet softness was gone. "Jenka, my Jenka," Ilioff could not resist even though he knew Ben-Zion disliked emotional displays. "I will keep this brief because I know that you are busy. Yasha was drowned in a river, Daniel fled captivity to Mandatory Palestine, and we want to leave Russia with Jenka."

"No way! Jenka is my son, and he will remain with me."

Ilioff had expected this answer. He'd come prepared with responses that would soften Ben-Zion's resolve.

"I know you are his father, and you will make the final decision," said Ilioff, thus neutralizing the first minefield. "But you have to think about what's best for Jenka. For years he hasn't studied in school. He's been dragged from place to place. He is already twelve years old and needs to study in an organized environment and make up all the material he has missed. The war, famine, and chaos in Russia may continue for years."

"You did not want me to marry Anna, and now you want to take my only son from me."

Jenka sat quietly and listened. He was hearing these things for the first time.

"True, but we learned to appreciate you and to respect you. We accepted you as our son, and for seven years, we funded your and Anna's studies and living expenses in Switzerland. I didn't think I would have to bring this up, but we are talking about education, profession, about Jenka's fate. He is more than just your only son; he is also the only grandson we have from our daughter."

Ben-Zion sat rigidly.

"If Jenka stays in Russia till the age of eighteen, he'll enlist in the Red Army, a young man with no education. A simple soldier. The party will never allow him to be an officer because, on his mother's side, he belongs to the bourgeois intelligentsia, to a family whose sons fought in the White Army, and whose uncles belong to the wealthy Jewish aristocracy. They will always suspect him of disloyalty."

"I cannot part from my son," Ben-Zion whispered.

"You don't have to. Jenka will travel with us. At the age of eighteen, he will decide what he wants to do. If he wishes to stay with us or return to Russia. He may even enlist in the Red Army. But then it will be his decision."

Ben-Zion sat silent. After a while, he turned to Jenka and asked him what he wanted. Ilioff had wished for this moment, he looked at the boy, praying that Jenka would answer that he wanted to go with his grandfather, but instead, he said, "I do not know." Maybe this was the answer that Ilioff should have expected.

"It's alright. I'll come back tomorrow. You can think about it."

Thoughts raced through Jenka's mind. He lay in bed that night and remembered how his mother would tuck him in every night, that she would read poems he didn't understand, and tell him stories. He asked himself what his mother would want him to do. He was searching for a sign, a hint to help him decide. And he remembered his mother's stories about explorers of unfamiliar countries. He remembered that she had said that one day he, too, would board a ship and sail off to discover foreign lands. That was the sign his mother had sent him. She wanted him to board the vessel departing from Odessa for a land he did not know. She had equipped him with a compass for the future.

The next day he announced resolutely that he would travel with his grandparents.

*

In October 1922, they boarded the ship called the "Gastein." Ilioff was sixty-three, Clara sixty, and Jenka thirteen. They left behind the horrors of the civil war that had claimed the lives of millions, the heavy famine, and the Bolshevik political persecution. They also left behind the body of Yasha, their youngest son, who was drowned by the Bolsheviks and was never returned to them for burial. Clara also left behind her family, not knowing what had happened to them. Jenka was happy to go.

When the ship left the Black Sea and entered the Mediterranean, the color of the sea changed to light blue, and the sun shone. Every day they walked on the deck, enjoying the chance to chat and get to know one another again. By October 31st, they could see the towers and rooftops of Jaffa in the distance.

Chapter 3: Out of the Frying Pan into the Fire

Leaning on the railing of the ship, Clara, Ilioff, and Jenka waited for their turn to get on the boats that would bring them to the fishing port in Jaffa. A sea breeze filled their lungs as their eyes followed the caravan of wooden dinghies leaving the harbor and sailing around the new breakwater that the British had finished constructing in 1920. The boats reached the deep water where the ship was moored. They were tied to the ship, and porters loaded the passengers' luggage onto the rocking boats, shouting to each other in Hebrew, Arabic, and Russian, before sailing back towards the port. A loud honk echoed, vibrating through the air, blaring once, twice, three times. Their gaze shifted towards an approaching ship adorned with an Italian flag. The anchor of the Italian ship was thrown into the water, and after it, a rusty iron chain fell, shrieking and clanging from the abrasion until it was swallowed by the silent water.

The heat made time pass sluggishly. The passengers waited, sitting in the shade, fanning themselves with their hats to create a light breeze. Others looked at the view along the harbor. Ilioff pointed to the British flag hoisted on a high pole atop one of the warehouses. "The flag of the Ottoman Empire with its crescent moon and eight-pointed star was flown from the rooftops of Jaffa for the 400 years that they ruled the Mediterranean Basin. The Crimean Dispute on the Black Sea between the Russian Empire and the Ottoman Empire lasted for decades," he explained calmly and clearly, like someone used to lecturing to an audience of students.

"The Ottoman Empire has dissolved," Clara beamed as she stroked Jenka's hair and nagged him to wear a hat.

"I lived under the Ottomans during the Great War, and they forced Jews to enlist in their military," said a tan young man. Everyone turned towards him, curious, wanting to hear more. "We were in serious danger. The Ottomans hunted down a Jewish spy network, rightfully suspecting that we actually supported the British. They hung all of its members, including a young woman. They shut down our establishments and our newspapers. Many Jews fled to Egypt and returned here only after the British occupied the country and received the mandate over Palestine."

"Why did the British decide to call the Land of Israel by the name Palestine?" Jenka asked. "In Russia, Christians call it the Holy Land."

"After the Romans defeated the Jews in the Bar Kochba revolt of 132 BC, they changed Judea's name to Palestine and combined it with the province they called Syria-Palestina. Maybe the British wanted to avoid the religious struggle that's been going on in the Land of Israel for centuries between Christians and Muslims," Ilioff suggested.

"Then, I am Swiss, Russian, Israeli, and Palestinian," said Jenka proudly. Clara smiled, and Ilioff embraced his grandson.

*

Their turn to disembark from the ship arrived. They sat squished together on the wooden plank benches of the small boat, leaving room for the sailors to paddle. They could finally see the wharf in detail, the large warehouses, and the new customs and administration house, built in a European style. As they got closer, they began to recognize relatives and friends, and the air was filled with exclamations in Russian, English, Polish, and Arabic. Ilioff spotted Daniel, who stood tall, wearing shorts and, on his head, a large straw hat.

The excited Jenka stood up and called, "Daniel, Daniel," gesturing broadly with both hands to try and catch his uncle's attention.

His movements rocked the little boat, causing the Arab navigator to raise his voice and shout in Arabic, "*Askut! Hus!*" The other passengers grabbed the boy and forced him into his seat.

The boat approached the dock. Muscly, tan arms grabbed the rope thrown at them from the boat, tied it to a dock cleat, and began helping the passengers disembark from the wobbling vessel. Street vendors approached, offering their wares – cold drinks and sweet oriental cakes. They shouted in Arabic seasoned with words in Russian, Italian, and English. A British officer greeted the passengers and instructed them to form a queue, beginning at the entrance of the nearby pavilion. Obedient, they hastened to line up and waited quietly. Some stood erect, excited, their faces beaming with joy, and if they hadn't been embarrassed, they would have kneeled down to kiss the Biblical ground. Others stood tensely, apprehensive about starting a new, uncharted chapter of their lives.

A group of Arabs with metal canisters on their backs came toward them and began spraying the whole queue with disinfectant. The startled passengers coughed, cried out, and covered their eyes. Clara froze. Throughout the entire voyage, she'd waited for the moment she would see her son and celebrate their safe arrival. She had worn her good dress and meticulously combed her hair, pulled it up, gathered it, and adorned it with a gold and diamond brooch, and now they sprayed her like a beast. She had never experienced such an affront. Ilioff, on the other hand, accepted the whole experience with understanding. He reassured her and those around them and praised the British, who were taking precautions to prevent the entry of diseases and parasites into the country.

"People come here from distant lands," he said. "Some of them are sick and carrying germs."

It was hard to convince the people who felt humiliated and insulted. But when he explained that in America, sick immigrants are quarantined, they shook their heads, unsure whether to believe him or not. If in America, the land of unlimited opportunity, where some of them would have secretly preferred to be; if in America where the Statue of Liberty, a virgin carrying a torch, welcomes new immigrants; if in America people are quarantined, who were they to complain about being sprayed? Some argued that Ilioff was lying, but when he explained that it was no rumor, that he had visited America thirty years earlier and experienced it himself, even the skeptics among them fell silent.

"You traveled to America?" marveled Jenka, who was learning new things about his grandfather every day.

"I'll tell you all about it another time."

The queue got longer. The passengers from Odessa were joined by the passengers who had arrived on the Italian ship. It was hot and humid. They finally entered the huge hangar. Heavy, long-armed fans spun lazily on the ceiling making a racket and failing to cool the air. It was crowded. The smell of sweat mixed with the odor of the disinfectant spray. People young and old stood on their feet, being interrogated by officials and filling out forms in incomprehensible languages while trying to hide their apprehension. They all feared bureaucratic issues that would somehow prevent them from entering the country. Impatient children ran around, hiding among the people, spooking each other and laughing. When their parents caught them, they grabbed them forcefully, and the children shouted and cried as if they were being abused.

When the Ilioff family left the hangar, Daniel was waiting for them with open arms and a massive smile on his face. As if like magic, the world suddenly seemed colored in optimism. Daniel, Daniel. They could reach out and touch him. He looked so rugged, muscular, tan. They hugged, crying. A horse-drawn cart was waiting nearby. With his long legs, Jenka climbed in easily. Daniel gave his parents a hand, helping them take a seat on the wooden bench over which he'd spread a blanket. Then he poured them each a cup of cool water from a big earthenware jug. Daniel also ensured that the luggage from the barges would be carefully loaded and tied to the cart. Clara took two wide-brimmed hats out of her suitcase and handed them to Ilioff and Jenka. For herself, she unpacked a colorful parasol. She opened it, sat up straight, and waited for instructions.

"We are going to Haifa to meet my wife Sarah and your first granddaughter," Daniel declared happily. Whipping the horses, he added, "On the way, we will stay overnight in Hadera." They nodded their heads obediently in agreement.

The cart crawled slowly along the dirt road. The wooden wheels bounced up and down, moaning, threatening to fall apart. The coastal plain unfolded before them. The flora was sparse, dry, and yellow. Soon, the cart joined a long, dusty caravan making its way north. A procession of camels laden with goods, Arabs wearing *keffiyehs* mounted on horses, Arab women in embroidered dresses, their faces covered by coins, carrying bundles on their heads, beating the donkeys walking alongside them with rods and shouting, "Giddy up." They could see Jewish people in the caravan as well, riding horses and leading carts filled with agricultural goods – wheat, barley, tomatoes, olives, potatoes, and chickens. Every so often, a British military automobile drove forward and overtook the line of wagons, leaving behind it a cloud of dust. Jenka was excited; he stood in the cart shouting enthusiastically, with Ilioff holding his hand, smiling at the sight of his happy grandson, and telling him about all the animals he was seeing for the first time. Meanwhile, Clara sat huddled over, shaking the dust off her clothes.

On the way, they stopped for a light meal. Daniel spread a blanket on the ground, sliced a loaf of black bread, and took a hunk of cheese and some vegetables out of the basket. Pesky flies quickly buzzed over, landing on the food, their faces, and their clothes. The family fanned them away, but it was no use; the bugs kept coming back. Clara and Ilioff lost their appetite and wouldn't touch the food. Daniel watched his parents, unable to discern if their crestfallen looks were from fatigue or despair. At least Jenka ate with gusto, went to pet the horse, and could not stop talking.

"We must get a move on. The road is long," Daniel ruled. So, they climbed back into the cart, and the horse began trotting forward slowly.

"On the ship, I was told that it's hard to find a job here. What about you, Daniel? Are you working?"

"I've started working at Lord Melchett's villa on the shores of the Sea of Galilee."

"Where is this *boibrik*?" Clara asked, surprised at herself for using the Yiddish word for a provincial town.

"It's where Jesus walked on water two thousand years ago," Daniel chuckled.

"How did you find yourself there?"

"When Lord Melchett visited British Mandate Palestine, his friend Chaim Weizmann took him to the Sea of Galilee. The Lord was so excited that he purchased 200 *dunams*."[2]

"He's gone mad," Clara sighed under her breath, but it was unclear

---

2 One dunam is 1,000 m^2.

to those sitting with her whether she was referring to Lord Melchett, Weizmann, or her son, Daniel.

"I am in charge of the farm, the garden, and the orchards. We grow oranges there, and there's also a packing house. Jews and Arabs sit on mats on the floor for hours and wrap each orange separately with paper. Then they then are exported to London from the Jaffa port."

"I do not understand how an English lord is willing to associate with a man who has as little pedigree as Weizmann."

Daniel halted the cart. He was used to his mother's arrogance but was unwilling to put up with it anymore. "Weizmann is an important leader. The English wanted to establish a Jewish state in Uganda, and Weizmann persuaded them to drop the idea. He said to Lord Balfour, 'Suppose I were to offer you Paris instead of London, would you accept it?' 'But we have London,' Balfour answered, and Weizmann retorted, 'That is true, but we had Jerusalem when London was a marsh.'"

"Weizmann is also very wealthy," said Ilioff, knowing that money was a sensitive topic for his wife. For her, pedigree and money went hand in hand. "Weizmann developed a fermentation process to produce acetone called the 'acetone organism' and patented it. The British needed acetone as a substitute for gunpowder during the war, and Weizmann made a fortune."

"What about your inventions?" Daniel asked, interested.

Ilioff sighed, "Russia is not Britain," and Clara nodded her head in agreement. "Do you remember how the Kharkiv Polytechnic didn't want to give me a professorship because I was Jewish? And how long it took for me to get one? After that, the Bolsheviks refused to allow me to register patents. They threatened that Clara and I would be sent to a re-education camp if I didn't cooperate. They confiscated the house and the money we had in the bank."

"They also drowned our Yasha in the river," Daniel added.

Everyone fell silent. Only the creaking and sighing of the cart could be heard.

"What happened to us? Life used to be so good and so beautiful," Clara whispered, leaning on Ilioff's shoulder.

"Look at the full half of the glass, Clarushka," said Ilioff, giving her a hug. "We managed to escape the Bolsheviks, Daniel is alive and married, we have a granddaughter, Jenka is with us, and you also have me."

Jenka sat raptly. All these years, his father had glorified the Bolsheviks. Jenka had never known that they'd drowned Yasha.

*

As they approached Hadera, the dunes began to appear as expanses of clean, pale-yellow sand mounds. Now and then, a small bush could be spotted, struggling for its life, tilted, yielding to the wind with tiny, withered, dry leaves.

"We should have stayed in Tel Aviv before embarking on such a difficult journey," Clara murmured. "I heard that a modern city is being built there, with wide, tree-lined boulevards. We could have taken a walk and sat at a café."

"That was the original plan. But before you arrived, the Arabs committed a massacre at the Immigrants House in Jaffa. The immigrants drove them back with iron bars they removed from the fence. Then, Arab policemen arrived, fired at the building's gate, and a mob burst inside and began killing and looting. The Arabs only retreated when a British officer arrived."

In his mind's eye, Daniel could see his parents' bodies tense up. "Don't worry. There is a rifle under my seat."

"A rifle? I know guns," Jenka said enthusiastically, "I was at battles that my father participated in and killed soldiers from the White Army."

Ilioff shushed him. "Daniel and Yasha belonged to the White Army. What's all this talk about?"

Daniel went on, "A year ago, Bedouins murdered Yosef Trumpeldor while he was defending the Jewish settlement of Tel Hai in the north of the country, close to Syria."

"How could primitive Bedouins kill a Russian war hero with a badge of honor for valor from the Czar?" Clara asked in disbelief.

"And what about a Jewish defense force? I know how to make Molotov cocktails," Ilioff suggested, thoughts racing through his mind.

"A Jewish force called the Haganah has been established. But it's limited in scope, lacks central command, suffers from a budget shortage, and various other issues. They have very few weapons and act as an underground force, is illegal under the British Mandate."

Clara shouted, "Ilioff, why did we come here? Out of the frying pan into the fire. What's next?"

"But this is our land," Jenka blurted out, surprising everyone, perhaps even himself.

The sun began to set, painting the dunes a magical gold. The color palette of the sky changed, fading to red, orange, and gray. When the sun sank into the sea, everything went dark, except for the star-filled sky. Ilioff and Clara fell asleep, their heads swaying to the rhythm of the cart's wheels like branches in the wind.

Daniel loaded the rifle. "It is dangerous to travel at night."

Jenka moved to sit next to him. "I'll be your eyes. I have experience spotting suspicious movements and noises."

*

The cart stopped at a roadside motel. Light flickered through the windows of a two-story stone building. Dozens of carts and coaches were parked in the courtyard. Horses and donkeys were tied along the fence, their heads stuffed in sacks of feed. Daniel woke his parents, helped them get down from the cart, and they dragged their feet heavily toward the building. When they opened the hostel door, they were blinded by the light of numerous kerosene lanterns and the sound of dozens of young people eating and speaking a mix of Russian, Polish, and Hebrew. Dima, the owner of the hostel, came to the door. He took one look at the exhausted old couple holding onto each other and leaning against the young boy. "Yes, we have a vacant room." He showed them to the stairs that led to the second floor. Dima opened a door and revealed a small room with four cramped beds covered with white mosquito nets. Despite the late hour, the air was still warm and humid. The windows had dense screens that made it difficult for fresh air to enter the room.

"The mosquito nets and the screens are to protect you from malaria," he explained in perfect Russian.

The old couple lay down on the beds and closed their eyes. Daniel and Jenka went down to fetch the luggage. They unloaded the suitcases from the cart, carried them on their backs, climbed the stairs, entered the room huffing and puffing, dropped the bags to the floor, and slammed the door behind them loudly, waking up the old couple.

"Could you please be quiet?" Ilioff begged. "We were already asleep."

"You must get up and come downstairs to eat."

"We're not hungry. We just want to sleep."

Daniel brought over a bowl of cold water. He washed their faces and their hands, disregarding their pleas to let them sleep. Eventually, they got out of bed and shuffled after him down the stairs to the dining room.

Dima greeted them and ushered them to a large table located in the corner at the edge of the dining room. His wife, Fanya, wiped down the table with a damp rag and cleared the previous diners' dirty dishes.

"Please, sit down," Dima addressed his guests with a smile. "Come, sit! It's not every day that older people, fresh off the boat, come to the inn. I have many stories to share with you."

"My parents are tired. They just want to eat and go back to sleep," Daniel said.

"I want to hear," peeped Jenka, sitting up straighter in his chair.

So, Dima began to tell his tale. "We decided to leave Russia when we realized that the Russians don't want Jews when they segregate and don't want them when they assimilate. The Hibbat Zion movement was established, determining that the only solution was the Land of Israel, which was part of the Ottoman Empire. This was during the Storms in the South pogroms of 1882."

"Eighteen eighty-two?" Ilioff opened his eyes. "The Russification, the assimilation into Russian society, which I so strongly believed in, shattered before my eyes during the horrible Storms in the South. I didn't believe in Zionism and thought maybe the answer was the 'Am Olam' movement that decided to move to America and establish agricultural communities there. We went to America, but we did not know how to cultivate the land there. Soon, quarrels broke out among us, everything fell apart, and I returned to Russia to complete my studies."

Dima nodded his head, empathizing with every word the old man said. "They didn't know how to cultivate the land here either, and there's also malaria here. Many people gave up and returned to Russia."

"How severe is the malaria?" Ilioff asked.

"The Hibbat Zion Movement purchased thirty thousand dunams of land from an Arab Effendi named Salim Khoury. But as it turned out, they'd bought malignant mud. And the young men and women, who'd come from Russia and Poland, contracted malaria."

"Luckily for us, we had Dr. Hillel Yaffe, who was an expert on the damn disease," chimed in Fanya, trying to cheer up the guests.

Like a wilted flower that had finally been watered, Clara woke up, sat up straight, and asked, full of curiosity, "Dr. Hillel Yaffe?" Everyone's eyes widened when they saw how attentive and interested she was.

"Hillel is a childhood friend of mine from Ekaterinoslav. I didn't know that he was infected with Zionist fervor. He comes from a good family. His father is an educated man and a successful merchant."

Dima looked at Clara. Despite her tousled hair and dusty clothes, it was clear that she was a true aristocrat. "Your friend was the first doctor here to figure out that Anopheles mosquitoes, which multiply in marshes, cause the disease. Baron Edmond de Rothschild consented to Yaffe's request to purchase two hundred thousand eucalyptus seedlings from Australia because their roots would absorb the swamp water and dry them out."

A hefty waitress placed a jug of water and a few metal cups on the table. Daniel, Jenka, and Ilioff poured themselves some and drank. Clara sat frozen in her seat, her hands clasped on the table.

"It was hot today. You need to drink even if you aren't thirsty," said Daniel pouring her a cup and serving it to her. Reluctantly she reached for the cup and smelled the water. Perhaps it had come from the marshes?

"If you are looking for mosquitoes, they are already dead. This water has been boiled." The waitress looked contemptuously at the spoiled old woman, who reminded her of her Polish mother, whose every letter was packed with warnings and pleas, begging her to return to Europe. Clara touched her lips lightly to the brim of her cup and began to slowly sip. Everyone was looking at her. When she finished drinking the water, she smiled at them all.

The waitress returned with a large bowl full of food and placed it in the center of the table. Daniel hurriedly filled himself a plate and started eating hungrily. Jenka also pounced on the food, wolfing it down quickly, but Ilioff and Clara looked at the food suspiciously, wondering whether to try it. Daniel urged them to eat. "The food is healthy and clean." He filled their plates, and they began to eat carefully as if looking for vermin or rocks. But they had to admit, the food was better than it looked.

"I like to see what I am eating. It is important that food be served to the table in a way that stimulates the appetite," Clara explained her hesitation.

"People here work hard and eat because they are hungry," replied Dima, who had changed his mind about her. She may be an aristocrat, but her haughty demeanor was unbearable.

"When everything is mixed together, it looks like scraps thrown into a bowl. Are they saving on dishes? Is there no one to wash them?" she looked down her nose as if she were scolding the maid.

Dima decided not to respond. If he were to snap back at her rude remarks, a quarrel would break out, and it was more important to him to continue recounting the story he'd already told dozens of times to every new immigrant who arrived at his inn. "Hundreds of young men and women arrived to work in the marshes. The water reached our chests. We held the seedlings between our toes and pushed their roots into the muddy earth. The eucalyptus trees grew, but the swamps remained. We all got sick, and every day we buried more dead."

Ilioff saw Clara's face contort, and she began to inhale heavily. He knew what was going through his wife's mind. She began to whimper, and he grasped her hand.

"After the Bolsheviks drowned our Yasha, not one day has passed that we haven't mourned," and the pained sighs of a bereaved mother erupted from her throat. "He wanted to immigrate to the Land of

Israel so badly, and we prevented him," she wailed. Then she paused, trying to digest her thoughts, "Now I know that if Yasha had come here, he would have laid in a tent on a shabby mattress, feverish with malaria and dying alone."

"Yes, Clarushka, it is possible that our Yasha would have died of malaria here."

"We should have gone to America." She burst out in heart-breaking tears. "A good, big, wealthy country. It's horrible here. Sand, flies, marshes, malaria, Arabs. They killed the Russian hero Yosef Trumpeldor, they will only get stronger, and there will be wars, many wars. What will happen to our children, to our grandchildren?"

Ilioff pulled Clara's head to his chest. "Why are you always so pessimistic, my Clarushka? We all love you, and you make life dark for yourself."

Clara and Ilioff went up to their room. Daniel brought them quinine pills and a glass of water. They were too tired to change into their sleeping garments.

"We'll sleep in our clothes," Ilioff said to Clara, stroking her hand. She had such soft skin. "You are right. Our Yasha would have died of malaria here," he said, and they both felt a glimmer of relief shine through their sea of pain.

*

In the morning, Daniel made sure that everyone followed his instructions, and wore clothes that covered their entire bodies, including their necks. After a few minutes of driving, eucalyptus trees materialized before them. A forest of trees whose roots were dipped in swamp water. Despite the early hour, the air was smoggy, and steam rose up from the bogs.

Ilioff gave an order to halt the cart, and Daniel protested, "Why take the risk? There are mosquitoes everywhere. You are elderly and can get sick."

But Ilioff insisted. He got down from the cart and walked towards the swamps. Some young people working there noticed and approached him.

"Good morning, grandfather. Are you looking for your son or grandson?" A lanky fellow asked in Russian.

"We arrived yesterday by ship from Odessa. We are making our way to Haifa," he replied.

"Congratulations, grandpa. I wish my parents back in Russia would come as well."

"What are you doing?"

"Digging channels to drain the swamps into the Hadera River."

"At the roadhouse, they explained to me that trees were planted to dry out the swamps," said Ilioff.

"The roots aren't deep enough. But it will be fine. The water level of the swamps have already started to drop."

He watched the young people standing in the marshes, taking mud from the bottom, forming it into bricks with their hands, and letting them dry. Others built walls for the drainage channels from the dry bricks. They worked quietly and devotedly, in reverence, like a religious sect.

"Cheer up, grandpa," they smiled at him. "We are all sick and taking lots of quinine. We have ringing in our ears, fever, convulsions, and vomiting. But within a year or two, the swamps will disappear, and with them, the malaria."

Ilioff recognized their ideological fervor. He had seen millions of Jews overtaken with the same zeal when they'd believed in the doctrines of Russification, Communism, and Bolshevism. Everything turned out to be a hoax. Tens of thousands of young Jews had sacrificed their lives for the sake of the Russian Revolution that then stabbed them in the back.

"Grandpa, cheer up. We did not come to be coddled. We came to build a homeland for the Jewish people."

For the first time, Ilioff understood the power of being a Zionist pioneer.

*

They arrived in Haifa in the dark. The tired horse hauled the cart up Mount Carmel. Daniel stopped the cart when they reached Nordau Street. "We're here." He got down from the cart, patted the horse affectionately, and tied him to the fence. Jenka helped his grandparents climb the stairs to the second floor, and they entered a modest two-room rental apartment.

"During the day, we keep the windows closed so that mosquitoes and flies don't enter," Daniel explained, opening the shutters and allowing a pleasant breeze to blow in. "You can shower before bed." He pointed to a tall pipe ending in a perforated circle.

Daniel turned on the tap, and water spouted out. He quickly undressed and proceeded to take a shower. The water splashed all over his body, and he let out a roar of delight, "Oh, it feels so good! It's wonderful!"

Clara couldn't believe her eyes. Her son stood before her, stark naked. Izzy Stanislavski's grandson, acting like a common farmer. He may have a muscular and rugged body, but to bare it before everyone? Oh, the shame. May God forgive him, she thought and averted her eyes, having already seen everything that intrigued her.

Jenka waited impatiently for his turn and got into the shower. The water was cold but refreshing. When he was finished, Ilioff took Clara's hand and led her to the shower so that she wouldn't slip. He washed her hair, dried her tenderly, then showered himself. The beds were simple, like the ones at the roadhouse, but the sheets gleamed with cleanliness. Ilioff wore pajamas, Clara a nightgown with lace trimmings, and Jenka put on a long cotton nightdress and wore a nightcap on his head. Daniel made sure everyone was in bed, then left the apartment, and quietly closed the door behind him.

*

Light flooded the room through the open shutters. The door to the small balcony was ajar, and a fresh breeze blew in. Jenka got out of bed and went out on the terrace. The Mediterranean Sea unfolded before him; the crescent-shaped bay framed by sandy beaches that kissed the water's edge. He took a deep breath. He removed his nightdress and felt the air caress his naked body. He indulged in the pleasurable experience. He closed his eyes and saw millions of glistening particles fly towards him rapidly from the sea. Merging together, they created a blurry image out of which his mother's face appeared. He thought he heard her speaking to him. He couldn't understand the words but recognized her soft voice. The gentle wind reminded him of her touch. He had never felt her so close to him.

There was a knock on the door, and Jenka opened his eyes. He hurried to lift his nightdress off the floor, covered his nether regions, and before he could open the door, Daniel burst inside with Sarah, who held the baby in her arms. Jenka apologized for forgetting to lock the door, but Daniel explained that no one locked their doors. There were no thieves.

"We brought you breakfast – egg, yogurt, tomato, and black bread." Daniel spread a checkered tablecloth on the old wooden table, lit the wick, and put the kettle on to boil water.

Ilioff and Clara woke up, apologizing that they weren't appropriately dressed for their first meeting with their son's wife. Clara approached the baby, took her into her arms, held her close to her chest, and kissed her. When she raised her head, a look of gratitude, for the wonderful little creature that her daughter-in-law had given birth to, brightened her features. Jenka declared that he, too, wanted to hold the baby. He sat down on a chair, and they carefully placed her in his arms.

"Her name is Anna, or Hannah, in memory of your late Anna." Sarah smiled and saw Clara beaming appreciatively at her. The baby woke up and started to cry. Sarah pulled out her breast and nursed her.

Clara was amazed. Was this how people acted? Only farmers whipped out their bosoms and breastfed in public.

"Women breastfeed their babies here," Daniel said. "Wetnurses are only employed if a mother can't produce milk."

"I'm continuously learning new things here," Clara chortled, and Ilioff joined in her laughter and embraced her.

The young woman finished breastfeeding and lay the peaceful baby on the bed. She surrounded Anna with pillows until she saw that the infant was asleep and breathing steadily, her hands spread out like a Hannukah *menorah*. They sat down on wooden chairs at the round table and ate breakfast. The weather was pleasant, a refreshing breeze blew in from the bay, and bright sunlight shone on the balcony and through the windows, creating an optimistic atmosphere.

"To sit with Jenka, Daniel, Sarah, and the baby," Clara said, happy, "is a miracle. I can't believe it."

Daniel was pleased that his mother had received his wife warmly, "You will see each other every day now. Sarah will stay in Haifa for another two months until the baby grows stronger."

"Where do you intend to take her?" said Clara curiously.

"As I told you, I work at the farm of Lord Melchett. Not far from there, Migdal, a new settlement we call a *moshav* is being built.

"What is a *moshav*?" Ilioff was interested.

"In each *moshav*, a group of farmers are united in a cooperative economic framework, mutually aiding each other, but each family is an independent economic unit," Daniel explained, adding, "I took out a loan and bought land there. When I finish my workday at the villa, I go there and work on building a house for us. Friends from the *moshav* have been helping me. Sarah and the baby will come once the house is ready."

"There is no doctor there and no running water," said Sarah looking straight at Daniel. "The trip from Haifa to Migdal takes at least three days. You can only get there on a donkey or a horse." Her voice echoed with the bitterness of a longstanding argument between them.

"Soon, a paved road from Tiberias, a town on the shores of the Sea of Galilee, to Migdal will be complete, and it will be possible to travel there by coach."

"My Goodness," Clara was horrified.

"Is there malaria there?" It was unclear whether Jenka's question was intended to decrease or increase the anxiety level in the room.

"There is almost nowhere here without malaria. We'll put screens on the windows and take quinine." Daniel knew that the malaria talk would lead the conversation to a negative place, so he spoke up in defense of the land. "The Sea of Galilee is magical. If you walk just a few minutes from Migdal, you can bathe in the lake. The water is lovely and pleasant, not cold like in Russia. The wild and ancient Arbel Cliff overlooks The Sea of Galilee. In just a few hours ride, you reach Lake Hula, a wildlife Eden. Migratory birds from northern Europe stop there on their way to Africa. Jenka will be able to come to visit us during the holidays. We'll go hunting."

Jenka's eyes lit up. "I'll be your hunting dog, and I can play with my cousin."

"Ilioff, why are you quiet? What do you think of all this?" Clara turned to her husband.

"This is a new country. This is their life, Clarushka. There is nothing we can say."

*

"We'll go to the Technion now," Daniel announced. "Jenka will stay with Sarah and the baby."

After a few minutes of leisurely walking, the Technion building came into view. Ilioff hadn't expected to see such a large and impressive structure, built in the style of northern Europe out of chiseled stones and decorated with oriental arches. As they approached, he recognized Professor Aharon Cherniavsky and his wife near the building's entrance and picked up his pace. A decade had passed since he'd met them at Anna and Ben-Zion's apartment in Switzerland. Cherniavsky had been an assistant at the Physics Institute and graduated in the same class as Anna and Ben-Zion. When had that been? In 1912. Only a decade had passed, and the whole world had changed.

Cherniavsky noticed Ilioff, ran towards him, and the two men hugged. "I was so excited when Daniel told me that you were coming to Haifa. I hope you won't be angry with me for snitching to some of my friends who have insisted on meeting you."

His friends didn't wait for an introduction with the distinguished guest. "I'm Shmuel Pevzner, the engineer," said one man, bowing to Ilioff. "I immigrated in 1905, I was a delegate to the First Zionist Congress, and today I am a dedicated friend of the Technion."

"I am Dr. Shmaryahu Levin, a native of Belarus, a loyal fighter for the Technion, and with no insult to this prestigious and important institution, I am also a devoted fighter for the Hebrew University in Jerusalem." Then he turned to Clara, with a broad smile. "I know your family from Ekaterinoslav. I served as Rabbi in the Jewish community there from 1898 to 1902. It is an honor to meet you."

"I see that the surveying engineer, Mr. Ephraim Krause, has arrived." Cherniavsky opened his arms wide to receive him.

"I recommend to our distinguished guests to stay on good terms with him," suggested Shmaryahu Levin. "His wife is Dr. Esther Shimkin, who works with Dr. Eliyahu Auerbach at Hadassah Hospital on the slopes of Mount Carmel. The only Jewish hospital in the city."

"Now we can start the tour," Shmuel Pevzner said, addressing everyone in eloquent Russian as he took on the role of the guide. A sloping stone railing flanked the wide staircase on both sides leading to the entrance of the building, giving it an air of dignity. They reached the foyer, a great hall with a high ceiling.

"I have visited a considerable number of Polytechnic Universities in Europe throughout my life, and I do not remember seeing such an impressive foyer," marveled Ilioff.

The building stood out from the simple and gloomy houses he'd encountered the day before. "The vision to establish the Polytechnic was Dr. Nathan Paul's, one of the founders of the Ezra Association in Berlin," Pevzner explained. "He visited the land in 1908 and realized there was an urgent need for an institution that trained technicians and engineers. He raised funds and approached the well-known Jewish architect Alexander Baerwald, who lived in Berlin, and came here specifically, where he founded the local architectural style. In 1913, the construction was almost completed, everything was clean and ready for the housewarming and for studies to begin, but then The Great War broke out, and everything fell flat."

They continued down to the basement to see the labs. The rooms were spacious, and light came in through arched windows near the ceiling. On the lecture floor, they passed through dozens of spacious, neglected rooms with shattered windowpanes, cracked floors, and walls defiled by heinous graffiti paintings.

"The structure served as a disinfection institute and a slaughterhouse for the German army," explained Dr. Shmaryahu Levin to his horrified guests. "Then the British used the building as a military hospital. When the war ended, we had to persuade the British to vacate the building."

"The building has undergone severe misuse," Clara declared.

"We are currently raising funds for the renovation and repurchase of the equipment," Pevzner said, trying to convey a positive perspective.

"When do you expect to start classes?"

"Evening studies are scheduled to begin in late 1923, and official classes should start in early 1924," disclosed Cherniavsky. "In the meantime, I am teaching at the Herzliya High School in Tel Aviv."

Dr. Levin noticed the concern on Professor Ilioff's face. "We are purchasing teaching equipment and machinery, selecting professors, and putting together a curriculum. With your scientific prestige and experience teaching higher education, it will now be possible to raise money to set up a chemistry lab."

"I hope so, I hope so," Ilioff said and fell silent.

They all went down to the grounds. Mrs. Cherniavsky led them to the shade of a large tree, beneath which a table was set, on it a glass jug containing cool lemonade, and a plate of cookies. They sat down to drink lemonade.

"Dear friends, I must find a job," Ilioff interrupted the conversation. "The Bolsheviks confiscated all my property, and, at my age, I cannot make my living by paving roads."

Clara's heart squeezed up in her chest; she felt the humiliation and pain of his words.

"I heard that there is a severe unemployment problem," sighed Ilioff, and everyone bobbed their heads in agreement.

"Pinhas Rutenberg is currently looking to hire employees," proposed Cherniavsky. "He intends to hook up the entire country to electricity. He's already gotten approval from Churchill, the Colonial Secretary. Rumor has it that he's already raised two hundred thousand *lira* in cash."

"I knew him back in Russia when he was still working in a factory in Ekaterinoslav. He's an entrepreneurial type," Ilioff's voice filled with hope.

"And a famous communist, too," said Pevzner, as Ilioff nodded in agreement.

Ilioff stood up. "I have a new granddaughter who is waiting for her grandfather."

On the way back to the apartment, Ilioff felt tightness in his chest. Daniel supported him so that he wouldn't fall. When they arrived at the house, Clara went to sleep, but Ilioff could not.

"Father, why are you so worried?"

"We have enough money left to live off for just a few more months, half a year at the most. A year after Anna's death, I deposited her share of the inheritance in a bank account in Switzerland, but that money is meant for Jenka. It would be terrible to take my grandson's money."

*

Ilioff sent a letter to Rutenberg, and within two weeks, he was invited to meet him in Tel Aviv. He purchased a ticket for a sizeable three-horse-drawn carriage, dubbed "Diligence." He was told that the trip would take six hours, including a stopover. The ten passengers sat crowded on benches on each side of the carriage. Some of the passengers asked to open the windows during the ride so that fresh air would come in, but others objected, fearing that pesky flies would enter. Sweat stains materialized under the armpits and on the foreheads of the passengers, filling the carriage with a repulsive odor.

Carrying the weight of the world on his shoulders, Ilioff sank deep into thought. What if he didn't get a job? There would be no choice but to travel to America. He'd spoken about it with Clara, but when Jenka heard, he objected firmly. The boy resolutely announced that he would not leave the country and that if they did, he would stay with Daniel. A man his age should be relaxing in an armchair, free from worries about earning a living, enjoying the fruits of years of his labor. Instead, he was looking for a job in a new place, in a language he didn't know. He arrived, exhausted, in the hot and humid city of Tel Aviv. He bought a soft drink and a sandwich at a small kiosk and sat down to rest on a boulevard lined by young trees. Above his head was a woven awning of leaves, through which the sun shined, playing games of light and shadow on the ground. The houses were nice and new. He watched the passers-by, and his mood began to improve. Then, he rented a carriage and went to the office on Allenby Street, utilized by the Tel Aviv-Yafo Electric Company Ltd.

He climbed the stairs, stopping for a light rest on each landing. When he reached the third floor, he saw young men crowded on benches, leaning against the walls of a long, narrow corridor. When they saw the old man, they quickly made room for him to sit. Ilioff listened to them talk about the severe unemployment, about a friend who'd found a job, about a friend who'd given up and returned to Europe, and about the letters they'd received from their worried parents back home. They could be his students, he thought, or even his grandchildren. Luckily none of them knew him. He sat hunched over, ashamed, attempting to hide, not wanting to be seen.

He waited patiently alongside the young folks. The door opened, and Rutenberg exited the room, glancing at those waiting as if trying to estimate how long it would take him to interview them all. Then, he noticed the odd figure of Ilioff sitting bent over in the corner.

"Please come in, Professor Ilioff."

Ilioff took out the scientific papers he had published from his satchel and placed them on the table, but Rutenberg waved them away, "There is no need. I know who you are. I met you at the factory where I worked in Ekaterinoslav. I was a young engineer, and you, a well-known scientist who served as a professional consultant. I am also familiar with your plan for building dams to generate electricity on the Dnieper River. The plan remained in the drawer during the Czar's reign, but now the Bolsheviks have carried it out and even consulted with me."

Ilioff felt considerable relief that he didn't have to explain all that he'd accomplished in his life. "Yes, I remember you, from when you were just beginning, back in the factory in Ekaterinoslav. After that, you became one of the leaders of the communist revolutionaries."

"Yes, I was among the leaders of the Social-Revolutionary Party. But that belongs to another chapter in my life that I wish to forget."

Ilioff realized that the conversation was heading in an unwanted direction for both of them. "Mr. Rutenberg, I do not wish to waste your time. There are young people sitting outside who desire to meet you. Can you offer me a job?"

"Professor Ilioff, you are the man I need. Come back here tomorrow, and I will take you to visit the power plant." Before Ilioff left the room, he heard Rutenberg shouting to his secretary, "Arrange a place for the professor to stay."

*

Rutenberg arrived in his car to pick up Ilioff from the hotel, and the two drove to the site of the power station. Rutenberg introduced the professor to his employees as an expert who would be helping plan the company's major projects. Then, he took Ilioff to see the two, five-hundred-horsepower diesel engines that had arrived from Germany.

"You cannot imagine the bureaucratic difficulties I have been experiencing: anti-Semitism, opposition from the British, the Arabs, and even from Jews. When we built the power plant, the residents of Tel Aviv would come to the site and mock me, saying I had delusions of grandeur. My workers couldn't stand there and take it and instead cursed back at them with the most colorful Russian vulgarisms. The most memorable story is about an elderly Jewish Yemenite man who explained to his wife, 'A huge pump will stand here and pour oil into the wires that reach our house, so you won't have to carry oil from the store anymore.'"

"I get the impression that your workers are very respectful and even love you."

"I take good care of my workers."

They went up to the office. They agreed that Ilioff would immediately begin to prepare a preliminary plan for a diesel station in Haifa, which would be built in two years, in 1924. He was to receive a monthly salary.

In the carriage back to Haifa, a pleasant sense of weariness spread over his limbs. It was the calm after the storm, and he fell asleep.

Chapter 4: Awaken My Brothers, Do Not Sleep

"I enrolled you in the Reali High School," Ilioff informed Jenka contentedly. "You'll have to make up the material you missed over the years that you didn't study, but you're capable, and I'm sure you'll succeed."

"I will make up the material," Jenka was quick to reply, "but I'm afraid of going to school. I still remember how Father would beat me with a belt when he wanted to educate me."

"The Hebrew Reali school is an innovative school. The teachers aren't allowed to cause physical harm to the student's bodies," Ilioff said, trying to reassure Jenka. "You are already thirteen years old and cannot grow up like an ignorant Russian farmer. You must enter an educational framework, learn to study, stick to a schedule, do your homework, and stop all your craziness, especially the Russian cursing, the prank-playing, and your other nonsense." He nodded his head apprehensively, "We'll see if the principal, Dr. Arthur Biram, can make you an obedient schoolboy."

Jenka learned to speak Hebrew quickly but had difficulty writing, which was not unusual. All the kids in his small class belonged to the city's Jewish social melting pot, and their mother tongues were

Russian or German. The only exception was Yardena Cohen, who was of the sixth generation of her family to be born in the Land of Israel. Her mother tongue was Hebrew, though she also spoke Arabic. She was the daughter of Pinhas Cohen, an agronomist, a man of nature, and a teacher at the school.

Jenka excelled in the sciences but got bored in his classes. He would sit in physics class with his eyes closed and his hands over them, half asleep, and then suddenly open his eyes and shout, "that's a mistake." He'd run to the blackboard and prove that the teacher was wrong, using equations and calculations. If he were not the grandson of Professor Ilioff, the teacher would have kicked the talented and cheeky boy out of the class.

A short-statured teacher named Arieh Kroch taught math. Kroch would call Jenka to the blackboard and stand before him, straightening up to his full height, reaching the long-legged student's belt. He would then scold Jenka subtly for doing his homework haphazardly. "When I was your age, I would have prepared my assignments better." Jenka was his favorite student. And the teacher understood his talented student. He knew Jenka prepared his assignments carelessly because they did not challenge him, and not only that, but he viewed them as an insult to his intelligence.

*

The other subjects didn't interest him. Before the exams, he'd cram all the material, in tiny handwriting, making sure to write clearly, on a piece of rolled-up paper, which he could hide in the palm of his hand. It was a much more significant challenge than actually learning the material, and for such a challenge, he was willing to put in a lot of time and energy. Once, they caught him with the scroll and threatened to tell the professor. Then, they caught him again. Dr.

Biram summoned Professor Ilioff and firmly but politely asked him to stop tolerating Jenka's cheeky behavior and pranks so forgivingly. Yet, the professor defended the honor of his orphaned grandson.

"Jenka is just bored," he criticized Dr. Biram. "You need to engage him! Surprise him!" When he got home, he told Clara about the conversation. "Dr. Biram threatened to expel Jenka from school. I defended our grandson, but we must set boundaries on his behavior." But Clara had long since made up her mind, "When I chose to raise him, I decided to give him whatever he wants. I will make him a bowl of porridge every night before bed so that the taste of his short childhood in his mother's arms will not be erased from his mouth."

*

Every morning, the rising ceremony was repeated. The old couple stood by Jenka's bed, patting the blanket gently, whispering softly that he should get up, that the school bell would soon ring. When that didn't work, the pleading stage began – the bell had already rung, and he would be late again. "Get up, Jenka, get up," became the morning chorus. "Ding-dong, the bell has already rung," Clara sang in a soprano voice. Jenka would get annoyed, toss off his blanket, jump out of bed, blurt out a string of colorful curses in Russian, and run to the bathroom, where he'd shut himself inside, cussing. His grandparents would run after him, trying to calm him down.

"It is no fault of the boy's that his Bolshevik father dragged the poor lad to Red Army camps around Russia where uncultured soldiers taught him to curse."

Jenka was sick of it. He decided to get rid of the bell once and for all. He planned the secret operation in detail. He understood that he wouldn't be able to do it alone and roped in his good friend David Ehrlich. At midnight, Jenka climbed the tower, disconnected the bell from the beam, concealed it in a large side bag, and carefully descended. David was waiting for him down below with a donkey. They rode together to the Kishon River and, with the first ray of sunlight, got in a boat and rowed to the middle of the river, where Jenka, shouting with joy, picked up the bell and held it like a priceless piece of art at an auction while David photographed him. After drowning the bell, they rode the donkey back to the city and managed to get to school just in time to stand with the other students in the schoolyard. Dr. Biram told them about the missing bell and called the police. Who would want to steal a bell? The riddle of the missing bell was the talk of the town for days to come. Dr. Biram never bought a new bell.

*

Jenka spent the holidays with his Uncle Daniel, whom he called Doc, on the farm in Migdal. When he was fourteen years old, he and his grandfather took the Valley Train that left Haifa three times a week, crossed the Jezreel Valley, and traveled as far as Samakh in the southernmost part of the Sea of Galilee. Professor Ilioff visited the Rutenberg power plant on the Yarmouk river, one of the branches leading to the Jordan River, in Naharayim, on the border with the Emirate of Transjordan. Jenka liked to join him and listen to the explanations. Before returning to Haifa, Professor Ilioff went to the mule company at the train station to see Jenka off, who got on a donkey and joined the caravan of mules making its way to Tiberias. Doc was waiting for him at the mule company's final stop in Tiberias, his cart laden with sacks of food and farm tools. On the way, Daniel updated his nephew on the changes to the farm, which already had two horses, a mule, chickens, goats who gave milk, and a large tool shed.

When they arrived in Migdal, Hannah ran toward them, barefoot, and jumped on Jenka, "We call her 'Bosa' after the Russian word 'barefoot,'" said Daniel, giving her a kiss. The nanny Riva, who'd joined the family after Yasha's birth, sat Jenka down at the large wooden table in the kitchen, served him lemonade, and sliced him a piece of fresh black bread, on which she spread a generous amount of jam made from fruit from the trees in the orchard. He always asked for extra jam, causing Riva to smile and boast about the array of preserves she'd made from seasonal fruits, which stood tidily on the pantry shelf.

Jenka accompanied Riva and the children every morning to bathe in the Sea of Galilee. Sometimes he went alone, submerging naked in the clear water, attentive to the sounds of the wind, the silence, the chirping of the birds, and the fish who suddenly emerged from the water before diving in again. Then he'd walk back to the farm to eat the meal Riva had prepared. One day they found a small black snake in the kitchen. Jenka took a bucket and positioned its opening next to the snake, "Come on, cute little guy." The frightened snake willingly complied with Jenka's request, slithered in, curled up, and waited. Then Jenka went outside, placed the bucket on the ground, and the little snake slithered away.

On days when Doc didn't have to work, the two would head out early in the morning to hunt at Lake Hula. They rode horses, a rifle slung over Doc's shoulder and a *shabria* dagger in his bag. Around noon they'd reach the Hula swamps, which were covered by algae and malaria mosquitoes. The putrid smell of rotten plants filled the air, which blew thick with humidity. Islands were scattered throughout the lake, covered in high reeds, homes to wild boars, swamp cats, mongooses, and frogs. The two would weave their way through the lush vegetation, sinking in the mud, and keeping an eye out for animals. There was a division of responsibilities. Doc was the hunter, and Jenka was the hunting dog. When Doc shouted, "Run, dog, run," Jenka would race over, disappear into the thicket, and bring out the lifeless animal. For dinner, Riva would cook up a feast of meat.

From the window of his room at Daniel's, Jenka could see the Arbel cliff, which was formed by a volcanic eruption and rose to a height of 1,278 feet above the Sea of Galilee. During their war against the Romans, the Jews built a fortress there inside the hidden caves. Yosef ben Matityahu, who documented the war in his book, *The War of the Jews*, wrote the following about Arbel: "These caves were discovered on steep mountain slopes, and the Roman army could not access them from any side, for only narrow and winding paths led up to the mouths of the caves from below, while just above the caves, there plunged a deep, steep abyss."

Doc had promised to climb there with Jenka, but he had to give first priority to his work at Lord Melchett's villa and at the farm. So, Jenka decided to brave the climb alone. He passed the caves hidden in the cliff, the vestibules, and the cisterns, reaching the cliff's edge, where a flat plateau was revealed before him. His eyes thirstily drank in the untouched landscape, the valley, the Sea of Galilee, the mountains imposing across from him, and the towering Mount Hermon, which was under French rule, all the way in Syrian territory. He listened to the sounds of nature.

He walked along the cliff and noticed a stone protruding from the abyss like a terrace. He stood upon it and took a deep breath, his arms lifted out to his sides, floating on air and growing wings. He closed his eyes. He was an eagle circling over the valley and the Sea of Galilee; he flew higher, reached the mountains, landed on a cliff, and surveyed his kingdom. He did not know whether he was a boy or an eagle. In the face of danger, his instincts woke up within him to disrupt the scene and save his body from his mind's compelling vision. When he opened his eyes, he was alarmed to discover where he was standing. He carefully stepped back and sat down, thinking, *I wish to be an eagle in my next incarnation.*

At dinner, Doc questioned Jenka about how he'd spent the day, and the boy shared that he'd climbed the cliff. Daniel stopped eating, put down the fork, and waited a moment so as not to lash out and strike the boy. Everyone around the table fell silent. Without raising his voice, Daniel explained that Jenka had been very irresponsible, that he could have fallen and been hurt or, God forbid, killed.

"Arbel is a wild place; if the animals smell blood, they will rip you to pieces. You are old enough to know that even adventuring must be done responsibly. You must be aware of the dangers a place poses and take the relevant safety precautions. There are adventures of the brave and curious, and there are adventures of fools. Yours was the latter."

Jenka listened. Doc didn't whip him with a belt like his father used to after such antics. His grandparents never scolded him. They never set boundaries. Doc spoke to him the way he wished his father would.

*

Kroch, Jenka's teacher, founded the Hebrew Scouts Movement, and Jenka, who had just turned fifteen, joined the "Haboneh," or The Builder" group, which was part of the "Meshotetei BaCarmel" tribe, which meant "Wanderers in the Carmel". The group's job was to serve as the technical squad of the tribe, namely, to set up tents, build wooden bridges, and renovate the tribe's nest. The group's belongings included a cooking pot, a large aluminum ladle, a small ax, a flashlight, and a tin garbage bin. The group bought a large hardcover notebook to serve as their squad journal. When Jenka told them he'd received a new camera for his birthday, the group decided he would be the squad photographer and manage the diary. He illustrated the title page with accurate engineering drawings. Scout meetings took place every Thursday and were logged briefly in the journal. For example, the group met at 3:30 pm near the Shemen oil factory beach, where the members did sports activities and then spent half an hour in the water. Sometimes lectures were given, such as that of Mr. Louis Cohen, who explained to them how to plant and care for trees. On another occasion, they learned to produce shade in open spaces using scout sticks, ropes, and blankets. Five months after the group was formed, they composed a group anthem, writing its lyrics to the tune of a popular song. These were the words:

> Awaken, my brothers, do not sleep!
> Awaken, young builders do not wait
> A hoe, a hammer – our weapons
> Our flag – a language, a people
> Work – our warfare it beckons
> Our hands shall not be feeble!
>
> Though little are our rows
> Our desire is limitless
> Despair cannot defeat those
> Who happily fight challenges!

After the thirteenth meeting, the group went through a hard time. Some left, new people joined, and the discipline became lax. They decided to unite the group by going on a trip to Caesarea's antiquities built by the Jewish king, Herod.

The trip was a great success, and the group members searched for a way to commemorate it as an important event in the group's history. After a brainstorming session, the group members approved a proposal to write up the trip in the language of the Bible as a chapter about the renewal of Israel. The first day was described thus: "And they shalt walk day and night, and in that day they shalt arrive at the fortress of the crusaders, may they be damned. And it was evening, and the sun was setting. And so, the head of the group spoke to the heroes, saying: 'Listen, heroes, to my words! Rise and be courageous, for it is a dark day, there is an abundance of work, and time is scarce. Rise, long-legged Jenka, and look to the south.' And the heroes heeded the voice of their commander. And they encamped on a high hill, set up their tents, and chose men to watch over them. And there was evening, and there was morning, one day!"

The group's problems still did not stop, so the Scouts' leadership decided to send Dr. Simon to the squad to find out the root of the problem.

"What do you talk about?" asked Dr. Simon in the tone of voice of a doctor striving to understand what ails his patient.

"We usually talk about day-to-day affairs and decisions concerning the group," said the bespectacled Itzik.

"It would be more suitable if your discussions were scheduled. Each meeting, a different member should present a serious topic such as socialism or political parties, instead of just discussing issues specifically of interest to the group," Dr. Simon explained as if it were a matter of the utmost importance. He concluded by reprimanding them: "The reason you do not have a fixed goal is because you do not have a fixed standpoint, same as all the youth in the Land of Israel."

The group sat with their heads bowed. A strained silence spread.

"I know I'm not a great thinker," said Jenka childishly, feigning ignorance, and making all the group members laugh, "but I thought we were going to get expert advice from you on how to penalize disobedient members, and instead, you are rebuking all of us."

"Spare the rod, spoil the child," voiced one of the group members, and all the boys burst out laughing.

Dr. Simon realized that the meeting was headed in an unpleasant direction and decided to change the subject. "The Scouts' leadership has instructed you to build a shed that will act as a home for the school scouts," and he left the nest pleased to have faithfully fulfilled his role as an educator.

The group stayed behind to discuss the shed.

"We don't have the tools to build a shed."

"We need money to buy them."

"We need money to fund our bicycle trip to Gaza."

"If the Scouts' leadership thinks we are so good that we can build a shed, they should pay."

And the log states that the group has approved its willingness to build the shed for a fee.

The cheeky demand for money caused a stir within the tribe and was communicated at the Scouts' leadership meeting, where it was rejected vehemently. The group did not give up and decided to take their trip early and build the shed when they got back. The leadership saw this act as a rebellion. They forbade the group to go on the trip. They were ordered to proceed immediately with the shed's construction. Furthermore, they were warned that "if the group didn't receive permission to go on the trip and did so anyway, they would be banished from the tribe." The group unanimously ignored the threat and decided immediately to go on their eleven-day bicycle trip. Satisfied with themselves, it was noted in the log: "And there began the sound of cheering and trumpets, the sound of drums and flutes. We are the builders, forewarning the haters, not afraid of obstacles and dangers."

An article was published in the daily newspaper *Davar* during their trip, under the headline "The Bicycle Trip." It read as follows:

"The members of the Boneh scouts group arrived here from Haifa by bicycle via Tel Aviv, and from here they set out on their bicycles to Gaza and arrived there safely on Friday. They will also cycle the entire way back to Haifa." Both the Scouts' leadership and the group continued to defend their respective stances. The group left the Scouts and tried to continue operating independently until they finished school in October 1926.

Chapter 5: Handsome as a Movie Star

Upon graduating from high school, Jenka decided to study at the Technion . The institute opened in February of 1925 and had two departments: one for architecture and the other for civil engineering. Professor Ilioff taught in the civil engineering department and also founded the chemistry laboratory. All of the lectures were required to be taught in Hebrew, and although he had many years of experience teaching chemistry, he had to toil for hours writing out his lecture on paper in Hebrew using Russian letters. He was not even sure that the students understood what he was teaching. After class, he'd go down to the yard and explain the lecture in Russian to the students. All the lecturers did the same.

Professor Ilioff valued modesty and simplicity. He still wore the same shoes and clothes he'd brought with him from Russia. He was the sole breadwinner of the family and worked several jobs. In 1926, he mustered the courage to start building a house and took out Anna's inheritance money that he'd deposited in the Swiss bank for Jenka. He used half of the amount to build a home that, when the day came, Jenka would inherit, and the other half he gave to Daniel so that he could pay off his debts on the farm in Migdal. Ilioff bought a plot of land on Pevzner Street in Hadar HaCarmel, near the Technion, and commissioned the architect Alexander Baerwald, who'd designed the Technion and many of his colleagues' houses.

Baerwald planned a one-story house for Professor Ilioff so that it would be easy for the elderly couple to cope. The house had a large living room that had a balcony with a door leading to a small garden, a spacious kitchen with an exit to a small balcony, a bedroom for Ilioff and his wife, a bedroom for Jenka, and a big room for Daniel's children for when they came to visit. When the construction of the house was complete, Jenka took on furnishing the place as his personal project. He designed each piece, determined its future spot in the apartment, took measurements, building the furnishings in the Technion's workshop with his own two hands. For the living room, he built a big round table made of light-colored wood with matching chairs, a small high table that stood on long legs and was made of an artful combination of different types of wood, and a large settee with rounded wooden seats. For his grandparent's bedroom, he built a large wardrobe, its doors decorated with geometric patterns made from different shades of wood, and a dressing vanity for Clara. He also built a large sideboard for the living room, with four doors and a display case where crystal bowls and vases were kept, decorative items that were the pride of his grandmother.

During vacations, Doc's three children came to Haifa to stay at their grandparents' house with their nanny Riva. In August 1929, during summer vacation, the riots broke out – extreme acts of violence between Arabs and Jews that claimed the lives of hundreds of people from both sides. The pogroms began in Jerusalem following the incitement of Mufti Hajj Amin al-Husseini, who spread the false claim that the Jews intended to harm the holy places of the Islamic people. When the riots reached Haifa, Doc ran to the store to buy food, and the whole family barricaded themselves in the house for several days. During the riots, 133 Jews were killed, 339 were injured, and Jewish settlements and communities across the country were destroyed and abandoned. On the Arab side, 116 were killed and 232 wounded. Back home in Moshav Migdal, 9-year-old Bosa told her friends that "people kept coming and telling us how many dead and wounded people were being brought to Hadassah Hospital. My three-year-old brother hid. I was scared, but I did not hide."

*

Doc came to Haifa to buy a motorcycle at the Sunbeam agency. Motorcycles were discovered to be an effective means of transportation on dirt roads. Jenka gazed at Doc's motorcycle enviously; it didn't occur to him to ask his grandparents for money to buy one. He knew that his grandfather worked hard to support his family. So, instead, he collected a few old, discarded British motorcycles, disassembled them in the backyard for parts, and constructed a motorcycle for himself. He would take it on short rides to check, listen, and find where it required improvement. When he returned, he would spend hours taking it apart and rebuilding, polishing, and brushing.

A group of motorcyclists was formed in Haifa. One of their frequent trips near Haifa was the ride to the white cliffs of Rosh Hanikra, at the top of which stood the French Lebanese border post. They would park their motorcycles on the rocks near the water and walk barefoot on the reef, scraped and limping. When they reached the edge, they would dive into the deep sea, swim into the giant caves below the cliff, diving over and under each other, they would make noises that echoed within the cave walls, explore the tunnels, and finally, return to the sea, and wait for the embrace of a wave that would assist them gently onto the reef.

Occasionally, Jenka would travel alone. He sought the quiet, taking all the time he needed to take photographs, play with the shadows, adjust the focus, and position himself at the best angle with the most optimal lighting. He wanted to capture his experiences encountering nature on film. Alone, swimming naked in the sea, he could feel the power of nature enveloping him. On one occasion, he went swimming in the caves, and a storm began at sea. Waves crashed against the cave's walls, and the cave's opening turned into a death trap. He could barely swim back out to the sea, and the giant waves hurled him against the reef before sweeping him back into the open sea. He began to feel weak, and his heart rate reached an insane speed. He understood that he was fighting for his life. Another enormous wave arrived, and his body was thrown onto the reef; he gripped it with all his might, pushing his body onto the sharp protruding rocks, and crawled over the reef, spitting up water, coughing, his eyes burning. When he reached the shore, Jenka stretched out, exhausted, grateful to have found his way back to the stable and supportive earth. He sat up slowly, groaning in pain. On his left shoulder was a big bleeding gash, and his whole body was covered in black and blue bruises. He soaked up the blood sprouting from his cuts with a towel and tore up his shirt with his teeth to bandage the gash on his shoulder. He had learned the limitations of his strength compared to the sheer power of nature.

*

There were few children in Moshav Migdal and its surrounding area, and the small school had only one class in which children of all ages studied together. So, Bosa, Yasha, and Riva, moved to Haifa so that the children could attend the Reali school. The Reali school's tuition fee was known to be expensive because it was a private school. However, Ilioff paid a nominal tuition fee for his grandchildren because he was a professor at the Technion. Life at the Ilioff family home was conducted around the dining table in the living room. Ilioff would sit and read, and Clara would do tarot, needlework, or crochet. In the corner of the living room was Ilioff's desk. Riva made sure that the house was always clean and that there was good food to eat. The only one who disturbed their domestic peace was Jenka with his "craziness." He was the only one who had his own room; he forbade everyone from touching his desk and forbade them from moving anything. There was a small notebook on his desk where he would write down all his debts, big and small. Everything that was paid was erased. He would shout and curse in Russian if he noticed that anything had moved in his room. "Jenka, look at yourself. Get dressed, shave. Change your torn socks already. Jenka, Jenka, what will become of you?" Riva would scold him and lecture Clara for always giving him what he wanted.

When he went out to ride his motorcycle, he would change into the clothes that gave him a meticulous look that honored the vehicle he rode. In the summer, he'd wear a well-ironed, light-colored button-down shirt with a collar and sleeves that reached his elbows, shorts down to his knees, shoes and knee socks, a flat cap, and a big leather bag strapped diagonally across his chest. On cold days he wore a fashionable leather jacket, a matching hat that his grandparents bought him, and aviator sunglasses.

The young ladies didn't remain indifferent to Jenka when he rode the streets of Haifa on his motorcycle, handsome as a movie star. But his experience with them made it clear to him that he had no idea how to talk to women. Everything that interested him, such as his motorcycle and photography, didn't interest them.

After resolving that one of the ladies, Rachel, was very beautiful, he invited her for a ride on his motorcycle to the Sea of Galilee because while riding, he wouldn't have to talk to the girl, and on sharp turns, Rachel would press her chest up against his back. At the start of the descent to the Sea of Galilee, Jenka swerved toward the Arbel plain. They got off the motorcycle and walked along the plateau, breathing in the fresh air of the fields. Jenka had no choice but to force himself to talk to her about this and that and listen to the latest gossip, pretending like it interested him. But eventually, he lost patience, grabbed her by the hips, and kissed her. But, when he began stroking her breasts, and he heard her sigh with pleasure, she pushed him away.

"I'm a respectable girl from a respectable family. You can't fool around with me unless you propose to me first."

"Okay," Jenka replied, a naughty smile on his lips. He walked ahead, increasing his pace, and she tried to match her steps to his. After fifteen minutes of brisk hiking, Rachel was wheezing and gasping. Jenka stopped. "Rachel, I have a surprise for you." She was glad he remembered she existed.

"Close your eyes and give me your hand." He covered her eyes with a handkerchief, and she smiled excitedly. Then he took her hand and led her a few tens-of-meters onto the raised plateau. He removed the blindfold when she felt the touch of rocks under her feet. Rachel opened her eyes, saw the abyss below her, and grabbed Jenka with all her might, not letting go until he had carefully helped her off the rock. They ended the romantic trip by swimming in the waters of the Sea of Galilee.

Since then, he made a habit of bringing girls to the Arbel Cliff

*

Every year, a Purim carnival was held in Tel Aviv, the famous *Adloya-da* procession that paraded from Herzl Street to Allenby Street. The motorcycle gang decided to go watch the carnival that had become famous thanks to the legendary dancer Baruch Agadati, who threw glorious Purim parties that included a vote for Queen Esther. One exhibit called "The Tower of Babel" was about the struggle for the revival of the Hebrew language. It was a tower carried on a horse-drawn cart with signs that read "Resurrection of the language = resurrection of the people" and "Our life and death are in the hands of our language."

They continued south after Tel Aviv. The few roads that were paved ended, and the motorcycles leaped down dirt paths, winding between mountains speckled with rocks and prickly thorns. They went to Hebron, where, according to Jewish tradition, the fathers and mothers of the Jewish nation were buried in the Cave of the Patriarchs. Then they went to Nablus and journeyed to Jerusalem, where Jenka photographed the Old City, the Western Wall, Al-Aqsa Mosque, the churches, the Tower of David, and the city wall while sheep munched on the grass at its foot. They went down to the Dead Sea, the lowest place in the world, and made their way along the water, where islands of clumped salt jutted out above the sea. They continued up to the cliff of Lot's wife, who, according to the Bible, turned into a pillar of salt after looking back on the destruction of Sodom, despite God forbidding them to do so.

They took longer trips as well – to Syria, to the antiquities of Baalbek, where the remains of magnificent temples built by the Greeks and Romans stood, to Palmyra, Tadmur, which was built near a fertile natural oasis, and to Aleppo, the largest city in the region. With a camera hanging around his neck, Jenka would run among the ruins, taking pictures all the while.

When he came home from his trips, Jenka took over the kitchen and turned it into a photography dark room. He learned how to develop photos himself, installed a red and yellow light, positioned trays full of liquids, and sat using a photo magnifier for hours. On the kitchen balcony, there were ropes for hanging laundry that Jenka used to hang his photographs. His photos reflected his sensitivity to aesthetics, his classic balance, and especially his love of nature. He bought albums. He pasted triangles precisely the size of each photo on every page, ensured they were equally spaced, and inserted the images inside the triangles. Each album was wrapped in parchment paper and put into a sealed cardboard box.

Doc's children asked permission to watch. Jenka agreed to leave the door open on the condition that they wouldn't speak and wouldn't move. They nodded their heads in agreement. Then they asked to look at the albums. He sent them to wash their hands and dry them well. When they returned, he checked if their hands were dry. Then he opened the albums, and they sat quietly, looking at the photos in fascination.

Chapter 6: I Never Fell Off My Motorcycle

Jenka got off his motorcycle and walked into the Sunbeam motorcycle company's showroom in Haifa. "I heard that the new model arrived." The eyes of the young twenty-one-year-old man darted toward the new motorcycle, which stood like a gorgeous fashion model on a podium. He approached it, circled it once and a second time, bent over, checked its wheels, admired its engine, then stood back and nodded his head enthusiastically but sadly, as if he were looking at a wondrous toy he couldn't afford to buy.

"Sunbeam is organizing a trip from Tel Aviv to London with the new model," voiced Yechiel, guessing what thoughts were running through Jenka's mind. "I can recommend you for it."

Jenka got on the motorcycle, took a deep breath, and sat up straight. Yechiel hovered over him, "It's a campaign tour to promote the new model," he whispered as if revealing a sweet, forbidden secret and handed Jenka the new motorcycle's catalog.

"A campaign tour?" inquired Jenka.

"It's related to the Maccabiada, a kind of Olympics for Jews that's set to take place in Tel Aviv in 1931," Yechiel nodded his head, pleased with the sporting event's description. "The idea was born when Yosef Yekutieli visited the international Olympics and saw how many Jewish athletes participated, representing their countries, and even winning medals. He appealed to the Olympic Committee to permit athletes from Mandatory Palestine to participate. Still, they refused, stating that athletes without a country couldn't participate in the Olympics," Yechiel explained. He enjoyed demonstrating knowledge and showing the young man that he was up to date on sports news, not just motorcycle sales.

"So, what does this all have to do with Sunbeam?"

"The company is stressed about all the press and advertisements about the Maccabiada. The Maccabi club sent a motorcycle delegation on a mission to recruit athletes for the Jewish Olympics. For some reason, the journalists who covered the story decided to point out that one of the delegation members was riding a 1928 Indian motorcycle made in America. And the journalists, who don't actually know much about motorcycles, noted that the model he rode was giving all other motorcycles a run for their money."

Jenka got off the bike, his hand gliding over the glorious machine, "And the company fears that Indian's press will hurt Sunbeam's sales?" he asked, browsing through the catalog. "This new model's performance is excellent. Who'll remember the Maccabi club's motorcycle trip to Europe a year ago?"

"I felt the same at first, but the Maccabi club is planning a second motorcycle trip from Tel Aviv to London to recruit more athletes. A date has already been set – May 23rd, 1931. The commotion in the press will start again soon," sighed Yechiel. "The Hapoel club is worried their athletes will abandon them for the Maccabi club."

"This is all an idiotic war between motorcycle companies and sports clubs," Jenka said and returned the catalog to Yechiel, exited the showroom, and got on his old motorcycle.

"Should I recommend you?" Yechiel called out to him.

"Do you really think I would miss a trip to Europe on the latest Sunbeam model?" Jenka smiled, revved the engine, stepped on the gas, and drove off.

Two weeks after the press release about the departure of the "Maccabi" club's second delegation to Europe, an article was published about another motorcycle delegation heading to Europe. This time, by the Hapoel club and sponsored by the British company Imperial Chemical Industries, which owned Sunbeam motorcycles. Furthermore, the article stated that the delegation would pass through Vienna on their way to London. And so, on June 7th, 1931, *Davar* newspaper reported, "Yesterday, a group of 12 Hapoel riders left for Vienna and the Diaspora for the dual purpose of building ties with Jewish youth in the Diaspora and with the global labor movement. They are all bachelors."

*

The construction of Haifa's port had not yet been completed, so the riders with their motorcycles boarded a flat-bottomed barge that then sailed slowly toward the ship, which was anchored in deep water. The barge was tied to another vessel laden with Arabian horses that stomped their hooves, shaking the boat. One at a time, each horse was harnessed in a "hammock" and attached to the ship crane's hoist rope, which lifted them onto the deck. Once the horses were tied up and loaded into their corral, it was time to hoist up the motorcycles. The bikes were pulled up without any particular issue and tied onto the deck. The sea was peaceful, and the ship arrived safely in Turkey after a two-day voyage.

In a line, one by one, in perfect formation, the caravan of motorcycles descended to the shore and, after a brief jaunt around the city, continued on their way to Vienna. Accustomed to the Middle East's yellow dryness and heat, the motorcyclists' eyes eagerly drank in the refreshing green shade of the forests, fields, and orchards. They looked longingly at the small villages covered in foliage, where every street was loaded with lush potted plants, and a myriad of flowers adorned each balcony. They looked enviously at the great rivers and lakes, thinking that one such lake, in addition to the Sea of Galilee, could solve the water shortage at home.

They arrived in Vienna and rode proudly in a row through the wide streets. They admired the magnificent buildings that stood on their mounds for centuries, which dwarfed the houses built on the sand dunes of young Tel Aviv. The good life, the luxurious cafés, the big stores full of wares they couldn't get back home, the elegant attire of the passers-by. They also encountered Jews who were so excited to meet them that they competed amongst themselves to host the visitors in their magnificent homes. Their hosts complained about the economic crisis that made the anti-Semitism worse, but they did not intend to leave Austria. After Vienna, they continued to Germany, riding along the Rhine, then onwards to the Netherlands. The awe of the abundant greenery of Europe, the plenitude of water, and the good life continued. They crossed the La Manche Canal on a ferry and reached Great Britain.

Imperial Chemical Industries announced their arrival, and journalists were waiting for them. *The Daily Herald* published a photo of them. *The Manchester Guardian* described their journey and quoted a member of the group, Avraham Ikar. *The Daily Telegraph* highlighted the fact that they'd ridden a British motorcycle that had successfully traveled 5,000 miles without tire or machine malfunctions. The group was invited for a publicized visit to the Sunbeam factory. Echoes of the trip's success, shared by the company's publicists, reached home, and on October 3rd, 1931, an article was published about them in *Ha'aretz* newspaper, stating that "The journey's benefactor, Imperial Chemical Industries, on whose motorcycles the visitors rode, threw a feast for their guests."

The time came to return home. They again crossed the channel, but this time off the coast of France. Every day they devoured stretches of the road. They reached the alps and ascended to the snowy mountain peaks where piles of snow that had been shoveled to the side of the way towered over two meters high. At the summit, they parked their motorcycles shoulder to shoulder in flawless symmetry and went for a trek. And as they were hiking up a glacier, they heard a shout and saw Jenka fall into a gorge about twenty yards deep.

"Jenka! Jenka!" The group members called down to him and began blaming each other for hiking up a glacier without tying themselves to one another with ropes, and for ignoring the "Entry Prohibited" signs.

And then, they heard a voice: "Can you hear me?"

"Are you injured?"

"I'm in pain, I can't move. It's completely dark here."

"Jenka, tell us what's happening."

"My shoulder blade hurts, and there is stabbing pain in my left elbow."

"Some of the guys went out to call for help. Hang in there," and they heard a string of Russian curses rise up from the bottom of the gorge.

Two men stayed behind near the opening of the gorge while the others rushed to the nearby village to call for help. The Swiss villagers didn't understand English very well and instead led them to another neighboring town where there was a tourist center. When the group explained what had happened, the Swiss assumed stern expressions and said they'd broken the law since hiking on the glaciers was prohibited. They agreed to send a rescue party but clarified that they would also be reporting the incident to the police. When the group members were told to hand over their passports to the Swiss, they understood the gravity of the matter and spoke amongst themselves in Hebrew, agreeing to make a run for it. Back in the village, they bought ropes and collected some discarded planks of wood, but by the time they reached the gorge, the sun had already set. So, they unloaded their equipment from the motorcycles, set up camp, lit a fire, and appointed one member of the group to stand guard and shout "Jenka, Jenka" every ten minutes and wait for him to answer, "I'm alive." But an hour later, they heard Jenka lament "I'm freezing." They threw two sleeping bags down to him and heard him swearing as he wrapped himself in them.

"Jenka, are you okay? Jenka, answer me already!" yelled the rookie, earning the irritable answer, "I haven't kicked the bucket yet!"

"We'll rescue you with the first light of the morning."

"I'll be a lump of ice by then. I'm freezing." As he waited at the gorge's bottom, Jenka remembered a small dog he'd encountered a few days earlier when they'd spent the night at a small road lodge in the Alps. He'd gone outside in the early morning and discovered the dog tied to an iron bar with a rope. The puppy was shivering. His fur was glued to his slender body. It was clear that he'd been trembling for hours, forced to spend the night outdoors in the alpine cold. It was so cruel.

He'd gone back inside the lodge and asked whose dog it was. "Your dog is freezing cold. He was tied up all night and couldn't even run around to keep warm or seek shelter."

A large fellow came outside, shouting, "It's my dog, and I'll do with him what I want! Mind your own business," and untied the puppy.

Then Jenka remembered how his father would hit him with a belt for running over frozen rivers, and how once the ice had cracked and they'd pulled him out, shivering. He'd been hypothermic then, whereas now the cold was creeping, permeating, painful.

He hit the organs he had ceased to feel. He saw his mother's face above him, radiating with love and warmth, and felt his body react, yearning for her, he surrendered in her embrace and let her ease the cold.

In the morning, they threw a rope into the crevice, cautiously trying not to cause an avalanche inside the gorge. One of the group members climbed down and tied Jenka to the rope. Slowly, they pulled him up, got him out, and sat him down by the fire to warm up. They took off his clothes and examined his body, which had changed colors. Some parts were pale white, and others blushed red. They poured hot water on him. They determined that he'd been pummeled severely but hadn't broken anything. They gently dressed him in dry clothes, like a baby, made him a cup of hot tea, poured some cognac into it, and finally, Jenka smiled. They decided to leave the site as quickly as possible, but not before blocking the entrance to the gorge with planks of wood and taking photographs next to it.

The bikers wanted to get home already and picked up their speed. They had gotten used to the beautiful views and the greenery, and their excitement had faded. In Istanbul, they boarded a ship bound for Haifa, and Sunbeam made sure to publicize their return in advance. As their ship approached the harbor, they were greeted by the Sea Scouts, who picked up their oars and saluted their comrades for completing their mission successfully.

*

The Hapoel sports club boycotted the Maccabiada after their demand for equal representation of their athletes with Maccabi sports club's athletes was rejected. Nevertheless, the Maccabiada commenced on its planned date, March 28th, 1932. Tel Aviv's mayor, Meir Dizengoff, rode his horse at the head of the parade made up of 390 Jewish athletes from 27 countries, including 60 from Syria, Iraq, and Egypt. Yosef Yekutieli, the man who initiated the "Maccabiada," declared in his speech, "In addition to the athletic trial, a national trial will occur as well. Hundreds and thousands of young Jewish people have come to the Land of Israel to participate in the Maccabiada. They will inhale the air of their beloved homeland, they will hear the revived Hebrew language ringing out loud and clear, and they will return to their homes full of vigor and courage to continue the work of their people in the Diaspora until their time comes to immigrate to Israel."

As a sign of appreciation to the Jews of the Diaspora for mobilizing and sending athletes, the Maccabiada organized a motorcycle delegation to Baghdad. The riders, Jenka among them, visited Rutenberg's power station in Aram-Naharayim, which began to supply the country with electricity that very same year. From there, the delegation continued on a paved road that crossed the whole desert and reached all the way to Baghdad. The trip's route was scheduled to the last detail, as were their visits and where they stayed. A considerable amount of the delegation's time was devoted to social gatherings and meetings with the community. Most members of the group loved these events, held in the homes of wealthy Iraqi Jews, but, Jenka stood in the corner, his look communicating a combination of boredom and disgust.

"What's on your mind?" Vefka Kandelman asked, approaching him. He liked Jenka. Unlike the rest of the group, who were academics from respectable families, Vefka was a junior technician for the electric company. He felt that the rest of the group didn't respect him and were arrogant towards him. But Jenka was different; he treated Vefka as an equal.

"I feel like I don't belong. None of this suits me," answered Jenka, pursing his lips.

"Let's go outside and talk," Vefka said, gesturing toward the terrace and grabbing his friend's arm. They went outside. A breeze that smelled like jasmine blossoms wafted toward them from the garden.

"I won't travel with a group anymore after this trip," Jenka said.

He continued frankly, "I love riding my motorcycle because it gives me a sense of freedom, to be who I am, to challenge myself, to be in nature, far from what everyone thinks and does. But here, with the group, I feel trapped, forced to go along with plans others decided for me. They barrel past beautiful sites and don't allow me sufficient time to take photographs while, on the other hand, waste time on chitchat, jokes, wisecracks about women, and all kinds of debauchery and gluttonous nonsense."

"Wasn't it the same on your trip to Europe?"

"It was like this there too, but I was less bothered by it then. It was the first time I went on such a long journey; I was proud to belong to a motorcycle gang, and I learned a lot from them." Jenka was quiet for a moment, but then he surprised Vefka with a secret: "I wish I was an eagle and could fly anywhere I wanted."

"You have a motorcycle, and you can ride wherever you want. Next time, when you plan your own trip, invite me along," said Vefka, and the two of them returned to the drawing room.

*

Back in Haifa, Jenka started working in the engineering department of the Iraqi Petroleum Company, known as IPC. The company laid down an oil pipeline 700 miles long from the Kirkuk field in northern Iraq to the Mediterranean Sea in Haifa, where they planned to build a deep-water port for the arriving oil tankers to dock. The wages were good, the hours were comfortable, and the Haifa girls smiled at him. But Jenka was restless. He kept searching for a new adventure that would inspire him. He came up with ideas, cross-examined them, and ruled them out. Like a hunter preparing to catch his prey, Jenka sharpened his senses to seize whatever opportunity fate decided to send his way.

One early evening, Jenka was riding on Herzl Street in Haifa when he suddenly saw Yosef Langutsky riding a motorcycle in front of him. Jenka invited Yosef to his home, where Riva treated them to some food she'd just finished cooking. Only after she made sure the young men were no longer hungry could the two finally lock themselves in Jenka's room, reminisce about their trip to London together, and look at the photos. "Originally, there was talk of returning home through North Africa and not through Europe," Yosef said as they flipped through the album.

"Why did they decide to go back through Europe?" asked Jenka, surprised.

"Most of the roads in North Africa are unpaved. The area is wild and dangerous. There are constant wars between the tribes, rebellions against the Italians, and simple robbers looking to kidnap a white man and demand a hefty ransom. It was a risk the company didn't want to take."

Jenka looked eager.

"It could be fascinating to travel to Europe from the opposite direction than we did then. We could cross Sinai, go through Cairo and Alexandria, continue along the coast of North Africa to the Gibraltar Strait, cross over to Spain, and from there go north to Norway. We could return home through the Balkans and Turkey."

Yosef's eyes gleamed. "What a journey. It sounds amazing. I wish I could join you, but I just got married, and my wife wouldn't like it if I disappeared for a few months, and work wouldn't allow it either."

"You need your wife's consent to embark on a journey?" Jenka was shocked.

"If I insisted, she would eventually agree, but it might hurt our relationship."

I would never give up a trip because of a woman, thought Jenka.

In the evenings, Jenka locked himself in his room, learning what routes existed, everything imaginable about each country along the way, where to sleep, and where to visit. He spread out maps of different scales on the floor of his room, calculating how many miles he could travel each day, debating his options, making decisions, and changing his mind. Unlike his trip through Europe, he would have to travel long, uninhabited distances in North Africa. There would be an issue finding places to refuel the motorcycles. Jenka wrote letters to the embassies of Britain, Italy, and France asking for permission to refuel at military bases. The letters he got back were sympathetic but only contained recommendations, subject to each base commander's consent. Jenka couldn't rely on goodwill, so he designed two more tanks to add to the two existing ones – one for drinking water, the other for gas, and attached them to his motorcycle.

He wrote up a list of equipment to bring on the trip. First priority was given to a tire repair kit, motorcycle repair tools, a first aid kit, photography equipment, canned foods, a blanket, and some essential clothing. He attempted to load the gear numerous times in his backyard, each time omitting more supplies. When he applied for a four-month vacation, his workplace was not happy. Still, when he showed them a map of his route, they considered it and decided they should be proud that a man like him was among their employees. They agreed to give him time off in July and August when the workday was shorter. July and August were the hottest months; he would burn to a crisp on his journey, but he couldn't come up with another solution. He asked Vefka to join him on the trip. Jenka thought Vefka was an honest, loyal, relatively disciplined fellow and, despite being a bit chatty, wouldn't cause any trouble.

Vefka was moved. His eyes widened, and he hugged Jenka, "You've made me a happy man. You won't regret choosing me."

Jenka nodded, smiling at Vefka's excitement, "Can you take a four-month vacation from work?"

"Yes, no problem. I have no tenure at the electric company. I can resign, and when I return, I'll be re-employed. Wiring the country for electricity is so much work; they always need technicians."

The pair left Haifa in July 1933. They rode up to Jerusalem and descended south in a straight line towards the Sinai Desert. On the second day of their trip, they started smelling gas fumes. They tasted their drinking water and discovered that the fuel tank was leaking into the water tank. Jenka looked for the leak's location, blocked it temporarily, pursed his lips, and, after a few minutes, resolved, "We need to head back."

Vefka felt the energy deplete from his body. "Go back? Maybe we should keep going and find a place to repair it along the way?" begged Vefka, who hated the idea of backtracking.

"When it comes to water and fuel, we can't take risks," Jenka ruled, getting on his motorcycle and turning around. Vefka followed him.

They arrived in Jerusalem and went to a garage, where the hole was welded, and the rest of the tanks were inspected. They were found to be in good condition, so the pair set off again. When they were traveling through Sinai, Jenka's camera stopped working. This was not the first time his camera had broken down on a trip; usually, he disassembled it, cleaned it, and put it back together again. But the date was Friday the 13th, the worst combination of all. Even if he uttered every curse imaginable, and even if he spat and knocked on wood, nothing he could do would be powerful enough to fight the evil authority of the day.

He sat worried, picturing all the possible mishaps they might encounter on their journey. "Only a serious sacrifice can undo the evil power of this day."

Vefka observed him, "What's the most precious thing you have with you on this journey?"

"My motorcycle."

"Excluding your motorcycle because, without it, there's no trip," Vefka clarified and saw Jenka eyeing his camera.

"No, no," Vefka was startled. "Maybe in Cairo we can find a fortune-teller? Maybe you can find a protective charm?" suggested Vefka.

"I won't take photographs," Jenka decided, resolutely removing the camera from his neck, and shoving it deep into his bag.

*

The closer they got to central Sinai, the more the disruptions intensified: connecters unfastened, and supplies fell off their motorcycles. They had to stop and improvise new ways of tying their belongings. Finally, they arrived in Bir el-Hassana, a British military base that had become famous during the First World War. The first air evacuation of wounded had left for hospitals in Jerusalem. They fueled up, tightened the ties on their equipment, and, the following morning, traversed a high mountain range that crossed Sinai. Large rocks were scattered across the road, piercing their wheels and forcing them to change tires numerous times. The descent from the mountains was difficult and dangerous, but they encouraged each other, reminding themselves that they'd be in the lowlands soon.

Exhausted, the mountains behind them, they discovered that their motorcycles were sinking into the soft sand while a strong wind began to blow the sand to their eyes.

"It is impossible to go on like this. We should rest and ride to Suez tomorrow," Vefka suggested.

"There are big, celluloid face masks in our luggage," Jenka shouted so that his friend could hear him and began unpacking the gear to reach the masks buried deep in the bag.

The wind started to blow the supplies he scattered; some things spread out in the air like kites, while other items rolled quickly across the sand. They picked up the gear, struggling to walk, their feet sinking with every step into the sand, got back on their motorcycles, and put on the face masks.

Just before sunset, they arrived at the Suez Canal. They were drained, but the lights of the city of Suez flickering beyond the canal awakened in them dreams of a shower, a good meal, and a comfortable bed to lay their weary bones. But, true to the custom of the Middle East, the ferry was late, and they only reached the city of Suez at midnight.

*

In the morning, they continued towards Cairo. The road was paved but full of potholes, and their motorcycle's exhaust pipes were broken. They went to a garage in the city to repair the damage. Jenka and Vefka stayed in noisy, bustling Cairo for four days. They visited all the tourist sites, and on the last night, Vefka insisted on going to see a belly dancing performance. He did not want to go alone, so Jenka did him a favor and agreed to come on the condition that they'd return to the hotel early. Vefka was excited, but his friend sat with his upper body resting on his arms and his head resting on his hands with which he covered his eyes. Not puritanically, he just wasn't interested. When he heard the crowd roaring, he opened his eyes, parted two fingers, and peered through the gap to see what everyone was so keen about. He saw nothing of interest, closed his fingers, and returned to his half-asleep state. But when the audience roared again and stomped their feet, Jenka peered through the gap between his fingers and saw a dancer spinning colorful beads that were attached to her nipples. It was intriguing, so he straightened up and kept his eyes open. At first, the breasts rotated parallel to each other to the right and then to the left. But the climax came when the breasts rotated in opposite directions. The dancer's body was so fully mobilized in her effort that it seemed like her breasts were about to detach from her body. The colored beads became confused by the intensity of their spinning and flew into the air, scattering across the floor as the wild crowd scampered to pick them up. Jenka was fascinated. He couldn't figure out how she'd managed to do it. He raised technical hypotheses on the matter for the entire walk back to the hotel.

"Stop it! Enough!" Vefka interrupted him, "I went out to see women dance, to get turned on, and all these theories about the spinning stunts don't interest me!"

Jenka fell silent. He knew Vefka as a quiet man, a trait he greatly appreciated. But now that it came to women, the guy suddenly had a lot to say.

Jenka patted his friend on the shoulder as if to show that he understood.

"Were you turned on by the dancer?" Vefka was curious.

Jenka thought for a moment, "A little," he said. Humming quietly, he shook his head from right to left, unable to decide. "I enjoyed myself, but it was nothing special."

In the morning, Jenka woke up full of vigor and opened the shutters to let in the sunshine. Vefka shouted, "Close the shutters!" and covered his head with a sheet to protect his eyes from the light.

"I told you that we had to get up early, but you wanted to see butts, bellies, boobs, and everything else," Jenka said as he finished packing his belongings.

"Let me sleep. It doesn't matter if I sleep for another hour."

"Are you trying to annoy me? You know how strict I am about keeping on schedule."

"Yes, I know, but right now, I'm sleeping."

But Jenka did not leave his sleepy friend alone and explained the dire consequences of a late departure. "The Egyptians will soon begin to water the land along the Nile canals. The water will mix with the red dust of the road and turn to mud."

Reluctantly, Vefka got up, took a shower, and then wanted to drink coffee.

Jenka got upset. "I'm struggling to complete the trip I planned for months, and all my plans will come to nothing because of you. The road will be muddy, we'll slip, and we'll end the trip in a pathetic hospital."

Vefka fell silent and dressed quickly with Jenka's string of Russian curses in the background. They got on their motorcycles, put on masks to protect themselves from the dust, and made it in time to cross the road before the Egyptians watered it because the Egyptians weren't on schedule either. When they stopped for a break, Vefka wanted to say to Jenka, "See, you were yelling and stressed for nothing," but he made up his mind to keep quiet. He was glad Jenka had calmed down and didn't want to upset him again.

They arrived in Alexandria in the evening. Before leaving home, they had been ordered to go to the British police's main headquarters to declare their arrival and fill out forms. When the people at the station heard they were headed to Gibraltar, they crowded around them. Everyone seemed to have warnings for them.

"The road west is tough and littered with rocks that will cause a lot of trouble for you."

"Did you bring enough replacement tires?"

"Do you know what danger you're are getting yourselves into?"

"Sandstorms cover the roads making people lose their way and die of thirst."

"There are Bedouins. There are robbers. They'll kidnap you, and the chances of finding you alive are slim."

Jenka stood resolute, a cold expression on his face, solid as stone in the face of an attack. Vefka eyed him with a pleading look, "Maybe we should stay in Alexandria a few more days. We can consider alternative routes."

Jenka narrowed his eyes and shot his friend a piercing look, and Vefka recoiled and shut his mouth.

"If you're determined to make the trip, you should at least carry a weapon," a British officer suggested and began filling out their forms.

"The British don't allow Jews to buy weapons and obtain a license in Palestine," Jenka replied.

The officer ignored Jenka's comment and continued to fill out the forms, asking for their personal details.

"There are several police stations along the way. You must enter each of them and announce your arrival. We will also inform them that you are coming. That is our only way of knowing whether you are alive or dead." They signed the forms and, at their own risk, set out again.

The British and Egyptians were right. The thick dust that rose up was unbearable. The maps were inaccurate, and they guessed the rest of the way, following a trail of broken fragments left by a vehicle that had passed before them. They had yet to reach the coastal town of Mersa Matruh and were going barely 20 miles per hour. After more than ten hours on the road, they got to the town, and the local British governor came out to greet them. He'd received a message from Alexandria notifying him of their arrival and took them to their hotel.

After a shower and a light meal, they lay in bed, their limbs sprawled out, and they closed their eyes.

"Do you hear that?" asked Vefka.

"Hush! I'm asleep."

"There is something going on in the yard," Vefka got out of bed and went out on the balcony.

"I don't hear a thing," Jenka said, covering his head with a sheet.

"They're lighting up the yard and setting up chairs in rows. Something is about to happen."

Jenka jumped out of bed, went out on the balcony, saw what was happening, muttered a few curses and ran downstairs, looking like he was about to blow a fuse, with Vefka in his wake. He caught the hotel manager's eye, hurried towards him, and in a threatening tone, announced in English that they were tired and needed to sleep. The hotel manager didn't understand what the commotion was all about. His English vocabulary included only the essentials, such as 'Thank you, sir,' 'Please, sir,' 'There is a room,' 'There is no room,' 'Do you want one girl?' 'Two?' 'It's even possible to have three, sir.' But how could he explain to these young men that on this night, every week, a theater performance takes place? He accompanied his broken English with pantomime that looked like it had been borrowed from a dramatic love scene. He cried, laughed, and even got down on his knees.

Vefka stood on the sidelines watching the two and thought to himself that the real performance was taking place before his very eyes and not on stage. The audience began to arrive, and the actors took the stage and began to dance, drum, and sing in Arabic. Suddenly, a shrill noise blared as the microphones were plugged into amplifiers so the whole village would hear the cry: "There's a show tonight!"

Jenka and Vefka demanded that the amplifiers be turned off. The owner of the place got sick of them and shouted, "Enough, *hallas*," shaking his fists and gesturing at them threateningly. People in the audience started yelling at them for disrupting the show and approached the two infidels to silence them by force. It could have ended very badly had it not been for one of the policemen at the hotel, who called the governor. He arrived accompanied by police officers, demanded that the show be canceled, and dispersed the crowd. The people were angry, demanded their money back, and approached the two strangers, insulting them. The policemen were forced to defend Jenka and Vefka with their bodies. Vefka and Jenka felt very uncomfortable about the whole affair, but in the end, they had no choice but to thank the governor and head back to bed.

*

The next day they continued west. The sun was shining, and the hot wind threatened to vaporize them. They drank more water than their budget allowed, fearing dehydration. And as if someone was answering their prayers, a mist began to creep up gently from the sea, bringing a pleasant coolness with it. But what started as a refreshing misty haze turned into a massive onslaught of fog. It got cold. They couldn't see a thing. They sat curled up in blankets beside their motorcycles, waiting for the fog to dissipate. And suddenly, as quickly as it had arisen, it faded, and the muggy heat returned.

After two days of rough riding over rocky roads, full of potholes and bumps, they arrived in Sollum, a shabby coastal town on the Libyan border that served as a commercial center for the Bedouin. They stocked up on fuel and food and decided to keep moving to compensate for the delay in their progress and get back on schedule. They rode to the border checkpoint, but it was closed. So, they looked for the customs official. However, when they asked the passers-by questions in English, they chuckled and answered in Arabic. Nevertheless, the rumor of their arrival quickly spread across the town, and the fat, sweaty customs official came out of his house and motioned for them to follow him to the checkpoint, where he signed the necessary paperwork. Meanwhile, night had fallen, so they decided to stay there overnight. They were given the "best" room at the inn, intended for foreigners. It had a wide double bed covered with a worn velvet bedspread adorned with gilded tassels along its edge. There were red shiny satin curtains on the windows, and beside the bed was a dresser with a large, cracked mirror. Heaps of filth were piled up in the corners of the room and under the bed, the shower was broken and turbid water dripped from the tap. Jenka and Vefka lost their appetite and went straight to bed.

Early in the morning, they rode up to the plateau that overlooked the town to report their arrival at the Italian military outpost. As they approached, they saw camels grazing, standing unmoving in their places, blinking their eyes, and pondering. But when the camels heard the motorcycle's noisy engines, they were panic-stricken and galloped in all directions. The camels' owners came out of nowhere, carrying clubs, their eyes burning with anger, and cursed at the strangers until they'd herded the whole caravan back. The Italians watched the affair indifferently, and after everything settled down, they approached the guests, welcoming them. It wasn't every day that visitors riding motorcycles arrived at such a place.

The Italians warned them of what lay ahead, of the large stones scattered over the bumpy road full of deep potholes and chasms. They were barely able to shift gears. In an hour and a half, they advanced only 14 miles. Just before dusk, they reached Bardia, a seaport known as the place that German submarines handed over weapons to the Senussi rebels in support of their campaign to expel the British and the Italians from the area. The small Libyan village sat on a cliff overlooking the banks of a bay. They got to the village, discovered one lone street, and pondered how to proceed. A group of men approached them, surrounded them, and started to touch them, curiously eyeing their motorcycles. Sensing some action in the sleepy hamlet, more people joined the mob which grew around them, trapping them in. Jenka and Vefka started waving their hands and shouting "Get out of here" in Arabic, but the ring of men with glowing eyes and smiling faces continued to tighten around them.

"They're fantasizing about how they can dismantle the motorcycles and sell them for parts." Vefka clung to the seat, just in case someone tried to knock him off his motorcycle.

"Let's get the hell out of here," Jenka shouted as he stepped on the gas, waking up the dozing engine, which sounded out a menacing growl.

The motorcycles loudly forced their way through the crowd as dozens of hands pulled at their luggage, trying to detach it. The two young men took a sharp turn to the backyard of one of the buildings, sped inside, and stopped with a deafening squeak before an abyss.

"Damn," cursed Jenka. "The houses are built into the cliff."

"We are in serious trouble," Vefka murmured.

"Shut up, or they'll hear you. The locals are looking for us. They will tear us to shreds," he said, anticipating the worst.

But the voices of the crowd were fading.

"They are silent, like hunters stalking their prey," whispered Vefka, huddling underneath his motorcycle.

"Maybe they think we fell into the sea with the motorcycles and went looking for us," Jenka speculated.

Darkness fell. The only sounds to be heard were the wind and the waves crashing onto the cliff. Like thieves in the night, they pushed their motorcycles back into the street. It was deserted. They jumped on their bikes, pushed the pedal to the floor, and made sparks fly. In the light of the moon, they saw antelopes jumping at their wheels and cowardly ones running in the opposite direction and watching curiously from a distance.

After riding urgently for about an hour, they decided to stop for the night despite having no idea where they were. They checked that there were no snakes or scorpion nests around them, covered the motorcycles with weeds as camouflage, and didn't dare light a fire. The next day, after six and a half hours of bumpy riding, having traveled 75 miles, they reached the town of Tobruk and hurried to tell the Italian authorities what had happened.

"You were lucky. We have an undercover agent in the village whose job is to report rebel groups to us, and he persuaded the crowd to disperse," an officer explained, noticing the shock on the two strangers' faces.

"This is a wretched country. The roads are terrible, and the rebels are always stirring up trouble," he complained.

More Italians chimed in, "We have to be here, but why are you here? Why don't you stay a few days and tell us what's going on in the world?" but Jenka was determined to keep going.

They rode west, their spines vibrating, every bump in the road giving them whiplash. They could see the unfinished roads the Italians were building. The local workers waved to them.

"We're the last people that will have to stomach these trails," Vefka shouted.

They neared the Italian fortress of El Gazala, which was located in the heart of the swampy marshlands. The fort also served as a prison for Senussi rebels. The Italians went above and beyond, hosting them for dinner, eager to talk about the world, Europe, Syria, Iraq, Jerusalem, any place that might help them forget where they were posted. The next day the fortress commander insisted on leading them through the marshes so they could continue safely on their way to Benghazi. They arrived in a big European-style city and could finally clean and oil their motorcycles at a proper garage. They kept west, and a sea of sand dunes unfolded before their eyes. They climbed the dunes on foot to plan out how they should cross them. Then, they returned to their motorcycles and rode higher to see more of the road ahead, their burdened motorcycles creaking over the sand. They reached the area where the dunes met the sea, and water burst through the sand, creating pools, some full, others muddy, and some that the sun quickly dried. They climbed each sand dune on foot, searching for a path through the dry pools.

They passed over many sand dunes since leaving Benghazi before reaching the town of Sirte. After resting for a few hours in the bulrush bungalow they'd rented by the sea, Jenka and Vefka went for a stroll. They met a local man who was dressed in European-style clothing and spoke some English. He immediately invited them to eat at his house when he heard where they were from.

The men sat at a table that was covered in bowls of food. The women sat huddled in a corner on the floor, and the men threw the leftovers at them.

"How can people who wish to be Europeans behave this way towards women?" Jenka asked, shocked, unable to restrain himself.

"This is acceptable to us." Everyone nodded in agreement, "such is our custom."

"But you wear European clothes," Jenka snapped at them.

"We have no choice. The Italians force us to dress like this."

They kept going west and reached the ruins of the Roman city, Leptis Magna. It was hidden under mounds of sand for hundreds of years, and the antiquities were well preserved. Jenka declared they were more beautiful than the Syrian ruins of Baalbek and Palmyra. From there, they cruised easily to Tripoli and in no time arrived at the stunning city surrounded by palm groves. A local man on a motorcycle approached them and volunteered to take them on a tour of the area and to dinner. And yet again, the men sat at a table overflowing with a rich local feast. Meanwhile, the women who'd prepared the meal sat submissively and quietly in the corner, waiting for food to be thrown to them.

"I will not touch the food if the women do not sit at the table," Vefka announced.

Their host stood up, a steely expression on his face. "You dog!" he yelled at Vefka in English. "Were it not for our noble tradition to protect our guests, I would cut out your insolent tongue and chop off your head."

Then he turned to the other honorable men seated at the table and translated the words of their heretic guest into Arabic. An uneasy silence filled the room. The women raised their heads, watching to see how the chips would fall. Everyone turned to look at Jenka. He weighed his options. If he supported Vefka, they would both be thrown out of the house in disgrace, but the food covering the table looked delicious, and he was starving.

He shook his head from side to side, struggling to make up his mind. Finally, speaking slowly, emphasizing every word, Jenka announced, "The old folks say, 'when in Rome, do as the Romans do.' That is, behave according to local custom, wherever you go." He went on, "Who am I? Just some infidel, some white man, a young idiot, with no manners." Hitting his hand on his chest as if confessing a sin, he concluded, "Who am I to judge you and your culture?"

The host translated Jenka's words to the other guests and came around the table to embrace him, while the old and honorable gentlemen smiled and praised the wisdom of Allah.

*

Vefka and Jenka arrived at the Tunis border checkpoint. They honked for about half an hour until a fat Arab in baggy pants came outside rubbing his eyes and, without even checking them, signed their passports and went back to sleep. They continued to the customs house, and the border police announced that the customs rates were determined according to the weight of each motorcycle and the luggage on it. No matter how nicely they asked, the police didn't agree to subtract the equipment's weight, so they took out the Sunbeam manual where the weight of their motorcycle's was listed.

"When you leave Tunis, the money will be refunded," the customs official explained.

"We can pay with a cheque," Vefka proposed.

"We don't accept cheques. They're not worth anything. You can't even wrap a pita with one."

Jenka left Vefka with his motorcycle as collateral at the customs house and drove to town in search of someone who would cash his cheque. The passers-by did not know English. They pointed him this way and that way, the girls giggling and the men checking out his motorcycle. Finally, he found a shopkeeper who knew English.

He picked up the cheque, scrutinized it carefully, and agreed to take it. He handed Jenka the money.

"You're short," Jenka said after counting the bills.

"I take a 30% commission."

An argument broke out between them, and turning his back offendedly on Jenka, as if about to walk away, the shopkeeper said, "If you don't like it, you can take your cheque and go." Jenka's hands were tied.

They kept west and, after 800 miles, reached the city of Oran, one of the oldest and wealthiest cities in Algeria, which was once the center of the Trans-Saharan slave trade. After leaving Oran, they crossed the border into Morocco. They soon came to Fès, a large, impressive city that was divided between an Old City and a modern, European-style city. They strolled through the market and along the walls of the Old City, where Jenka bought postcards, and in the evening, they returned to the modern part of the city. A policeman stopped them, looking suspiciously at the white-skinned young men in shorts.

"What are you doing here?" the officer asked in French as he snatched the postcards from Jenka's hands.

They did not understand what he was saying.

They repeated the word "tourists" over and over again.

"Where are your passports?" he answered in a combative tone. "Passports, passports," he repeated again and again.

They gave him their passports.

They signaled to him to give them back their passports. But instead of doing so, he came down hard on them in French, and all they understood was the word police. They turned to the passers-by, who had gathered around them, intrigued by the scene, looking for someone who spoke English, but everyone in Morocco knew not to mess with the police. The officer handcuffed them and called over a police car. They had no choice but to get in and sit down. Jenka and Vefka spoke among themselves, trying to understand what they were being accused of and what would happen if they were thrown in jail. They'd heard that no inmates left Moroccan prison alive. They'd tried to think how they could notify the British embassy to come and save them.

"Silence," the officers ordered.

They arrived at the police station, and in flowing French, the officer explained to his superiors how he'd caught the criminals while they all examined the bewildered young men.

Jenka and Vefka requested to telephone the British embassy.

"The British won't help you here. Morocco is not a British colony," he answered in French.

They were taken to the precinct commander's office. He knew some English, and, for the first time, they heard that they were being accused of coming to Morocco with no money and engaging in the illegal trading of postcards. They emptied their pockets on the table, taking out cash and checkbooks. Apologizing profusely, the commander released them.

In a heatwave that reached 46 degrees in the shade, they rode 290 miles from Fès to Meknès, then headed north until they arrived at the Strait of Gibraltar. There, they boarded a ferry to Spain and, at long last, arrived in Europe, elated to have escaped the heat.

Finally, there were good roads, accurate maps, gas stations, drinking water, and pleasant weather. They burnt up the road. They toured Segovia and San Sebastian in Spain, crossed the Pyrenees, crossed the border to France, saw Bordeaux and Paris, and, from there, continued north to Belgium, the Netherlands, Denmark, Sweden, and Norway. They even reached the Norwegian fjords. They headed back south and rode to the town of Neuchatel, which had a Sunbeam factory next to it. They submitted their motorcycles for inspections and repairs that lasted five days. And from there, they rode on to London, Calais, Geneva, Tyrol, Florence, Rome, and Naples, where they were thrilled to see the volcanic Mount Vesuvius erupt in their honor. They rode to the other side of the Italian boot to the port city of Brindisi and boarded a ship home. Their trip wasn't covered in the press, not in words or photographs, but Jenka left behind a 12-page long travel journal, written in cramped handwriting. He summed up the four-month-long journey, the 12,000 miles, with these words: "I never fell off my motorcycle."

Chapter 7: Tales to Tell Our Children

One day, an Indian gentleman arrived at the motorcycle club in Haifa. He shared that he'd endeavored to cross from Kenya to Egypt through the Nile countries on his motorcycle but to no success. He explained that the geographic society hadn't fully explored the area yet, so there were no maps or water and nowhere to refuel. Still, he could provide general information he'd gained from his experience. Jenka was inspired by the idea and started planning a trip to the Nile and India – a journey of about 18,000 miles. With a letter of recommendation from the British Chemical Company in hand, he began corresponding with a transport company in Nairobi and with the Western India Automobile Association to get details about the appropriate season to make the trip, the road quality, where to refuel, taxes, and more. To avoid the wet season in Africa and India, it turned out that he needed to leave Haifa in December and travel counterclockwise. In other words, he would travel from Haifa through Sinai, Egypt, Sudan, Uganda, Kenya, and Tanganyika, where he would board a ship to Bombay, ride up to Ceylon and down to Kashmir, and return through Iran, Iraq, and Syria.

The issue of refueling motorcycles was even more severe on this route than on the trip to North Africa. Now there would be stretches where they'd need to cover a distance of 700 miles with nowhere to refuel. The issue of drinking water was also more severe. Jenka designed four tanks of the same size to attach to each motorcycle, three tanks of gasoline, each containing 23 liters, and the fourth tank intended for drinking water. Another smaller container contained 7 liters of oil. In addition to the tanks, he added photographic equipment, essential clothing, blankets, and food. The weight of the baggage came to half a ton. He invited Vefka to join him, and the two decided to depart in November 1934.

*

At the wedding of his good friend from the Technion, Shlomo Grozovsky, Jenka met Tzipora Arbel – Tzipkeh. Tzipkeh was a member of the first pioneering families, called "*bilu'im,*" in Rishon LeZion and worked in editing and translations. She was widely considered the most beautiful and intelligent girl in Haifa, and he couldn't understand why she was so eager to spend time in his company. After the wedding, he offered to escort her home, and by the following morning, he was enamored by her charms.

She liked to get on his motorcycle, sit behind him and hug his waist, feel her hair blowing in the wind, and see the jealous gazes of the other Haifa girls. When Jenka took her to the cave near Rosh Hanikra, which was on the border of what was then French Lebanon, she seduced him. He continued lying on the cold ground, shaken by what he'd just experienced for the first time, as she danced before him naked at the cave's opening. The light shining in from outside created a silhouette from her beautiful, supple body.

"Why don't you take a photograph of me?" She continued bouncing around, enjoying the way he was looking at her.

He grabbed his camera and searched for the perfect angle, "Don't move, don't move."

"I can't stay still anymore," she whined, standing on one leg, her other knee raised and bent, her back arched forward, and her nipples grazing her leg.

"I'm trying to get your body shape to merge with the shape of the cave's opening." He kept changing positions, lay on his side, walked over to her, and corrected her pose. "Now, don't move."

"You're torturing me," she giggled. "Soon, I'll punish you for your behavior."

"You moved. I can't take pictures if you move."

She was tired, and the initial excitement she'd felt from the shutter clicking had passed. She pushed him to the ground, told him he was a bad, bad, bad boy, and made love to him.

Ilioff and Clara were fascinated by Tzipkeh. She felt at home in the Ilioffs' modest villa, coming to Jenka's room, desiring to make love until the wee hours of the morning. She would make an upset face when he said, "I have to wake up in the morning for work." When he tried to explain to her logically that he loved her, yearned for her, but needed eight hours of sleep, she would mock him. "Where is your sense of adventure?"

When he showed her the route of his next journey on the map and explained the details, he could see that she was bored. She asked him again, ""Who do you like more, me or your motorcycle?"

When he asked, in too naive a voice, "What does it matter?" She insisted he answer, so he jokingly said, "The motorcycle," and she slapped him lightly on the cheek.

"You don't even know how to lie."

"And what's wrong with that?" He hugged her. "I hate liars."

"You don't deserve a woman like me." she looked up at him with a naughty smile, wrapped her arms around his neck, and quickly undressed him. "You are too thin," she whined. "But you have a beautiful face, high cheekbones, and glowing eyes. Do you have Tatarian blood in you?"

"Maybe from my father's side." He made a menacing face.

"I love that you are wild and adventurous. You are different."

"So are you."

He proposed to her, and they decided that the wedding would be held when he returned from his journey.

*

The residents of Haifa accompanied the two motorcyclists, who were the talk of the town, to their point of departure. Tzipkeh stood beside Ilioff, wearing a long fashionable coat and a white beret on her head, as befitting for the woman engaged to marry the professor's grandson. The first few hours of the trip were more difficult than Jenka and Vefka had expected. The weight of the baggage shifted toward the back of the motorcycles and caused instability and vibrations. After about 60 miles of riding, one of the motorcycle's chains broke. They had no choice but to lessen the weight of the luggage. They unpacked all the gear, placed it neatly on the ground, inspected each item repeatedly to decide if it was truly essential, compromised on a minimal amount of vital equipment, and had the rest sent home. After that, they crossed the Sinai desert in two and a half days without any particular problems. They continued on to Cairo, purchased firearms, and after giving a considerable sum of money to the authorities, received a departure permit. They were told that the money was intended as collateral in case they got lost in the desert, and the government had to organize a search party. Sunbeam motorcycle company publicized the trip, and the Egyptian newspaper, *La Bourse Egyptiènne*, published an extensive article about them, outlining their previous trips and the route they were taking this time.

The motorcycles were loaded onto a small sailboat, one of the thousands of vessels cruising south toward the stone-carved tombs of the pharaohs. They arrived at the site, went ashore, took pictures, and returned to the sailboat to continue to Komombo, but the wind had stopped, and the boat refused to move. Along with the 15-year-old captain and the two 12-year-old sailors, they attempted to row forward, but the boat just wouldn't move. In the end, they lost patience and declared that they wanted to disembark and continue along the East Bank of the Nile on their motorcycles. The three boys burst out in tears, their bodies trembling with emotion.

"Our father will beat us if we don't bring home money," they cried, revealing bruises from beatings on their bodies as their faces distorted exaggeratedly in pain. "Who are we to blame for the wind stopping?" they wailed on.

The boys looked up at Jenka and Vefka pleadingly, straining to smile, "But the wind always comes back. Always. If not today, then maybe tomorrow, maybe the day after tomorrow. If Allah wills."

"We will pay you the full amount even though you didn't bring us to our destination," Jenka said. The boys got down on their knees and kissed the young men's feet.

They went down to the beach with their motorcycles, but before they revved up, they looked over at the boys, "I'll give *baksheesh*, a tip, if one of you joins us to show us the way," Jenka suggested.

The boys hastily jumped off the boat, vying against each other for the new job opportunity.

"We'll take the skinniest one, the one who weighs the least," Vefka joked and started lifting each of them to check how heavy they were. Jenka seated one of the boys before him, and after a two-hour drive between cotton fields and irrigation ditches, they reached the village.

It took them two and a half days to cross 300 miles of desert to reach the Abu Simbel antiquities. They rode over the desert roads covered with a thin layer of pea-sized quartz stones that bounced up and injured them, hitting their engines and causing the motorcycles to make sharp, uncontrolled deviations from the path. Further on, the road was covered in sands of varying density which often slowed down their velocity as if the pistons had stopped working, and when they accelerated, they flew over hard sand at perilous speeds. They left behind miles of scar-like stripes in the soft sands, making the dunes look like deeply plowed fields. They discovered that whenever one of them stopped in the sand, the motorcycle began to sink, and when he revved up, he would dig himself in deeper, needing help from his friend to get out. But, if the friend stopped, he too would get stuck. They learned the hard way that they could only stop on hard sand, but the difference was hard to discern with the naked eye. As they approached the ancient temples of Abu Simbel, the road became littered with sharp rocks and large stones, the top layers of which had eroded.

Jenka and Vefka kept south along the Nile, and the motorcycles flew over the rocks and sank into the sandy pits. Exhausted, they noticed a small village called El Nadi in the distance, where they could rest and stock up on water and fuel. As they approached, they saw a black cloud of mosquitoes shrouding the entire village. Hurriedly, they refilled their water and two tanks of gas, and with faces and hands swollen from mosquito bites, they got the hell out of Dodge. Gripped by frenzy, they accelerated over and down dunes of soft sand, their necks aching from the continuous whiplash. At night they slept under the open sky at the foot of a heap of stones, one of the dozens of rock cairns that served as landmarks in the uncharted desert. They gazed up at the stars and were happy to be among the handful of people in the world following their dreams.

When they started the motorcycles in the morning, sparks of fire shot out of the exhaust pipes. "*Yob tvoyu mat*," Jenka swore in Russian, biting his lips, before letting out another barrage of curses. "Because of those damn mosquitoes, we filled the water tank that still had water in it with gas and filled two fuel tanks that still had gas in them with water." They had no choice but to empty the fuel from their motorcycles and fill them with the only untainted gas tank. They were left with no water and moistened their lips with sips of cognac. At twilight, they started searching for a well but lost their sense of direction of travel and decided to continue their quest the following day. They slept in shifts, for they heard dogs barking and thought they saw the movements of a caravan of camels and when morning broke, they spotted the well about a mile off.

If North Sudan is a desert, South Sudan is a vast swamp covered in a cloud of mosquitoes. The White Nile is so wide that sometimes they couldn't even guess which direction it was flowing. To protect themselves against malaria, they swallowed large quantities of quinine pills until they heard ringing in their ears. They barely made it over 60 miles a day. They passed by dilapidated villages and saw people tall, thin, and naked. A meningitis epidemic was raging in the area. After riding about 350 miles, they reached the city of Khartoum. Exhausted, they decided to stay in town to rest for a couple of days.

From Khartoum, they rode south for several weeks on a road that wound between the banks of the river and the woods. They could see elephants, hippopotamuses, and hundreds of crocodiles sunbathing in the light, all facing the water. After about 1,140 miles, they arrived in the city of Juba, and the British authorities gave them back the money they'd deposited as collateral in Cairo in case they were lost in the desert. When they entered the town of Torit the next day, Jenka stopped to take pictures, and Vefka overtook him. Then, Jenka noticed a big commotion ahead of him and saw his friend lying on the ground beside his motorcycle, surrounded by locals. Sensing trouble, Jenka fired two shots into the air and rushed to the aid of Vefka.

When he got closer, he found Vefka sprawled on the ground, surrounded by a group of giggling women. At first, he was confused, but after a few moments, Vefka explained what had happened. "I saw you had stopped to take pictures, so I overtook you and noticed these cute young women in the bushes. They came up to me, smiling. They have such perky breasts. Each of them gave me fruit. I ate the fruits, and we all laughed. I felt like King Solomon."

"So why are you lying on the floor, your highness?"

"Female jealousy." Vefka sat up, an expression of one who understood the ways of women on his face.

Jenka never understood why women were actually attracted to Vefka. After all, he was shorter than Jenka, and his appearance was less impressive than Jenka's. Maybe, with the help of their feminine instincts, they could feel that Vefka wanted them.

"What did you do this time?" Jenka teased him.

"Another girl came out of the bushes, approached me, and gave me a piece of fruit. I couldn't eat anymore and rejected her gift. The other women laughed at her. She was offended, begged me to take her fruit, clung to me, and I had to push her away. She got angry and pushed her hand into my mouth, grabbing the fruit of the young woman before her and shoving her fruit into my mouth instead. I lost my balance and fell."

When they crossed the border into Uganda, a British colony, they discovered another world, abundant in animals, vegetation, wide roads, and cultivated fields, where the locals were clothed in shirts and trousers that gleamed with whiteness. They arrived in the city of Kampala, crossed the new iron bridge over the Victoria Nile, and went to see the Ripon Falls, flowing with the waters of Lake Victoria. From there, they continued cruising leisurely to the town of Nakura, named after a small lake. A strip of yellow shoreline bordered the body of water, and mountains that seemed as if they were painted blue surrounded it. In the middle of the lake was an enormous pink circle made up of millions of flamingos flapping and fluttering in the water. Jenka drove his motorcycle closer to take a picture and realized he was sinking in the swampy mud. Vefka helped him out, and they both lay down under a tree, their clothes hanging on a branch to dry.

"We'll certainly have stories to tell our children," Vefka said and brushed away a procession of ants that had climbed on his leg.

"True. There will be tales to tell," Jenka agreed, covering himself with a cloth and crushing the ants that were climbing on him.

"What stories will you tell?"

Lying on his back and closing his eyes, Jenka contemplated the question, "I will tell them that I went with my good friend Vefka Kandelman to Africa, that we went deep into the jungle, and there I was kidnapped by cannibals who dragged me off and tied me to a tree. At night, they carried me to a large clearing in the middle of the forest where a bonfire was burning. They put a large pot of water on the fire, and everyone sat around drumming and singing. They pulled me to the fire against my will. The sounds of the tom-tom drumming grew louder. They stripped me of my clothes, preparing to throw me into the boiling pot of water. The tribe's chief came up to me, circled and groped me, stood before me glaring, and then spat on me. '*Ptui, ptui.* No meat! It's better to eat an animal than a white man who is skin and bones.' And that is how I survived."

"Do you really think your kids will believe you?"

"Don't children ask their father to tell them a story every night before they go to bed? I will tell them how the cannibals didn't want to eat me."

"What makes you think your children will believe such a story?"

"Why not? Don't kids believe in witches who ride broomsticks? Don't they believe in mice that turn into horses? Why wouldn't they believe that savages almost ate their father?"

They reached Nairobi, the capital of colonial Kenya, and from there continued to the Nananya river. Seeing that there was no bridge over the river and the sun had already set, they decided to sleep in the riverside hostel. Unfortunately, it was full, so the owner of the establishment offered them accommodation in a hut on which they had not yet put a roof. She promised they wouldn't have to pay if it rained at night. Lo and behold, in the middle of the night, lightning lit up the sky, and deafening thunder clapped over and over. The skies opened, and heavy rain wouldn't stop falling. The hut's floor turned into one big puddle, and all their gear floated around them.

Soon the rain filled the river, making it impossible to cross it on their motorcycles. The only choice they had left was to dismantle them, carry the pieces over their heads across the river, and reassemble them on the other side. They finished taking the first motorcycle across and went back to disassemble the second motorcycle and move it as well. But when they were just about to enter the river, Jenka noticed a tail peeking out of the bushes on the other side. He called out to Vefka, and their well-trained eyes determined that they were seeing a lion advancing toward them. Not willing to risk it, Jenka fired at the predator several times and, out of the bush, jumped a frightened little donkey with a long tail instead of a lion. Luckily, the shots alerted the locals, who helped them move the other motorcycle over the river without their needing to disassemble it.

Between leaving southern Sudan and arriving in the British colony of Tanzania, the motorcycles had covered over 900 miles. Although they were riding through an equatorial area, the climate had been pleasant because of the high altitude. The snow-capped view of Mount Kilimanjaro accompanied them on their travels. The humidity became more and more awful as they began their descent to the port city of Mombasa, which was located on a small island in the Indian Ocean and connected to the mainland by a bridge. They decided to freshen up by taking an athletic swim from the port to the mainland. They dove into the water, the sea was calm, and they progressed quickly. People gathered on the shore, shouting at them and waving their hands to get their attention. The police arrived, too, swiftly lowered a boat into the water and rowed towards them with all their might, shouting, "Sharks, sharks," in Arabic, English, and French. Startled, Jenka and Vefka started swimming furiously towards the boat, occasionally looking around to make sure that the sharks hadn't arrived yet. Sturdy arms grabbed them and pulled them onto the boat, and one policeman scolded them as if they were wayward children. They sat huddled over, not saying a word in their own defense. When they arrived on shore, Jenka whispered in Vefka's ear, "That really could have been an idiotic death."

Three months after leaving Haifa, a crane loaded their motorcycles onto a ship called "Kenya." And after nine days of sailing, they arrived at the port of Bombay in India.

Chapter 8: The Venom of the Scorpion and the Web of the Spider

A letter from Tzipkeh was waiting for Jenka at the central post office. The letter began with declarations of how much she missed him, all sorts of loving nicknames, and bits of idle chitchat. It ended with the laconic proclamation that she had moved into a rental apartment with Boris Zackheim, a family friend.

In his enthusiasm for the trip, Jenka had almost forgotten Tzipkeh, and he felt ashamed of himself. Yes, some nights, he wished he could make love to her. So, he too, wrote her a letter, in which he began by professing how much he missed her and went on to describe the route of their travels and some interesting anecdotes. He wondered whether to respond to the news that she'd moved into an apartment with a young man and consulted with Vefka.

"I wouldn't allow my fiancée to live in the same apartment with a young man for several months, even if he is a family member."

"What are you afraid of? That they'll sleep together? After all, she could have hidden it from me and not written about it at all."

"If she wrote about it, it's a sign that something's going on between them."

"Nonsense. Tzipkeh is an honest woman."

"What makes you so sure?"

"When we met, she told me, by her own initiative, that she's had many men in her life. She could have concealed it from me."

"So now she's openly cheating on you."

"No way. She told me that no other man makes her feel the way I do. She said that I drive her crazy. When I take her on my motorcycle, she feels like the queen of the world."

"Jenka, I wouldn't believe a single word that comes out of her mouth, except that she's slept with many men."

"Thanks to her experience, she is very free and drives me crazy with her erotic fantasies, although she would prefer me to be less skinny."

"Your Tzipkeh has you wrapped around her little finger."

"Once, I went away for a week, and when I came back to pick her up, she wasn't at her apartment. At first, I got upset, but then she told me she'd missed me so much that she ran away so I would look for her and feel what longing was like."

"Jenka, you are so naive. Write to her saying you're jealous and don't approve. Tell her that if money is the problem, you are willing to finance the rent of the second half of the apartment."

Jenka thought it would be inappropriate to show jealousy. So, instead, he ended the letter by declaring his love for her.

*

From Bombay, they rode south toward the Island of Ceylon. The road crossed through parched valleys and poor villages for hundreds of miles. There were no gas stations to be found, but thanks to the letters of recommendation they'd received from the British authorities back home, they could refuel at the British army bases along the way. Advancing slowly over the dusty main roads, from time to time, they got stuck behind two-wheeled wagons drawn by oxen, laden with the local agricultural produce that swayed from side to side. Sometimes the wagons bore piles of bamboo rods, which blocked the way, and made Vefka and Jenka hesitant to ride around because the dust billowed and obscured the road in front of them, even just a few tens-of-yards away. Groups of villagers walking to the market also joined the caravan, among them, *fakirs*, who carried red wicker baskets full of snakes. One of them toted two baskets attached to the ends of a pole that rested on his shoulders. His toddler son sat in one basket, and in the other basket, to maintain balance, sat a bunch of snakes. Snakes also crossed the road unhurriedly while others lay sunbathing. Vefka ran over them, and when he came across a particularly large and non-venomous snake, he got off his motorcycle and lifted it high in the air. Jenka, on the other hand, zigzagged so as not to hurt them.

The further south they traveled, the more the tangled jungle took over both sides of the road. It took them hours to overrun the twisted greenery. In other parts of the route, the ground was muddy, tall trees with massive trunks blocked the light, and fog rose among them.

After a long stretch of riding, Jenka and Vefka were hungry. They stopped at a local restaurant in a small village and ordered cooked rice. The owner of the restaurant brought them large leaves, which they took to be an appetizing local salad. They devoured the leaves quickly but were disappointed with their flavor. When the restaurant owner returned with the rice, he was horrified to see that the guests had eaten their plates, which were made of the leaves, for the area was plagued by cholera, and to avoid it, people should eat only cooked foods. The next day Jenka and Vefka felt terrible, but luckily, they didn't contract cholera. From then on, they made sure to eat only cooked food and not to be tempted by uncooked vices. However, a religious holiday took place in the following days, and because of their custom, the locals refused to sell them cooked rice.

They had not expected to encounter any problems getting food in India and hadn't stocked up on cans. With no other choice, they sustained themselves by eating bananas and drinking coconut water.

*

Jenka and Vefka kept north along the coast, joining a caravan of dozens of carts laden with bamboo rods, harnessed to oxen. One of the oxen was startled by the motorcycle's noise, so Jenka quickly rode to the shoulder so the bull wouldn't destroy the cart. Unfortunately, in the process, he bent the rear wheel of his motorcycle. He had no spare tires left, so he spent half the day taking apart and reassembling parts of Vefka's front wheel to improvise a temporary fix that would allow the damaged motorcycle to keep riding. As evening set in, they arrived in a small village, tired and filthy, covered in layers of dust from the road. They couldn't find a place to bunk there because the only bungalow for guests was being repaired. They planned to sleep under the stars, but the locals warned them not to sleep outside because there were a ton of snakes. A local man, a driver for a travel company, invited them to sleep at his house. In the room were two large copper bowls full of water, and they hurried to bathe in the bowl with the cleanest water. As they were about to leave the room, the cook entered and filled a cooking pot with water from the very same bowl they had washed in moments earlier.

"The cook is too lazy to go outside to the well to fetch clean water," Vefka stated.

Jenka was just about to shower Russian curses on the cook when he noticed that at the bottom of the bowl, the words "for drinking only" were written, and they both fell silent.

*

The road to the city of Calcutta was flooded, so they loaded their motorcycles onto a train. Their arrival was announced in a photo published on April 6th in the Times of Calcutta. They made their way back inland to the temple-studded Ganges Valley. Hundreds of people and cows stood immersed for hours on the steps leading to the holy water of the river. They went to see the Taj Mahal and the ancient observatory in Delhi. They continued northward to the highest mountain peaks in the world, heading in the direction of Kashmir. They crossed deep ravines and climbed mountains on muddy roads that passed by plunging abysses. A few days earlier, there had been an avalanche of snow, and they had been warned not to approach the area, but they decided to take the risk. On either side of the way, piles of snow were heaped up to a height of thirty feet. That night they slept in a small mountain hut. The next day, the weather started to warm up, and the heaps of snow began to melt. As they rode down the mountains, the melting snow water turned into waterfalls, and the air became freezing cold. When they reached the base, they drank hot coffee in the cabin. From there, they continued to the Kashmir Valley. All around them, trees bloomed, and pools of water reflected the snowy mountains and the wooden houses and painted boats. They crossed the border into Iran and visited the ruins of Persepolis, the ancient capital of the Persian kingdom.

It started to rain heavily in the evening, and the road flooded. About eighteen miles before Natanz, Vefka slipped, and his motorcycle fell on him, breaking his leg. "I cannot leave you here. Cars don't normally pass by here and certainly not in such weather." Jenka picked up the motorcycle as Vefka cried out in pain. "I'll leave your motorcycle here and take you on my motorcycle to a place where you can receive treatment."

He surrounded Vefka's motorcycle with big stones so that it wouldn't be swept away by the downpour. Jenka picked up Vefka, who was screaming in agony, and put him on the motorcycle. By the light of the flashlight, he rode through the flooded area, sharp stones hid under the water, and one of them punctured a hole in his tire. In order to repair the flat tire, he had to remove Vefka from the motorcycle, lay him in the puddle, fix the flat in the dark, and put Vefka back on.

They arrived at a small village, and Jenka went to search for the home of the Mullah, the leader of the village. He carried Vefka, who shivered with cold and wailed in agony, to the house, removed his wet clothes, changed him into dry ones, and laid him in bed. Immediately afterward, Jenka rode to Natanz, where he was told there was a telephone. He called Kashan, the biggest city in the district, hoping to order a taxi for the following day to pick up Vefka from the village and bring him to a hospital. But he didn't speak a word of Persian. It was late in Kashan, but Jenka set out to look for the Mullah, whom he believed would know Arabic. He explained to the Mullah in broken Arabic that he needed a car for his wounded friend. The Mullah understood and agreed to order the taxi for him on the phone but demanded a hefty sum of money for his services. Jenka hurried back to the village where he'd left Vefka to inform his injured friend that a taxi would arrive in the morning. Then he walked to the scene of the accident where they'd left Vefka's motorcycle alone on the ground. He found that the motorcycle's headlight had been broken in an accident and rode to the village by the light of the moon. But the cascading flood covered the path, and he accidentally ended up on the wrong bank of the river. He looked for a bridge, rode on to the village, and took apart Vefka's motorcycle so he could load it onto the taxi. He didn't close his eyes all night.

In the morning, the taxi arrived in the village, a Ford automobile with a driver who waited outside the Mullah's house. Jenka carried his friend to the cab, then loaded the motorcycle parts onto it. The

Mullah instructed the driver to drive a hundred and twenty miles to Tehran and take the wounded man to the hospital. The taxi set out, and Jenka, who was dead tired, went to sleep for a few hours. When he woke up, he discovered the car had broken down after driving just a few yards. There were no other cars. Jenka found a truck and, with a small sum of money, persuaded the owner to leave behind some of his cargo and make room for Vefka and the motorcycle parts. For two hours, he drove beside the truck, which advanced slowly behind a caravan of wagons and people, until he determined to stop and stay overnight in one of the villages along the way. He was overcome with fatigue. The next day he drove to Tehran and went to the hospital. Vefka told him that, along the way, the truck driver had collected more goods, sacks of wheat, cages of chickens, and bundles of bamboo, some of which fell on him. He had screamed in pain, but the truck's engine roared, and the driver could not hear him. Six fractures were discovered in his leg at the hospital.

The doctors determined that Vefka should return home on a flight. Jenka reassembled his friend's motorcycle and sent it to Baghdad, where there was a truck route on the Baghdad-Haifa line. He rode to Baghdad to oversee the motorcycle's delivery to Tel Aviv, then crossed the yellow and dusty Mesopotamia Valley, barely stopping except to sleep and refuel. In Baghdad, the trucking company had tried to persuade him to join them and load his motorcycle on the truck, too. They said he shouldn't dare cross the Syrian desert alone. Jenka had no patience for journeying with a slow caravan of trucks. He was required by the authorities to sign a declaration that he took full responsibility for his own life. He set out into the desert alone, heading for Damascus. On the trip, he slept under the open desert sky and was stung by a big yellow scorpion. He understood he was living on borrowed time and needed to get to the hospital in Damascus as quickly as possible. The pain was intense; his leg swelled up, drool dribbled from his mouth, he sweated profusely, and he had difficulty breathing. He fought for his life, for every minute he had left before the allergic reaction to the venom would cause seizures and damage his heart and nervous system. With the rest of his strength, clinging to life, barely conscious, he reached Damascus and received medical treatment.

When he got to Haifa, his friends held a surprise party for him in the yard of the Ilioff family home. Everyone applauded when he arrived, and Tzipkeh ran into his arms. Everyone was delighted, saying that the bravest fellow had won the heart of the most beautiful, talented, and intelligent lady in town.

Davar newspaper published an extensive advertisement for British and Levant agencies Ltd. The headline read, "Only the Sunbeam Could Do It," and below it, the routes of their three big motorcycle trips were detailed alongside a photo of Jenka and Vefka. Photographs of the two on motorcycles starred in Sunbeam's catalogue, and the editor of the prestigious National Geographic Magazine approached Jenka, asking him to write about their trips to Africa and India, even paying him £500.

*

Rumors of their extraordinary journey also reached the ears of Lord Melchett. He held a dinner party in Jenka's honor at his villa, which stood at the entrance to the Druze village of Ussefiya. Jenka bought new clothes and shoes for the Lord's event. He sat at the table beside the distinguished British guests who took great interest in his expeditions and even sang in his honor:

For he's a jolly good fellow, for he's a jolly good fellow
For he's a jolly good fellow, which nobody can deny!
For he's a jolly good fellow, for he's a jolly good fellow,
For he's a jolly good fellow, and so say all of us!

Jenka's shoes were too tight, so he kicked them off. When they finished the main course, the Lord invited his guests to proceed into the drawing room for a dessert of coffee and cake. As they stepped into the next room, they noticed the guest of honor wearing only his socks. Their British etiquette prevented them from commenting on his lack of shoes. What's more, they attributed it to the oddness of the unique man. The Lord, too, widened his eyes in alarm at the sight of the white socks protruding from underneath Jenka's trousers and approached the young man discreetly. At the height of British courtesy, the Lord asked if Jenka had no objection and would be willing to accompany him out of the room for a few moments. He explained to Jenka that the maid had found shoes under the table and that if he was not mistaken, she had found them under Jenka's seat, and he believed they belonged to him.

*

Jenka wanted a simple wedding, but Tzipkeh longed for lavish nuptials. She ordered an extravagant wedding dress from Europe. A tuxedo was sewn for Jenka. New clothes were made for each family member, even Doc's children. It was one of the city's most impressive and noteworthy weddings. Even Vefka, up and walking with the help of a cane, arrived on time, fresh off his flight from Tehran.

When the last of the guests went home, the couple got into a fancy car that drove them, with all their presents, to their new rental apartment. Jenka had taken care to equip the place to every last detail. Everything was new and of the finest quality. He had even placed a bouquet of red roses on the table in honor of the bride. They got into bed and lay cuddled, chitchatting, joking about the guests and the presents.

"I have a secret I want to tell you," she said, stroking his nose.

"What secret?" He asked, curious as a little boy.

"I won a bet."

"What bet?"

"About you."

"About me?"

"Do you remember when we met at Shlomo's wedding? I'd seen you before that many times riding on your motorcycle. You looked like a movie star. A lot of girls desired you, but you didn't seem interested. You looked unattainable. Only motorcycles, cameras, and travels."

"But I wanted you, my darling."

"I bet my girlfriends that I'd be able to get you to the *chuppah*[3]."

"Do you hear what you're saying?"

"I bet with Ruchala, Shoshana, Naomi, and Sarala that I would seduce you and marry you. I came to Shlomo's wedding to entrap you in my web of temptations," and she put her hand on his crotch.

"You made a bet with those blabbermouths that you would marry me?" He removed her hand and sat up, dumbfounded.

"Yes. And now you're mine." she cuddled up to him.

"Do you mean to tell me that this entire extravagant wedding was to celebrate a bet with your idiotic girlfriends?"

"What are you so worked up about?"

"Are you saying everything that happened between us was part of the bet? Was everything fake? Lies?" On his face was a look of shock and repulsion.

---

3 A Jewish wedding is performed underneath a "chuppah," or "wedding canopy."

"Jenka, calm down."

"You bet on me like I was a toy? Of a spoiled brat? Or some household pet?"

"It was a joke, I was kidding."

"Weddings are a joke to you? Emotions are a joke?"

Naked, he got out of bed, locked himself in the bathroom, and took a shower. Tzipkeh knocked on the door. He did not open it. When he got out, he went to the chair where his tux was neatly arranged so it would not wrinkle and angrily pushed it to the floor. He went over to the closet. He put on simple clothes. Tzipkeh clutched at him, and he pushed her away. He left the apartment and slammed the door behind him. He paced alone through the dark streets. He'd often wondered why she had chosen him; she had so many suitors. All her talk about loving him and his craziness for motorcycles, photography, and travel, had been part of her plan to win the bet. He remembered that Riva, the nanny, had never shown enthusiasm for Tzipkeh. He sat down on the bench and cried. He realized that, in fact, he did not know her at all. Then he returned to the apartment and slept on the couch in the sitting room.

They decided to get divorced but continued to live in the apartment together temporarily. One day he came home early because a meeting was canceled and found her in bed with Boris Zackheim. Scared, the guy jumped out of bed, grabbed his clothes, covered his privates, and ran out. Emotionless, Tzipkeh remained in bed and pulled back the sheets, revealing her naked body, waiting for Jenka to fall prey to the temptation.

"You were sleeping with him when I was in Bombay?" He recalled the letter he'd received from her saying she'd moved in with Boris, and he remembered Vefka's warnings.

"We were sleeping together before you even left on your trip." She knew she was hurting him.

"What did you think? You could be my wife and continue sleeping with your lover?" He shouted and threw the sheet at her.

Tzipkeh got up, put on a white silk robe with rainbow-colored flowers, tied the sash, went to her dressing table, sat up straight, and began brushing her hair.

"If you wanted him, why did you marry me?" He grabbed her hand and snatched the hairbrush from her.

"If I hadn't married you, I would have lost the bet, and my friends would have publicized my failure. There would be no way for me to deny it. And who would have married me if the bet had been made public?"

"What if you'd gotten pregnant? How would you know whose child it was?" Jenka's face contorted with rage.

"Calm down. I'm not pregnant." She went back to brushing her hair.

Jenka moved back into his room at Ilioff's house. He wandered around like a shadow of himself. How could he have been so blind? He had wanted to start a family of his own with Tzipkeh. He had been so naive, so innocent, untouched, devoted to her body and mind. Since his mother had passed away, he hadn't experienced a normal family setting. He'd wanted kids, wanted to grow old with her, like Ilioff and Clara. When Riva probed at him, concerned, he shouted at her to leave him alone. He saw the old couple looking at him worriedly and locked himself in his room.

Six months after the wedding, they divorced. Tzipkeh spread a rumor that she could not stay with him because he was gay. Who would believe him if he tried to tell the truth about what had happened? He was considered an oddly behaved man. She would have the time of her life making up lies. He decided to keep his mouth shut. To ignore it. He never mentioned her name. Erased her. He resolved that if he married again one day, it would be to a simple girl. He no longer wanted a beautiful, talented, and intelligent girl. Tzipkeh remained in the headlines of the local press and announced her marriage to Suhail Shukri, an Arab, the only son of the Mayor of Haifa, Hassan Shukri, who supported coexistence with the Jewish people and had survived several assassinations attempts by Arab extremists.

Chapter 9: Tragedy at the Port

It was1936. More and more Jews attempted to flee Nazi Europe. The gates of the world closed before them. The Arab revolt broke out in Mandatory Palestine. The Arabs demanded independence from the British Mandate and a halt to Jewish immigration. During the uprising, spurred by cries of "*Itbah al-Yahud*," or "slaughter the Jews," Jews, British, and Arabs were killed. The British established a commission headed by Lord William Peel and invited Arab and Jewish representatives. The Arab representative, Mufti Amin al-Husseini, declared that the Jews had no right to the land and asserted the false claim that the Jews seek to eliminate any trace of the Muslim's religious and historical right to exist. Abdullah I, the Emir of Transjordan, sent a letter to the Partition Committee denying the rights of the Jews to the Land of Israel and stating that it belongs to the Arabs. Chaim Weizmann explained to the commission members that since the destruction of the ancient Kingdom of Israel, the Jewish people have been scattered around the world and persecuted. The commission imposed a ban prohibiting Jews to continue purchasing land from the Arabs. The British continued to issue certificates to Jews, but their number was limited. The Arabs demanded an immediate cessation of Jewish immigration, and the uprisings continued.

Despite the Jewish community's disappointment over the Peel Commission, they still had reason to cooperate with the British so that they would continue to allow European Jews fleeing the Nazis to immigrate. Therefore, retaliatory actions against the Arabs should be avoided so as not to upset the British, and energy should be focused on defending the Jewish settlements. On the other hand, members of the Etzel accused the Jewish leadership of cowardice and of giving up the Land of Israel and demanded actions against the Arabs. The hatred between the two Jewish groups was extreme, and the disagreement brought the settlement close to a civil war. Although Jenka was a member of the Haganah, regarding the issue of restraint, he agreed with the Etzel. He thought that so long as the Arabs believed there was a chance to oust the Jews, they would do so and that they would interpret the Jewish people's restraint as weakness.

As the Arabs became bolder, switching to organized guerrilla activity and hit-and-run ambushes, the supporters of the Haganah became apprehensive and whispered that perhaps the time for passive defense was over. It was time for bold actions. They encountered skeptics who claimed that even in ten generations, the Jewish settlement wouldn't understand how to design a bomb because what did they know about explosives? And let us not forget the British, who were watching their every move. But, as the successful ambushes of the Arabs intensified, the Haganah was left with no choice but to set up a special unit headed by Munya Mardor. The unit's job was to plan retaliatory operations and supply the required weapons. Munya recruited the engineers Yosef Zaretsky, Shmuel Wilensky, Amit Ziniuk, and Jenka. The group had a basic knowledge of explosives and welding iron pipes, enough so that they could attempt to assemble a simple bomb.

In 1938, the Night of the Broken Glass attacks occurred in Germany. Many Jews were killed, and thousands more were arrested and sent to death camps. The Jewish people were in a state of desperation. The following year, in 1939, the British issued a policy paper called the Third White Paper. The document stated that a bi-national state would be established in the territory of the British Mandate, with the governing power given to the Arabs. Two-thirds of the population would be Arabs and one-third Jews. The legal immigration of the Jews would be first reduced and then halted entirely within five years unless the Arabs agreed that it could continue. The purchase of land by Jews would be limited to 5% of the Mandate's total area. The Jewish community in Mandatory Palestine held demonstrations, and the illegal immigration of Jews on rickety ships bursting full of immigrants continued to arrive on the country's shores. Some drowned, some were captured by the British and returned to Germany where they were sent to death camps. Others managed to make it to safe land.

Munya Mardor would often come to Ilioff's house and lock himself in a room with Jenka, where the two would talk for hours, throwing ideas around. They would leave the house stealthily at night and go to the workshop at the Technion, where Jenka would present the experiments he was working on. Riva, the nanny, assumed they were talking about classified things and that no questions should be asked, but Ilioff thought Munya was enticing Jenka to go to prostitutes. Neither of them bothered to correct him.

*

Shifra got up early. She went to the kitchen, drank a glass of water, put an orange in her bag, and hurried to the sea. She had her own locker in the quiet changing room on the beach. She took out a bathing suit, towel, and bathing cap and took off her new dress, folding it carefully, so that it wouldn't develop creases in her locker.

The blue sea unfurled before her. She took a deep breath and ran in, surrendering with pleasure to the coolness of the water. She swam back and forth from the shore to the buoy six times, did her exercises, and concluded with a headstand. Then she hastened to shower, put on her dress, shoved the wet swimsuit into a cloth bag inside her purse, and raced to catch the bus.

When she got off at the station near Bank Hapoalim, she was pleased to see that the bank's gates were still closed, and she joined the workers crowding at the entrance. When the security guard opened the doors, she pushed her way to the bathroom, took the wet bathing suit out of its bag, and hung it up to dry at the window. Standing in front of the mirror, she fixed her hairdo, pulled her dress down, and re-tied her belt. She was pleased with what she saw in the reflection. A gorgeous woman of about 23 years old, tall, with a perfect figure, green eyes, black hair, and a swan-like neck. She wondered why men rarely pursued her, why they preferred women less beautiful than her.

"You are special. You have class," her friend Sarah explained. "When men see you, they know they need to be serious about you. When they see me, they know there's the possibility of necking on a bench in a public park on the first date."

Shifra took her place at the bank's counter, sat down, and began filling out forms. The bank manager came up and praised her beautiful handwriting, large, curling, like an illustration for a poem. Maybe her penmanship was the reason they'd hired her; after all, she had no professional secretarial training, and she didn't know how to type on a typewriter.

Shifra finished writing and sat waiting for the customers. Whenever she was unoccupied, her thoughts wandered toward Ezekiel Wollensky. His family and her family had come from the same town in Russia, and both settled in Haifa. When they were children, their families used to socialize together, and she and Ezekiel played, fell in love, and even discussed marriage. But then the Wollensky family decided to send Ezekiel to Europe to study medicine. Shifra had thought that before he went off to school, they would get married and that they would go to Europe together. There she would be able to learn a profession and maybe even work and chip in for their living expenses. But his family had ignored her, acting as if she did not exist, and had made it clear that she had nothing to look forward to. When doctor Ezekiel returned, he would marry a girl with money and pedigree. It destroyed her. She begged her father to send her to Beirut to study nursing. "What do you need to learn to be a nurse for? Do you think you won't get married if you aren't a nurse? We have two more girls in the house who need to get married," he replied. Every time she recalled his words, pain pierced her chest.

An older woman approached the counter and looked at the wistful young woman, "Can you exchange one hundred for twenties?"

"Of course." Shifra came back down to earth. The workday had begun.

She didn't hurry home after work. Sometimes she went to Etzel meetings and lectures; there were modest refreshments and a friendly atmosphere. That night she got home late, quickly climbed the stairs to the second-floor condominium, took off her shoes, and quietly entered the kitchen. Her mother stood cooking soup over the kerosene burner.

"I couldn't fall asleep," Miriam mumbled. Shifra observed her mother. She saw a short, hunched-over woman with a wrinkled face and her head tilted to the side. A woman in whom all the joy of life had dried up, like a rotten tree trunk, empty inside. She walked over and hugged her.

"Sit down and eat some vegetable soup," said Miriam, filling a bowl with steaming hot soup without waiting for her daughter's answer.

"The soup is delicious," Shifra said and ate with gusto. Her mother sat across from her, her eyes planted on the floor, her feet off to the sides and her knees slumped inward.

"Mother, why did you marry him?"

Miriam took a deep breath, filling her lungs with air and releasing it slowly. Only then did she speak. "It was a different time. We lived in a small village in Russia, and everyone listened to their parents. I was an only child; my father had passed away. I studied to be an arithmetic teacher, and I wanted to marry Shmuel, who had also studied at the teacher's seminary. He was an intelligent and gentle man. My mother objected. She was a strong woman and said that she knew what was best for me."

"You were a good, obedient girl."

"At first, I objected. But my mother pressured me. She spoke enthusiastically about Zalman, an attractive redheaded man who was a talented trader with a bright future ahead of him."

Shifra held her mother's hands. "She did you a terrible injustice. She chose for you the husband she wanted for herself."

"She convinced Zalman to marry me. He never loved me. I gave him three daughters, and he was ashamed of me. He never raised a hand against me, but he looked down on me, belittled me."

"He did all of that so he wouldn't feel small compared to you," whispered Shifra, stroking her mother's hair.

"He shouted that I only gave birth to girls because I was an educated woman."

"Is that why Father doesn't want me to study to be a nurse?"

Shifra's eyes filled with tears, and she didn't know if she was crying for her mother or herself.

Miriam clasped her hands tightly together, with her thumbs crossed over each other. "Then we ran away from Russia, but when we were crossing the Polish border, they shot at us. A bullet pierced my neck."

Shifra caressed Miriam's head and kissed her thin, pulled-back hair.

"Mother, I hate him for what he has done to you and to me."

"Zalman is also unhappy. Don't hasten to judge him so harshly. He would have liked a beautiful young woman to give him sons. Selling car batteries is not what he aspired to do in life, and he comes home from the garage in a bad mood every day and takes it out on me. He only feels good about himself at the synagogue. He donates money and is well respected."

Shifra finished her soup, washed her plate, cleaned the counter, and went out to the small balcony off the kitchen to get some fresh air. Then she locked herself in her room and opened her wardrobe. She couldn't wait to get her salary every month. After receiving it, she gave a share to her father and then went to Ilka, an expensive clothing store in Haifa that imported clothes from Europe. Everything she tried on looked terrific on her and made her feel better.

*

An ad hung in the basement of the Etzel, exclusively for its members: "Join the Aviron Aviation School's pilot course, held on Kibbutz[4] Afikim in the Jordan Valley. Studies will be funded by the Etzel."

When Shifra arrived, everyone was sitting with their chairs leaning against the wall, listening to all the details about the course. "Aviron operates domestic flights," Yair explained. "But they also do security missions, including patrol and liaison, warning about Arab attacks, transmitting information to isolated settlements, and evacuating the wounded."

At the end of the meeting, she approached Yair and told him that she would like to take the course but that she worked at a bank.

---

4 A "*kibbutz*" is a Jewish collective living arrangement in Israel, based on principals of communal living.

"Take unpaid leave during the basic training course. And after that, the additional trainings are held every weekend at the Aviron branch on Mount Tabor. It's all funded by the organization," he said, gazing at her. "You will make a beautiful Hebrew pilot."

Her father, of course, objected, but she stood her ground. "You didn't agree to let me study nursing, so I 'll become a pilot instead!"

He shouted at his wife, "Why did you give me only crazy girls?"

The aviation studies brought her joy. When she completed the introductory course, she made sure to come to the additional training near Mount Tabor, overlooking the Jezreel Valley. The site's director took her on a tour of the location and introduced her to the flying instructors. They went inside a big glider repair hut, and there she saw him. He stood, concentrated on fixing a glider, glanced at her, and returned to work.

"The Haganah sent him to us," the director explained to her. "Jenka studied in Cairo and received a certificate authorizing him as a glider pilot. We published a book he wrote called, *Chapters on Pilot Theory*."

She saw him during training, so handsome in his flight suit, hat, and sunglasses. He looked like a movie star. She didn't dare approach him.

During one training session, a warm eastern wind blew. Shifra didn't feel well but didn't give up. The experience of gliding gave her life meaning. She glided off Givat HaMoreh, feeling dizzy; the horizon swayed, the ground stretched out above her, and then suddenly, it was in front of her. The glider plunged down, she heard a breaking sound, the air came out from under the wing, and she fainted. Her comrades who were watching ran to the scene and carried her out. Her face was green, her right eye huge; they poured water on her, and she complained of pain in her ribs and had difficulty breathing. They carefully placed her on a stretcher and hurried to the path where an ambulance was arriving that rushed her to the hospital. They stayed by her side while she lay in bed, bandaged and sore. When everyone left, only Jenka remained, placing his hand on the bed sheet that covered her.

"You were lucky that only your ribs were broken. I'll fix the glider, don't worry."

She never went back to flying after that. But soon, Jenka started waiting for her under her building on Arlozorov Street with his motorcycle. Zalman would go out on the balcony to watch his daughter get on the motorcycle, wondering why Jenka didn't come upstairs to the apartment to make the proper acquaintance with her father.

Jenka consulted with Riva, the nanny, asking what she thought of Shifra. She had told him more than once that he was naive about women and that if he had consulted with her about Tzipkeh, she would never have let him marry her, but Shifa was a good woman. She would come to Ilioff and Clara's house after work and talk to them with the scant Russian she knew from home. Clara would spend most of her day in the terrace garden, sitting in an armchair. Shifra would listen with great interest to Clara's stories about the wonderful years in Ekatrinoslav, the carriage drawn by four horses, the etiquette she had learned at the girls' school in Switzerland, and her family pedigree. Sometimes Clara would burst into heartbreaking tears over her young son, Yasha, whom the Bolsheviks had murdered and thrown into the river, and over her large extended family, whom she'd left in Russia and had no idea of their fate.

When Jenka proposed that Shifra move into his room, she did not refuse. Something was soothing about her – her noble beauty, her maternal tenderness, and her eyes, which reminded him of his late mother's eyes. He appreciated her integrity and her modesty. And she adored him; whatever he said or asked of her, she did. He liked that she was obedient. When she looked at him, a sweet smile shone in her eyes, behind which hid a thin veil of sorrow, as if she were afraid of being happy. He photographed her sitting in the living room, leaning against the door to his room. She was dressed so tastefully. He laid out a rug and created a backdrop of pillows in his room. He photographed her sitting barefoot in her undergarments, so feminine, with a sensitive, vulnerable look on her face, desiring his presence to feel protected. When he asked her to marry him, she hugged him. She could not have hoped for more.

"I want a small wedding with family."

"Alright."

"We shall continue living in my room at Ilioff's house."

"As you wish." She was surprised that he didn't want to rent an apartment.

The wedding was held at the Ilioff home. In attendance were Daniel and his family, the Lifshitz family, Ilioff's colleagues from the Technion, and some of Jenka's friends. Shifra refused to let her father invite his friends from the synagogue. When the wedding was over, she lay in bed, her palm supporting her head, her elbow resting on the pillow. She wore a white silk nightgown trimmed with delicate lace that she'd bought especially for the occasion. He stood by the lamp, watching his wife radiate with love and tenderness.

"I intend to travel to Spain to join the Civil War." He turned off the lamp.

"What are you talking about?" Shifra thought her ears had deceived her or that he was jesting.

"I also don't want children." He got into bed and turned his back to her.

"Jenka, what's going on with you?" she asked, withholding the urge to scream.

She tried to force him to turn towards her, but he stayed rooted in his place. She froze as if struck by lightning and cried quietly into her pillow. Whom could she turn to? To her parents, who were glad she'd left home? She lost her smile that night. In the morning, as they had planned ahead of time, they went to have their portrait photographed. His hopelessly serious gaze and her sad, empty eyes remained frozen in the picture frame.

That evening Shira sat in the sitting room to read a book, trying to hide her emotional turmoil. Ilioff approached her and asked her to join him for a little walk in the fresh air. They did not say a word all the way to the Technion. They sat on a bench under a streetlight.

"What happened?" Ilioff asked. Shifra couldn't fight the tears welling up in her eyes. "He wants to travel to Spain to join the civil war."

"He's back to his old craziness," Ilioff sighed, enveloping her hand in both of his hands. "Occasionally, he gets ideas like that into his head. Don't worry; the Haganah won't give him up so easily. He won't go."

"That's not all," Shifra said and burst into bitter tears. "He doesn't want children."

Ilioff was caught off guard. He hadn't expected this.

"What should I do?" Her question reverberated with pain and despair.

"Jenka is my grandson, the only child born to my late daughter, may she rest in peace. I am shocked by his behavior."

"It's so cruel," Shifra's voice broke.

Ilioff paused for a few seconds, then spoke in a calm and balanced voice. "Jenka's first marriage left him deeply scarred. He is taking out what his first wife did to him on you. As if he is afraid you will hurt him." Shifra looked into Ilioff's wise eyes. "He is a good man – honest, loyal, hardworking, and very talented. He had an extremely difficult childhood. He was orphaned by his mother at a young age. His father was very hard on him and dragged him into battles of the Russian Civil War. He witnessed things that children should not see. We raised him, but grandparents cannot replace parents."

"I know about his difficult childhood. I will not give up on having children," she whispered resolutely.

"Jenka wants kids, too. He just needs time. You will have children."

"His eyes are as cold as ice. He seems unreachable."

"He loves you in his own way. You and your patience have the power to heal him. There is not always a logical solution to every situation. There will come a time when you will know what to do. I believe in you. You have an inner strength you are unaware of," he said and gazed at her reassuringly. She nestled in his arms. Her father only shouted at her and shamed her, but Professor Ilioff believed in her. She looked into his intelligent and sincere eyes and felt calm.

They fought constantly over the next few months. She couldn't forget the things he had said to her on their wedding night. She decided to establish her independence. She had never left the country before, and in mid-August 1939, she decided to travel alone to France. When she arrived in Marseille, she discovered that the city was full of refugees seeking to flee France. Everyone told her she was crazy to suddenly go to France when a world war was about to break out. She continued on to Paris, and only there did she truly realize the gravity of the situation. She sent a postcard to Jenka that read, "Jenka, my wonderful husband. I'm coming home, and we can fight again." She traveled quickly back to Marseille and managed to board the last ship to leave for the Middle East before the war began.

*

Towards the end of 1940, the British caught three large illegal immigrant ships: the Milos, the Pacific, and the Atlantic, which were carrying 3,500 unlawful immigrants from Germany, Austria, and Czechoslovakia. One thousand eight hundred of them were forcibly transferred to a deportation ship called "Patria," which was docked at the Haifa port. Before the war broke out, the British would send the refugees back to Europe, and since the outbreak of the war, they started sending them to a detention camp on the nearby island of Cyprus. However, this time, they decided to send them to the Mauritius Islands in the Indian Ocean. The leadership of the Jewish settlement agreed that resistance to this course of action must be displayed so that the deportation of illegal immigrants to distant lands wouldn't become a permanent policy.

The idea to perform a minor attack on the Patria arose in the Haganah's special operations department. They would create a hole with a maximum diameter of roughly 20 cm, which would cause the steamer ship to sink slowly so that they could safely get the illegal immigrants ashore. The ship's repair would take time, and meanwhile, they would take political action to prevent further deportation. Shaul Avigur was appointed operation commander, and the bomb's preparation was entrusted to the engineering team of Yosef Zaritsky, Shmuel Wilensky, and Jenka.

Munya searched for a way to contact illegal immigrants on the steamer to inform them of the plan. He hid the bomb in a small barrel so that a member of the Haganah who worked at the port could smuggle it onto the ship. However, the attempt to bring the bomb to the port was unsuccessful due to the meticulous security check at the gates. Ultimately, he managed to arrange a job at the port for himself and waited for the perfect opportunity. When the ocean liner's oven broke down, Munya joined the group of port employees who boarded the ship to fix it. Aboard the Patria, he contacted Hans Wendel and Tova Ferger, the leading activists, and instructed them where to place the bomb.

The explosion occurred at nine o'clock in the morning when the deportees were eating breakfasts in the deck dining room. The explosive caused an entire board from the ship's side to detach and created a massive hole. Suddenly, large amounts of water burst in, and the ocean liner tilted to the side and began to sink rapidly. Within ten minutes, the Patria disappeared underwater, and only her tip could be seen protruding. Meanwhile, the Haganah command, including Operation Commander and the engineering team, stationed themselves on the Carmel slope and watched what was happening at the port with binoculars. Screams escaped their mouths when they witnessed the tragedy. They looked at each other in horror; they had no plan prepared for such a disaster.

"Disperse everyone! Go home and act normally. Do not arouse any suspicion," Shaul Avigur ordered.

Jenka arrived home. The nanny, Riva, greeted him shouting, "The Patria has sunk!"

Seeing his pale countenance, she asked, "What happened to you? Are you ill?"

"I have a headache. I left work early."

"Who could have done such a terrible thing? The ship was full of families, elderly people, children, and babies."

Riva looked at him suspiciously. She knew of his covert activity.

"Riva, I do not know. I have a headache. Let me be." Jenka locked himself in his room.

In the evening, Shifra returned from work. Jenka was lying on their bed motionless. She caressed his head.

"It's the Patria, right? The Etzel did it. It was scheduled for tomorrow, but they decided to do it today."

"How do you know?" He opened his eyes.

"I have friends there."

He didn't like her ties with the Etzel. He'd tried to convince her more than once that their method of terrorism was immoral. Her words meant that the blame would not fall on the Haganah, but he was angry that she was revealing the Etzel's secrets.

"I would not tell you Haganah secrets," he declared. "Your friends trusted you."

"You are right, my wonderful husband." She stroked his pale face.

He got up and went into the bathroom. He looked at his reflection in the mirror. Had the mark of Cain appeared on his forehead? The calculations for the bomb's size went through his mind time and time again. The calculations had been correct, but they had not known the ship was so rotten. If they'd known all the details, they would have calculated differently. He leaned with his hands against the sink, his head dropping downwards. At that moment, he wanted to die but remembered Shifra's words. The Etzel had also been planning to attack the ship; the Haganah had been one day ahead of them. He wished they would have been the ones to do so, not the group he belonged to.

Most of the people who were on the ship jumped into the cold water. Some were injured. Others who remained stuck inside the ship drowned. Women swam distances with their children under their arms until the lifeboats arrived. Some did not know how to swim. The search for the missing continued for three weeks, and the bodies kept piling up. Two hundred sixteen illegal immigrants drowned, including eight children who were buried next to each other in the Haifa cemetery. About 1,600 passengers survived. The press was full of a mélange of horrible and heroic stories. One story was about a baby who survived. Her parents lined a basket with a large pillow and tied it around her tiny body. When her father saw that people had begun to jump into the water, he threw the basket into the sea, held his wife, who could not swim, and jumped in along with her. The basket managed to reach the shore. One of the sailors saw the basket, opened it, and discovered the baby, whose body was completely blue. He resuscitated her, and she survived.

The Jewish settlement was struck by astonishment and rage. How had the ship sunk so quickly, and who was responsible for the horrific act? The communist newspaper *Kol Ha'am* wrote on December 12th, 1940: "All the communities of the settlement are debating the question of who holds responsibility for this blood-shed and mass murder. The various Zionist parties are attempting to place the blame on each other. The Haganah declares that the Etzel is to blame, while the Etzel points to the agency organizing these illegal immigration crossings as the main offender. From all of the debate, one thing has become clear, that the perpetrators of this heinous crime are in the Zionist camp." An inquiry commission was set up in which military personnel, ocean liner experts, and survivors participated. They concluded that the hull of the Patria was rotten; therefore, the impact of the explosive on the ship's body was immeasurably more significant than could have been calculated for a steamer its age. The nails were rusty and could not withstand the pressure caused by the explosion. The cause of the ship's rapid sinking was discovered, but who was to blame for the bomb?

The leadership, led by the Workers' Party of the Land of Israel, painted the victims as heroes who had sacrificed their lives to build the land. Berl Katzenelson, one of the party's leaders, told Avigur, "The Patria tragedy is our modern-day battle of Tel Hai.[5] Patria is the biggest Zionist act accomplished in recent years." The surviving illegal immigrants did not dispute this narrative.

Meir Haimon, one of the survivors, said, "The operation was justified. We must not give in to the British. We have a responsibility towards illegal immigrants who are yet to come. We believe that the intention of the Jewish settlement organizations was pure and that the man who gave the order simply did not think it through. But human beings make mistakes."

---

5 On March 1, 1920, a battle took place between Arab irregulars and a Jewish defensive paramilitary force protecting the village of Tel Hai in the northern Galilee.

Chapter 10: Giving Up on the Female Harem

Shifra did not give up and kept conveying to Jenka that she wanted a child. He no longer objected in principle but raised new arguments. "This is not the time to have a baby. The Arab Mufti of Jerusalem lives in Berlin and is close to the Nazi elite, the SS and Adolf Eichmann. He met with Hitler, and it was promised that the German interest in the Middle East would be the extermination of Jews. Rommel's German army advanced through North Africa on its way to Cairo and, from there, plans to come to Mandatory Palestine. The Haganah is preparing a frantic emergency plan, a 'Masada[6] on the Carmel.' The Germans will hunt us down. There will be mass suicide."

"There will never be a suitable time. As long as World War Two rages on, there won't be a suitable time. The war could reach us here, you could be killed. The war could drag on for years. If we don't have a baby now, we may never have one." She grabbed him gently, pulled him to her, and kissed him for a long time.

In May 1942, a baby girl was born at Molada Hospital on the Carmel. They named her Ruth, a common name in those years. A short, biblical name. Shifra got her smile back. The young family

6 Masada was the location of a Jewish rebellion against the Romans in 73 AD, where it is commonly believed that the rebels committed mass suicide rather than be captured.

continued living in Jenka's room, and the new father was excited to photograph the baby girl laying on her back, on her belly, and lifting her head. Ilioff loved to take his great-granddaughter into his arms. He was proud of her and showed her off to his friends at the Technion. "Look what smart eyes she has." Everyone agreed. Jenka liked to hear their excitement about the baby. Maybe she really was special. Deep inside, he thanked Shifra for insisting on having a child.

*

British warships arrived at the port of Haifa, and the city filled with soldiers from every country in the empire on their way to the front. Some of the ships had been damaged in battle. The Iraqi Oil Company, where Jenka worked, loaned him out to the British Army to work on repairing the vessels. He was the subordinate of a senior British engineer named Mr. Stoke, and they became friends. Stoke shared memories of World War One in which he had been a submarine commander, and Jenka told Stoke about his motorcycle trips. They also discussed the heavy British losses in the war, and from time to time, Jenka came up with ideas for weapons that could be developed to help the British.

"I want to introduce you to a high-ranking British officer," Mr. Stoke said.

Jenka considered how to react. He always feared that some Brit would make the connection between him and his activities in the Haganah.

"You should not trouble yourself for me. I do not deserve such an honor," Jenka said modestly.

"Stop being modest. He will come to visit the port tomorrow morning."

When Mr. Stoke arrived the next day, he was accompanied by another British officer, Mr. Smith, whom he introduced to Jenka.

"You Jews have all kinds of ideas. You are smart," Officer Smith said. "I want you to try and test your rocket idea. You may use explosives from the British Navy."

Jenka knew it was an immature, almost stupid idea. After all, his knowledge of explosives was just basic. He tried to evade their offer, but the officer insisted. Having no choice, he designed a primitive rocket and threw it down from the grounds of the Technion. The rocket exploded, making a loud noise, and some windows in the neighborhood shattered.

"Think of another idea," Mr. Smith said.

A week later, the officer arrived, escorted by additional officers. "We like your idea of creating a bomb with an anchor structure attached to the bottom. The bomb itself would be lighter than the water and could float vertically to reach the ship." Jenka knew it was a ridiculous idea, but the British officers thought otherwise. Stoke would not stop nudging Jenka to enlist in the British Navy. He understood Jenka's dilemmas regarding the British policies of the White Paper. Still, he eventually persuaded him by repeating Ben-Gurion's famous words: "We will fight the British as if there is no war against the Nazis and cooperate with the British as if there is no 'White Paper.'"

On the appointed day, Jenka arrived at the British headquarters along with dozens of other male and female recruits. All the recruits stood in a row in the great courtyard, waiting to hear where they would be stationed. The British called each of the volunteers by name and ordered them to go in the same direction. In the end, Jenka was left standing alone. A terrible fear came over him. They must have discovered that he had been an engineer who made bombs for the Haganah. He imagined the noose wrapped around his neck. They took him to a hallway at the far end of the camp and shoved him into a room.

"We have a different plan for you." The officer in the room examined the tense young man.

"What plan?" Jenka wanted to find out as much as possible so he would know how to fight for his life.

"Don't argue, and don't ask questions," the officer scolded him.

"Yes, sir," Jenka said and fell silent, but he kept his hands clenched into fists.

"Take an envelope. You shall travel by train to Egypt, and when you reach Suez, hand it over to the military commander."

He saluted, took the envelope, turned sharply, and hurried out of the room. He decided not to board the train before informing Munya of the unexpected development. Maybe the Haganah would have ideas on how to undo the unfortunate decree. Jenka returned home. Shifra was surprised. Just a few hours ago, they had said their goodbyes.

"What happened?" She paled, fearing that the British had discovered his past activities.

Just then, Ilioff entered the room, "Did you desert?"

Jenka was exhausted and collapsed onto a chair. Riva brought him a slice of bread with marmalade that she'd just finished making.

"The British separated me out from the other engineers. They have another plan for me. I do not know what it is, but I have a very bad feeling." He watched as Shifra took the crying Ruth in her arms.

"If they wanted to kill you, they would have done so right away," Shifra reassured him as she pulled out her breast to nurse. "They would not have entrusted you with a letter declaring that your death sentence be carried out in Alexandria."

"Such cruel games are not characteristic of the British. It is more typical for the Bolsheviks to let a messenger deliver a letter ordering his own death sentence," added Ilioff.

Jenka approached Shifra, "You will have to raise the girl without a father. Just as I was afraid of when I said I did not want children."

"Who said you were going to die? By the time you get back, I'll have raised the wonderful gift you have given me." She embraced him, and he kissed the baby. "Let Munya know about this development. Maybe the Haganah will find a way to undo this unfortunate decree."

On his way out of the room, Jenka turned around for a moment and looked at Shifra. "I know that I have let you down."

"You have not let me down, my wonderful husband."

*

In Suez, he handed the envelope to the local British commander, trying to hide his concern. The officer opened the envelope, looking at the tall, slender Jewish man standing before him, raised his eyebrows in puzzlement, and invited Jenka to sit down.

"Do you know why you're here?" the officer asked.

"They told me not to ask questions and forbade me from opening the envelope," Jenka replied, sitting up straighter.

"You will join an elite group of brilliant minds recruited by the British Empire from across the colonies. You will be stationed in a secret scientific unit in southern England."

Jenka was dumbfounded, "Me? Are you sure?"

"You were recommended by Mr. Stoke and another group of Navy officers. You also passed all the security clearances successfully."

"I passed all the security clearances?" Jenka tried to conceal his astonishment.

"We have a file on you. We know everything about you."

"What do you know?" He asked in the calmest and most innocent voice he could.

"The crucial thing is that we know you do not support those despicable Zionists," he said and flipping through Jenka's file, he added, "there is a letter here in which you requested to rejoin your father in Russia."

"Yes, I submitted such a request," Jenka confirmed, recalling those days of yearning for his father.

"A Zionist would not return to Russia." And that was the end of the conversation.

The British destroyers suffered heavy losses at the hands of German submarines. To get to England unharmed, the British destroyers that would leave Suez for the British Isles planned to make their way around the entire continent of Africa – a route considered the least dangerous. When the destroyer that Jenka was scheduled to board arrived, it was full of hundreds of Polish nurses who'd been recruited to help the war effort. Men attacked the ship in an attempt to board. Naval officers begged Jenka to trade places with them. He had no problem giving up on the female harem and boarded the next destroyer instead.

*

An Admiralty officer was waiting for Jenka at the military port in Portsmouth when he disembarked from the ship. He drove Jenka to the Navy fleet's lodgings and showed him to his room. After ensuring that Jenka had everything he needed, the officer bid him farewell, saying "Mr. Ratner, you're a lucky man."

Jenka felt he was lucky, too. He hadn't been hung, and he wasn't vomiting his heart out on a destroyer that a German submarine might sink at any given moment. He had been stationed in the scientific department of the British Empire.

"The room is great," Jenka replied with satisfaction.

"You haven't heard the news?"

Jenka continued to survey the room, handling objects and getting used to his new surroundings. "What happened?"

"The destroyer carrying the Polish nurses hit a naval mine. There are no survivors. It took us a while to realize that you'd switched ships. At first, we thought you had drowned."

A heavy silence fell. Jenka sat down, clasped his hands tightly together, and propped his chin upon them, and closed his eyes. He'd been spared again. Ever since he was a child, the angel of death had been stalking him. He recalled how the officers back in Alexandria had envied him for being placed in the destroyer along with the Polish nurses. He tried to remember the face of the naval officer who had switched with him. He hadn't even reached the age of twenty. What was his name?

In the dining room the following morning, he met a group of several dozen young men who had gathered from all across the empire. He joined one of the tables, and all the men introduced themselves in English, each with a drastically different accent. They were all excited to be in the British Isles for the first time. Jenka shared that almost a decade earlier, he'd joined a group who had ridden motorcycles from Mandatory Palestine, crossed Europe, and come here.

"So, you're a motorcyclist?" They looked at him in admiration.

In the following days, they underwent an underwater naval mining course, and all the knowledge the British had on submarine warfare was revealed to them. He thirstily drank in the material they were learning and stayed up late every night, studying and internalizing the meaning, his eyes gleaming with excitement. Meanwhile, the trainees were looking into which scientific unit they should ask to be integrated into. They had all been warned that under no circumstance should they ask to be placed directly under the terrible demon, the chief engineer of the scientific unit, the Vice-Admiral, Sir Oliver Thornycroft. The various members of the group managed to find excuses to be placed in faraway units until the only person remaining was the Jewish fellow from Palestine. The feared man's office manager invited Jenka into the room. Jenka had never met such a high-ranking British officer. He straightened up to his full height, inhaling deeply, and stepped inside the large room, the walls of which were decorated with photographs of British destroyers. Sir Thornycroft sat behind a large desk. His eyes were hard, alert. On the wall behind him hung photographs of King George VI.

Sir Thornycroft observed the young man who stood tense as a rubber band before him. "So, you are the brave fellow who was placed with me. I heard all the others ran away from me like little mice. I suppose you couldn't find any other position. What does that say about you? We shall see. You may sit down."

Jenka sat down, erect and waiting for instructions.

"At least you're not a big talker. That's already a virtue."

"Yes, sir."

"I divide people into two types: the majority are people I do not trust and whose lives with me are hell. Then, there is the minority who have proven themselves, with whom I can maintain a tolerable, or even, pleasant relationship."

"I promise to do the best I can."

"What did you do in Palestine that made the officers think you were so talented?" The Vice-Admiral leaned back in his chair.

"I had a stupid idea to develop a special bomb designed for airplanes to drop on ships. They experimented, and it didn't work. I also had other idiotic ideas."

"Who, pray tell, was the foolish British commander who thought that would work?"

"I only realized how truly ludicrous it was during the course here."

"We have ten proximity fuses that are causing problems. My engineers haven't been able to decipher and rectify the issue. Let's see what you can do?" And with that, the Vice-Admiral gestured for him to leave.

Jenka got up, saluted him, and left the room thinking that "the demon" was not so terrible after all. He appreciated that the man had gotten straight to the point and assigned him a task. Already up to date on their conversation, the office manager handed Jenka the sketches, ordered a soldier to accompany him to the bunker and show him the proximity fuse storehouse, and reserved a small bunker for him to dismantle them and figure out what the problem was. Things move fast here, Jenka thought with satisfaction. He took apart the broken fuses, reassembled and disassembled them several times until the issue became clear to him, and only then went to sleep.

He rose early the next morning, ate breakfast, and rushed to the secretary to ask for a room with a drawing table. She informed him that he would be sharing a room with two other engineers. The room was spacious and had a large window. Each engineer had their own workspace with a drawing table and state-of-the-art drawing tools. The other two men had not yet arrived, and Jenka stood alone in the room. He approached the drawing table and felt the adrenaline flooding his body. His eyes twinkled, his thoughts focused, and he tackled the assignment. He sketched the fuses with the repairs necessary for each one. He took the sketches to the workshop, sat all day beside the people crafting the parts, and made sure that their work was accurate. The next day he took the fuses to the testing site and fired them. They all worked perfectly.

Sir Thornycroft was pleased and assigned Jenka additional tasks. He liked Jenka's brilliant and aesthetic solution to the complex design problem. He never praised Jenka to his face but confessed to his colleagues that the "bloody Jew" was better than the rest of his engineers. Jenka never imagined that he would work at such a high-level, professional place. He also appreciated the English spirit of mobilization in the war against the Nazis and admired the English character. They were men of action, not just all talk, unlike the

Jews who argued over everything. In the evenings, the unit would go to the pub and drink beer, and Jenka would charm them with stories about his motorcycle travels through Africa and India.

Sir Thornycroft appointed Jenka as Chief Project Officer and recommended that he be promoted to the rank of lieutenant colonel. The Admiralty agreed on the condition that he receive British citizenship, but Jenka stalled with his reply. Sir Thornycroft presumed Jenka was undecided because he had a wife and daughter in Palestine to whom he planned to return someday. He thought the solution should be romantic – Jenka should be introduced to an English girl, someone he would fall for.

*

Clara passed away a few months after Jenka left for England. That day, as usual, she sat in her armchair on the terrace facing the garden, dreaming of the happy days of her youth: the proms, the dresses, the jewelry, and the four-horse-drawn carriage. Suddenly, she stood up, smiled, took a few steps, fell down, and died. Ilioff loved her until the day she died. For him, she'd always remained the same beautiful social butterfly who had enchanted him at their very first meeting, gliding between the guests at a ball in her parents' palace in Ekaterinoslav. He had wanted her to be happy so badly, but how could she have been? But how could a mother whose daughter had died of an illness at 26 years old, whose youngest son had been drowned in a river during the Russian Civil War, who did not know what had happened to her family members under Bolshevik rule, and under the Nazi occupation, be happy? Clara had never felt at home in the Land of Israel.

Ilioff passed away later that year. The funeral was respectable. The Technion praised him in their newsletter and named the Chemistry Laboratory after him.

Bosa, Daniel's eldest daughter, was accepted to the Hebrew University, but she met a security guard near Migdal, and they decided that establishing settlements in the Land of Israel was more important than their studies at the university and joined the group that founded Kibbutz Ma'agan Michael. Yasha, Daniel's youngest son, attended the Kadouri agricultural school. Only Gideon, the youngest of Doc's children, who was already sixteen, returned to Moshav Migdal. Shifra was left alone with the toddler, Ruth, and the funds at her disposal were insufficient to maintain the house and support herself and her daughter. Having no choice, Shifra realized that she had to return to her parent's home.

When she arrived at the apartment door with the baby in her arms, Zalman received her with a sullen look. "I thought I had already married off one daughter. There are two more unmarried ones at home." Her mother, and her sisters, Shulamit and Tova, stood behind him. The expression on her mother's face begged her not to talk back.

"Well, come in already." he motioned for her to enter. "Where do you intend to sleep? In the kitchen? There's no space to move in this house! Your mother and I sleep in the living room! We gave your room to Shulamit and the spare room to Tova!" Shifra watched the color drain from her mother's face.

"So, that's how it is at the Professor's?" Zalman shouted, stretching his arms out to the side. "I thought you married into a family with money, to an educated man, an engineer! Could they not look after you?"

"Shifra can have my room," said Tova.

Zalman asked, "Where do you think we can fit two more beds?"

"Shifra can sleep in my bed, and we will add another small bed for Ruth," she explained.

"And where will you sleep? On the floor?" asked Shulamit.

"I volunteered for the British Army. I won't be needing the room." Tova held her breath.

Zalman approached her. "Have you gone mad? All the girls in the army are prostitutes. The next daughter to return home will be carrying a bastard."

"I leave for Cairo in two weeks."

Zalman was about to slap Tova when her mother stepped in between them, but he pushed her aside. Shifra couldn't stand it any longer. She ran out of the apartment and slammed the door behind her, shouts accompanying her down the corridor. She sat sobbing in the stairwell, holding baby Ruth and kissing her. She needed fresh air. She climbed up the stairs to the roof. The laundry of the building's occupants hung on the lines, drying in the sun. Shifra hadn't remembered that there was a laundry room on the rooftop that wasn't in use. She brought her belongings upstairs and settled in the empty laundry room. News of the uprising in the Warsaw ghetto arrived. She remembered Jenka saying that babies shouldn't be brought into the world in such times, and she hugged Ruth tightly.

Shifra would often go down to the mailbox on the ground floor of the apartment building, collect the letters, and hand to her parents those addressed to them: electricity bills, water bills, and thank you notes for generous donations to the synagogue. In his rare letters, Jenka wrote that he was happy with his post and that he often went out with his friends from the unit, most of whom were single, though there were also a few married men. They had come to the conclusion that British girls were the most attractive. This hurt her feelings, but she had expected him to sleep with a girl from time to time. She couldn't exactly forbid him from doing so.

Among the letters addressed to her parents was a letter from Tova, her sister, in which she reported that she was working at a military hospital. She had met many new people, including Noa Eshkol, the daughter of Levy Eshkol, chairman of the Workers' Party of the Land of Israel. Noa recommended that she study to be a physical education teacher. She was not yet decided on the matter. She was content. They shouldn't worry about her.

The only letter left in Shifra's hand was from Jenka. The whole family nudged her to open the letter. She opened it, skimmed the text, and her complexion paled.

"What happened? Is Jenka injured?" Zalman asked.

"No. Jenka is fine," mumbled Shifra.

Zalman snatched up the letter and read that his son-in-law was writing to his daughter to tell her that one of the other officers had introduced him to his sister, a nice girl and that he had started seeing her.

Zalman began to yell, "While you sit here in my house, your husband has already found another wife! You were always stupid, and you've stayed that way! You are going to your husband! Now! I won't let you stay here for another minute!" Zalman threw the letter at Shifra.

Shifra picked up the letter. She wondered why Jenka had told her about the woman. She'd already received letters saying that he and his friends went out to the nightclubs to meet English girls. But now, he was going steady with a girl. She would soon convince him to divorce Shifra. Jenka was naive regarding women.

Zalman did not leave her alone. "You better sit down right now and write to him that he needs to bring you to England."

She needed time to think about what and how to write to him. She tried to talk some sense into her father. "We are in the midst of a world war. Armies are traveling from front to front, families are separating, and you expect the British Admiralty to ship me to England because my husband wrote that he's been spending time with a girl?"

He continued to insist, and Ruth started crying. Miriam took the girl into her arms.

"You will not leave this room until you write to your husband." Zalman slammed the door behind him.

Shifra began to write:

My beloved Jenka, my wonderful husband,

When I received your letter, I kissed it. I think about how much I love you and miss you every day. Ruth is growing nicely but lacks a loving father to photograph her, to develop the photographs, and to put them in the album.

I'm glad you're happy with your job and aren't lonely. My circumstances are dreadful. I was forced to move back in with my parents. Back when we first met, I told you how much I suffered at home, and now that I've returned with the baby, Zalman won't stop abusing me emotionally. Now he's declared that he plans to throw us out of the apartment. As you know, I have no money to rent an apartment. It will take months for Ilioff's will to take effect.

I wish I didn't have to turn to you in this matter, my wonderful husband. However, I have no choice but to ask you to bring us to England. I know it's unrealistic and that there's a world war, but life doesn't always proceed logically. What is it you always say? Sometimes miracles happen. Please don't be angry with me, brave and extraordinary husband of mine. I have no one I can count on other than you.

Forever Yours,

Shifra

Jenka requested to meet with Sir Thornycroft. He knew his request was unrealistic. He was mortified by the mere act of appealing to Thornycroft. When he entered the office, he could barely say the words.

"What's the matter, Jenka?"

Jenka clenched his fists, bit his bottom lip, sighed, and squirmed.

"Whatever is wrong with you?"

"I apologize in advance for bothering you and appealing to you on this matter which is so insignificant during these days of the war effort." When he finished the first sentence, Jenka stood up straight like a good soldier.

"Speak already," Thornycroft commanded, looking perplexedly at Jenka.

"I received a letter from my wife."

"What does she want?"

"I know it's impossible, frankly impudent, and I'm already ashamed of the appeal in advance, but she wants me to bring her and our daughter to England," he grimaced, his eyes bugged out awkwardly as if his request were absolutely delusional.

He expected Thornycroft to hit the table, order him to leave the room, and his body stiffened, prepared to accept any punishment lovingly.

Thornycroft was silent as he absorbed Jenka's request.

"I will look into the matter," the Vice-Admiral replied calmly.

"You intend to consider this disgraceful request?"

"Yes. At ease. You're free to go."

Sir Thornycroft thought this was a superb idea. How had he not thought of it before himself? With the woman and toddler in England, Jenka wouldn't refuse their offer of British citizenship. He picked up the phone and asked to be transferred to the head of the navy, explaining the unusual request. It was approved.

*

In January 1944, Shifra and her two-year-old daughter boarded a British destroyer. She was the only woman on the ship full of soldiers, and they all cared for and pampered her and Ruth. No one believed that she was joining her husband, an engineer serving in the science department. They all assumed it was a cover story for something much more important and confidential. Some even joked that she was related to some royal family or perhaps a member of the Rothschild family.

Shifra got off the destroyer at the docks of Portsmouth with Ruth in her arms. She spotted Jenka waiting for them, taller than the English men, wearing a three-piece suit, tie, and hat, and holding a bouquet of flowers in his hand.

"You look like an English lord, my wonderful husband," she said as he hugged them both.

An Admiralty automobile drove them to their home, a two-story house with a large living room that had a fireplace and a glass window facing the street. Jenka threw a match onto the wood waiting in the fireplace, and a flame leaped up, warming up the room.

"This is a suitable house for raising a family," proclaimed Shifra.

Chapter 11: One Blind and the Other Deaf

The German submarines continued to sink the Allies' destroyers and supply lines in the Atlantic Ocean and the North Sea. One day Captain Walker, one of the most esteemed naval commanders, came to the scientific unit. He asked to meet with Vice-Admiral Thornycroft to report on the occurrence of a bizarre incident. Jenka was also invited to the meeting.

"I was in command of two destroyers that got caught in a storm," Walker began. "The Sonar to detect submarines stopped working in one of the destroyers, and in the other, the system for dropping depth charge bombs into the water broke."

"So, you had a blind destroyer with combat capability and another destroyer that could see but lost its ability to fight," the Vice Admiral concluded.

"Naturally, I ordered both destroyers to return to England to be repaired." Jenka nodded in understanding.

"On the way, the destroyer with the functional sonar discovered a nearby group of submarines down to their exact location. I ordered the ship to keep its distance from the submarines because it could not defend itself, and I ordered the crew to report the location of the submarines to the blind destroyer."

"Correct orders. So, what happened?" asked the Vice-Admiral, his curiosity blooming.

"The 'seeing' destroyer used its sonar to follow the second destroyer, which quickly reached the submarine, floated over it, and was about to drop its depth charge bombs. Then, the bizarre thing occurred – the destroyer with the working sonar discovered that the submarine had made a sharp turn and escaped, without the destroyer above it being aware."

"Even if the ship's sonar were functioning, they wouldn't know about the turn because sonars cannot detect anything below them that isn't moving," the Vice Admiral explained to Jenka.

They fell silent.

"The submarine knew that the destroyer had discovered it and had no chance of escaping, so they didn't try to escape. They waited for the destroyer to reach them, literally seducing it to get on top of them, in order to blind the sonar, and then changed direction, to shoot a torpedo and drown the destroyer."

Jenka made room on the table and picked up two pencils of different colors and a fountain pen. "The red pencil is the destroyer with the functioning sonar, the blue pencil is the destroyer that can fight, and the submarine is the fountain pen."

They moved the objects around on the table, according to Walker's report.

"Your analysis is right. Now comes the remarkable part of the story," Walker said, trying to keep his composure and not to get too excited. "The 'seeing' destroyer reported the sudden deviation of the submarine to the blind destroyer. There was no point in dropping the bombs then, for the submarine had changed position. Next, the 'seeing' destroyer told the other destroyer where the submarine had fled, and in turn, the blind destroyer chased after it, reached it, and drowned it."

Jenka continued moving the colored pencils and the fountain pen as Walker described what had happened.

"My two disabled destroyers sank all four submarines using a minimal number of bombs," Walker concluded.

It was quiet as they all attempted to understand the tremendous significance of what had been accidentally discovered.

"German intelligence knew that the destroyer's sonar was blind to the submarine below it."

Thornycroft narrowed his eyes as he comprehended the gravity of the situation. "How could we make such a mistake? We've paid such a terrible price for this blunder. When I think of all the thousands of soldiers who drowned at sea over the course of the war, burned alive in the tar of their ships." He stood up, horrified. "Our destroyers dropped their bombs believing they were above German submarines because they had correctly navigated themselves towards the submarines. But they mistakenly assumed that the submarines would continue in a fixed direction."

Submarine warfare theory was forever changed. It was also decided to equip the submarine chasing destroyers with new devices that allowed them to drop their depth charges from long-range, thus helping them to avoid unnecessary risks. Sir Thornycroft devised a comprehensive solution and instructed Jenka to head the task force that would develop the idea in detail, conduct experiments, and execute its design. Jenka and the group of engineers hurried to complete the solution and built a three-barreled mortar, placed at the destroyer's bow rather than its stern, which they called the "Squid." Each barrel was a different length, which achieved a diverse range, and the middle barrel also shifted to the side so that the barrage of the three barrels together formed a triangular-shaped impact spread. Next to each one was another Squid that created a mirror-image impact spread to the first so that together they formed two triangles in the shape of a hidden "Star of David." On average, it took two barrages of six depth charge bombs to sink one submarine instead of taking 120 depth charge bombs like before the invention of the Squid. The weapon was effective and, to a large extent, removed the threat of German submarines.

*

Sir Thornycroft continued to urge Jenka to accept British citizenship, and he began to consider responding in the affirmative. Shifra, however, vehemently objected. They lay in bed, and he brought up the subject as he stroked her legs, which he had always thought were the most beautiful legs in the world.

"The British brought you and Ruth to England during the war, which is completely unheard of. They did it so that I would accept British citizenship. I'm happy here."

"Within a year, the war will end, and they will no longer need you. There is anti-Semitism in England, and you will go back to being treated like a worthless Jew from Palestine," Shifra said. "The Haganah needs you."

Jenka was silent.

"The English don't care about us," Shifra added. "I showed you that article from the underground newspaper about a Jew who managed to escape a death camp and revealed the truth about the gas chambers and the mass extermination. There was even a photograph of the gas chambers. The next day the newspaper shut down, and no more stories have been published about the Jewish genocide since. The British are doing everything they can to hide the facts. And they refuse to consider bombing Auschwitz to slow down the death rate."

Jenka understood the many reasons against accepting citizenship firsthand but was grateful to Sir Thornycroft for his trust in him and the complex and fascinating projects the Vice-Admiral had authorized him to head. But, Shifra would not let it be. "Your employment will end when the war ends, and we will have to return home. You can contribute there, as well. Also, I am pregnant and don't want our two children to grow up English."

She'd surprised him yet again. How had she managed to set him up? As he caressed her belly, he whispered, "Who said women aren't malicious?"

Shifra's attempts to form friendships with their English neighbors were unsuccessful. Their husbands had all been drafted, and most of them were serving overseas. The losses were heavy, and the women felt resentment towards the Jewish foreigner from Palestine whose husband was by her side, also a soldier, but serving in the Admiralty, out of mortal danger. Her English wasn't that of an Englishwoman; she made mistakes and had an accent. The women were unkind and made her feel like a foreigner, a native from one of the British colonies. She was afraid to open her mouth. From time to time, she even heard anti-Semitic remarks. In contrast, Ruth felt like an English girl for all intents and purposes. English was her first language; she had many girlfriends and was always invited to birthday parties.

Danny was born a sweet baby with light hair. Caring for the children and keeping the house was all Shifra's responsibility. Jenka presented her his entire salary, and as far as he was concerned, with that, his duty ended. Sometimes Shifra reminded her husband that he had a daughter and needed to pay her some attention. He took her for a walk to the neighborhood park, where she met friends. While they played, he sat on the bench, opened his little notebook, erased the tasks he had already done, and wrote in new tasks scheduled for the following day. He heard shouting. Ruth and her friend Elizabeth writhed on the ground, screaming. He walked over to them, looked at their scratched knees, assessed that their injuries weren't severe, and helped them get up. Their cries and shouts annoyed him. He commanded them to stop crying. Ruth lifted her head, pursed her lips, and stopped crying. Jenka held Ruth's hand in one hand and her friend's in the other.

The three of them walked slowly to Elizabeth's house, who continued wailing the whole way. When they arrived, Elizabeth's mother came outside, and the little girl amplified her cries as if what had happened was the worst thing in the world. All the while, Ruth walked beside him quietly, limping, not wailing, holding back her tears. For the first time, he felt that Ruth was truly his daughter. Before bed, she insisted that he tell her a story. Her mother knew how to read stories, but Ruth preferred to hear about her father's adventures in Africa and India. She especially loved the story about the cannibals who had caught him in Africa, who had already prepared a big pot of water to cook him in, but when they saw how thin he was, they said, "*ptui, ptui,*" and threw him out.

*

The Second World War came to an end. The members of the scientific unit were released from the army, and Jenka received a letter of appreciation for his contribution to the war effort.

He [Mr. Ratner] was a designer of outstanding merit and was responsible for, and indeed actually prepared and designed certain intricate weapons and equipment which subsequently proved highly successful and were of great importance. Mr. Ratner was an officer of high personal integrity who provided extremely satisfactory service.

Chief, Royal Naval Scientific Service

Before his release, Sir Thornycroft had tasked Jenka with the Limbo Project – the development of an even more sophisticated and long-range mortar for future submarine warfare. For the first time, he encountered difficulties mobilizing the team to show enthusiasm for the work. Work ethic had dropped drastically. Thousands of discharged soldiers had returned home. Unemployment rose. Strikes broke out as the unions demanded better wages. Foreigners began to be accused of taking returning soldiers' places and were no longer welcome. Jenka's good days in the science department were over. Anti-Semitism had raised its wicked head.

They knew that as May 1948 approached, the scheduled date of the cessation of the British Mandate in Palestine, the Arab majority would attack the Jewish minority in an attempt to eliminate them. The Mufti of Jerusalem, Haj Amin al-Husseini, was the champion of Egypt and Palestine. In 1946, Hassan al-Banna, the founder of the Muslim Brotherhood, called Husseini "a hero who challenged the Zionist Empire with the help of Hitler and Germany. Germany and Hitler may be no more, but Amin al-Husseini shall continue the fight."

*

Jenka contacted a London-based Zionist family who often hosted senior members of the Zionist leadership. When they informed Jenka that Moshe Sharett, secretary of the political department of the Jewish Agency, was stopping over in London and staying with them, Jenka drove there in secret and met Sharett, Berl Locker, the chairman of the Jewish Agency, and Haim Slavin, the director of the Haganah's Military Industries. Jenka showed them sketches of the weapons he'd developed and said, "We all know that when the British leave Palestine, a war will break out. The Jews are a minority. I could develop weapons."

They were alarmed by the idea. "You shouldn't dare. The English have eyes and ears everywhere. They will hang you and hang us," they warned him.

"What's the point of developing weapons? At Military Industries, we copy guns and pistols," Slavin added.

Jenka returned to Portsmouth and told Shifra about the meeting. "Nothing has changed with the Jews. It's always the same debate about restraint. They don't understand why we need to develop weapons. I am fed up with our people."

Shifra listened. She knew her people well. He continued, "If the Jews in Palestine cannot unite and won't acquire weapons, the Arabs will finish what the Germans didn't have time for," he predicted darkly. Shifra knew he was right. The world would stand aside, condemning actions with words alone but doing nothing.

Jenka's sleep was troubled. He fell into depression. His predictions for the future were bleak. The meeting in London, the disregard for his ability to contribute, and the lack of comprehension had left him with a feeling of deep despair. He contacted the U.S. Embassy and asked what he would need to do if he wished to immigrate, become a permanent resident, and find employment in the defense field there. They informed him that he could receive a national interest waiver within a few days. He had been born in Switzerland, and the quota for Swiss immigrants wasn't full. Then he received a message from the Zionist family in London informing him that Teddy Kollek would be stopping at their home on his way to raise funds in the U.S. Jenka feared that he would again face condescension, but Shifra urged him to go nevertheless. With no expectations, his face emotionless, his heart heavy, Jenka traveled to London. He met with Teddy and presented the developments he had created for the Admiralty. Then and there, Teddy called David Ben-Gurion, who gave Jenka a direct order to return home posthaste.

But how could he leave England? He had been exposed to national secrets about cutting-edge weapons for years. He knew they would not let him go easily. He requested to meet with Mr. Sutton, the officer who'd replaced Thornycroft. The new supervisor was not interested in technical work and focused instead on administrative procedures. The relationship between them was cold.

"I humbly ask your permission to leave England and return home," Jenka announced as he stood at attention.

"Are you unhappy here? Have you not received the required funds? Do you not have the necessary manpower?"

"I have no complaints. But the war is over. I have successfully completed the development of the 'Limbo.' It is time for me to return home. I contributed to England in my own humble way during the war." Jenka knew he hadn't convinced Sutton.

Mr. Sutton examined the tall, slender man, narrowed his eyes, and surveyed him suspiciously, "I'm sorry, but I cannot allow you to return to Palestine. We have enough trouble there, and the last thing we need is for the Arabs to accuse us of allowing a weapons development expert to come to and help the despicable Jews."

Jenka bit his bottom lip, "I humbly ask to consider the matter," he persisted, not prepared to give up.

Sutton had no intention of giving Jenka another project. Jenka was even quite sure that Sutton would be happy to be rid of him so he could appoint a British man in his place.

"I'm prepared to allow you to go to the United States."

Jenka had not expected such an offer. Sutton warned him, "If you try to escape and go to Palestine, we will find out and prevent it. We have our ways," and with that threatening sentence, the conversation ended.

Jenka and Shifra knew that Sutton's threat was real.

He made an appointment with a doctor, and before entering the clinic, he wounded himself in the mouth. "I'm dying. I have tuberculosis. I'm coughing up blood," he complained. The doctor performed an X-ray and found a scar on Jenka's right lung. Jenka had expected this. He knew about his old scar, which could look like tuberculosis. He also knew that the doctor was anti-Semitic.

"All I ask is that you help me leave England." He knew the doctor understood he was faking his illness. But correctly assumed that the doctor would want to do England a favor and get rid of another foreigner. With a letter from the doctor in hand, he appeared before Mr. Sutton.

"I was thinking about your offer regarding the USA, and I would be happy to accept it, but unfortunately, there is no chance that the Americans will agree to accept me. I have tuberculosis." He coughed and handed over the doctor's note. Sutton realized it was all a performance but couldn't ignore the doctor's decision.

"You will be allowed to return to Palestine after completing the Limbo prototype experiment successfully." Jenka remained expressionless, pleased that he was able to exemplify the English composure at its best.

"I also suggest that you stop coughing. Otherwise, I shan't be permitted to continue to employ you for fear that the rest of the staff will catch your dreadful disease."

Jenka saluted. As he stepped toward the door, he heard Sutton warn, "Don't you dare join the vile underground Zionist ranks there. If you do, we will eliminate you."

*

The 'Limbo' prototype experiment was successful, and the British Army adopted it as their latest naval destroyer weapon for years to come. Sutton kept his promise, and on the 17th of April 1947, Jenka was released from the British Army. His friends in the unit held a farewell party in his honor. Sutton arrived at the party and announced sadly, "Jenka is ill and will be returning to Palestine." No one believed he was sick; he had been working with them at full steam for the past few months. Everyone wondered how he was being permitted to return home with everything he knew. Their memory was still fresh from the heinous act of the Jewish guerilla group, the Etzel, who had planted a bomb at the General Secretariat of the Government and the British military headquarters at the King David Hotel in Jerusalem. About 90 people were killed, including roughly 15 Jews. They had intended to give Jenka a new slide rule as a gift but, after some thought, decided to wait until the next day. They brought the slide rule to his home. He invited them in, did a few calculations to check out his new toy, and put it back in its bag. Before they said goodbye, they suggested he read the dedication they'd written on the back of the rule. It read, "Don't Shed British Blood."

*

Jenka, Shifra, and the children boarded a ship to Palestine. Jenka would walk with Ruth on deck every day. She loved walking beside him, proud of her tall father. At one corner of the deck, they discovered a thick rope curled into a coil, creating a hollow tower inside which Ruth would hide and pretend she was in a cave in Africa. When the ship arrived at a port in Italy, the deck filled with Jews, Holocaust survivors, quietly huddling, curled up in ragged clothes, wrapped in blankets. One of them approached Ruth; he had a peculiar look in his eyes, and she ran away. She didn't want to walk on the deck after that.

The sea was peaceful, and the ship docked at the Haifa port by the end of April 1947.

Chapter 12: The Painter's Studio

The morning mists dissipated, and they could see the British flag waving over Haifa's port. As the ship was slowly pulling in, they noticed that new neighborhoods had climbed up Mount Carmel. Soon the city's arms would reach up and meet the new neighborhoods atop the mountain. In the middle, lay wild plots of nature doomed to a fate of imminent construction. The ship was secured to the wharf. They were glad to be home. Breathing in the familiar air, they slowly descended the narrow staircase off the ship. The young family followed the sign leading to the Border Police and joined the line. Shifra noticed a glimmer of tension on Jenka's face and knew he feared the British detectives would find an excuse to have him killed. They arrived at the counter and handed their passports to the clerk.

"You are returning to Palestine after a five-year stay in England?"

"Yes," replied Jenka, standing upright, taut as a rubber band.

"What did you do there for so many years?" asked the clerk as he flipped back and forth through the pages of Jenka's passport.

"I was an officer in the Admiralty's scientific unit."

"Where is the official naval authorization proving that you have been discharged and are permitted to return to Palestine?" Jenka took the certificate out of his bag and handed it to the clerk.

"Please wait a moment." The clerk handed the documents to a

man wearing a suit and dark glasses who stood behind him, and they disappeared into the adjoining room.

The people in line peered at the tall man, trying to guess what trouble he was in. The man in the suit with the dark glasses came out of the back room, walked back to the counter, and studied Jenka. "It says here that you are fatally ill." He did not seem at all convinced. "You look fine to me," he muttered.

"He has advanced tuberculosis," Shifra was quick to explain.

"The illness began when I was a child and was dormant for several years. It broke out again during my service in England because of the cold and the humidity."

"Where will you live?"

"We don't know yet."

"We require an address." They gave him the address of Zalman's apartment in Haifa, and the clerk stamped their passports.

Waiting outside was Doc, who had come specially from his farm in Migdal, as well as Zalman and Shifra's sisters, Shulamit and Tova. They ran towards Jenka and Shifra when they saw them exit the building, waving their hands and shouting their names. They embraced, admiring the toddler with the blond hair. Uncle Doc, who remembered Ruth from when she was a baby, picked her up. She was startled by the strange man and asked in English to be put down, clinging tightly to her father's legs.

"She only understands English."

"You didn't speak Hebrew with her?" Doc was surprised.

"She will learn Hebrew here." He recalled the many arguments with Shifra, who had also insisted that Ruth should speak Hebrew in England.

"Why didn't Mother come?" Shifra looked at Tova, troubled.

"Mother is ill. She is waiting for you."

*

The shutters were closed, a dim glow shone through the few tiny open cracks, and the smell of medicine filled the air of the unventilated room. Miriam's face was swollen, her thinning hair was pulled back, and an immense, ugly, elongated growth clung to her neck. Shifra kissed her face, took her hand, and cried because she had not been able to get Miriam out of that house and give her a better life. She sat Danny on the bed so her mother could touch him, and he burst out crying. Ruth refused to sit on the bed. She looked at the old woman's face, backed away, whispered fearfully, "She has the face of a witch, and there's a snake wrapped around her neck," and ran from the room.

Jenka stood waiting for them in the corridor, a stranger in the Lifshitz residence. A wave of longing flooded over him. He missed the little house on Pevzner Street, Grandfather Ilioff, Grandmother Clara, Riva the nanny, his bedroom, the kitchen where he would develop his photographs, and Doc's kids. He continued to stand sternly, patiently, as they all sat around the table covered with a white embroidered tablecloth, on which sat a pot of tea and some cake. Shifra called him over to join them, but Jenka refused with a brusque shake of his head. She knew that all the stress he'd experienced that morning at the border checkpoint might come up, and she got up, apologized, grabbed his arm, and together they left the apartment. She climbed the stairs to the roof of the building to show him the laundry room.

"This is where we lived when you went to England. We can live here again temporarily." He checked that there was running water and electricity. "The toilet is outside." Shifra pointed to a small hut at the corner of the roof; he checked if the toilet flushed, and on his way back to the laundry room, grabbed the iron railing of the roof to see if it was strong, to make sure there was no danger of the children falling.

"We'll live here temporarily. It will be crowded for the first few days with the four of us here, but I will leave soon, once I receive instructions from Haganah."

"You know I'm not spoiled."

He liked her answer.

"We'll build our own house with the inheritance money I received from Ilioff."

She smiled.

"We will wait for you, my wonderful husband."

He almost answered, "I love you."

*

In a small notebook with graph paper, Jenka wrote a list of tasks he had to do. His first task was to contact the architect, Professor Yohanan Ratner. They were not related, but people often confused them. He knew Yohanan from before he'd gone to England. Yohanan was already a senior officer in the Haganah and a senior faculty member at the Technion back then.

Jenka rang. Yohanan picked up the phone, and Jenka recognized his voice; he had the Russian accent of someone who, in his youth, had served as an officer in a Cossack unit.

"I have arrived." He waited for Yohanan's response.

"You will be contacted," he said and with that, the call ended. Jenka took out the notebook and scribbled crowded circles over the line until it was impossible to see what was written there.

The next task was to enroll Ruth in Rebecca's Kindergarten, which was a short walk away. They entered the kindergarten. It was on the ground floor in an apartment building with a small adjoining garden.

"This is my daughter," he said, and he introduced Ruth. "She was born in Haifa. We recently returned from England, and I would like to enroll her in kindergarten."

"Too bad you didn't inform us in advance, but we will accept her anyway." She turned to the girl, "What is your name?"

Ruth backed away, clinging to her father.

"She speaks and understands only English," Jenka explained, "but she will learn Hebrew."

"We accept children who are new immigrants. We have a child at the kindergarten who speaks only Yiddish and another who only knows Polish, and it's not easy for them. But a girl who only speaks English? The other children will think she's English, and they hate the English here."

He still thought it was better to speak English than the languages of the Diaspora. "We will speak only Hebrew with her at home," he promised and asked, "Can I go now and pick her up at noon?" Rebecca nodded in agreement, and Jenka translated for Ruth.

The kindergarten teacher introduced Ruth to the children and explained that she had returned from England and spoke only English, but that no, she was not English. She is Jewish and was born in Haifa. The children looked at Ruth, and she looked at them. No one invited her to play. She went to the toy shelves, selected a game, and played alone. She saw the children whispering. One of the girls made an ugly face, all the boys laughed, and Ruth gathered herself, holding back tears. When she needed to use the bathroom, she went up to Rebecca, who called over her assistant, thinking maybe she would understand what the girl was asking for in English.

"Pee," she shouted. "Pee! Pee!" she squeezed her thighs together and jumped up and down, trying to hold it in. If she peed in her pants, she would be too ashamed to return to the kindergarten ever again.

"Oh, pee-pee," the woman realized, grabbing the girl's hand and leading her to the bathroom.

Two days later, Ruth refused to go to kindergarten. She burst out in tears, yelling that she wanted to return to England. "All the kids here are mean. I will never go back to Rebecca's Kindergarten."

Shifra was busy with Danny, the toddler, and Ruth was happy to spend her days on the roof, daydreaming. Six ropes stretched from one side of the roof to the other, attached to wooden pillars that were planted into the concrete floor. The laundry of the buildings' occupants hung dancing from the ropes. The laundry on each rope would often get tangled with the fluttering pieces of laundry above or below it, and Ruth would jump around in circles, crawling and speaking to herself, synchronizing with the movements of the laundry. When she grew tired, or the weather became too hot, she would build tents from sheets and blankets tied to the railing with a rope. She would sit under them and invent stories about fairies and imagine herself performing heroic deeds in the jungles of Africa. This was how Ruth finished her kindergarten years.

Jenka's third task was to build a house. A realtor took them in his car to a neighborhood called Carmelia on a spur of Mount Carmel, descending toward the beach. Recently, a dirt road that surrounded the area had been paved and in the center was a hill covered in groves of large pine trees with a view of the sea. They saw the lot only once before Jenka decided to buy it.

"The location is beautiful, but it won't be convenient to live there," Shifra said, trying to rein in his enthusiasm.

"The area will develop."

"There's no grocery store there, no bus there. You have to climb the entire hill to reach the bus on the main road." She saw that Jenka was getting annoyed.

"I hate to put things off," he said, and she knew it was true. "Any day, someone will come for me from the Haganah, and I do not know when I'll return home. There is no time."

When he saw that she was silent, he waved his hands, "If you don't want it? Then who needs a house anyway?" She knew he was stressed because the Haganah hadn't contacted him yet and that he still feared the English would have him killed.

"The money is mine. My inheritance from my mother. And I have decided that this is the lot that I want."

"Okay," Shifra nodded in resignation as she accepted the verdict.

He designed the house by himself and showed Shifra the plan when he was finished. A large living room, a spacious kitchen with a balcony, and two bedrooms with exits to another shared balcony that faced west towards the sea. He patiently explained the details to her, as he would explain an engineering sketch to technicians. He clarified the considerations he'd taken and rotated the plan so she could understand where North, South, East, and West were. He elaborated on the air circulation and the view.

She watched and listened, keeping quiet.

"If you have any comments or changes, I want to hear them now."

"I need to think, to consult."

"Tomorrow, I may not be here anymore, and you keep wasting time."

"Why did you buy a lot so fast? Why do you want to build the house that you'll live in your whole life so fast?"

"What whole life? The English may capture me at any moment and hang me."

"The money for the house has been lying in the bank for years. It can wait a little longer."

"No, it cannot." He softened, explaining his considerations. "In May, the British Mandate ends, and war will break out when the English leave. Banks could fail, and the leadership may seize the money to help survive the war."

"Okay." She didn't like making decisions until she was sure. She preferred to wait until things became clear and then make a choice.

"I don't want you to wake up tomorrow morning and say that you regret it and want to make changes. It's final."

"It's final," she said pacifyingly. "If we don't build now, we might never build."

"I want to make sure that you and the children have a home." He hugged her, erasing the third task from his notebook.

*

Aharon Donagi, who everyone called Aharonchik, dropped out of high school at the age of seventeen. That was in 1942: he just could not sit at a desk and study for his matriculation exams. The world was at war, Jews were being massacred in Europe, and the British were hunting down ships full of illegal immigrants and deporting them from Palestine to the island of Mauritius in the Indian Ocean. He learned that a year earlier, the Haganah had established the Palmach elite combat reserve brigades with no budget and reliant solely on volunteers. He joined the Palmach, which had begun preparing for the horrible possibility that the German army would invade the country, too. He took a squad commanders course and then a sapper course. By the time Aharonchik was 23, he had already been incarcerated in the British prison several times under different names. Each time, he was released after a few months. Under the command of Professor Yohanan Ratner, Aharonchik engaged in "top-secret assignments." His black eyes, thick flowing black forelock of hair, tanned skin, and whole demeanor radiated with explosive energy, shrouded in mystery.

"A weaponry specialist has arrived here from England," Yohanan informed him. "He must be transferred to a hiding place quickly so that he can begin working."

"Roger that. I'll take care of it," he replied.

"Oh, and one more thing," the professor added. "He came to the country under the pretense that he was terminally ill and about to die."

An envelope with no stamp was waiting for Jenka in the mailbox. He opened it carefully, taking out a note signed by someone named Aharonchik, who asked about his health. He wanted to meet Jenka the following day at ten in the morning on a bench in nearby Binyamin Park, a short walking distance away, perfect for a terminally ill man hoping to sit in the park and get some fresh air.

The next day, Aharonchik went to the park and saw a tall, thin man sitting on a bench. He estimated that the man was in his late-30s; he had high cheekbones and was balding, with black hair remaining only on the sides of his head. The description matched Jenka.

He sat down beside him and whispered, "I am Aharonchik," and the man didn't move a muscle. "I put a letter in your mailbox."

The man turned to him, "Who sent you?"

"Professor Yohanan Ratner," whispered the young man. "Shall we go talk in the nearby café?" Jenka obediently stood up, walking alongside him as they crossed the park. When they got to the café, they scanned the area to make sure they weren't being followed and quickly ducked inside.

"What would you like to drink?" Aharonchik asked.

"I don't want anything," Jenka replied, his forehead wrinkling. "I have a few questions I want you to answer for me briefly and concisely. Then I'll take off."

"What do you want to know?"

"Information about you."

"I am a sapper. My job is to travel around the country, investigate requirements, and report back to the leadership."

"What do they know how to do?"

"Simple things, like detonators and time pencils."

"What about Military Industries?"

"They copy and manufacture rifles, pistols, and the Sten submachine gun, including ammunition."

"Where am I to fit in this whole operation?"

"Ben-Gurion has decided to set up a science department captained by Professor Ratner. The professor recommended you as head of the weapons development. Your direct commander will be Shlomo Gur, and I have been assigned to be your operative, to obtain materials and contact the laboratories and workshops."

"Shlomo Gur?" Jenka sighed with relief. He'd been worried he would have to work with some *politruk*. "We studied together at the Technion. Shlomo is a hard-working, honest guy and an excellent coordinator. He established fifty-two Tower and Stockade settlements in one day, establishing facts on the ground."

"Ben-Gurion asked Shlomo how many people were in the science department, and he answered 'one and a half. He meant you and me. You're the one, and I'm the half," Aharonchik chuckled.

"What about laboratories?"

"There are small workshops scattered around, especially in Tel Aviv. They know how to produce simple, imprecise things."

Jenka looked worried, "It will be difficult to develop complex designs without good workshops."

"Everyone is eager to learn."

"I understand," he said, comprehending the magnitude of their expectations and of the responsibility he would hold.

"The department will be established in Tel Aviv, and I've been sent to bring you there today." He wasn't sure how Jenka would react.

"I need to go home to collect my things and speak to my wife."

An hour later, they were already on the road to Tel Aviv. Aharonchik spoke, and Jenka listened, his eyes opening and closing. Aharonchik couldn't tell if he was awake or asleep.

*

The car stopped near an apartment building in central Tel Aviv. They climbed to Shlomo Gur's apartment on the second floor. Aharonchik knocked on the door five times, waited for five counts, and knocked five more times. Shlomo opened the door, checked that no one else was in the corridor, ushered them inside hastily, closed the door, and bolted it. He hugged Jenka warmly. "I remember you from the Technion! Your motorcycle trips to India and Africa and how all the girls fawned over you."

"I'm not sure the girls will be as keen on me nowadays." Jenka rubbed the bare patch at the top of his head.

"Everyone was worried about you. We were afraid of what the English may have done." he turned to his wife Rachel and said, "This is the friend I told you about." Shlomo took Gali, his three-year-old daughter, into his arms and introduced her to his friend.

Aharonchik said his goodbyes, and Jenka and Shlomo sat down at the kitchen table.

"Are you hungry?" Rachel asked Jenka.

"Yes," he nodded his head and folded his arms on the table as if waiting for food.

"What would you like to eat?"

"My wife makes me oatmeal every evening."

"I thought porridge was only for babies," Rachel laughed.

"My late grandmother would make me oatmeal every evening, as does my wife, Shifra."

"I have some semolina porridge left over that I used to make for Gali when she was a baby," Rachel said as she searched the pantry.

"Maybe something else?" Jenka suggested. Eating old baby porridge didn't appeal to him.

"I can make you an omelet."

"An omelet would be nice."

Rachel took two eggs out of the ice box, placed an aluminum

pan on the kerosene Primus stove, made an omelet, chopped up a tomato and a cucumber, and sliced two pieces of black bread, spreading one with white cheese and the other with jam. When he finished eating, he requested a strong, hot cup of tea. Then Rachel went to put the girl to bed.

Finally, it was quiet, and Shlomo and Jenka closed the kitchen door.

"The British are about to leave," Shlomo said. "They will take all their weapons with them. They know the Arabs plan to slaughter us as soon as they leave. The British expect us to beg them to stay and protect us. We can only trust our own."

"What is the state of weapons in the Jewish settlement?" Jenka rested his elbow on the table, placed his chin on it, and leaned forward with his whole body, listening intently.

"The Haganah have pistols, rifles, several Sten submachine guns, and some explosives in their storehouses. There are no land mines and no anti-tank weapons." Shlomo continued, "Ben-Gurion has assigned you to develop weapons."

"What do we need most urgently?"

"Mines," Shlomo was quick to answer as if he had reached this conclusion after debating the subject at length. "We need to surround the kibbutzim with landmines so that the Arabs won't be able to infiltrate them."

"I only know naval mines," he said, interlacing his fingers and rubbing his thumbs together rapidly, "but if anyone can describe what land mines look like, I can develop them."

"I know a fellow named Mordechai Sharoni from Kibbutz Kinneret. He served as a sapper in the Jewish Brigade during the Second World War."

And with that, the matter was settled. Shlomo stood up and said, "I'm going to sleep," he turned off the light walked out of the kitchen.

Jenka followed him in the dark waiting for orders. But when

Shlomo opened the door to his bedroom, Jenka rushed toward him and asked, “What about me?”

“Oh, I forgot to tell you that you’ll be staying in Gali’s room. We’ve set up another bed in there for you.”

“You want me to sleep in a room with Gali?”

“We only have two rooms. Would you rather sleep in my room with Rachel and me? We can’t put a bed in the kitchen. Only Gali’s room is left.” He opened the door to the toddler’s room. Jenka saw the bed they had made up for him.

“I need a desk to work on,” he whispered to Shlomo so as not to wake the girl.

Shlomo whispered back to him, “Start on Gali’s little wood table.”

“Do you mean the tiny table covered in pictures of teddy bears eating honey out of little round bowls?” Jenka quickly suggested an alternative. “Maybe I can work on the kitchen table?”

“No, no.” Shlomo looked apprehensive at the very thought. “Do you want Rachel to throw us both out of the apartment?”

Shlomo closed the door to Gali’s room and walked Jenka down the hall. “Listen, Jenka. We were all waiting for you to reach Palestine in one piece. We were very concerned. Tomorrow I’ll rent out a floor in an apartment in central Tel Aviv where you can work with your team.”

Jenka entered the girl’s room quietly. He had a nightshirt and nightcap in his bag but decided not to bother. Wearing a full suit of clothes, he lay down on the small bed with his long legs hanging in the air and fell asleep. He got up early in the morning, sat on the pink wooden stool, folded his legs like an Indian fakir, took some of Gali’s blank drawing papers, placed them on the teddy bear picture, and got to work.

*

Shlomo hastened to sign a lease on a rental located on the fourth floor of an old building on Frug Street. The street was known as an artist's hub and was close to the Habima Theater, which corresponded perfectly with Jenka's cover story – they'd decided he would pretend to be a painter to explain why he was living in Tel Aviv and working from a studio. Aharonchik borrowed a pickup truck and, with the help of his assistants, David Fruman and David Barak, loaded the disassembled drawing tables on it and then carried them to the fourth floor on their backs. They furnished the kitchen with basic utensils and brought a coffee table and some chairs. A staircase led from the apartment to the roof, where there was a small bedroom with a bed and a wardrobe.

Shlomo and Jenka left for the building under cover of darkness. Using a secret code, Shlomo knocked on the door, Aharonchik opened it, and four smiling people welcomed them.

"This will be your studio," said Shlomo, pointing to the drawing tables, proud of how fast they'd arranged everything, "and this is Mordechai Sharoni, a former brigade man, and these are the two Davids," he said, patting their shoulders fondly.

They all sat down around the small table, awaiting Shlomo's instructions.

"Jenka will design weapons, and you will assist him with anything he needs. He worked as a lieutenant colonel in the British Admiralty's weapons development unit. The British are looking for him, and they must not find out he is here."

"We've taken the necessary precautions," Aharonchik reassured them. "We've stationed an undercover guard from the Haganah near the entrance of the building. If he sees a British investigator, he needs only to pull a wire that will ring a bell in the studio. It will take the British time to walk up to the fourth floor. When they reach us, we'll have turned all the drawing boards to look like painting easels.

I also suggest that you start studying painting." They sat listening earnestly and nodded in agreement.

"The course of action will be as follows: I will receive demands for weapons, and I will pass them on to Jenka."

Shlomo looked at him, and Jenka quickly confirmed, "Whatever Shlomo asks, I will do. I will receive instructions from him alone and not from anyone else."

Shlomo was pleased that the message was clear and proceeded to explain, "There will be no organized paperwork detailing our orders. Instead, we'll receive notes with orders here and there. Generally, we have to wait for the Haganah's approval, but we'll also get direct inquiries from the field in order to bypass unnecessary bureaucracy. We will also receive ridiculous demands that we won't be able to fulfil. We'll decide what to do and what not to, what's possible and what's not. I will accept full accountability. I know there will be people in the chain of command who will resent me."

Jenka smiled. He liked Shlomo's matter-of-fact tone. He remembered British bureaucracy. You had to wait to get permission before starting work on any project, and he'd been reprimanded many times for beginning assignments before getting the green light.

"Together with David Furman and David Barak, I will obtain all the materials and equipment that Jenka needs," Aharonchik declared.

"You should also spread the projects over different workshops and laboratories. Experiments will be carried out on the beach in Herzliya, Bat Yam, or elsewhere." And with that, Shlomo concluded the meeting. It was late. Everyone stood up, ready to head home.

"Sharoni, stay behind with me, and we'll work into the night," Jenka said.

The others left the studio, covertly slipping out of the house, one by one, engulfed in the darkness.

Jenka and Sharoni sat down at a drawing board, “In England, I worked on naval mines. I need you to describe to me what a landmine looks like so I can sketch a composite drawing of one.”

Sharoni’s face broke into an impish smile. “You want me to describe a landmine the way that people describe criminals to the police?”

He began to describe the mine as Jenka drew, changing the sketch according to his instructions. “No, wait. Yes, maybe, I don’t remember exactly.” Suddenly, Sharoni held his hands to his head and shouted, “I can’t believe I forgot! I have some mines at the kibbutz that I took home as souvenirs after the Second World War.” Jenka chucked all the composite drawings in the trash and called Shlomo. They decided to go to Kibbutz Kinneret in the morning, and Sharoni left, hoping to catch a few hours of sleep.

*

In the morning, Shlomo arrived at the studio with Sharoni. Jenka was already waiting outside, always punctual and on schedule. “You’ll sit behind me,” Shlomo said and opened the back door.

“What about my long legs?”

“I’ll move the front seat forward so you can straighten them.” He saw the dissatisfaction on Jenka’s face and went on, “If the British police stop us, they’ll turn first to whoever’s sitting in the front, and it would be preferable if they didn’t notice you. At the very worst, we’ll be arrested. But you will be hanged.”

Jenka got into the car, cursing under his breath. Shlomo then passed each of them a gun. “Arab gangs roam the back roads. We don’t want to become another newspaper story about more Jews murdered on the highways.”

They took the main road to the valley. The road was paved with one lane for both directions for slow-moving buses and trucks carrying goods. There weren't many private cars. Every time they had to bypass another car, Aharonchik honked his horn, scared of the cars coming toward them. Jenka drank in the view thirstily, remembering the motorcycle trips he'd taken around the country as a young student at the Technion. He was surprised by the number of new settlements being built and by the many cultivated fields. In the afternoon, they began their descent down the winding road to the Jordan Valley, over 200 yards below sea level. There they headed towards the kibbutz, which sat on the lake's southwestern shore. As they glimpsed the roofs of the kibbutz in the distance, the heat became so terrible that it felt like they were baking in an oven.

"How can people live in a place like this?" Aharonchik wondered aloud, exhausted.

"It's hard, but you learn to live with it," Shlomo answered while they all absorbed the sheer beauty of the place. "The situation here is good compared to other settlements in the Jordan Valley. There's a lot of water here, and the trees grow fast, providing us shade. It's close to the Sea of Galilee, and you can jump in the water to refresh yourself."

They drove through the kibbutz gate and found a shady place to park the car before hurrying to Sharoni's apartment. For a moment, Sharoni feared he had given the mines to some friend whose name he couldn't remember. But lo and behold, the mines lay in the closet, carefully wrapped in a clean cloth, waiting for them. The four men fell onto the couch, drained from the heat.

"They're serving lunch in the dining hall right now," Sharoni said and urged them to get up.

They followed him obediently, dragging their feet on the burning hot ground. When they got to the dining room, they washed their faces in cold water and saw the huge ceiling fans spinning around lazily, making a racket but not cooling the hall one bit. They sat down at a long table, and various kibbutz members approached

Sharoni, asked how he was, and welcomed the visitors kindly. It wasn't every day that strangers came to the kibbutz. They did not ask questions. They knew that Sharoni was involved in security.

The fish from the Sea of Galilee were delicious, and Sharoni ate with gusto. The other two men, however, had lost their appetite due to the heat. Equipped with freshly filled bottles of water, they quickly followed Sharoni back to his apartment, loaded the landmines into the car, drove out of the *kibbutz*, and fled the valley, opening the windows to let in the breeze. On the way, the British police stopped them and asked to see the identification of those sitting in the front.

Jenka sat in a back seat, quiet and huddled over. Shlomo's words resonated in his mind: if his friends were caught, they would be sent to jail, but if he were caught, he would be condemned to swing in the noose. They passed the ID check without a hitch, but Shlomo decided they shouldn't risk taking the mines all the way to Tel Aviv. He had friends at Kibbutz Dalia. They went to the kibbutz and explained to his friends that they needed a private room to take apart a confidential weapon. They brought over a wheelbarrow, loaded the mines into it, and covered them with tree branches. Sitting in the private room, Jenka slowly dismantled the mines, sketching each part according to the order in which he'd disassembled it and numbering each piece so that he would know how to put them together in Tel Aviv. Meanwhile, darkness fell, and the curfew started, so they had to sleep at the kibbutz. Early the next morning, they left for the studio on Frug Street in Tel Aviv. The rest of the team waited for them with large straw baskets, put the disassembled mines inside, and carried them up to the fourth floor.

Jenka worked at a rapid pace. He didn't care how he was dressed or what he ate. He continued to work even after everyone went home at night. His enthusiastic spirit infected everyone around him. He designed a mechanical mine made of wood, sketched the whole composition, and technicians designed the different parts. Aharonchik and the two Davids gave each workshop a separate piece of the drawing so no one would know exactly what they were working on. When the new parts arrived at the studio, Jenka placed them neatly on the table, and everyone stood around him like young medical residents learning through observation of a chief surgeon's work. He looked at the sketch he'd made with the instructions on how to assemble the mine and began to attach each part. "*Yob tvoyu mat*," Jenka swore in Russian; the pieces would not fit together.

With passion and determination, Jenka educated and trained his assistants on how to supervise the various laboratories and workshops so that the results would be accurate. He explained to them about fits and tolerances and permissible deviations from the nominal degree, crucial calculations that workshop technicians did not know anything about. When the parts arrived from the workshops the second time, everyone observed as Jenka put them together. Then, he directed them individually to disassemble and reassemble each model. This method of education proved itself.

Cases in which they required engraving machines that weren't available in the country arose, but the engravers showed great improvisational ability and successfully replaced the missing lathes with good, old-fashioned manual workmanship. Their great willingness to learn, dedication to work, the symbolic prices they asked for, and the spirit of volunteering they displayed all impressed Jenka immensely.

When the wooden model mines were ready, they experimented at the beach in Herzliya and invited the Haganah's head armorer. The models exploded. They made a considerable racket. They raised a cloud of dust. The armorer was impressed, and they were ordered to start the immediate production of 100,000 landmines. The team and the workshops rallied to the task.

A few days later, Shlomo arrived at the studio, his face downcast.

"The Haganah has ordered us to stop production. The kibbutzim aren't prepared to plant landmines that operate with an automatic mechanism in their fields. They tend the fields and fear they may step on the mines themselves."

Jenka looked at Shlomo gravely, "*Kibinimat.* I hate when requirement specifications are changed." He paused, filling his lungs with the air, debating. He nodded his head and said, "Their claim is warranted. What now?"

"The kibbutzim have heard that there are electric mines that can be neutralized by turning off their electricity while they work in the fields. They can turn the mines back on when they finish the work by reconnecting them to the electricity." The team again rallied to design and produce what was needed.

The number of orders reaching the studio continued to grow, and students, alumni, and university faculty members came to assist them. Among the prominent men to join the team were Stef Wertheimer, a long-standing Haganah member, Chaim Singer-Ron, a famous Palmach sapper, and Chaim Moro, the mechanical engineer. Jenka sketched the models at the offices of Ze'ev Rechter's architecture firm, but he needed model builders, so Rechter sent his son Yaakov and his son-in-law Moshe Zarhy. The whole team worked around the clock, getting in a few hours of sleep here and there.

*

Three months after moving to Tel Aviv, Jenka went to visit his family. On his way there, he got caught in an unforeseen curfew and was chased by British soldiers. He managed to reach the building on Arlozorov Street in Haifa and hid on the ground floor. The soldiers entered the building, searched each apartment, and left. When it got dark, he climbed to the roof, to the laundry room where Shifra and the children lived. He saw her taking laundry off the line and folding it into a large basket. He approached her quietly and hugged her from behind. She didn't panic. Recognizing his hug, she turned around with a happy smile lighting up her face.

"You aren't angry at me for not letting you know of my arrival in advance?"

"I'm here. There's no need to notify me in advance," Shifra laughed.

"My friends' wives demand to be informed in advance about when they plan to come home."

"I have no suitors."

She opened the door to the small room, and he saw Ruth and Danny sleeping. He approached them, bent down, saw the calm expressions on their faces, and quietly walked away so as not to wake them. They left the room. He appreciated that she was raising the children alone and didn't complain that he'd been away from home for so long.

"What's new?" Jenka asked matter-of-factly.

"I've visited our lot in Carmelia several times. It's hard to get there taking public transportation, and when it gets dark, the jackals leave their dens, come to the lot, and howl. It's scary to walk around there alone and I'm scared I'll step on a snake."

"I don't want to hear any more complaints," he said decisively. "I have greater concerns on my mind."

But she did not let up. "There's no grocery store nearby."

"The realtor said that a milkman comes to Carmelia every two days with milk, cheese, and eggs. The iceman also comes with ice for the ice box. You'll have to walk to the grocery store once a week. How far is it? A mile?"

"The contractor wants more money."

"Alright."

"What? No. You have to pay him according to his progress. You also have to get collateral and have a lawyer supervise." She saw that the conversation was tiring him, but she continued. "I worked at a bank. That's what they do at the bank. They get collateral. You have to be more involved."

"What are you talking about? A war is about to break out, and if we're not prepared, the Arabs will slaughter us all. They won't even keep us alive to clean their toilets."

"Fine. Give the contractor all the money. It's your money," Shifra said, accepting his verdict.

Before leaving for Tel Aviv, he took some of the photographs from his trips to India and Egypt. He planned to paint the photographs. If the British came to the studio, he needed to have some artwork to show.

Chapter 13: Forgotten in the Wadi

On November 30, 1947, the United Nations held a vote on the division of Mandatory Palestine into two states: a Jewish state, and an Arab state. The vote was broadcast live on the radio. Charts were prepared to mark which countries were in favor of the partition, which countries opposed it, and which abstained. Shouts of enthusiasm or disdain followed each country's vote. They reached an outcome with a majority of thirty-three nations in favor of dividing the land into a Jewish state and an Arab state. Thirteen countries voted against the division, including Lebanon, Egypt, Syria, Iraq, and Saudi Arabia, as well as most of the Islamic nations, including Iran, Afghanistan, India, and Turkey. Ten countries abstained, including Britain, the Republic of China, Argentina, and Yugoslavia. The great build-up of tension in the Jewish community was released into an outburst of abundant joy. People ran outside and filled the streets, hugging, praying, and dancing. And not only in the Jewish settlement in the land of Israel but also in Jewish communities across the Diaspora. In Rome, they gathered for a prayer of gratitude before the Victory Gate built by Titus after he defeated the Jewish people approximately two thousand years earlier.

The next day, the Arabs of Palestine launched an attack on the Jewish community. They were joined by volunteers from the Arab League and the Muslim Brotherhood. The attacks were predominantly focused on routes leading to isolated Jewish settlements and on settlements where Jews and Arabs lived together. The Jewish forces engaged chiefly in defending their settlements. They knew it was just a warm-up for the colossal attack that the Arab countries would launch in May when the British left the country.

*

On Ben-Gurion's desk was a letter from a Jewish scientist who claimed to have invented a weapon called the "Compart" during World War II. He said the weapon hadn't been tested in the field because the war had ended first, but he'd still received an honorable award for the innovation. When he arrived in Palestine, he contacted Professor Aharon Katchalsky from the University of Jerusalem, who, in turn, contacted Shlomo. They both checked and concluded that it was an idea that would work only in laboratory conditions and could not be transferred to an industrial stage. Ben-Gurion heard about it through the grapevine and turned to Military Industries to look into the matter, but they too rejected the idea. Ben-Gurion didn't give up and summoned Shlomo, who tried to evade him and come up with excuses.

"Running experiments on something like this will cost a lot of money, and it will take time until we can allocate the funds. It will be impossible to do it in time."

"The idea is excellent, and I demand that you carry it out." Ben-Gurion banged his fist on the desk.

Two days later, Shlomo received a phone call from Ben-Gurion's treasurer telling him to go to Bank Hapoalim, where the money needed to plan and produce the Compart awaited.

The science unit increased its staff, brought on chemists, and added more drawing tables. They even took the risk and imported supplies from Europe despite the British confiscating suspicious products left and right. There were endless problems, but Ben-Gurion had insisted.

In one of Shlomo's nightly meetings with the commander of the Haganah, he was told about a recent gathering of the People's Council, in which the impending war and the fear that the Jewish settlement would have to fight against the entire Arab world had been discussed. There was a general feeling that disaster was approaching. The atmosphere had taken a gloomy turn when Ben-Gurion declared that there was nothing to worry about because they had a secret weapon.

"Tell me, Shlomo, are you producing the secret weapon?" whispered the commander.

"We have nothing."

A few days later, Ben-Gurion's secretary, who had also been at the gathering in question, met with Shlomo and asked, "Do you know what the secret weapon is?"

"I don't know anything."

"Shlomo, you will jeopardize our friendship if you don't tell me what you know."

"I don't know anything."

A few days later, they met again, and Shlomo asked his friend, "What did Ben-Gurion say exactly?"

"We have a secret weapon. There is nothing to fear. The scientific unit is developing it."

Shlomo suddenly felt sick.

"Ben-Gurion must mean the Compart." Shlomo decided that Ben-Gurion must be notified of their progress, "It's extremely dangerous for the 'Haganah' to be under a false illusion of safety."

He resolved to invite Ben-Gurion to the workshop where the experiments were being conducted. He arrived discreetly, early in the morning, and before entering the workshop, Shlomo told

Ben-Gurion that the experiments were failing. Ben-Gurion's look hardened, and he did not answer. Later, he heard details from Jenka, the chemists, and the engravers, who all told him the weapon was nothing more than a fantasy. He left the workshop with his face downcast.

Shlomo accompanied Ben-Gurion to his car and stated, "There are times when the things we want are impossible to achieve. It is important not to develop false illusions."

Ben-Gurion sat in the car and looked at Shlomo. "I am very disappointed in you."

*

The Haganah received alarming reports that the Arab Legion was stationed and armed with tanks in the Arab village of Beit Nabala near Ramla. The Haganah didn't have anti-tank weapons. Ben-Gurion set an urgent meeting with Yaakov Dori, the commander of the Haganah; the head of weaponry; Chaim Slavin, the director of Military Industries; and Shlomo and Jenka from the Science Unit.

"What can we do to stop the tanks?" asked Ben-Gurion, deeply troubled.

Jenka didn't hesitate for a second and said, "Only the PIAT can help. It's an anti-tank weapon that the British used successfully during World War II."

Slavin quickly contradicted Jenka, "All the stories about the British supposedly using the PIAT successfully in Africa are completely made up."

Jenka replied, "You are wrong. During World War II, the British produced thousands of PIATs and transferred many to the Soviets and the Polish and French resistance forces."

Their disagreement would have continued if Shlomo hadn't interrupted them. "And what will happen when the tanks reach Tel Aviv?"

They fell silent.

"We would have to surrender," some of the men in the room whispered. "A suicide mission. We'll have no choice but to take the women and children and go toward the sea."

Shlomo and Jenka burst out in a string of curses.

"I refuse to sit here and listen to such vulgarisms," shouted the head of weaponry and left the room. Ben-Gurion pursued him to the stairwell and called to him to come back, but he couldn't catch up with him.

"I will try to create a shell similar to that of the PIAT, something that can penetrate 50 mm steel," Jenka promised Ben-Gurion.

Slavin narrowed his eyes.

"I expect a pilot demonstration in 30 days," Ben-Gurion ruled.

*

Jenka hadn't developed shaped charges in England. He knew the subject from studying and learned from documents he'd brought with him. But the PIAT was a land weapon, and he'd only studied and read about naval-shaped charges. His time was short, and he wanted to see how the PIAT's launcher was designed. Shlomo couldn't find a launcher in the Haganah warehouses, so he turned to Alik Suchshaber, director of the Hebrew University's laboratory, for help. A few days later, Suchshaber provided Jenka with a launcher he'd obtained by bribing an English officer with £70, an amount three times his monthly salary. In order to continue the development of the PIAT, Jenka needed 5 kilos of a type of explosive called TEN. The only place that could provide such a thing was Military Industries.

Still, just the thought of Jenka made Slavin,rage like a bull before the fluttering red flag of a matador. The negotiations between Jenka's people and Slavin's people regarding the delivery of the TEN reached a dead end. So, Shlomo asked for a meeting with Ben-Gurion.

The two parties came to the meeting, each accompanied by their assistants and supporters, uttering a quick "hello," then sat on either side of the long table. When Ben-Gurion entered, everyone straightened, gearing up for the opening shot.

"What is there to say? I'm listening," Ben-Gurion said. He hated quarreling between the Jews and knew of the enmity between Slavin and Jenka. Aside from often referring to Jenka as the "Illusion Salesman from England," Slavin was also angry about the Science Unit's industrial military production, which bypassed Military Industries.

Slavin fired the opening shot. "I did not agree to give the little TEN that I have, because there is no chance in the world that anyone could design a PIAT shell without the original sketches." Slavin turned to look at Shlomo. "And I am no longer willing to put up with your arm-twisting and pressure to deliver the goods."

"If Jenka insists on obtaining TEN, let someone else give it to him," the head of weaponry chimed in.

The tension persisted. Ben-Gurion didn't say a word but frowned at Slavin.

"If I have to give over the TEN, I'm leaving the meeting." Slavin exited the room in a huff. Shlomo ran after him, dragged him back to the room, and Slavin agreed to give them three kilos of TEN.

The thirty days that Ben-Gurion allocated to prepare the pilot had passed. It was decided that the test would be held in the wadi near Kibbutz Dalia before a distinguished entourage that included Ben-Gurion, the Haganah leadership, and Chaim Slavin. In order to demonstrate the PIAT shell's ability to penetrate steel, the scientific unit prepared two steel plates, each 25 millimeters thick, and attached them to each other, thus forming a 50-millimeter steel plate. The spectators stood waiting in anticipation. An explosion sounded, and they watched as the shell penetrated both plates. The people encircling Jenka exclaimed joyfully and embraced one another while Slavin and his group yelled in dismay.

"Look what this charlatan did!" shouted Slavin, shoving Jenka. "Do you all believe that it truly penetrated? Can't you see that the fraud from England made the hole in advance? It doesn't look like a shell perforation at all."

Some others approached the hole, scrutinizing it like doctors examining a tumor with a magnifying glass.

"It's impossible," Slavin's men whispered to themselves. They tapped the plates, listening to the metal's sound, suspicious that the boards were not steel. Soon an argument broke out between the two groups.

Jenka stood on the sidelines throughout, watching the Jewish warring and not saying a word. The corners of his mouth turned up slightly, smiling at the absurd sight, but his eyes revealed his concern over what the quarreling would cause. It was starting to get dark.

"The curfew is about to begin. We need to get out of here quickly," said Shlomo, and on that matter, everyone was in agreement. At once, all the arguing ceased; everyone collected their various personal belongings, hurried to their vehicles, and fled. Meanwhile, Jenka approached the steel plates and put his palm over the hole, evidence of a successful development. When he turned back around, he realized that everyone had driven off. They'd forgotten him behind in the wadi. Then, all by himself, he dragged each 12-kilo plate and hid them in the field, covering them with stones.

When he finished, Jenka started walking toward Kibbutz Ein Hashofet. He couldn't see the lights of the settlement, only the light of the stars in the sky. He weaved his way through the wild and tangled vegetation, the thorny bushes and rocks, with dozens of green eyes of howling jackals tracking him. He held a stone in each hand in case the jackals tried to attack him. After hours of walking, he arrived at the kibbutz and called Professor Yohanan Ratner. The following morning, an automobile arrived at the kibbutz, and Jenka led it to where he'd concealed the steel plates. They loaded them onto the vehicle and drove to the studio in Tel Aviv. Jenka continued to refine the shell until it could penetrate 200-millimeter-thick steel, and the Haganah ordered 1,000 PIAT launchers and 100,000 PIAT shells.

They celebrated at the studio. Jenka was pleased but showed restraint. They sat at the small table on which sat modest refreshments of drinks and cookies. Soon came the time for telling stories. Jenka told them about his stay in the Admiralty and about his motorcycle trips through Africa and India. He felt comfortable, and they drank in his stories thirstily, feeling team pride about doing important work for the impending country's security and about working with a unique human being. When the team left, he locked himself in his room and wrote a poem. He didn't understand where these spontaneous verses were born from, medleys of ten to sixteen stanzas written in rhymes. He hid them in a large envelope that read, "Personal, Do Not Open." Aharonchik and Shlomo had once discovered him in his room writing poems. He had made them swear to keep it a secret.

The science unit moved to Givat Rambam in Givatayim and established the Hill camp. There were Arab snipers camped about 900 yards away, and the booming of shots could be heard from the hill. There were remnants of a farm at Camp Hill, built by Germans who were ousted by the British during World War II. The unit prepared the site, and the architect Yaakov Rechter designed the camp. A small truck arrived under the cover of darkness with the drawing tables from the studio. Likewise, a large truck delivered wood to build cabins, tents, and furniture. Avraham Berman, formerly commander of the Jerusalem branch of the Haganah, was appointed camp commander. He demanded that the Haganah pitch a fence around the camp. They denied his request on the grounds that there were more urgent priorities. It was far more crucial to build fences in the individual settlements in the Negev than in Givatayim.

At Camp Hill, the work went on day and night, and they got few hours of sleep in between. The Haganah needed them to develop a five-inch mortar with a range of up to three miles. Their endeavors to find a suitable pipe for the barrel, one that would withstand the pressure of the blast, were unsuccessful. Having no other choice, they decided to use a six-inch diameter pipe, which weighed more than the shell, causing the mortar's range to be limited to two miles. The test was scheduled for Friday the 13th, which, as far as superstitions go, is the worst combination of all. Fridays and the 13th of any month are both prone to calamities, and Jenka considered their combination to be the most ominous by a long shot. Despite Jenka's warnings, the group set out on the trial run in four small 4X4 trucks loaded with mortars, and he joined reluctantly, prophesying unfortunate events.

The group reached the beach in Bat Yam early that morning and got settled in. They fired the first mortar, and it worked fine.

"It's Friday the 13th, and everything is working perfectly," Jenka's group members gloated.

"You're not finished yet," Jenka responded, watching them.

They tested the second mortar, and the experiment was successful too.

"It's Friday the 13th, and everything works fine," the group members teased him.

"You're not done yet." He muttered a string of curses hoping to soften the impending disaster.

They tested the third mortar, and the experiment was successful yet again.

"You're not finished yet, and the day isn't over." He knocked on wood three times, just as he did when a black cat crossed his path.

They checked the fourth mortar, and this time, like all the rest, the experiment was successful. The group burst into cheers.

"Wait, wait. You aren't done yet." Jenka looked around anxiously, unsure where the disaster would strike. Nevertheless, he had this lingering feeling that he should wait for a disaster, so he did.

Around six that evening, they loaded the mortars on the trucks, revved their engines, and alas, the first truck sank into the sand.

"It's Friday the 13th," Jenka stated.

The second truck also got stuck.

"It's Friday the 13th, too." Downcast, he shook his head in concern, uncertain how the matter would be resolved.

The third and fourth trucks also got stuck. The 4X4s stood in a train one after the other, all sunk in the sand and unable to move. The group members grabbed shovels and began digging, but whenever they started the engines, the trucks' wheels dug in deeper. Jenka stood up straight as if facing the curse head-on. They all approached him and apologized for their mockery. After eight hours of work, the trucks began to drive. From that day, some of them started believing that Friday the 13th and black cats caused bad luck.

*

Jenka hadn't been home to visit his family in weeks. Shifra cared for the children alone and supervised the house's construction. Construction ceased, the workers enlisted in the Haganah, and the contractor disappeared with the money. She had an emergency phone number she could reach Jenka on; she'd never used it, but she had to speak to him this time.

Jenka was called to the phone.

"Who died?" Jenka asked.

"No one died."

"Then why did you call?"

"The contractor ran off with the money. The suppliers are demanding their pay and have asked the court to issue a bankruptcy order for the sale of the house."

Shlomo knew it was Shifra on the phone and noted the concern on Jenka's face.

"Is there anything I can do to help?" Shlomo asked and suggested to Jenka, "Tell Shifra to move into the house with the children and live there. To establish facts on the ground, like with the Tower and Stockade settlements."

Jenka's face lit up.

"Shifra, I spoke to Shlomo. Move into what exists of the house with the children. Establish facts on the ground. They wouldn't dare throw a woman and her two children out of their home because of debt when her husband is away serving in the army."

"There are foundations, no windows, no doors, no flooring, no electricity, and no water."

"When they established the 'Tower and Stockade' settlements within one night, the conditions were no better."

Shifra was silent.

"Shifra. You can do it. You were the only woman in the course who learned to fly a glider."

"I see that there's no other way," Shifra said, her voice quiet.

"Move tomorrow, even today, if you can. If city inspectors come, go out to the yard with the children and drive them away."

Shlomo grabbed the phone. "Shlomo here. Shout at them, yell, 'You should be ashamed of yourselves! My husband is risking his life for this country. I have nothing to feed the children. Shame on you, shame on you, don't you dare come back here!' Be dramatic, make a show of it." Jenka could not believe his friend's advice; he took the phone and said, "I'm sorry, I can't help you more. I love you."

When she heard that he loved her, Shifra began to cry. How had the sky not opened up? How were no angels flying around with trumpets, announcing that Jenka had told her he loved her?

"Don't delay the move, and do not tell a soul."

She packed their clothes in suitcases that very day, put the kitchenware in a cardboard box, and wrapped the rest of their belongings in a large sheet. The following morning, she called a taxi, loaded their effects into the trunk, and rode with the two children to Carmelia, to the concrete skeleton of the house. She covered the windows with plastic, improvised a door to close one room, and slept there with the children. When darkness fell, she lit the kerosene lamp and cooked dinner on the burner. Outside was a tap attached to a long flexible hose, which she used for drinking, cooking, and bathing.

With Danny sitting in his stroller, Shifra would walk a mile to the convenience store to do some shopping. She would pack the stroller full until only the toddler's head could be seen popping out between the groceries. The ice cart stopped coming, so she dragged ice blocks home, too. Without tiling on the floors, Danny was left to crawl around the sandy foundation of the house. Shifra had to keep an eye on him at all times for fear that he would find stones or shells in the sand and put them in his mouth. From a polite English lass, Ruth turned into a creature of the wild outdoors, vanishing from the house, running around the hills and wadis, climbing trees, and daydreaming that she was the princess of a savage African tribe. Without a husband by her side or a supportive family to lean on and alone in an isolated neighborhood surrounded by untamed nature, Shifra was left to face these hardships by herself. She had no one to turn to for help.

When Ruth turned six years old, Shifra enrolled her in the Reali school. Shifra was willing to take food from her own mouth to pay the pricey tuition of the private school, which was known for its high standard of education compared to Haifa's public schools. Jenka was an alumnus of the school, and Shifra wished to give her daughter the education she hadn't received from her own parents. Within the first few days, it became clear that Ruth lacked the preparation other children cultivated in kindergarten. She had no listening skills, her Hebrew was inadequate, she didn't understand what the teacher was explaining, she wouldn't do her homework, and when she got home, she would throw off the light blue dress with the school's crest, run out to the fields, and disappear. On Parents' Day, Ruth got a report card with three failing grades. Shifra feared her daughter would be held back a year.

*

On May 14, 1948, the last day of the British Mandate, Ben-Gurion declared the establishment of the State of Israel. The next day, active armies from seven Arab countries raided the settlement. The Jewish fighters had weapons developed and manufactured in Israel by a science unit, rifles from the Czech Republic – the only country willing to sell weapons to Jews – and weapons manufactured in Israel by IMI, which were copies of weapons used in the Second World War.

In October, the newly formed Israeli Defense Forces carried out Operation Yoav, aiming to break through to the Negev, which was detached from the rest of the country, and to push out the Egyptian army, whose forces had weakened. In November, Operation Hiram began, during which the IDF seized control of the Upper Galilee's center and parts of the Lower Galilee. In December, Operation Horev was launched in the Negev and eastern Sinai against the Egyptian Expeditionary Force. With the exception of the Gaza Strip, the IDF managed to oust the Egyptian army from the entire

State of Israel. During Operation Ovda, the last operation of the War of Independence, the IDF conquered the southern Negev and the Jordan River Valley, including the city of Eilat at the southernmost point on the Red Sea, Kibbutz Ein Gedi on the Sea of Galilee, and the ancient Israel fortress of Masada. During the Armistice Agreements, the UN established an agency to supervise and ensure that the ceasefire agreements were being kept.

The War of Independence ended. Out of the Jewish population comprised of about 650,000 people, six thousand men and women fell in combat. About 700,000 refugees from Jewish communities in Islamic countries arrived in the young nation. And just outside the borders of the newly declared state, refugee camps were established, full of Arabs waiting to return and take revenge.

Chapter 14: The Fairy Tale Apple

At the foot of Mount Carmel, at the entrance to Haifa, a huge refugee absorption camp was established for the new Jewish immigrants, most of whom had come from Islamic countries. The refugee tents were hot as a furnace in the summer, and in the winter, the occupants froze from the strong winds blowing up from the sea. The rains turned the campground into one big puddle. Many of them were educated people, merchants who'd been allowed to immigrate only if they left all their possessions behind. Others had escaped in secret. They spoke Arabic, English, and French.

High on the Carmel, near the Reali high school in Beit Biram, another refugee campground was set up. The camp had a fantastic view of the Jezreel Valley, the agricultural fields, and the oil refineries' two cooling towers. Strong winds blew in the winter, threatening to uproot the pegs, as the tent covers fluttered and whipped loudly. Young men and women, the latest refugees from Romania and Hungary, lived in the camp. Some of them spoke Yiddish. They were very thin, looked older than their age, had a strange look in their eyes and numbers tattooed on their arms. Parents warned their children that they had been through horrors at the concentration camps, some of them had lost their minds, and their behavior was impossible to predict.

These were the years of austerity, and each household was allotted a ration of points according to the number of family members and the children's ages. People could buy clothes and essential food and supplies with the points, using coupons. Long queues stretched out of every grocery store. A lucky few received food packages from relatives in the United States. At home, people ate simple foods: omelets, *leben* yogurt, eggplants, cucumbers, and tomatoes. Many of the fruits and vegetables were inedible, infested with worms; only the oranges, grapefruits, and lemons were spared. The cafés that had prospered under the British Mandate, where the ladies who'd immigrated from Germany and Austria before the rise of the Nazis would sit, chatting with friends at five in the afternoon, remained empty. Little "Tnuva" restaurants popped up like mushrooms after the rain where small shops had been. For a fair price, any soul could eat an Israeli meal of a one-egg omelet, a salad, a cup of tea or coffee, and a slice of fresh black bread. Salaries eroded.

The milkman was released from reserve duty and started coming to the Carmelia neighborhood with his donkey-drawn cart again. He would knock on each door with a little pad and pencil in hand to write down the orders, collect the empty, clean glass bottles, rush back to his cart, put a large funnel in each bottle, hoist up a huge iron can, and pour milk into the bottles. Hidden underneath a pile of ice, he had small glass jars of yogurt and cream cheese wrapped in parchment paper, stamped with the green Tnuva Company logo. The milkman would put everything in a large bag and run back, hobbling from the weight of the load, in a rush to deliver the produce, glancing behind him fretfully at the dripping wet cart. The goods had to be sold before the ice cubes melted.

The Ratner family home was the sixth structure built on Carmelia's mountain ridge. Before it, stood a guest house built on the mountain's steep, south-facing slope with a spectacular view from the sea to the ruins of the Crusader fortress, Atlit Castle. A hill with tall pine trees rose past the inn, and vacationers would spend their mornings there, sitting on comfortable chairs, gazing at the view, reading a newspaper or a book, and enjoying the sea breeze. During the austerity years, private citizens couldn't afford their own vacations, so large companies, such as "Egged" the bus company, "Shemen" the oil company, or "Ata" the clothing brand, sent their employees on a recuperative week to eat well and put on some weight. At lunch, there were four courses, a truly gourmet meal: eggplant and tahini salad, chicken or vegetable soup, a main course of chicken thighs or *schnitzel*, or sometimes meat goulash with rice, mashed potatoes, or barley. The dessert was either apple or chocolate cake or strawberry jelly. There was always seltzer water on the table. After taking an afternoon nap, the guests would walk on the road that went around the ridge and watch the beautiful rainbow palate of the sunset. It was possible to use the phone at the Carmelia guest house in an emergency. When the Ministry of Defense installed a telephone at the Ratner family's home, the residents realized that Jenka must be doing important defense work. They understood that they shouldn't keep questioning Shifra about her husband's job.

Jenka would only return to Haifa on Friday afternoons until Saturday, before heading back to Camp Hill on Sunday mornings. Jenka's earnings were modest, most of the money was allocated towards finishing the house, and Shifra decided to rent out a room in their home to the guests of the Carmelia Hotel. The hotel was a fifteen-minute walk away, a pleasant stroll in the morning, muggy in the midday heat, and terrifying after dinner with jackals howling in the dark. The hotel wasn't too keen on the idea, but Shifra didn't give up and lowered the price until they couldn't resist the temptation and began referring guests to her. She bought new sheets and towels, emptied the wardrobe, washed the floor daily, tidied the room, and aired it out. She cleaned the bathroom several times a day. She would greet them wearing a starched white apron with lipstick on her lips. She did her best to endear herself to the guests so they would recommend to the hotel to send her more people. At noon, when the guests went to nap, Shifra would beg Ruth to be quiet, to stop fighting with her little brother, explaining how much they needed the money. But after a few minutes of silence, the fighting would start up again, and the ritual would repeat itself.

In 1949, Shifra gave birth to Michal. Jenka joked that "his wife set him up" and grimaced as if he didn't understand how it had happened. He decided that the children needed a swing, designed a frame of pipes to hang it from, calculated a margin of safety, and brought the structure home on the roof of his car. Then he dug four holes, planted the frame's legs, encircled them with concrete, and painted the pipes a light gray. Several children could climb on the swing set at the same time, hanging on the pipes and swinging. Ruth stopped climbing trees after that.

When the construction of the house was completed, Jenka moved the wooden furniture he had designed for Ilioff's home into the large guest room: a large settee with wide wooden armrests, a wardrobe with doors adorned with geometric patterns made with different shades of wood, a round table with a glass top, and four matching chairs. It was quality furniture that would last for a lifetime and for generations to come. There was also a unique small high table that stood on long legs and was made of an artful combination of different types of wood. Jenka designed a light, narrow, long wooden sideboard for his seashell collection that would fit in the wall nook. The sideboard had a large glass door, and on its shelves, Jenka placed each shell in its designated place, ensuring equal spacing between each row and each shell. Jenka also ordered a special cabinet with iron siding that could withstand fire and protect its contents. On the weekend, he picked it up from the factory, tied it to the roof of his station wagon, drove home, took it off the roof, loaded it on his back, cursing, carried it home, and placed it in the living room.

"An iron cabinet in the living room?" Shifra vehemently protested as she watched him meticulously clean the inside of the cabinet and check that the key and the spare key were working properly. Then he dragged in gray iron boxes that he'd been storing in the house, positioned them in a straight line, opened them one by one, took out dozens of cartons, and carefully pulled out his albums, which were each wrapped gently in parchment paper. He checked thoroughly that after twelve years of storing them, moisture hadn't penetrated the photographs, rewrapped them in the paper, replaced any wrapping that had yellowed, and returned each album to its carton. He lined the cartons up in the closet, stuck a sticker on the back of each one in the exact same spot, and wrote down the year and location of the photos in each carton. When he was done, he locked the cupboard and went to his wooden worktable; it had also been made special and could turn into a drawing table. There were three drawers on its side, each with its own key. When he removed the bottom drawer, a secret drawer could be spotted, hidden behind it, and it was there that he hid the key to the cabinet. On rainy weekends, when it was unthinkable to walk outside, he would open the cabinet and place the albums and photographs on the round table. He would send Shifra and the children to wash their hands, and when they returned, they would hold out their hands for him to check that they were dry. Then he would open the albums and tell the story behind each photo.

*

Ben-Gurion summoned General Yohanan Ratner to his home in Tel Aviv. Paula served tea and a single biscuit to each of them.

"My wife only gives one biscuit. It's how she keeps me healthy. You're thin. You can eat more. Would you like another?"

Yohanan waved his hand in refusal. He'd heard the stories about Paula and the health regimen she led at home.

"I want you to head the committee overseeing the scientific operations in the defense field. You did so in the past, and you know the people involved very well."

"I would be happy to do so." Yohanan finished the biscuit.

"I've decided to call the new division 'The Science Corps.'"

Yohanan, the pleasant-mannered, civilized man with the European etiquette, jumped as if bitten by a snake, "That's the name I suggested. You stole my name," he banged on the table with his fist so hard that the glass shattered.

Yohanan reported to Jenka that a science corps had been formed and said it was called HEMED for short.

"It sounds more like Helem – the city of fools – than like HEMED, which is so similar to '*hamud*,' the word for cute. Maybe we can change the name."

"Ben-Gurion isn't talking to me because of the name. Please, don't ask what happened."

Shlomo was appointed the commander of HEMED and Jenka the chief engineer. Both received the rank of lieutenant colonel. Chaim Kara, a Hungarian engineer with excellent knowledge of ballistics, was appointed head of the weapons department and received the rank of major. Aharonchik also received the rank of major. They kept coming to Camp Hill in their civilian clothes. Jenka would show up unshaven, wearing worn shoes, sweaters with holes, and faded pants that he adamantly refused to part with. Before the Friday meetings at General Headquarters, he would lock himself in the bathroom for nearly an hour, shaving and cursing as the razor cut the sensitive skin of his face. Then he would put on his freshly ironed uniform with its shining insignias. He'd walk into the General Staff meetings standing fully erect. The female soldiers would smile as they served tea and cookies to the tall, handsome lieutenant colonel.

*

When Ruth started the second grade, she became good friends with Edna Zilberstein, a girl from a wealthy family whose father was an agent who imported electronics from outside Israel. Edna lived in a big fancy house near Carmelia. Dita, Edna's mother, was known for being a beautiful, elegant, blond-haired woman. The two girls would walk home together, chatting. Ruth would make up stories and tell them to Edna. When she got home, Ruth would throw down her school bag and change clothes. She never wanted to eat the food her mother prepared, which included an omelet, eggplants in tomato sauce, and salad. She hated omelets and despised eggplants even more. Ruth would run over to Edna's house.

"Have you done your homework already?" Edna's mother would ask, looking at the unwashed girl wearing old, un-ironed clothes. "Does your mother allow you to go to friends' houses before you finish your homework? Before you eat and comb your hair?"

Ruth wouldn't answer. She would go into the house and see the family eating lunch cooked by a housekeeper – a delicious meal with meat and, for the final course, a dessert. She would grab a chair, make room for herself, sit next to Edna, and eat with them.

When the meal was over, Dita would send Edna to do her homework, and Ruth would wait for her to finish.

Back home, full of admiration, Ruth told her mother and father how beautiful Edna's house was, what delicious food they ate there, how many games she had, and what nice clothes. She told them that Edna's mother was beautiful and about her blonde hair and all her many clothes and shoes.

"I know Edna's mother. I studied in the same class as her at school," Shifra said when she heard Ruth marveling at Dita so. "She wasn't that pretty at school. She married an electrical appliance importer who makes a lot of money."

"Your mother is much more beautiful than Edna's mother," Jenka declared, firmly adding, "I don't want to hear that you're jealous of Edna." Shifra, on the other hand, understood just how Ruth felt.

Before summer vacation, Edna told Ruth that her whole family was going on holiday abroad. Only the extremely wealthy could afford such things. On Saturday afternoon, Ruth wanted to enter her parent's room when her father and mother were in bed, but the door was locked.

"What is it?" asked her mother.

"I want to travel abroad like Edna," Ruth said.

They didn't answer. Ruth repeated her request over and over again. She knocked on the door repeatedly and shimmed the doorknob, trying to open it. Then suddenly, the door opened. Her father grabbed her arm, lifted her in the air with one hand, and spanked her on the behind with his other hand. His blows were hard and hurt very much. Ruth screamed.

Shifra cried out, "You're going to kill the girl. Stop!" And she tried to free Ruth from her father's grip.

He let go. Shifra caught Ruth and embraced her.

"Stop crying!" her father commanded.

"Ruth just wants a good life like her friend has. There's nothing wrong with that," Shifra snapped at Jenka.

Ruth stopped crying.

Jenka calmed down. He knew he was wrong to take out his frustration on Ruth over all those looking to make easy money. He hated them. He sat down next to Ruth. "We are hardworking people who make do with what we have. We live modestly. We don't envy the families of electronic importers or agents or brokers. We don't worship money," he explained while holding her hand in his.

*

The first guest to visit the house in Carmelia was Zalman's brother and Shifra's uncle, Uncle Yona, who was called Yoyneh in Yiddish. He arrived on a passenger ship from America that docked at Haifa's port, occupying a large section of the pier and towering over the rooftops of the buildings near the port. The giant ocean liner from America could be seen from every house in Haifa that faced the harbor, and on its deck stood Americans: wealthy and maybe even lucky enough to have met Hollywood movie stars. Shifra prepared the guest room, spread an embroidered white tablecloth on the round table, and put out cold drinks, oranges, and cookies.

When Uncle Yoyneh arrived in a taxi, he pulled green dollar bills out of his wallet, pushed them into the driver's hands, and asked him to wait. Zalman hurried outside to be the first to greet him, hugged his brother, led him to the living room, and everyone stood up in honor of the guest. Shifra offered him a drink and a cookie.

"I just finished eating breakfast on the ship." Yoyneh said and put his hands on his stomach.

Ruth walked over to the man who'd come from the other side of the world. She thought he was no different from the other people she knew, but his complexion was shiny, like a person who eats well and is satisfied with his life. "What did you eat on the ship?" What a strange question, Yoyneh thought, looking at the girl. He inserted his hand into his pants pocket and took out a big and shiny red apple. Ruth grabbed the apple, looked at it in awe, and held it close to her chest.

"It's an apple from fairy-tale-land, like Snow White's." She bit into the crisp fruit and closed her eyes with pleasure.

Uncle Yoyneh was surprised. "Don't you have any apples here?"

Ruth answered with her mouth full, "They are small, green, and full of worms, and I hate them."

Zalman was unhappy with where the conversation was going and decided to get to the point. "So how is it over in golden America?"

"It was hard at first," answered Yoyneh in Yiddish mixed with English. "I had a small cart, and I drove between the towns and villages selling goods."

"It sounds like the hard life back in Russia. Is that how it is in America?" Zalman did not believe that Yoyneh was telling the whole truth.

Yoyneh saw that everyone was waiting. "One day, I picked up a man who asked me to take him to the nearby village. When we arrived, he got off, and I continued on my way. The sun set, it got cold, and I looked for a blanket. Then, sitting under the blanket, I found a suitcase full of money that the man had forgotten."

"A man must go to America to get lucky." Zalman nodded his head as if his brother's story had confirmed what he'd always known.

"In the morning, I drove back to the village and returned the suitcase full of dollars to its owner."

No one had anticipated such a turn in the tale, "You don't say? What do you mean? You returned all the money?"

Yoyneh hastened to reply, his eyes shining, "And the stranger hugged me and said that he'd never met and would surely never meet a person as honest as me in all the world. And he made me a partner in his business."

"Where else in the world would he find such as honest man?" Shifra clapped her hands, walked over to the table, selected an orange, peeled it, divided it into segments, carefully arranged it on a plate, and served it to Yoyneh.

Jenka, who was sitting with his hands covering his eyes, lowered them. He was doing Shifra a favor by even agreeing to be present, but he liked Yoyneh's story. "I, too, have often slept under the open sky, and at night, all kinds of suspicious types nosed around me. It's lucky you weren't robbed and murdered."

"I would make a movie about it like in Hollywood," Ruth said earnestly and approached Yoyneh, but he glanced at his watch and turned to Zalman. "Now I want to hear what brought you to the Land of Israel and if you are content."

"Me? I have nothing to tell," muttered Zalman. "I also wanted to go to golden America. But I was married and the father of three daughters. In order to receive permission to immigrate to America, I needed an invitation and the Jewish communities there only wanted butchers. I went to a butcher to learn kosher butchering, and he pushed a chicken into my hands. She jumped from my arms in a panic, I chased around the yard after her, I grabbed her, and the butcher shoved a big cleaver in my hand and shouted at me to cut her neck already." Zalman went pale and choked up.

Shifra and Tova watched him. At home, he was rude to everyone, desperate for respect. They had never seen him in such a pitiful state.

"What does he have to do with slaughtering chickens?" Shulamit came to his defense, and Zalman went on.

"With my left hand, I held the hen tightly to my chest, and with my right hand, I held the knife. The butcher shouted, 'Zalman, only wound her, don't chop off the whole neck.' My hand shook, the knife slipped on her neck, the hen broke free, ran bleeding around the yard, flapping her wings like mad, and all the hens in the coop squawked, panicked, knowing they were to be slaughtered next. I fainted."

Uncle Yoyneh came up to Zalman, took a wad of dollars out of his wallet, and pushed them into his hand. Zalman kissed his brother's hand with tears in his eyes.

Shifra escorted Yoyneh to the taxi waiting outside and whispered in his ear, "Things are hard here. It would help if you sent packages of food." She knew Jenka was watching and would be ashamed of her.

A package arrived from America. When they opened it, they saw soft sheer tulle fabrics in shades of pink, stiff glittering taffeta, belts threaded with colorful plastic rhinestones, and costumes of imaginary characters as if from a movie set. It was not what Shifra had expected, yet each package that arrived caused great excitement. She invited a seamstress to her home, sat by her side, took the costumes apart at the seams, ironed the fabric, and with a Singer sewing machine, made new clothes for the whole family. When there were holes in the soles of their shoes, she went to a cobbler to glue on a new sole; when a child's foot grew, and their shoes started to press, she cut the front part off to make room for the growing toe. When there were holes in their socks, she darned the holes, and when a sweater frayed at the seams, she glued on a piece of leather.

Chapter 15: The Secret Camp

Professor David Bergman stood by the window of his spacious office at the Ministry of Defense in Tel Aviv. Outside, it was raining cats and dogs, and he gazed at the stormy sea. "It's good for agriculture. The water level of the Sea of Galilee will rise," he muttered to himself. The cold seemed to penetrate his bones despite the fact that he was wearing a thick sweater his wife had knit for him. He took out a box of matches, and with a decisive motion, he dragged the head of the match along the striker of the matchbox and gave life to a small flame. The professor hurried over to the gas heater and stepped on its pedal. The smell of kerosene climbed into his nose, smoke puffed out of the heater, and he waited until he saw that the fire was burning evenly. Then he opened the door so the smell of gas and smoke would dissipate, left it ajar, and walked back over to the heater to warm his hands. He heard footsteps, stepped out into the corridor, and saw a straight-backed man walking towards him in a freshly ironed uniform. He patted the man on the shoulder. "I see that you've made a marked effort to shave and wear your uniform, all in my honor."

Jenka entered the room and was drawn toward the dozens of photographs hanging on the wall. The professor proceeded to explain to Jenka who all the distinguished colleagues he was photographed with were, where he'd met them, and what he thought about each of their expertise. Afterward, they sat at a large desk with stacks of papers piled on the right side. Each stack had a note that read, "Weizmann Institute," "Hebrew University," "Students," "Defense," or "Bureaucracy." On the left side of the table was a tall stack with the note "For the Automobile" written on it.

"For the automobile?" Jenka wondered as he surveyed the orderly stacks with satisfaction.

"Unfortunately, I spend a lot of time traveling between the Weizmann Institute in Rehovot, the Hebrew University in Jerusalem, and the Ministry of Defense in Tel Aviv. I have a vehicle with a driver, and I've turned the back seat into an office. I installed a small tray table, the kind they serve room service on at hotels, and attached a small lamp to the ceiling of the automobile. That way, the time doesn't go to waste."

He rang a small bell. A girl came in holding a tray with two cups of tea and some cookies, placed it in the center of the table, and left.

Jenka was astounded. Drinks and important documents on the same table? He pushed the documents to the edges of the table carefully.

"You're right. Papers and liquids don't go together. I should ask for another small table for the room." The professor got up, closed the door, went to the cabinet, took out a bottle of cognac, and poured some into the tea, changing the color to a lighter shade. "I've embraced your practice of drinking tea with cognac," he said, and they slowly sipped the steaming drinks with the smell of liquor rising up into their nostrils. "I'm concerned about what's happening in the Science Corps, and I wanted to consult with you."

Jenka nodded his head in agreement and continued to sip.

"They are discharging the reserves. The Science Corps is shrinking. How many people do you have left at Camp Hill?"

"Maybe a hundred. There used to be six hundred." Jenka pushed his empty glass to the center of the table and said, "But that's not what I'm troubled by."

"What's troubling you?"

"Talk about Ben-Gurion meeting representatives of various institutions, who present to him all kinds of idiotic ideas, has reached my ears."

Bergman removed his glasses and cleaned off the steam from the tea. "I am aware that various organizations have their eyes on the Science Corps' funding."

"There is also a disagreement regarding the objectives of the Science Corps. The army wants the Corps to continue exclusively providing immediate solutions to issues that arise. That may have suited our capabilities in the past, but now we must consider the long-term."

"I have always believed in combining science and defense," the professor reminded Jenka. "We must accomplish long-term projects that stand at the forefront of technology."

They started throwing around ideas, enjoying each other's company as they evaluated the required infrastructure and the skills and scope of manpower they would need.

"I'm glad we're in agreement." The professor stood up and escorted Jenka to the door. "Before you go, I wanted you to know that I'm leading a campaign to have the research of the Science Corps transferred to the Weizmann Institute."

Jenka stopped. How hadn't he guessed? The man he trusted was working behind his back to move the country's defense research to the Weizmann Institute. Feeling Bergman pat him lightly on the back, he slowly turned to the other man. "Why are you telling me?" Jenka answered with the innocence of a child asking questions at a Passover Seder.

"I wouldn't want to make a move against your wishes."

"I'm just an engineer, and you are the decision maker," he said and walked away with long strides, disappearing quickly down the corridor and out of the building.

He thought about stopping to call Shlomo on the way to Haifa. But decided to refrain. It would be better to calm down and not call him in a rage. When he got home, he went straight to the phone and meticulously reported on the meeting.

"It's not at all certain that Bergman will succeed," Shlomo tried to lift his spirits. "Professor Weizmann, who runs the institute, believes that we are entering an era of peace and thinks there's no need for a science corps anymore, here or anywhere else."

"You really think Weizmann won't agree to it?"

"He won't agree."

"Usually, your assessments are correct," Jenka said and went to the kitchen.

His mood had improved. Shifra had already prepared his oatmeal porridge. He knew she'd heard everything but didn't say a word. He appreciated that she was not inquisitive. She set the porridge on the table, he ate heartily, and when he finished, he tickled her belly button affectionately and went to bed.

Shlomo returned Jenka's call a week later and reported, "The two professors quarreled, Professor Bergman resigned, and Ben-Gurion appointed him Scientific Advisor to the Prime Minister and the Minister of Defense."

Tzvi Dar, the new director of Military Industries, also wanted to engage in defense research, and a meeting was held with the top defense officials. When Shlomo heard that Tzvi' intended to invite Jenka to be his chief engineer, he couldn't hold back.

"Do you have no shame? All these years, you've harassed him, called him every derogatory name in the book."

Tzvi answered, "That all belongs to Slavin's time."

But Shlomo persisted. "And why would Jenka agree?"

Tzvi didn't hesitate. "If you recommend it, he will agree."

"You think I would recommend it?" Shlomo's back hunched like an animal ready to jump on its prey. "I object." He stood up and approached Ben-Gurion. "If you transfer Jenka to Military Industries, then there may as well be no Science Corps."

Ben-Gurion watched the incessant quarreling among the Jews thoughtfully. Shlomo knew Jenka was extremely loyal to him and wouldn't leave him willingly. Still, if Ben-Gurion demanded that he transfer to Military Industries, he wouldn't be able to refuse.

As the man who concocted and executed the Tower and Stockade operation, he decided not to let various committees determine the fate of the Corps. He needed to establish facts on the ground. On the weekend, he went driving with Aharonchik. When they passed near the Kurdani intersection in Kiryat Motzkin, 9 miles north of Haifa, they discovered a big abandoned British Armed Forces camp on the side of the road, covering 90,000 square yards. The buildings were neglected and dirty, and in some of them, abandoned British laboratory equipment lay covered in dust. But when they reached the camp's borders, they found themselves on the seashore. They walked on the hard sand as the waves of the sea grazed their bare feet. They sat down on a sand dune overlooking the water. The sun was about to set, and the colors of the sky changed to red, orange, and gray.

"The English used to come here to swim in the sea." Shlomo looked out at the quiet Mediterranean. "Now, it will be the camp and testing site of the Israeli Science Corps."

It started getting dark, and they walked back to the car, adrenaline rushing through their veins, discussing which building they would renovate first and how they would discreetly transport essential equipment from Hill Camp.

On their way out of Haifa, Shlomo made a U-turn and began ascending Mount Carmel. "We are going to see Jenka."

They asked where Carmelia was and received the answer that it was a neighborhood located in one of the new areas of Carmel branching down towards the sea. After driving around and around, they reached the steep descent of Rachel Street and headed down towards Carmelia. From every side, the howling of jackals could be heard, some very close by. The car's headlights illuminated the small, isolated house. They walked carefully to avoid falling on the rocks and knocked on the door.

"Who's there?" they heard Jenka's voice.

"Aharonchik."

Out of the darkness, a tall figure wearing a white nightdress and nightcap appeared.

"You haven't changed your nightshirt?" Shlomo was astonished when he saw the ghostlike figure. "That's the same nightshirt that you wore at my apartment in Tel Aviv."

"What's going on?" Jenka asked, ignoring Shlomo's comment. They stood at the threshold outside and told him about the abandoned camp they had discovered. They couldn't tell if he was indifferent or just pretending to be, but his only comment was, "Whatever Shlomo decides, I will do."

They began to transfer basic equipment from Hill Camp to the camp near Kurdani. They personally contacted people to convince them to stay in the Science Corps and move with them to the new camp. But the academic institutions had beat them to it, promising respectable salaries, academic prestige, and publication in scientific journals in Israel and abroad. Many deliberated.

Shlomo realized he needed to act quickly and summoned the engineers and technicians. They sat on chairs in a semi-circle, curious to hear what Shlomo had to say. So many whispers had already circulated about the secret project.

"I know the Technion, the Weizmann Institute, and the University have contacted you. You will write many words, publish theoretical articles, gain respect, and be exposed to the simple pleasure of the jealousy of academic competition. You know our friendly atmosphere, and most importantly, we'll be at the forefront of technological innovation, and if you stay, you'll see how designs are produced and how plans are fully realized. The real thing."

They fell silent. They darted looks at one another.

"What's on your mind?"

"It's not just us who have to agree." Yaakov built up the courage to speak. "Some of us are married or have girlfriends. They also have to agree to leave Tel Aviv, their jobs, their studies, so that we can work at an abandoned British camp north of Haifa, the future of which isn't guaranteed in the slightest."

"You are young. Why are you in such a rush to settle down?" Shlomo took on the role of the parent, the experienced mentor who has seen a thing or two in his life. "And regarding your concerns about the location, the new camp is nine miles north of Haifa. It takes less than half an hour to get there from Haifa. The time it takes to get to Tel Aviv from Herzliya, Rishon LeZion, and Rehovot," he added, "There will be a shuttle that will pick you up near your place of residence in the mornings and drop you off in the evenings."

Still, a tense silence prevailed in the room.

"All the work is secret and confidential," Yair complained. "I want to continue my studies on to a Master's degree and maybe a doctorate. At the academic institutions, we can publish our research. We can move up in life."

"We heard that all of your activities there are being done without permission. Maybe it's all a hoax," peeped Meir, tilting his head and scrutinizing Shlomo suspiciously.

"Jenka is with us." Some of them looked shocked. "I want to tell you that he gave up a secure career at Military Industries, where they offered him the world. He will be our chief engineer. In addition to your work in the Science Corps, you can continue studying for your degrees, and you can work as guest lecturers or assistants at the Technion," Shlomo said, pitching them further temptations. "Jenka, too, will soon begin lecturing at the Technion, teaching a 'Weapons and Ammunitions' course. So, what do you say?"

Hanoch Paroz announced that he would join them. Moya Epstein, Chaim Kara, and a few others were also persuaded. Cracks were forming in the wall of resistance to the move.

"I'm not so keen about working with Jenka. He splits people between those he trusts and believes in and those he tries not to see, and I'm among the latter," Hanan said and admitted, "sometimes I'm afraid of him.'"

Elad, the redhead, added, "He's also the champion of cursing in Russian." It wasn't clear if the comment was one of admiration or disdain.

"That's just folklore," Moya replied. "Take it easy, my friend. Look on the bright side. Think how much you can learn from him."

Shlomo decided they'd exhausted the matter, "Whoever is coming with us to the new camp, raise your hand."

One hand flew up, two more hesitantly joined, and little by little, one after the other, they all raised their hands.

Whispering quietly to each other, the architects Moshe Zarhy and Yaakov Rechter approached Shlomo and asked to step outside the room with him.

"What concerns you?"

"That's what we want to talk to Jenka about."

"On the weekends, he's in Haifa at the new house he built in Carmelia."

They drove to see him on Saturday and brought a bouquet of flowers as a housewarming gift. When they arrived, they saw him working in the yard, making a stone path leading to the house. He was wearing a sleeveless shirt, tight shorts, and a bucket hat on his head. He picked up heavy stones and positioned them on the path, dripping with sweat despite the chilly weather. When he saw them, he smiled, walked over to the green plastic hose, and washed his body with cold water. They stared as he soaped himself with vigor, emitting strange sounds from his mouth to keep warm. He explained that he always showered in cold water in the mornings to immunize his body. When he finished, he entered the house dripping wet and yelled, "Shifra! Towel!"

He went into his room to change clothes and asked them to wait in the hallway. Then he led them to the kitchen, and they sat down at a large simple wooden table that used to be a carpenter's table.

The young architects presented the flowers to Shifra and politely congratulated them on moving into their new home.

"I can't remember the last time someone bought me flowers," Shifra said, holding the beautiful bouquet.

She turned to Jenka. "Have you ever brought me flowers?"

"I don't know," he admitted. Suddenly he remembered, "Every time we hike in Carmelia, I pick the pinkest primrose and give it to you. At home, you put it in an empty glass yogurt jar."

"What should I do with these big, beautiful flowers? I don't have a vase."

"Put them in a pot," suggested Jenka.

And she placed the large aluminum pot, with the flowers in it, on a table.

It was lunchtime, and she made omelets for the three of them and asked if they wanted eggplants in tomato sauce. She didn't wait for an answer before filling their plates. While they ate with gusto, saying that the eggplants were delicious, Shifra explained why actually, this time, the eggplants didn't come out well. That she hadn't made them like the time when they did come out well.

While eating, Jenka explained that the house wasn't plastered, wasn't connected to electricity, and that they brought in water from the hose outside. He told them that Shifra didn't want to plaster the outside of the house so that the city officials wouldn't demand property tax.

"If the house looks nice from the outside, they'll say that I live in a fancy villa, and they'll want lots of money," clarified Shifra while trying to convince the two architects that she was right.

"Isn't it hard for you to live with such conditions?" asked Zarhy.

"Wouldn't you like to live in a nice, well-kept house?" added Rechter.

"I've gotten used to it. The contractor ran away with the money, and for over a year, I lived with the kids in the frame of the house."

Feeling embarrassed, the two young men looked at Jenka.

"Regarding the plaster, I don't know if Shifra is right or not. She can do whatever she pleases," Jenka announced.

They finished off the meal with a drink of hot tea with lemon and a drop of vodka.

Then, they were left to their own devices.

"What's the matter?" Jenka asked.

Moshe Zarhy began, "Jenka, don't be angry. I feel terrible, it's actually hard for me to say out loud, but I've decided not to continue in the Science Corps. As has Yaakov. We want to work at Ze'ev Rechter's architecture firm," Moshe said, holding his breath as if waiting for Jenka to burst out in a rage.

"Architects." Jenka shook his head. "Want to be architects."

They knew he looked down on architects. To their great surprise, he smiled. "Ze'ev Rechter is an outstanding architect who designs buildings on pillars. It makes sense because the pillar floor at ground level creates an open yet covered space and expands the sidewalk area while still exposing it to the wind."

"How do you understand architecture so well?" Yaakov asked.

"I designed our house here and explored the subject a bit. We have pillars here too, but at the back of the house because of the slope of the mountain."

"Jenka, you don't understand how hard it is to say goodbye to the team and especially to you. Maybe we can find some way for me to continue to serve part-time in the Corps?" Moshe wondered.

Jenka suggested that they take a hike with him around Carmelia on the dirt road that circles the mountain range. After the rain, the fields were full of poppies, primroses, crocuses, yellow chrysanthemums, and purple gladiolas. Here and there stood a cluster of towering pine trees. A breeze blew up from the sea. The view was spectacular. Jenka picked three perfect pink primroses to bring home to Shifra.

When they got back to the house, Jenka walked them to the car and patted them both on the back affectionately. "Be fine architects. That is how you can serve our country."

*

Ben-Gurion opened the drawer of his desk, took out a notebook, flipped through the pages with amusement, and showed Professor David Bergman.

"I made a list of Hebrew names from the Bible. People who represent the country will be given Hebrew names. There will no longer be Jews from the Land of Israel who bear Germans names like Katzman – man of cats, or Zisman – sugar man, Trepengelender – the stair railing, or Ashner – the ash man."

"I wish to keep the name Bergman," the professor answered.

"What is so wonderful about the name Bergman – mountain man. What connection do you have with mountains, exactly? Are you a muscular man who climbs mountains? We have chosen the ancient Hebrew name for a wise man for you."

"I signed every study I've ever published over the years with the name 'Bergman.' How will I explain that I have a new name now and that the person who signed and is quoted in scientific literature under the name 'Bergman' is also me?"

Ben-Gurion put his notebook back in the drawer, "Oh, the academic sensitivity," he exclaimed. "I have more important things to deal with," he interrupted and lifted his chin up in a sharp motion that ruffled his white hair. "You may leave. And be sure to close the door behind you."

As for Jenka, Ben-Gurion did not give up so quickly. He gave him the Hebrew name Gideon Rav-Tal. When Jenka came home and told his wife about the name Ben-Gurion had given him, Shira said, "Say the name again?"

Ruth burst out laughing. "Rav-Tal is such a funny name! What does it mean, 'the rabbi of the dew?'"

"No, not 'rabbi of the dew,'" Shifra explained. "It means 'rich with dew.'"

"I don't like the name, but Ben-Gurion said that he looked for a suitable name for me, and it took him a while to find one, and finally, he decided on Rav-Tal. How could I refuse? In any case, it's just to represent the country when we go abroad."

*

The Commander in Chief of the military, Yigael Yadin, undertook the establishment of an army reserve force. He feared that the Arabs would recover from the defeat they suffered during the Independence Day War and reorganize and attack the country. Ben-Gurion approved the significant budget Yadin needed, believing that if there was a strong reserve force, they would be able to cut expenses in the rest of the defense force. Yadin opposed the budget cuts and resigned. Ben-Gurion appointed Mordechai Maklef in his place, who had been the head of the Israeli Defense Force's Operations Division and who agreed to implement the budget cuts, but only under the condition that he would serve as Commander in Chief for just one year. Soon the Science Corps' turn for budget cuts arrived. Shlomo objected, so Maklef fired him and removed the Science Corps from the army, transferring the unit to the Ministry of Defense, where they would be Ben-Gurion's direct responsibility. In 1952, Ben-Gurion and Professor Bergman established the "Research and Design Directorate," or, for short, the Hebrew acronym, "EMET," which was made up of five institutes. Professor Bergman was appointed the Chief Scientist and Munya Mardor the General Manager.

Munya refused to accept the position. He had recently been released from the army after 15 years of service, he had started a business and bore a son. When Ben-Gurion continued to pressure him, he explained that he wasn't interested in being a subordinate administrator to Professor Bergman. Ben-Gurion promised to come to an agreement with Bergman, ensuring that Munya would be able to outline his own independent policy of action. Munya was still hesitant.

When Shlomo learned of what was happening, he determined to go with Jenka to Munya's apartment. He knew about their excellent working relationship. Munya opened the door and greeted them warmly. Lenka, Munya's wife, looked at them suspiciously and then shot a menacing look at her husband. It was a small apartment with no sitting room to entertain guests, so they went into the kitchen and closed the door.

"Munya, we came to you because we want you to take the position of general manager at EMET."

"When I heard that you were coming, I promised my wife that I wouldn't be tempted by you and that I would keep my promise to her. She deserves it. She's waited many years, and each time I denied her requests. I cannot disappoint her again."

"If you don't take the job, they'll just pass it on to some politician." They knew how much Munya hated the dishonesty of politicians.

They saw they'd touched a sensitive spot and triggered Munya's conscience. Shlomo took advantage and reinforced their argument. "You know that we are in the middle of a formidable fight surrounding the objectives of the Science Corps, and no politician will fight like you. You know how important it is that we establish objectives at the forefront of technology. Only you, together with Professor Bergman, can convince all the morons, who lack understanding and vision, of the needs of the future."

Lenka came into the kitchen and offered them cold, refreshing watermelon. They ate hungrily while she chatted with them about this and that, trying to divert the conversation to other matters. She knew that her husband would be unable to give in to them in her presence. Munya went up to her and asked to talk to her outside the kitchen. They left the room, but their arguing could be heard through the entire apartment.

"We will be guilty of causing a divorce." Jenka and Shlomo fled the kitchen, quickly passed the couple in the hall, and got out of the apartment.

When Ben-Gurion informed Munya that he would be able to manage his own policy at the Research and Design Directorate, his wife's pleas were no use, and he accepted the position. Furthermore, his wife hailed from an affluent family, and Munya was content with a symbolic salary of one pound a month.

*

Munya battled over the assignments allocated to EMET. It was decided that a meeting would be held in the company of Ben-Gurion, Professor Bergman, prominent officers from the army, and Munya. On the day of the gathering, they were informed that Ben-Gurion had a cold and had requested to hold the meeting at his home.

Ben-Gurion's wife, Paula, opened the door with a glass of milk in her hand. "Come in, come in. He'll join you in a minute."

They sat down, staring in amazement at the extensive library full of books on history, Judaica, and philosophy, and at his big, impressive desk. They stood up when Ben-Gurion entered wearing an old gray dressing gown and house slippers, with a handkerchief in hand to wipe his runny nose. He sat down in an armchair, and Paula handed him the glass of milk.

"Drink carefully. It's hot. I stirred in honey to ease your cough."

"Paula takes care of me," he said and sipped obediently.

"If I don't take care of you, who will? The state?" she looked straight at the people seated around the room.

"Paula, offer refreshments to our guests."

"There is a jug of cold water with freshly squeezed lemon, and I bought waffles and pretzels in your honor."

"Paula doesn't bake cakes," he apologized to his guests. "She claims that cakes are unhealthy and that I need to maintain my weight. She cooks me healthy food and makes sure that I get enough sleep."

"The refreshments are perfect." One of the officers poured himself some lemon water.

"Paula, we wish to begin." She exited the room like an obedient soldier, understanding that she was not to enter until he called her. "I'm aware of the matter at hand. Munya, you begin."

"At the Research and Design Directorate, we need to think long-term. This is the time to invest in infrastructure and laboratories, to educate the younger generation, who have no practical experience. We need to hold advanced study trainings and to send talented young folks to study abroad to familiarize them with contemporary innovations."

An officer butted in, interrupting Munya, "The entire IDF is undergoing extreme budget cuts, and here you are, requesting funding for developments that will take years. Who knows if they'll even bear fruit or if all the money will go down the drain?"

Munya cautioned, "If we don't think four to five years ahead, in a few years, we will still be in the same place that we are today."

"It's smarter to equip ourselves now, quickly, with ready-made weapons that have been tested by other armies," argued the contrary officer.

Munya did not give up. "I thought we learned our lesson. On the eve of the War of Independence, we discovered that the world's vital procurement sources were unavailable to us. We can never be sure that external sources will agree to sell us the weapons we need and whether they'll arrive on time."

The debate could go on forever.

"Silence, my friends," commanded Ben-Gurion, his voice hoarse, and all eyes turned to him. "Our advantage over our enemy, who outnumber us ten to one or more, is the Jewish brain. Is science. We have no alternative but to develop independently and to stop relying on external sources," and with that, he stood up and left the room, hunched over.

On their way out, they heard Paula order her husband, "Now you go straight back to bed, and I'll bring you a cup of hot tea with lemon."

*

At 7:00, buses left to pick up the employees and take them to work at Institute 3, one of the Research and Design Directorate's five institutes and the largest of them, located near the Kurdani junction.

Most of the employees were unmarried, some were Holocaust survivors, and to ensure they ate breakfast, the buses would arrive in time for the morning meal, which was served between 7:30 and 8:00. The meal consisted of porridge, omelets, white cheese, jam, fresh black bread, and coffee or tea. At 8:00, they started work. They also ate lunch at the institute, and at 4:00 p.m. when the workday was over, the buses drove them back. Many of them worked after hours and never considered asking for overtime.

Institute 3 continued to grow and brought on new employees. It became known in Haifa and across the north as 'The Secret Camp.' New people coming to the camp were told to "take a bus or taxi from Haifa and ask the driver to get off at the Kurdani junction station. Then walk half a kilometer north on the path leading to the gate of The Secret Camp." After a time, when passengers asked the taxi drivers to get off at the Kurdani junction station, they would reply, "You don't look like new immigrants who want to go to the immigrant camp at Kurdani, so I'll drop you off at The Secret Camp."

Jenka continued coming to work unshaven, wearing shabby civilian clothes and an odd brown beret on his head. When he arrived at the institute, he would change into a short-sleeved white button-down shirt and threadbare shorts. In the winter, he wore long pants and a ratty sweater. Shifra kept mending the sweater, but it continued to unravel. Jenka firmly refused to part with it. He always wore a serious expression and was often seen walking alone in great haste. When visitors came to Institute 3, they couldn't understand why this homeless man was roaming freely and didn't believe it when they were told that he was the chief engineer and had the rank of lieutenant colonel, one of the few in the nation at the time.

When working in his office, he needed total silence. In the studio and at Camp Hill, everyone had known that when Jenka was in a planning trance, it was forbidden, under any circumstances, to go near him. They had respected him and didn't interfere. But many new people had joined Institute 3, and occasionally one of them would walk down the hall whistling joyfully. When Jenka heard whistling, he would jump up as if bitten by a snake and run down the hall, cursing Russian and shouting, "stop whistling!" Silence would fall. Everyone would hide in their offices like mice in burrows. When Jenka had ensured there would be no more whistling, he would return to his office, slam the door, and go back to work.

Despite the PIAT's excellent performance in the War of Independence, there were complaints that the mechanical spring was rigid, and as a result, the shooters had to lie on the floor and push the 90-kilo spring with their feet. So, Jenka developed the RMATW, a rifle-mounted anti-tank weapon to replace the PIAT. The RMATW could be launched from any Czech rifle, which was the type of rifle used in Israel, and the penetration ability was more significant. Soldiers from the IDF complained that the shooter received strong blows to the shoulder due to the muzzle blast. The complaints didn't cease. Jenka got fed up and went out to a test site with the RMATW, watched by a group of young soldiers and their commanders. He pressed the rifle firmly to his shoulder and fired 80 shots in a row with good results. His shoulder blade wasn't hurt by the impact of the shockwave, and he turned to the soldiers. "If an old man like me, at 45 years old, can shoot without any issue, any young soldier can, too," and that was the end of that; no one complained anymore.

As the tank armor became thicker, reaching 400 millimeters, finding new solutions for anti-tank weapons became crucial, and Jenka began to develop the super-bazooka. He didn't have the blueprints of the American weapon, so he redesigned it, increasing the diameter of the shaped charge and the impact depth, and used aluminum instead of iron. There was no problem with the impact of the muzzle, but the blast of the projectile erupted from the back of the weapon after each shot. To protect the shooter from the blast, Jenka installed a protective screen on the super-bazooka. He went out to the beach at Institute 3 and performed the first tests, shooting from his shoulder. Everyone cheered, and Jenka smiled contentedly and told a joke.

From time to time, visits were made to the institute. When the guests were important, Jenka would shave in their honor. If very important guests were scheduled to arrive, such as the Commander in Chief or Ben-Gurion, he would inform Shifra a few days in advance that she should wash and iron his uniform. On the mornings of such visits, he would hog the bathroom for nearly an hour, shaving with a razor. He often cut his skin, after which a string of Russian curses could be heard throughout the house. He would accompany them on a tour of the institute, making sure to walk a step behind them to show respect. They would ask him to explain about the weapons he was developing, and only then, as everyone around him stood listening in awe, would his body relax.

Chapter 16: Jenka's Boys

The growth of the organization's infrastructure gained momentum, and Professor Bergman invested funds in the education of the institute's employees. For the first time, a research hierarchy was initiated, and professional fields of research were established: Mechanics – Jenka; Electronics – Dr. Yaakov Shekel; Chemistry – Dr. Dov Katz; and Physics – Dr. Binyamin Sturlesi

Among the new people to join Institute 3 was Dr. Moshe Feldenkrais, who'd earned his doctorate at the Sorbonne in applied physics and was appointed head of the physics department. Although he didn't leave a mark on the development of weapons at the Research and Design Directorate, he was known for herding all his subordinates outside at ten in the morning and laying them on the grass, where he instructed them to do exercises on one side of their body, explaining that the other side "would learn by itself." Rumors of this peculiar practice reached Ben-Gurion's ears, and he invited Moshe Feldenkrais, who taught him how to do a headstand. Feldenkrais immediately became well-known, so he left EMET and devoted himself to developing his exercise method.

There was Dr. Fidia Piatelli, an aeronautical engineer from Italy who immigrated to Israel after World War II. During the Mussolini era, due to racist laws, he was fired from his job and banned. He survived the Holocaust thanks to his wife, Heike, a Protestant with a Buddhist perspective on life. When they arrived in Israel, he worked refurbishing gliders for the Maof Company, and in the early fifties, he joined the Research and Design Directorate. He was the first aeronautical engineer to design missiles launched from airplanes to be used by the Air Force against ships and land targets. In 1957, Piatelli went to pick up his wife from the airport, and on the way, stopped in Tel Aviv to watch the film "A Man Escaped" by Robert Bresson, which was showing at the North cinema. While Piatelli was standing in line at the counter, a young man robbed the cash register, and while he was trying to carve his way through the crowd and run away, he fired his gun indiscriminately. Piatelli was injured, taken to a hospital and operated on, but sadly died a few days later. The murder shocked the young nation when it was revealed that a Holocaust survivor was murdered by a young man who was also a Holocaust survivor.

And there was also Chaim Kara, the engineer who developed a submachine gun to replace the British STEN. Kara was already at an advanced stage of development and had already designed 12 models of the new submachine gun when a young man, who had his own ideas for designing a submachine gun but lacked the professional background, asked to join him. The young fellow, Uzi Gal, gained insight into the work of an expert. A year later, Gal transferred to Military Industries, where he continued to work on his submachine gun, the Uzi, replacing the rounded bolt conceived by Kara with a square bolt. He presented the submachine gun as his own original development at Military Industries. In 1953, a committee headed by Yitzhak Rabin was formed to compare the performance of Kara's submachine gun model from the Research and Design Directorate and Uzi's model from Military Industries. It was determined ahead of time that Military Industries would begin production on the model selected by the committee. The committee concluded that both models were excellent and therefore asked Military Industries to price each of the models. Military Industries reported that the production of an Uzi unit would cost 14 pounds sterling, while the development of a Kara would cost 17 pounds. Because of the 3-pound difference, Rabin's committee recommended Uzi Gal's model, and the machine gun was named after him. Kara fought the committee's decision to award the Israel Defense Prize solely to Uzi Gal and demanded to be included as well. The committee denied Kara's appeal, so he sued in civil court for intellectual property theft. In the end, he gave up. The injustice committed had broken him. After Kara's case, the Research and Design Directorate began registering intellectual property patents.

*

Ruth reached the 6th grade and was having a hard time learning mathematics. "You need to help Ruth. She's failing all her tests," Shifra said one evening, serving Jenka his favorite porridge before bed. When he finished eating, he meticulously cleaned the table of all the crumbs, sharpened his pencil, and fetched a clean white piece of paper. Ruth sat next to her father, who drew a perfect circle on the page.

"This is the entire cake," Jenka explained to Ruth, and, in her mind's eye, she saw a big round chocolate cake with frosting. "Now I am dividing the cake into two halves," he said, drawing a straight line down the middle of the circle.

Ruth pictured the imaginary cake sliced in half; she could see the nuts inside and smell the chocolatey aroma of a freshly baked confection. Her mouth watered, and she licked her lips.

"Do you understand?" Jenka asked, and Ruth nodded. "Now I'm dividing the cake into four parts and then into eight parts." he drew lines cutting the slices of cake, and beside each piece, wrote two numbers, one on top of the other, separated by a small line.

Ruth looked at the numbers and pictured the scrumptious cake in her imagination but could not understand the connection between them. When Jenka saw that Ruth didn't understand, he drew an orange and divided it into segments. Ruth saw the orange with its orange-colored peel in her mind's eye and saw how her father divided the orange and marked each of its segments. Jenka painted a watermelon, an apple, and every fruit Ruth asked for. And she still didn't understand.

In math class, the teacher calculated equations with one unknown variable. "A train left the station traveling at one speed, and another train left half an hour later, traveling at a faster speed. When will the trains meet?" The teacher wrote the equations on the board, and the class listened diligently. Then the teacher asked if they understood, and everyone nodded in assent.

Jenka sat next to Ruth at the kitchen table, writing down numbers, and she stared blankly, gaping at the page. She saw the first train in her imagination, envisioned its colors, and heard its chugging. Then she turned her head and pictured the second train leaving; she could count the number of cars and see people through the train's windows. She saw the second train passing by the first, but how could she write down what she imagined in her mind in numbers? Jenka explained again, sketching patiently, over and over. And Ruth still didn't understand.

The school's secretary entered the classroom jittery with excitement. "Mr. Schlesinger, the math teacher, is ill. Mr. Kroch, the principal of all the school's branches, will teach his class today. It is a great honor."

Mr. Kroch entered the classroom, and Ruth looked at the old, short, chubby man. He took a seat at the teacher's desk, opened the class log, and began calling out the students' names. Each student raised their hand so that Mr. Kroch would know who was who.

When he read out the name "Ruth Ratner," he stopped. "I had a brilliant student named Jenka Ratner; he was extremely mischievous, but I liked him very much." Kroch's eyes twinkled, and he went on, "I see that you have the same last name."

"That's my father. I'm his daughter," answered Ruth. The gentleman peered at her and nodded his head, pleased.

Mr. Schlesinger was still sick when the next math class rolled around, and Mr. Kroch substituted for him again. He entered the classroom and proclaimed, "Ruth Ratner to the blackboard," before he even sat down to take attendance.

Ruth approached the board, her heart beating anxiously, but it was beyond her control.

"Jenka's daughter shall tell us what time the trains will meet." He sat up in his chair eagerly.

Ruth said the answer.

"Good," Mr. Kroch praised her.

"Now explain to us how you reached the result," he said, folding his arms.

Ruth was silent.

"Well, young Ms. Ratner, we're waiting," Mr. Kroch berated her.

"My father explained it to me, but I couldn't understand," whispered Ruth, on the verge of tears.

Mr. Kroch looked at her in disappointment. "So this is Jenka's daughter? And they say that the apple doesn't fall far from the tree, but here there's a tree but no apple. You may return to your seat."

When she got home, Ruth told her parents what had happened, so her father cleared the table of the dinner dishes, brought over a piece of paper and a pencil, and explained it to her again. But it was no use, for Ruth still didn't understand.

*

Every morning, Jenka drove to work in the station wagon he'd received from the Research and Design Directorate. The other two senior executives to receive cars were Munya and Professor Bergman. Jenka would drive the station wagon slowly, mulling over work matters until a string of vehicles extended behind him and started honking at him to speed up. He had vacation days he hadn't used. So, he drove the station wagon to bathe in the hot springs of Tiberias, hoping to relieve the arthritis he had begun to suffer from. His head finally unburdened by work matters, Jenka went heavy on the gas pedal. A police car sped up behind him and gave him a speeding ticket At the institute, it was decided that Jenka's driving issue needed to be resolved. So, two drivers, Berkovich and Malmud, were assigned to him. Every morning, Berkovich waited for him in a car outside the house to drive him to work, and every night Malmud would drive him home. He formed friendships with the drivers. He had always felt comfortable with honest, hardworking folk. They told him about their families, and he listened and tried to help.

On sunny winter days, the family would hike on the road that circled the neighborhood. Ruth would skip alongside her father, eagerly drinking in the tales about his motorcycle trips to India and Africa. When he went looking for the pinkest primrose, she would run after him and pick the 3 primroses that were chosen after undergoing a thorough inspection to ensure that they had no imperfection. Back at the house, Shifra would put them in water in an empty yogurt jar and look around the kitchen for the perfect spot to place them. On Saturday evenings, they would climb the mountain trail on foot up to the main road and head to the unpretentious Moriya cinema. There they would watch Hollywood films starring Deborah Kerr, or Esther Williams in a bathing suit, accompanied by dozens of girls, swimming in a pool or in the ocean off some exotic island. Sometimes they saw Italian films with Sophia Loren or Gina

Lollobrigida – the Italian beauties. And there were also French films with Brigitte Bardot, the famed sex symbol, who boldly exposed her back and her behind.

Sometimes they went hiking in the Galilee on Saturdays. At the eastern exit out of Haifa, there were still swamps with thousands of white daffodils, the mountains were studded with rocks, and here and there, giant machines began to carve out the large stones to create a field that could be cultivated. At the entrance to the Arab villages, dozens of barefoot children walked in front of the station wagon dressed in rags, with runny noses and eye ailments. The children would gather around the car and ask for money: "*Bakshish.*" Open sewer trenches flowed down the main dirt roads of the villages. A sewage canal also passed through the big market in the city of Acre. Flies jumped from the sewage to the stalls on either side of the canal, which were loaded with fruits, vegetables, lentils, and spices in every color.

*

On one trip, Shifra felt unwell. The tests revealed that she had gallstones. She needed surgery and was hospitalized. Jenka appointed twelve-year-old Ruth to look after eight-year-old Danny and five-year-old Michal. He promised to come home from work every day in the afternoon and gave her a phone number to call in case of an emergency. Lunchtime arrived, and Ruth decided to prepare a meal. She found a large piece of frozen liver in the ice box, took a pan, filled it with lots of oil, waited for it to boil, and threw the liver inside. The oil splashed and spattered everywhere, lighting a big fire. Ruth got scared. She called the neighbor Dibaleh, an elderly woman with plenty of meat on her bones who lived in a newly constructed home. Dibaleh thawed the liver, cut it into slices, fried onions, and put the pieces of liver on top. It was a delicacy. She told the girl that she would make chicken soup and asked that she call her father and request that he go to the Talpiot, Haifa's big marketplace, on the way home from work, buy a whole chicken, and tell the butcher to make sure it was clean of feathers.

Ruth hesitated. She didn't remember her mother calling her father on the phone. Certainly not regarding food.

"Call him," Dibaleh encouraged Ruth, her ample curves moving and jiggling as she washed the dishes. "When my Yankeleh was still healthy and going to work, I would call him several times a week at his job to ask him to go to the market on his way home and buy everything I needed. He did so willingly. Your father will be glad to do so as well."

Ruth walked over to the drawer, took out the piece of paper with the phone number written on it, and called her father's place of work. "This is Jenka's daughter, Ruth, speaking. I would like to talk to my father, please," said Ruth clearly, feeling very mature.

"Hold, please. He'll be here soon," answered the operator.

Dibaleh took a break from washing the dishes, patiently waiting with Ruth for her father to come to the phone, smiling, nodding her head, encouraging the girl for taking her advice and working up the courage to call her father.

An urgent note was sent to Jenka's secretary. He was seated at his table, leading his research meeting, when the secretary whispered in his ear. He immediately stood up, exited the room, striding quickly, and rushed to the phone. Avraham Levi, the administrative manager, darted after him, their eyes serious, dreading an emergency.

"What happened?" asked Jenka, anticipating the worst.

"The neighbor Dibaleh asked that you pass through the market on the way home and buy a chicken," said Ruth.

Jenka's words stuck in his throat.

"Don't forget to tell him to check that the butcher cleans off the feathers thoroughly and that I'll cook you a chicken soup," Dibaleh whispered in Ruth's ear, prompting her to continue talking.

"See that the butcher cleans the feathers well," Ruth repeated Dibaleh's request, and the neighbor stood beside her, pleased.

It was as if the sky cracked open, lightning struck, and thunder clapped. "You called me for that? How dare you listen to Dibaleh, that idiot!" Jenka shouted.

When his words reached Dibaleh's ears, she froze in astonishment, cowered like a mouse, and let out an offended squeak. "Instead of thanking me for cooking for his children and being willing to make them soup, he insults me." She hastily left in a huff. "What an awful man."

Ruth began to cry.

Avraham Levi grabbed the phone out of Jenka's hands.

"Ruth, Avraham Levi speaking. My wife will come over soon and bring food with her. Next time, ask for me if you need anything at all."

*

A group of young people began to assemble around Jenka. They soon came to be known as "Jenka's boys." They were talented, hardworking, and responsible; he loved working with them and invested time and effort into educating them. Some of them were natives of the land, like the engineers Moya Epstein and Olly Lavi or the technicians Yoel Tepper and Stef Wertheimer, the workshop supervisor. Others were Holocaust survivors, such as Hanoch Paroz, who had recently completed his studies at the Technion, and Moshe Ritterband, who was just as talented a technician but had no formal education. They voluntarily stayed late at work with him every night, and he would drive them in the station wagon back to their residences in Haifa. Some of them were lonely young men who had been children in the death camps and lost their entire families. He resolved to speak with Shifra on their behalf.

"What do you think about inviting a few of the young folk who work with me to live in the big room that we sleep in? We can move to a different room and the three kids can share a bedroom. They'll drive to work with me in the morning and come back with me at night."

"You want to rent them the room?"

"You want me to ask them for money?"

"There are properties for sale in Carmelia at extremely low prices. I want to buy a lot."

"You want to buy a lot?"

"I've been scrimping and saving every dime."

"You plan to do business?" He looked at her in disgust.

"We have three kids. They'll get married someday and need apartments."

Jenka was dumbfounded. He almost left the house, spewing curses, when Shifra spoke again.

"Fine. I'll agree to them moving in with us, but they should pay. They have jobs and earn good money. The room is large, and three or four people can live there comfortably. They can split the rent."

"You expect me to ask them for money? Have you no shame?"

"The rent will also include dinner during the work week."

Jenka scratched his bald head, debating whether to propose such a thing to them. How could he ask them for money?

"It will also include meals on the weekends."

"Alright, I'll talk to them."

The next day, four of Jenka's boys came to live in the big room that Shifra and Jenka had vacated for them. Shifra fed them, forced them to shower, washed and ironed their clothes, and soon, they started to call her "Mother."

*

Ben-Gurion viewed the settlement of the Negev Desert in the south to be a national mission. Thousands of high school seniors from every school in Israel gathered at the stadium in Tel Aviv. Ben-Gurion stood on stage and declared energetically to the students that "we must make desert bloom." As usual, he omitted the connecting article "the," so his speech sounded odd and funny to the student's ears. And what did he truly know about the needs of the youth in 1953? Ben-Gurion was troubled and disappointed by the reception of his oration. He searched for a solution that would incentivize good people to move to the Negev, hoping to attract a younger crowd by proxy. That was how the idea to move the Research and Design Directorate to the Negev arose. The employees congregated for his arrival. Jenka shaved, put on his uniform, and took care to walk a step or two behind him. Ben-Gurion spoke about Zionism, about responsibility, and about settling the Negev desert, where he would build them a modern, state-of-the-art base.

The employees of the Research and Design Directorate conveyed that they would be willing to move under a few conditions:

"We want a good school to educate the children."

"I agree," said Ben-Gurion.

"We want a film to be shown once a week."

"I consent," said Ben-Gurion.

"We want a swimming pool."

"That is totally unreasonable," said Ben-Gurion angrily.

At night, while giving her a foot rub, Jenka told Shifra about the gathering with Ben-Gurion.

"Would you be willing to move to the Negev?" she asked him.

"Yes. Ben-Gurion has requested me to, and in the desert, I don't suffer from arthritis."

"And what of our home in Carmelia?"

"What about the house?" he asked, not understanding her question.

"We have a house here."

He shook his head from one side to the other, "We can sell, we can rent, we can do this, that, and the other, we can do whatever you want, I don't care."

Ben-Gurion held firm in his stance against the swimming pool, so the Research and Design Directorate remained in Kurdani.

*

On her birthday, Ruth saw a dance performance by several girls from her class who studied ballet with Miriam Bat-Artzi. The ballet teacher taught in the living room of her apartment near the water tower, roughly half an hour's walk from the house in Carmelia. The girls went to the classes in tutu skirts, leotards, and pointe shoes with hard soles so they could stand on their toes. They did splits, bent their backs backward into a bridge, and slithered their arms. Shifra sewed a tutu with fabric from Uncle Yoyne's care packages from America. Ruth wasn't flexible, it hurt her to stand on her toes, but she loved to invent her own dances. At school, she announced to her class that she was a dancer, and invitations to perform at birthday parties poured in. Shifra starched and ironed Ruth's tutu, sewed a new outfit for a gypsy dance, hung the costumes on a hanger, and proudly accompanied her little ballerina to every performance.

Jenka's daughter wants to be a dancer? Where? There are no ballet troupes in Israel. Shifra decided that they needed to hear the opinion of an expert. Jenka was not enthusiastic about the idea, but Shifra was determined.

"You can't just work, work, work and work all the time. You also have a daughter and must consider her needs."

In the end, he gave in. "I think that Ora Ratner, Professor Yohanan Ratner's wife, was a dancer in Germany and even performed here several times."

"Invite them to our house, and Ruth will dance for them."

Jenka called Professor Ratner, apologized for bothering him, pronounced unpleasantly that his daughter desired to be a dancer, and explained that he would be exceedingly grateful if they would agree to come to Carmelia to see the girl dance. To his great surprise, Professor Ratner and his wife happily accepted the invitation.

That Saturday, Jenka's boys dragged their beds out of the big room. They carried in the round table, the chairs, and an armchair and rolled out a carpet. Shifra bought fruit and good-quality cookies. By the time the professor and his wife arrived, Shifra and Jenka were excited. They hadn't hosted distinguished guests since Uncle Yoyneh visited from America. After some unavoidable small talk, Jenka decided it was time to get to the point.

Jenka turned to Ora Ratner. "Ruth wants to be a dancer. Shifra and I don't know anything about dance. We wanted to hear an expert's opinion."

Ruth wore her tutu and put on her stiff pointe shoes, Shifra put on a record that played music, and the girl started to dance.

When Ruth finished, Ora's expression was impossible to read.

"Would you agree to perform a dance of your own, barefoot?" Ora asked.

"A dance of my own?"

"Yes. Invent a dance. Pretend that you are a sad girl, that you're in pain, or maybe imagine that you are the blowing wind, whatever you like."

Ruth didn't hesitate.

"Alright. This is how I dance during my performances at birthday parties. I will dance a sad girl who was once a princess, and then I'll dance a ghost who is sometimes a fairy."

Jenka was embarrassed.

Shifra knew Ruth's dances and set the needle to the record with the music that went with each dance. Jenka watched as Professor Ratner and his wife looked on in interest. Then, he also looked at Ruth, trying to understand what compelled them so.

"That was much better," Ora said, smiling.

"I really enjoyed it," added the professor.

Everyone sat down to hear the final verdict.

"It seems that Ruth has talent," Ora ruled. "There is a Russian ballet teacher named Valentina Arkhipova-Grossman who teaches in Hadar HaCarmel, at the foothills of Mount Carmel. I suggest that you sign Ruth up to study with her."

"I think Ruth should also learn to play a musical instrument, such as the piano," suggested the professor.

"An excellent idea. It will contribute to Ruth's musicality," Ora added.

Jenka and Shifra accepted Ora's ruling as the word of God on earth and set out to follow her advice. Shifra made an appointment at Arkhipova's ballet studio. She nudged Jenka to come with them. The teacher was Russian; he should speak fluent Russian with her. After all, Shifra's Russian was rusty. He should come dressed in uniform so the teacher would see his rank.

"I don't intend to come."

"You have time for work. Even in the middle of the night, you get up and call Munya. You drag him out of bed and talk to him loudly for hours. I don't know how he agrees."

"I'll check when I have free time," said Jenka, exhausted.

"The ballet teacher already set a date, and you better be there. Are you Ruth's father or not?"

On the scheduled day, he shaved and came home early from work to drive Shifra and Ruth to the ballet teacher's studio at 33 Masada Street in Hadar HaCarmel. It was the first time Ruth saw a dance studio. There was a wood floor, wooden barres along the walls, and a grand piano. Jenka spoke to the teacher in Russian and explained that they had come to her on the recommendation of the dancer Ora Ratner, wife of Professor Yohanan Ratner. To his surprise, not only was she unfazed by the professor's name, but she didn't even know who Ora Ratner was.

Arkhipova raised her hand dismissively as if expressing that such a dancer wasn't worth her attention, "Maybe she belongs to Gertrude Kraus's company or perhaps she's one of those modern, expressionist style dancers from central Europe."

Jenka and Shifra had no idea who Gertrude Krauss was and didn't know the difference between ballet and modern dance.

Shifra courageously cut into the discussion. "We don't understand dance, but Ora and Professor Ratner believe that Ruth has talent."

Arkhipova looked straight at the girl's parents.

"I know prodigies. Over the years, the prodigy disappears, and the girl remains," interrupted the ballet teacher with a self-important air. And so, Ruth became Arkhipova's student.

*

As the experiments at Institute 3 became more complex, the narrow coastal strip on the sea that had served as their testing site no longer sufficed, and they started to hold tests in the Negev desert in the south of Israel.

Lieutenant Colonel Aharonchik was responsible for all testing matters, and he designed a master plan for the future testing site. Elyashiv Shacham, an institute member and a geologist, knew the Negev very well and determined that the most suitable place for the site was a plain surrounded by hills on which viewpoints could be positioned.

Jenka liked going to experiment in the Negev. He would wear khaki shorts, a white short-sleeve shirt with buttons, a khaki hat, and closed shoes. The joint pain he suffered from in the humid Carmel and during the heatwaves disappeared in the dry air.

In the Negev, he would wake up every morning full of energy and shout, "Why aren't you all ready?" During the tests, everyone knew their role, and when each test was done, they would all walk down to the valley to review the results on-site. They collected the scattered pieces from which they learned whether the artillery fuses had exploded and if they hadn't, then why? It was also essential to pick up everything so sightseers wouldn't come upon dangerous materials. Sometimes they didn't find all the parts. In those cases, they trusted the Bedouins would find them and put them up for sale at the weekly market in Be'er Sheva, the capital city of the Negev, where institute representatives would wait to purchase them.

On the way back from the tests in the Negev, everyone would call their wives at home to let them know everything was fine and to ask how they were and how the children were. The wives were always curious about what time of night their husbands were expected to arrive home. Jenka didn't call and didn't understand why the others did. He told Shifra, and she replied, "You don't need to call. I don't have any secret admirers. You'll always come home and find me asleep under the covers."

*

Lieutenant Colonel Avraham Levi, the deputy project chief of Jenka's department, completed Jenka personality-wise. He was a good compromiser, had excellent problem-solving skills, and was always in good spirits. About one month before a vital experiment in the Negev, Aharonchik entered Avraham's office in a frenzy.

"The date scheduled for the tests falls on the 13th of the month. What if Jenka refuses to come?"

Aharonchik knew that Avraham Levi always bent over backward so that no tests would fall on the 13th, but this time something had gone wrong, and the problematic date had gotten the better of him.

"We'll change the date," Avraham hissed between his teeth and picked up the phone to inform Jenka. Aharonchik hastened to stop his hand, "This experiment cannot be postponed. Additional troops are taking part in it. We coordinated months in advance. There's no way I'm informing the other troops that the experiment is being postponed because Jenka is superstitious."

Avraham Levi, who knew Jenka extremely well, pondered for a few seconds before opening Jenka's daily planner, in which each day appeared on a separate page. He flipped ahead to the following month until he reached the 13th. Avraham lifted his head and looked Aharonchik in the eyes. Aharonchik nodded in consensus, and Avraham tore out the pages. Then he cut several papers to exactly the size of the diary's pages, punched holes on one side, and threaded them in, replacing the missing pages but conveniently skipping the 13th of the month.

They both inhaled deeply, praying Jenka wouldn't discover the ruse before the experiment.

When the designated day arrived, Jenka decided to take Ruth with him. They got up while it was still dark outside, and Shifra made them sandwiches for the road. At the entrance to the Institute, a caravan of command cars was waiting. Jenka sat in the first command car next to the driver, with Ruth beside him. When the caravan arrived at the appointed site in the Negev, they saw that the testing team, run by Aharonchik, had prepared large military tents ahead of time. The camp consisted of a tent for storage and test analysis that was equipped with cameras, a tent for sleeping, a kitchen tent, and a tent with two long wooden tables and matching benches.

Ruth got bored during the experiment. She went to the kitchen tent where they were preparing lunch. They were cooking chicken soup, a meat stew, mashed potatoes, and chopping vegetables for a salad, haphazardly throwing the skins into a large garbage bin surrounded by buzzing flies. At mealtime, everyone sat down at the long wooden tables. Moshe Ritterband, who was responsible for conducting the test, handed Ruth a bowl of soup and sat down next to her.

Ruth was pleased. Her mother didn't make soup at home because it was expensive to buy chicken. She ate heartily until a fly fell into her bowl.

"Why aren't you eating?" Moshe asked.

"There's a fly in my soup," the girl replied in disgust.

Moshe chuckled and picked the fly out.

"I won't eat soup that had a fly in it," Ruth declared.

"This is good soup. It will make you strong. When I was a kid in the camps in Germany, I dreamed of a piece of bread. Soup was unimaginable, with or without flies."

"You can pour out the soup," she said, about to stand up.

Moshe grabbed her hand. "We don't throw away food," he said decisively.

"My mother says we don't throw away bread, but she never said anything about soup with a dead fly in it," Ruth answered him.

"Don't throw away food!"

She couldn't ignore the determination in his eyes and the perseverance in his voice. Ruth picked up her spoon and ate the soup, grimacing with disgust, pretending to vomit, and enjoying that everyone at the table was looking at her. When she saw her father approaching in the distance, her performance quickly came to a close, and she hurried to finish the soup as if nothing had happened.

The test was a success, and Elyashiv took Jenka and Ruth for a jeep ride in the desert. Holding a camera, Jenka scanned the landscape through the lens, telling Elyashiv exactly where to stop so that he could capture the best lighting. Ruth jumped out of the jeep, quickly climbed the hill, and stood upright, motionless, facing the sun with her eyes closed.

Elyashiv was amazed. "You raised your daughter well," he said, observing her perfect posture.

Jenka nodded his head with pride.

"Why are you photographing Ruth on the hilltop? You can't see her face."

"I need someone to function as a scale to compare the height," Jenka explained.

"Now I see why you brought your daughter to the Negev," chuckled Elyashiv.

"Next time, I'll put you up on the hill," Jenka said, and Elyashiv stopped laughing. He knew Jenka meant it.

From the hilltop, Ruth shouted, "Take the picture already!"

"Don't move!" yelled her father. Only when he was satisfied with the composition he'd created of the girl and the hill did he bundle on follow-up instructions: "Open your eyes! Raise your head! Move half a step to the right! That's too far! A little further back! Smile!" Then he clicked the shutter button.

*

In the mid-1950s, there was a rise in terrorist acts committed by the Palestinian *fedayeen*. In March 1954, a bus left Eilat for Tel Aviv carrying eleven men, women, and children and four IDF soldiers serving as security guards. As the bus slowly wove up and down the steep winding roads of Ma'ale Ha'aqrabim in the Negev desert, terrorists boarded the bus and started shooting, killing all of the passengers. A nine-year-old boy and his five-year-old sister hid underneath the bodies. After the terrorists got off the bus, the boy stood up, called to his sister, and asked, "Are they gone?" One of the terrorists heard his voice, ran back, and shot him in the head.

Israel's political position in the world was in the dumps. In 1955, a conference was held in Bandung, Indonesia, with many African and Asian countries in attendance. Their goal was to wage war against colonialism and build economic and cultural cooperation among themselves. Israel was barred from participating. One of the keynote speakers was the mufti of Jerusalem, Hajj Amin al-Husseini, who had been in contact with Eichmann during the Second World War and had encouraged him to exterminate the Jews of Europe and to occupy Palestine and eradicate the Jewish settlement. The conference sided with the Arabs in the Arab-Israeli conflict. Over in Egypt, Nasser forged major deals to purchase state-of-the-art weapons from the Soviet Union, nationalized the Suez Canal Company, and blocked the narrow passage between the islands at the entrance to the Red Sea, called the Strait of Tiran. This meant that Israeli ships sailing from Africa and the far east couldn't pass to the port in Eilat.

In October 1956, Operation Kadesh, or the Sinai Campaign, began. British and French forces took control of the Suez Canal, while the Israeli army occupied Sinai and made their way to the canal. Israel's hopes that Sinai would be demilitarized after the operation dissolved but the United States of America and the Soviet Union demanded that Israel vacate the Sinai Peninsula, using threats. The Soviets went as far as to sever their relations with Israel. The operation resulted in a shift in Israel's approach to weapons development. Two years later, in September 1958, Ben-Gurion decided to turn the Research and Design Directorate into the Rafael Armaments Development Authority, or Rafael for short. No one disputed Rafael's vocation to carry out large projects at the forefront of innovation this time. And Jenka was promoted to the rank of colonel.

Many outstanding young engineers joined Rafael, among them Eliezer Gon, Reuven Eshel, and Saadia Bahat. During one of Ben-Gurion's routine visits to Rafael, Saadia's name came up.

"I would like to meet with Saadia," Ben-Gurion said, his mane of white hair fluttering in the wind. "I have a dream that one day there will be a Yemenite Commander in Chief, and perhaps your Saadia is the man for the job." No one said a word.

Saadia was called over, a short, light-skinned young man. "Your name is Saadia?" Ben-Gurion asked, unconvinced.

"Yes, that's my name."

"You don't look Yemenite."

"I was born in Lithuania."

"Why did your parents name you Saadia?"

"I don't know."

"Aren't you curious as to why they gave you a Yemenite name?"

"Even if I wanted to ask, it isn't possible. My parents perished in the Holocaust."

"I'm sorry to hear that," said Ben-Gurion and left feeling utterly dispirited.

Chapter 17: A Special Gift

Once a year, Jenka went for some rest and relaxation in Safed, a city on Mount Canaan, in the Galilee, known for its fresh, clean air. Along the road to the mountain top, dozens of small hotels and guesthouses grew side by side like trees. Even in the austerity years, vacationers were served cream for breakfast and dined on a portion of meat or fish daily. Shifra disliked going with Jenka on these recuperative trips. She used to claim she had nowhere to leave the children, and eventually, he stopped asking her. When Ruth reached the age of sixteen, Shifra suggested that he take the girl with him. Unlike twelve-year-old Dani and nine-year-old Michal, who were very attached to Shifra and rarely spoke to their father, Ruth was deemed "Jenka's girl" and considered "similar to him." She didn't see how she resembled her father, but it flattered her, nonetheless.

Jenka had a regular hotel that he went to every year on Mount Canaan. This time he rented two adjacent rooms with a connecting door between them. Around dinner, before sunset, the main street in Mount Canaan would fill with vacationers going for short walks, dressed in their best clothes, sauntering slowly, chitchatting about this and that. Jenka and Ruth followed a pair of giggling women who were walking arm in arm. From time to time, one of the women would turn her head to look at them.

"What do you think of her?" Jenka asked.

"What should I think of her?" Ruth wondered.

"Don't you think that she's extremely beautiful?"

"Beautiful? She's ugly." Ruth didn't know why she said what she said. She actually thought that the woman was quite pretty, a classic, natural beauty, with no makeup on. Since when did her father look at women?

At night, Jenka and Ruth each went to sleep in their respective rooms. Jenka got under his blanket wearing a long nightshirt, a nightcap to warm his bald head, and woolly socks so his feet wouldn't get cold. In the morning, Ruth entered her father's room and saw that he was already wide awake, puttering around the room, still in his nightgown.

"Did you see anything odd at night?" he asked.

"No."

"Something really embarrassing happened," he said, making an innocent childish face.

"What happened?"

"Do you remember the woman you said was ugly? I found her in my bed at night."

"Really?" Ruth opened her eyes in surprise.

"What was she doing there?"

"I do not know."

"What did she want from you?"

"I do not know."

"So, what did you do?"

"I chased her out of bed and knocked on wood three times as if she were a black cat."

Ruth believed him, and they laughed together.

The following day they went to Kibbutz Ginosar Beach at the Sea of Galilee. In her bathing suit, Ruth stood on the rounded stones that stuck out of the water, and Jenka photographed her, demanding that she turn her face to the sun, not blink, smile, not move, and she obediently did what she was told. On the way home, the conversation shifted to Jenka's travels in India and, from there, to the Hindu belief in reincarnation.

"I would wish to be an eagle," said her father in complete seriousness.

"Why an eagle?"

"It's a big, strong bird that can fly far, view the landscape from above, soar wherever it wants. It has no foes in the sky."

Back home, when Shifra was with Ruth cooking in the kitchen, she asked her daughter, without turning toward her, "Did your father meet some woman at the hotel?"

"No. Of course not!" answered Ruth, and Shifra continued to cook, brooding.

*

"Shdema," Rafael's official testing range, managed by Aharonchik, was established in the Meishar Valley in the Negev. In one of the experiments, Moya Epstein, head of the Luz Project, a powerful surface-to-surface missile, asked Jenka to design the part of a bomb called the 'warhead,' where the explosive materials and the fuse that activates them are found. A problem arose when the missile fell too close to its launch point. They had to go over to the missile and detonate it, so it wouldn't pose a danger to tourists hiking in the Negev. Jenka sat in a jeep beside Elyashiv Shacham, who knew the area very well. He raced the jeep over the rugged terrain, ascended hills, and descended into wadis. The jeep bounced and creaked as if it was about to fall apart. Sometimes, it seemed as if it were about to turn upside down. Jenka's eyes drank in the wild desert landscape thirstily, and when they reached the warhead, they detonated it.

During another experiment, they tried to test the warhead's strength. The team fired the missile toward a cliff, but yet again, it didn't explode. Jenka and Elyashiv rushed to the ridge and discovered the undetonated missile near the bottom.

Jenka grabbed a rope and started running to the cliff, shouting, "I'll start heading down."

Elyashiv looked at him anxiously. "Come back up. You're long past the age of twenty."

Jenka, who was already nearing the cliff's edge, said, "You mean I'm already half dead?"

Elyashiv followed him up and when they reached the top of the cliff, they saw where the shell was stuck. It was lodged in an alcove several yards further down. Elyashiv lowered the rope that Jenka, hanging in the air, was tied to. Jenka reached the missile, disassembled it, and put the fuse into the large side bag he was carrying before Elyashiv carefully pulled the rope back up. They returned to camp, their eyes gleaming with excitement. Elyashiv told the team how Jenka had submitted himself, like a baby, and agreed to be let down, hanging from a rope. He even exaggerated a bit and said that baby Jenka sang in Russian all the way down.

That evening, he told them about his motorcycle travels. "Sitting here together, it's fascinating to speak with you, Jenka. Why do you usually avoid people?"

He had never been asked such a question before. "I try to stay away from human-related issues," he explained. "I have very little patience for all kinds of things that are unfortunately extremely common in this country and drive me crazy. I thought the best possible service I could provide was to stick to the job myself and inspire the people working with me to do the same, without bringing in personal problems."

After successful tests, Elyashiv would take Jenka on jeep rides to remote spots in the desert that Jenka immortalized with his camera.

Kikion, the manager of Rafael's Mathematics center, took the initiative and developed Jenka's photographs of the Negev landscape to 35 cm x 50 cm. He then glued them onto wooden placards and decorated the walls of his office. Everyone at Rafael was jealous and wanted copies of the photos, too. Jenka and the photographer Yossi Sternberg were enlisted to carry out the assignment. They spent numerous hours of overtime, working into the night in the dark room. When the photos were ready, all the departments at Rafael competed against each other to decorate their walls with photographs of the Negev.

*

During geography class at the Reali high school in Beit Biram on the Carmel, Ilana, the teacher, showed the class a map of Africa. She lectured about the mountains, the rivers, the mines, the tribes, the climate, the new countries that had formed, and at the end, she mentioned in passing, "that once upon a time there were tribes in Africa that ate human flesh."

Ruth raised her hand. The teacher gave her permission to speak. She stood up and said, "There were still cannibals in Africa twenty-five years ago."

Ilana was astonished and asked, "How do you know that?" her voice dripping with disdain.

"I know because they almost ate my father."

The other students, even the ones who were dozing, lifted their heads, interested.

"What do you mean by almost ate? That they only ate his arm? His leg?" The teacher snickered.

Ruth took a deep breath so as not to lose her temper and confidently responded, "He was already in the pot, but when the savages saw how thin he was, they threw him back out."

Silence reigned in the classroom. They had never heard such a tale. Had an African tribe almost eaten the father of a girl from their class?

"It isn't true. It's a story your father told you before bed," the teacher's voice softened.

Then, Avi Brosh, who sat behind Ruth in class, stood up and, without asking the teacher for permission to speak, declared, "Ruth is telling the truth. My father knows Ruth's father. They were in the motorcycle club together, and Ruth's father's expedition was published in the newspaper. If Ruth says that they almost ate her father, then they almost ate him."

The teacher was suddenly less confident in her resolve. Ruth was a quiet, dreamy student, but Avi Brosh was an outstanding pupil and shouldn't be underestimated.

The teacher pursed her lips, batted her eyelids, and ran her hand over her hair, muttering quietly, "I didn't know that twenty-five years ago there were still cannibals in Africa."

That evening, as her father ate his oatmeal porridge, Ruth told her family what had happened in class, "...And the stupid teacher said it was just a story that my father made up to tell his daughter before bed."

Jenka stopped eating the porridge, pressed his lips together, and raised his eyebrows as if caught in a lie and wondering what to do. He waited a bit, turned to Ruth, bent his head, and said, "I plead guilty. I invented the story."

Ruth cried out, upset, "I believed you!" Her face contorted in pain, she couldn't control her emotions, she hit the table with all her strength, the bowl of porridge flew to the floor, broke, and the porridge scattered everywhere. Ruth ran to her room and locked herself inside.

*

The alumni of the Reali school's third graduating class decided to throw a reunion. They combined the event with the 80th birthday celebrations of Dr. Biram, the founder of the school and its first principal. The party was hosted by Professor David Ehrlich, who was Chief of Surgery at Rambam Hospital, the biggest hospital in Haifa. His home had enough space to comfortably accommodate all sixteen members of the class along with their spouses. A white tablecloth was spread over the living room table and scattered on it were colorful bowls designed by Maskit and produced by Mizrahi immigrants containing peanuts and sunflower seeds. There were also two large dishes of chopped salad, and trays holding small sandwiches and fresh seasonal fruit. In the center of the table was a giant birthday cake with the words "Happy 80th Birthday" written on it in frosting. When Dr. Biram entered the room, everyone clapped excitedly. They cleared a path to the cushioned armchair they'd prepared for him. He walked erect, with no cane, reaching out to shake the hands of alumni who introduced themselves and animatedly guessing the names of others. They hadn't expected this. Many of them had elderly parents, who were shut up in their homes, had difficulty walking, and needed help eating and constant care. Everyone agreed that he had an extraordinary character, even those who'd never liked him back in the day at school.

As the party was coming to a close, Jenka cleared his throat, "I have an announcement to make. I have a special gift for Dr. Biram."

They all knew Jenka and were surprised. "You brought a gift? Have you become polite since we last saw you?"

He pulled a small box out of his big old bag. "Can anyone guess what's in the box?"

"Perhaps a wood carving of Dr. Biram?" suggested Yardena Cohen, a famous dancer known for producing and performing in open-air holiday shows at kibbutzim. She was wearing an embroidered Bedouin dress and silver bracelets, and her red hair flowed freely down her back. Leah Kessel, a piano teacher, came up to Jenka, tapped on the box, and noted that it was made of simple cardboard, so how impressive could they really expect the gift to be?

Jenka ceremoniously handed the box to Dr. Biram, who had trouble opening it.

"Let me help you." David Ehrlich took the box, removed the wrapping paper with the precise motion of an experienced surgeon, opened the box carefully, and pulled out the small contents as if he were extracting a stone from a patient's kidney.

"What is it?" asked Dr. Biram.

"It's an electric bell," Jenka explained.

"A bell?" Dr. Biram wondered aloud.

Jenka smiled mischievously. "Do you remember when the school bell disappeared?"

"The police never solved the theft," murmured Dr. Biram.

Jenka stood up straight, prepared to deliver the critical information. "I am guilty of the heinous deed."

Dr. Biram looked at him. "I don't understand. Why ever did you steal the bell?"

Jenka flinched with embarrassment. He wore an expression like that of an actor playing someone displeased. "I don't like to admit it, but the bell annoyed me because it reminded me that I had to get up every morning to go to school."

Dr. Biram didn't let him off so easy, "So, where is the original bell?"

Jenka took out a photograph from his old brown bag. In the picture, a young man sat in a small boat in the middle of a river with a triumphant look.

"Here's the bell before I threw it into the Kishon river."

The room was silent for a moment, but the astonished Dr. Biram soon came to his senses, stood up, and continued with the investigation. "Who took your photo?"

This time it was Professor Ehrlich's turn to writhe in discomfort, and about to burst with laughter, he admitted, "I'm the second delinquent, the one who documented the drowning of the bell."

*

In 1959, Jenka received the Israel Defense Prize together with Michael Shor from Military Industries. He arrived at the ceremony clean-shaven, in an ironed uniform, with shiny polished insignias, and Shifra and Ruth by his side. At the reception, Ben-Gurion approached the seventeen-year-old Ruth, "So you're Jenka's daughter? What grade are you in?"

"I go to the Reali school and am about to finish 11th grade." Jenka stood straighter when he saw that Ben-Gurion was showing interest in his daughter.

"What are your plans for the future?"

"I want to be a dancer." Jenka held his breath.

"I saw a dance performance by Martha Graham, when she visited Israel." Jenka and Shifra had never heard the name. "I also saw an Indian dancer named Shanta Rao. Batsheva de Rothschild, the producer of Graham's dance company, insisted that I see her performance and even wrote me a letter afterward asking my opinion. I admit that I didn't understand it one bit." Ben-Gurion lifted his head and looked Jenka in the eyes. "Very interesting that you have a daughter who wants to be a dancer."

On May 29th, *Ha'aretz* newspaper quoted Ben-Gurion's words: "I am sure that we will not fall behind large nations whom with we cannot compete when it comes to the large sums spent on serious weapons that cost a great deal of money... But I believe we will not fall behind them in our intellectual and innovative abilities because science also requires, apart from reason, creative imagination."

Davar newspaper also quoted the prime minister: "Perhaps this notable prize is owed to those who work in defense science because they accomplish feats the scope of which are unknown to the public, and that merits special recognition."

Chapter 18: Father and Son

It was 1967. Dr. Ben Zion Ratner sat for hours in the living room of his home in Kharkiv, his eyes glued to the TV screen, watching Soviet news broadcast on the war that had broken out between Israel and the armies of Syria, Egypt, and Jordan. He heard Arab spokesmen announcing their intentions to destroy the Zionist state of the Jewish people. He was horrified.

"They aren't even willing to mention the name 'Israel,'" he told Sofia, his wife, who sat beside him.

"I know you are worried about Jenka." Every so often, she took his hand her hers, attempting to comfort and support him.

"I devoted my best and strongest years to communism. I chose it over my only son. And now, my country supports the Arabs. We learned in the Holocaust that when someone threatens to destroy Israel, it must be taken seriously."

Sofia nodded her head in agreement. "Jenka is already 58 years old; he's too old to be a combat soldier," she reassured him.

"Turn off the television. I cannot listen to my country announce the severance of their relationship with what they call the 'criminal' state."

Within six days, the Israeli army had run the Egyptian army out of Sinai and reached the Suez Canal, regained control of the Golan Heights on the northern border with Syria, drove off the Jordanian military from the east, and liberated East Jerusalem, which had fallen into Jordanian hands during the War of Independence. There was a sense of historical closure, and the people of Israel prayed and blew the shofar near the Western Wall, all that was left of the ancient Second Temple. The Israeli government offered to return the occupied territories in exchange for peace. Yet, at the Arab League summit in Khartoum, in which eight Arab countries participated, it was resolved that there would be no peace with Israel, no recognition of Israel, no negotiations with Israel, and insistence on the rights of the Palestinian refugees to return to Israel. With no peace treaty in place, religious Zionists began to settle the West Bank – the lands of Judea and Samaria from the time of the Bible. As the magnitude of Israel's victory became apparent, the hate and defamation of Israel on Soviet TV only increased. Ben Zion's apprehension turned into relief and pride. But he also felt alienated from the Soviet Union and gained a sense of belonging to Israel.

Friends started coming by Ben Zion's apartment; Jews who hid their ethnicity from the public. They felt the need to speak about what was happening, to stop being "the Jews of silence." Meetings were also being held secretly in the homes of other Jews. In the past, they'd never dared to do such a thing. Feelings of strength and courage began to grow in them. A group of Jews sent a letter to the Supreme Soviet demanding to be permitted to immigrate. More and more groups of Jewish people requested to leave the Soviet Union. Around the world, Jews and non-Jews alike held demonstrations demanding that Jews receive the right to immigrate, carrying banners and signs that read "Let My People Go." The Soviet Union denied the applicants and fired them from their jobs; some were even thrown in jail, where they held hunger strikes.

"By the time the Soviet Union allows Jews to leave, if they ever allow it at all, I will already be in the next life," Ben Zion muttered to himself after returning from one of the meetings. He sank into his armchair, exhausted.

"Perhaps you can try and meet with Jenka," suggested Sofia.

"What do you mean?"

"I mean, don't sit around waiting until the Soviets succumb to the pressure. Instead, you can submit a request to meet with your only son in another country, in Paris, for example." Her eyes lit up as the name of the city left her mouth. "It will be the dying request of an old man, a Russian patriot, a senior member of the party who devoted his whole life to his country, asking to meet with his son one last time before he dies."

"I'll think about it." He looked at her affectionately, "You take care of me. You're a good woman," he said, and Sofia chuckled.

Ben Zion picked up the phone and called the home of Professor Sergei Kaminsky, the director of the hospital where he'd worked until his retirement. Sergei picked up the phone, surprised to hear Ben Zion's voice on the other end. He'd always liked Dr. Ben Zion, who'd been an attending brain surgeon at his hospital for many years. Still, their relationship had tapered off over the past few years.

"I would like to speak to you about a personal matter," declared Ben Zion; he always got straight to the point, skipping the opening pleasantries.

Sofia stood beside him, pleased that he was finally following through with her idea. "Send my regards to Natasha," she whispered to him.

"Wait one moment," I'll check with Natasha. They heard Natasha's voice in the background saying, "Invite them over this weekend."

"We would be happy to host you at our house this weekend," said Sergei kindly, repeating his wife's words.

The next weekend, Sofia supported her husband's arm as she and Ben Zion climbed the stairs to the second floor of the building where Sergei lived. Natasha opened the door, embraced them, showed them to the small sitting room, and ushered Ben Zion to the large armchair by the window. When Sergei entered the room, Ben Zion tried to stand up in his honor, but Sergei murmured, "Sit, sit. No need to make a fuss."

Natasha served cookies and hot tea, and they conversed politely about this and that.

Sergei sat up straight. "What did you want to speak to me about?" he asked in the matter-of-fact tone of a manager with limited time.

"It's a personal matter. May I speak to you in private?" Ben Zion turned to face Natasha, fearing that she would be offended.

"It's fine," replied Sergei. Natasha, who'd grown up during the communist regime, understood, didn't argue and hastened to exit the room. Sofia followed her out.

Ben Zion and Sergei were alone. Sergei was prepared to listen and waited to hear his friend's request but saw that Ben Zion was looking at the ceiling, studying the room.

"There is no one eavesdropping. At least I hope not," whispered Sergei. He stood up, walked to the cabinet, pulled out a record of the opera "Rigoletto," and placed it on the victrola. "This is my favorite opera, beautifully performed by our Bolshoi Theater," he said and walked back to sit with Ben Zion.

"I heard that you are going to participate in a medical conference in Paris," said Ben Zion, and Sergei nodded in the affirmative. "Then, I've got a request for you, and if you refuse, I will understand."

"What do you need?"

Ben Zion took a deep breath and said, "I'm sure you've heard about the war in Israel."

"Since the war, several doctors, whom I wouldn't have believed were Jews, announced that they were Jewish and defended Israel during discussions in the doctors' lounge. Two of them even submitted immigration applications. I had to fire them, of course."

"I have a son in Israel. My only son. He's named Jenka. The last time I saw him, he was thirteen years old. He immigrated to Mandatory Palestine in 1922 with his grandfather. I refused to leave the Soviet Union. I was a Bolshevik patriot."

Sergei smiled. "What do you want from me?" Ben Zion detected a hint of discomfort in Sergei's voice.

"I don't know how much longer I have left to live. I want to see my son before I die." Ben Zion's voice shook with emotion, and his eyes filled with tears. "Jenka was orphaned by his mother at age five. I dragged him all around Russia while I served as a doctor for the Red Army. I was hard on him. I married for the second time in the twilight of my life, but Sofia and I have no children. Jenka is my only son." Ben Zion went quiet. He pressed his lips together as if he were ashamed of the intensity of his emotions.

Sergei put a hand on Ben Zion's shoulder, trying to calm him down and show him that he understood.

"If you agree," whispered Ben Zion, "I will give you a short letter and ask that if you meet a doctor from Israel at the conference, you give him the letter and ask him to find my son. I have an old address for Jenka, but I don't know if it's up to date."

"How will he find him?"

"He will, Israel is an extremely small country," Ben Zion elaborated.

Sergei fell silent.

"I know it's risky." Ben Zion looked deep into Sergei's eyes. "If you refuse, I will understand."

Sergei looked pensive.

"I am asking you as a father. You also have just one child."

"Give me the letter." Sergei stood up and quickly hid the letter between the pages of a book from his library.

*

Jenka picked up the phone.

"Dr. Yoram Klein here. Have I reached Jenka Ratner?"

"Speaking." Jenka felt uneasy. His work in the defense field had made him a cautious man.

"I've finally found you. I can't convey how long I've been looking for you and what investigations I had to undergo to obtain your phone number. It's all confidential."

"What do you need?" Jenka asked matter-of-factly.

"I was at a doctors' conference in Paris, and a well-known professor, the director of a hospital in Kharkiv, approached me and secretly passed me a letter his friend had given him for me to pass on to you."

"Who is the letter from?"

"I don't know. I can't read Russian." Jenka's heart skipped a beat.

"Listen, Jenka. I see from your phone number that you live in Haifa or its vicinity. I can bring you the letter if you give me your address."

Jenka was hesitant. "We can meet tomorrow at seven o'clock in the evening at the entrance to Moriah Cinema." To be polite, he added, "if that's alright with you. And I thank you, of course."

"That works for me. I'm free tomorrow evening. I know the movie theater."

The next day they met outside Moriah Cinema, and Dr. Klein handed Jenka the letter. Jenka saw his father's handwriting on the envelope. He rushed to the wooden street bench, which stood under a lamppost in the public park near the movie theater. He opened the letter and realized that his hands were shaking.

My dear son Jenka,

I hope my letter has reached you safely and that you and your family are well. Not a day goes by that I don't think about you since we were forced to cut off our correspondence due to political constraints. There isn't a day that I don't try to imagine what you look like and what my grandchildren look like.

About a decade ago, I married Sofia Romanovna, a psychologist, widowed by her husband several years earlier. She has no children from her first marriage, so you are our only son.

I am already 80 years old. My life has been full of action, hopes, and disappointments, but the thought that I will die before I see you again is difficult for me to bear.

It's been many years since I last heard from you, and I have no idea if you'd even want to, and if you can find the time, to meet me in some European city. For example, Paris. I shall be extremely happy if you consent, and I will apply for a visa.

Maybe they won't refuse an old man like me, who just wants to meet his only son whom he hasn't seen for 45 years.

Father, Ben Zion

Jenka's eyes filled with tears, and he let them fall. He felt his chest fill with intense longing, bound to the same longing his father felt all those thousands of miles away from him. He read the letter over and over again, trying to interpret what wasn't written down, what lay between the lines. He was aware of how careful they had to be with the written word in the Soviet Union and how unnecessary details had to be omitted in case the letter reached the hands of the KGB. Then, he carefully folded the letter, inserted it into the envelope, went home, told Shifra, and sat down to compose a letter to his father.

Dear Father,

I've been hoping to hear from you for a long time. I'm glad you're healthy and happy that you remarried and aren't lonely. I've been dreaming of meeting with you for years. Paris is an excellent choice. I can arrange to arrive on any date that suits you.

If you need money for the trip, I can buy you a ticket or two if you can bring Sofia, whom I would love to meet. I will do everything conceivable to ensure that we can see one another.

Attached is a photo of your grandchildren, Ruth, Danny, and Michal.

Your son,

Jenka

Over the next two years, Ben Zion submitted numerous applications for a visa. He filled out forms from the Ministry of the Interior, from his former workplace at the hospital, from the communist party, and underwent personal investigations. When he turned 83, he finally obtained the visa, and he and Jenka set a departure date and reserved a hotel in Paris. Sofia was unable to acquire a visa. About a week before Jenka's flight to Paris, he received a letter from Sofia.

Dear Jenka,

I have difficult news, and I hope it reaches you before you leave for Paris. Ben Zion, your dear father and my beloved husband, has passed away from a stroke. He died quickly and didn't suffer. During his final days, he was busy getting ready to meet you in Paris, which filled him with great joy.

Your father spoke of you with so much love and longing over the years. Although we haven't met, I feel you are my son, too.

Sofia Ratner

The struggle of the Jews in the Soviet Union for the freedom of immigration and the help of demonstrations by thousands of students and citizens resonated internationally. In 1970, the same year Ben Zion died, the gates were opened for Jewish immigration. Over that decade, 200,000 Jews immigrated to Israel from the Soviet Union. If Ben Zion had still been alive, he would have been able to immigrate to Israel under the "Law of Return," which states that every Jew can receive Israeli citizenship. He would have also been able to bring Sofia with him, even though she wasn't Jewish. Jenka continued to correspond with Sofia and made sure to send her money every month until the day she died.

*

About one year after the Six-Day War, a new position, called "Rafael Consultant," was created for Jenka. He knew he didn't belong with the new generation of sophisticated projects full of electronics, computers, and electro-optics, and the new job allowed him to choose what assignments he wanted to work on for himself. Following the heavy losses to Israeli tanks during the Yom Kippur War, Jenka promoted an idea initially presented by a German researcher named Manfred Held, who'd tried to convince the Germans to develop a reactive armor, an undertaking that many countries had rejected in the past. Jenka designed the mechanical part of the reactive armor, covering the tank with square brackets. The squares were assembled like a sandwich: two steel tiles with a thin layer of a unique explosive substance between them. When the tank is attacked, the explosives in the sandwich detonate, counteracting the fiery jet of the attacking missile and neutralizing its penetration. In the First Lebanon War, the reactive armor proved beneficial, and the American army also decided to protect their armored vehicles with the newly tried technology. During the war, an Israeli tank fell into Syrian hands, and a few years later, the Russian army's tanks were covered with reactive armor, too.

After finishing the complicated project, Jenka felt tired, physically and mentally. He liked to rest at Shdema, the testing range in the Negev desert. His good friend Elyashiv, who had become the range manager, gave Jenka his bed and slept beside him on a field bed or a mattress on the floor. In the mornings, Jenka would join in the experiments, and in the afternoons, Elyashiv would drive Jenka, equipped with his camera, in a jeep to secret spots that only a true Negev man would know. Sometimes he and Elyashiv would walk to the ridge at the southeastern end of Shdema's northern station. Jenka would gaze at the Negev landscape spread out before him and close his eyes.

"After I die, I dream of being an eagle in the sky and being able to view the entire landscape like a map below me. If possible, I wish to be buried here." Elyashiv nodded his head.

*

Jenka decided the time had come to exercise his rights and use all the vacation days he'd accumulated to take a sabbatical leave and bring Shifra on an extended trip around the world. He booked expensive hotels so that she could get a taste of the good life. And after asking friends what the most prestigious cosmetics company in Paris was, he called the head branch of "Elizabeth Arden" and scheduled a facial for Shifra. While on a stroll around the city, he led her to Place Vendôme, where she saw the storefronts of the leading fashion houses and most expensive jewelry shops in France.

"I have a surprise for you," he informed her.

"A surprise?"

"I booked you a treatment at 'Elizabeth Arden.'"

"Really?" She could see that he was pleased that she was surprised.

"How much does the treatment cost?" she asked, both curious and apprehensive.

"One doesn't ask the price at places like this," Jenka answered as if scolding a child who asked the wrong question.

They entered a grand hall, which had a gigantic glass chandelier hanging from the center of the ceiling. There were elegant sitting areas along the walls with round tables embellished by gilded trim and chairs upholstered in velvet, standing on thin, rounded legs. Shifra eyed the well-dressed women who sat sipping coffee. She noticed their expensive clothes, shoes and purses in matching colors, diamond rings, and pearl necklaces. Behind the reception desk stood beautiful young women dressed in black uniforms, who greeted them with a smile.

"I wonder who paid for all this extravagance," Shifra muttered under her breath, and Jenka frowned, rebuking her.

"I brought you to an establishment that most women can only dream of entering. Please behave as is expected of a proper European lady."

He approached the reception desk to announce their arrival. Shifra followed him hesitantly, feeling like a country girl who'd come to see the Queen of England. A young woman with a shapely body and light hair led Shifra down the corridor, on the walls of which hung photographs of famous women expressing gratitude for their incredible treatments.

During the facial, the cosmetician, speaking English with a heavy French accent, explained to Shifra, "Madame has neglected her skin for many years." Shifra nodded her head in agreement.

"Is there anything to be done?" Shifra asked in English.

"I will make a list of ointments for the Madame to purchase so that your skin will look young again," she answered delicately. Then she escorted Shifra back to the grand hall.

Jenka saw them, stood up, and walked quickly to the counter before Shifra could beat him to it.

The cosmetician took out dozens of boxes of different sizes, "These are the ointments the Madame needs," she said, smiling at Jenka. Before Shifra could say a word, Jenka declared, "I'll buy them all." Even when he heard the price, he didn't bat an eyelid, and like a knight, prepared to sacrifice his life for his beloved, he paid the full amount. They left with Jenka carrying a heavy bag full of parcels on his arm. Shifra didn't speak to him all the way to the hotel.

When they entered their room, she ambushed him, shouting, "How could you waste such a large amount of money without asking me?"

"I've always told you that you have the most beautiful legs, but what can I say? Your face is the face of a 57-year-old woman." He moved closer to her face, scrutinizing her wrinkles.

"And why exactly do you think I have wrinkles? Did you ever do anything for our family?"

"I finally bought you a gift, and this is how you repay me?"

"When did you learn to buy gifts anyway?"

"I admit. I don't know how, but I've decided to try," he said, nodding his head.

"You're wasting money on nonsense." She emptied the bag onto the bed, and the boxes scattered to and fro. "All these years, you gave me your entire salary so I could manage it myself, and nothing mattered to you. Suddenly you are in charge of all the money. I wanted to buy a plot of land in Carmelia so we would have something to bequeath to the children, and you wouldn't let me. The shops here a filled with things I would love to buy, but you get mad when I walk into the stores. Why did I marry a man like you?"

"Maybe I did you an injustice when I asked you to marry someone like me," he answered earnestly.

During the flight to the USA and throughout their stay there,

Shifra barely spoke. She wanted to know how much Jenka paid for every expensive hotel they stayed at, and her heart sank. She calculated everything she could have bought with the money.

They left for Japan, and there, towards the end of the trip, Jenka finally gave her some money. She bought a pearl necklace, a black mohair sweater, and embroidered handbags for each of her daughters and for herself. When they returned home to Israel, she emptied the suitcase of her few purchases and let go of her frustrations over the money he hadn't given her.

Shifra knew that Jenka had also returned home frustrated, but not because of their arguments. His frustration began when the representative of Rafael in the US held a reception in their honor and invited American Jews from the industry. One of the people, a man in his early forties, approached Jenka and introduced himself as the senior engineer of a large technology company.

The man opened up to Jenka. "I'm a Zionist, and I wish to immigrate to Israel. Can you help me find a job in Israel?"

"Why are you asking me, and not the embassy or the Ministry of Immigration and Integration?"

"I did. All I got was empty promises from Israeli bureaucrats. They want me to immigrate to Israel. But I can't leave my place of work and move my family to Israel without being sure ahead of time that I have a job waiting for me, a career in which I'll be able to contribute significantly to the country."

Shifra noticed Jenka's face become melancholy. "There are many others like me," added that engineer. "I really want to do something for my people in Israel."

As they were getting ready for bed at the hotel, Shifra could see that Jenka was upset. "Do you remember that when World War II ended and I nudged you to return to Israel?" asked Shifra, who had finished brushing her teeth.

"I'll never forget how I met in London with senior officials from the Jewish Settlement, how I showed them what I'd developed in England, and how they disregarded me. Now history is repeating itself with talented Jewish engineers from the United States who want to immigrate to Israel," he said, slipping into his nightshirt. He got into bed and turned off the light. "Maybe I was wrong to return to the country that rejected me." Jenka turned on his side.

"You contributed so much to the country," she told him as she climbed into bed. "I know you're depressed because of the conversation with that engineer."

"He's not the only engineer who approached me saying similar things."

Shifra sighed. "Let's go to sleep," she said, stroking his head.

"If it hadn't been for that meeting with Teddy Kollek in London, I doubt I would've returned to Israel," he whispered.

*

By the mid-1970s, Carmelia had become a sought-after neighborhood to live in, and the surrounding nature of fields and hills metamorphosed into sites of accelerated construction. Only the wadis still retained wild vegetation. Jenka and Shifra sold their house in Carmelia to a contractor who built a condominium there, and in exchange, they received three small apartments in the newly constructed building. Shifra demanded three apartments, but the contractor argued that she didn't deserve that many. So, she persuaded each of the children to chip in some money to give to the contractor. "This is an opportunity," she said, her eyes shining, certain of her path. When one of the children wanted to switch to a bigger apartment, she asked the other two to help in exchange for the promise to help them in the future. Some of them didn't like mixing business with family; they said it was a recipe for conflict. Still, it was impossible to say no to Shifra, and her powers of persuasion prevailed. That was how she finally expanded the family's property. Jenka didn't like it, but he chose not to interfere.

After she purchased the inheritance rights from her sisters, she and Jenka moved into the small, modest one-bedroom apartment where Shifra's father, Zalman, had lived until he passed away. Ruth was married to Reuven Eshel, who was head of the aero-mechanical division at Rafael and supported Ruth's unconventional career as a professional dancer. They had two children together. Michal made a beautiful bride at her wedding to a talented physicist named Danny and the two soon gave birth to a daughter. And Danny, Ruth's younger brother, married Ora, a Yom Kippur war widow who was left with a three-year-old girl and a baby boy born during the war.

After their miserable trip around the world, Jenka came to the conclusion that the only way to atone for his disgraceful behavior towards Shifra over the years was to do everything she asked of him.

"I want to move the wardrobe between the table and the bed," she decided.

So, he took a measuring tape, measured the wardrobe and the space between his desk and the bed, and with the air of an expert ruled, "It won't fit."

"It'll fit. It'll fit. I'll show you." She started backing up into the closet and pushing it with her behind. The wardrobe didn't budge. She pushed with her legs bent and pushed with her legs straight. She tried pushing with her back to the closet and then facing the closet, but it wouldn't move an inch.

"Why aren't you helping?" She turned to him, frustrated, and saw Jenka looking at the closet deep in thought, planning the optimal pushing position and calculating how they should divide the labor of pushing between them.

Finally, as if it were a science experiment, he ordered, "I'll stand here, you stand there. Yes. Like that. Don't move." Then he shouted, "Push! Harder! One more time!"

The wardrobe began to move, groaning and leaving grooves on the floor behind it, but it still wouldn't fit between the table and the bed.

"This is what happens when you think after doing," Jenka complained, exhausted. "Make me my porridge, and I'll go to sleep."

"After you eat your Quaker porridge, we'll push one more time," Shifra answered excitedly and hurried to the kitchen.

She returned with a large bowl full of oatmeal. "I added a spoon of honey and a slice of butter, to give you strength." She watched as he smiled at her, eating heartily. When he was done, they resumed their game of rearranging the furniture.

*

Jenka would drive Shifra to pick up their young grandchildren every morning during the week. She insisted on taking care of them at her house because she knew where everything was. She would bathe them, wash their clothes, and cut their hair so it wouldn't get in their eyes. Jenka would help her. Then, in the afternoon, he would take her to return the squeaky-clean kids. At lunchtime on Fridays, she would invite the children and grandchildren to come and get cakes that she baked for them. She knew that if she didn't tempt them with sweets, they wouldn't come.

They would arrive at the small apartment with their spouses. Shifra would show them the cookies and cakes they were to receive in the cramped kitchen after they ate the meal she'd prepared for them. There was no room in the apartment, so they would eat outside in the hall, sitting on the stairs that led to the apartment. The food was simple and delicious, and Shifra would bustle around the kitchen in constant movement refilling their plates while explaining that this or that dish wasn't as good as last time. When they finished, she packed them all cakes, cookies, and other treats but didn't let them go before they promised they would come again next week when she would bake even tastier cakes.

From time to time, early in the morning on Fridays, Shifra would hurry to buy a newspaper. Excitedly, she'd open the paper to the page of ads posted by immigrants who'd decided to leave Israel and were selling their belongings. She would nudge Jenka to drive her from apartment to apartment, and he'd stand waiting, hidden in a corner, his eyes closed, his heart breaking as he watched Jewish American Zionists leaving the country. But Shifra was happy; she bought blankets and pillowcases, pots and pans, and even games for the grandchildren, never forgetting to make sure that everything was made abroad. Then Jenka would carry it all home. He also lugged crates full of carrots from the busy Talpiot market in Hadar HaCarmel. Cursing, he'd look for parking, choose the freshest carrots, and climb the stairs to the second floor with the heavy crate in his arms as Shifra explained the miraculous medicinal properties of carrot juice.

Chapter 19: The Strikebreaker

Jenka was troubled by the rise of Arab propaganda in the world. He saw their version of the narrative becoming broadly accepted as the truth and watched as Israel became increasingly politically isolated.

In 1961, Adolf Eichmann, the man responsible for sending the Jews of Europe to the death camps by train, was discovered hiding in Argentina. He was smuggled into Israel and brought to trial in Jerusalem. Holocaust survivors took the witness stand and communicated what they had been through for the first time. The entire trial was broadcast on the radio, giving every family in Israel the chance to hear the horrors from firsthand witnesses. The trial also uncovered information they already knew but had perhaps overlooked – the connection between Jerusalem's mufti, Hajj al-Amin, and Eichmann, who'd planned to exterminate the Jewish settlement in the land of Israel together. In June of that year, Jenka wrote a letter to the secretary of the Prime Minister's Cabinet:

1. During Adolf Eichmann's trial, the relationships of Mufti Haj Amin al-Husseini and his entourage (i.e., the Arab Higher Committee) with the accused and other higher-ranking German officials responsible for planning, initiating, and implementing the mass extermination, became apparent. It is regretful that the above points weren't emphasized enough. Eichmann's sentencing may be the last opportunity to highlight the Arab's' guilt.

2. It became clear at the Bandung Conference (held in Indonesia for African and Asian countries) that the very same group of criminals, who call themselves the Arab Higher Committee, continues, even now, to supposedly represent the blameless refugees, and the entire world worries for their safety.

3. I am worried that we aren't taking advantage of the current opportunity to attack Gaza. It seems that instead, we will concede to being accused by the United Nations. And meanwhile, from the UN's point of view, a legitimate stage is gradually being set to justify an Arab military attack on Israel.

Sincerely,

E. Ratner

In October 1973, the Yom Kippur War broke out, catching Israel by surprise. A coalition of Arab states attacked Israel, led by the armies of Egypt, Jordan, and Syria. In the war's early days, it seemed that Israel, nicknamed the Third Temple, was about to fall. But the Israeli Defense Force recovered and turned the tide of battle. Jenka believed that the war was an extraordinary achievement, from a purely military perspective, of course. His reasoning was that Israel suffered a tremendous blow, proportionally to its size, but was able to recover after three days.

He felt that the fact the Arabs had been successful in surprising them was due to internal neglect on Israel's part but didn't blame the late Commander in Chief, David Elazar. He had known the man personally and thought he was a first-class soldier, one of the best in Israel. He recalled the pressure and demand to downsize the army's reserves, reduce the army's budgets, and the faith that everything would be fine. Jenka understood that, as in the past and in the future, the success of the war would be measured internationally according to Israel's political standing, which remained poor.

In the mid-1970s, workers across the country went on strike. The commander of the Air Force somehow obtained a wage hike for his corps, hoping to attract the best and brightest individuals, and the defense industry wanted to follow suit. For the first time in Rafael's history, the company's workers went on strike, demanding an increase in their pay. Although the private sector paid more, they had always been honored to work at Rafael, maintaining the importance of their jobs for the country's defense. They had taken pride in doing quality work that was professionally challenging. They had never cared that the salary was low and the working hours long. On April 25, 1975, the day of the strike, Jenka hung a letter on the dining hall door.

Idolatry in Israel

The outlandish war on the standard of living is cruel because our poor and besieged country is incapable of answering these demands.

The war on the standard of living has become a national sport, a competition in having a talent for extortion. It shall be no surprise when the champions of this "contest" are the very same powerful groups that effortlessly hold the country and the public on a string. The worst part is that the real motive for these despicable wars is not even greed but jealousy that borders on sibling rivalry and is causing internal strife...

The entire nation shall stand united against those who act as fifth columns and servants of the Palestine Liberation Organization.

Those who truly care about defense research will not strike, even if we are deprived. I would like us at Rafael to be viewed as different, for us to join together and break this vicious cycle by volunteering to have our wages reduced. We mustn't blindly follow foolish leaders driving the Israeli public mad. Where is the intelligentsia for whom we request educational compensation and funds for advanced study?

Sincerely,

E. Ratner

Jenka crossed the picket line, went to work, and cautioned that if the strike persisted, the people of Israel would end up scrubbing Arab toilets. He spoke passionately, and the younger generation didn't understand who the strange old man was and what he was talking about. Others, who knew him, were heartbroken by his conduct. He received a letter from the worker's committee: "Due to the seriousness of the act of repeatedly breaking the strike despite receiving a warning, and in the desire to prevent future deviations against the decree, the board has hereby resolved to terminate the strikebreakers from the worker's committee." At the bottom of the letter were the words: "The employees reserve the right to appeal against the board's decision, within two weeks from the date of the decision's publication."

As Jenka read the letter, he became enraged and began composing a reply on the back of the same piece of paper. "It's difficult for me to accept that I, who founded this institute and the field of defense research in Israel on the whole, owe an explanation for my conscientious behavior to those whose 'pre-planning' didn't exist when I began my work in defense."

After he calmed down, he composed an official reply to the committee:

> *I don't care that you threw me out of your committee because I don't think it's suitable for me to be part of a group managed by a strike committee... I am extremely unhappy about the salary increase. I will keep the 850 pounds from the last few months in a separate account, and I won't give it to my family. I will find out if we would've received the money even without the strike, which would deem the money uncorrupted. Still, your strike was disgraceful, unnecessary, and idiotic. If it turns out that the strike really "achieved" something here, I will have to treat the money as a dividend of organized crime... I will deliberate which respectable defense organization to donate it to, and I shall ask everyone conscientious at the institute to follow my lead... Envy consumes us. It will be challenging to turn this extortion contest into a volunteering contest.*

The strike damaged Jenka's health. He began experiencing chest pains.

"What are you fighting for? People want to live better, to have beautiful homes, to enjoy life," Shifra said.

"I'm not against people having better lives. But there's a competition to see who can squeeze more out of the country."

"You shouldn't have agreed to have your salary decreased. You know I save every penny so that our children will have apartments."

"If it were up to me, I would donate all our property to the country."

"You're crazy," said Shifra, but she knew he was capable of doing so, and the fear that he would follow through accompanied her for the following years.

At the Rafael conference in July 1975, just a few months after the strike, the director of Rafael, Ze'ev Bonen, shared that the organization was in danger of laying off multiple employees. He also communicated the fear that those who remained would soon be unemployed, too, because there was no money left to buy their materials. Jenka thought that the employees should give up a little of their salaries to help prevent the impending scandalous situation at the David Institute – the establishment formerly called Institute 3, which had been renamed the following the death of Professor David Bergman. So, he went to Rafael's director and suggested that the management initiate a fundraiser. Ze'ev replied that at a time like this, the public wouldn't look favorably upon such an initiative coming from the management. He instead proposed that Jenka continue the endeavor himself. Therefore, Jenka started a volunteer function and set a personal example, writing accordingly:

Following the Rafael conference, it has become clear that the salary burden on Rafael's budget has put the company at risk of layoffs and hidden unemployment. Therefore, in my opinion, we must form a group of people at the David Institute who are willing to set a personal example by being prepared to work hard and tighten their belts. I, therefore:

a) Agree to work without compensation at least 6 additional hours per week for a period ending on December 31st, 1976.

b) Request that my gross wages be reduced by 15% until the day my employment at Rafael ends.

c) Give up 50% of my advanced study fund.

d) Would like my name to appear in the list of volunteers if it is published.

May this fundraiser be a success,
E. Ratner

He collected 60 signatures, which, according to the administration, were only signed as a personal tribute to Jenka. He kept his promise of setting a personal example. He received a letter from the accounting department explaining that "all the amounts above were deducted from your salary and will be transferred to a special fund. We will inform you separately what the money will be used for. We thank you again for volunteering to contribute."

*

As Jenka grew older, his concern for the country's fate increased, and he decided to put his thoughts into writing. One of his essays dealt with the State of Israel's primary destiny historically, and he divided it into three parts, emphasizing the important words:

> *The Age of the Diaspora*
>
> *This long period was founded on the assumption that Jews are inferior creatures. The Gentiles believed this, and despite being "The Chosen People," the Jews themselves did too. Those without a conscience murdered Jews, those with a limited conscience contented themselves by spitting at them, and those with a fully developed conscience showed signs of affection that were actually based on self-superiority and a hidden contempt for the Jewish people. The Gentiles refused to accept the Jews. Mixed marriages only happened when Gentiles needed Jewish money. Obliterating the Jews was difficult, for they were scattered across the globe. Barred from blending in with their surroundings, the Jewish people remained fortified behind religion and tradition. They continued "living a life of exile" (which is seven times worse than death) for two thousand years.*
>
> *The Primary Historical Purpose of the State of Israel*
>
> *The primary purpose is to eliminate the concept of Diaspora or exile and everything related to it. This goal is being partially achieved already. The establishment of the state of Israel raised*

the position of the Jews on the hierarchical scale significantly. There is no lack of people who hate Israel, but the mockery of Jewish people has ceased. The Christians are willing to accept the Jews both in first-world countries and also in places like the Soviet Union. Those who don't especially hate them treat them as equals and are prepared to marry them – hence a surge in intermarriage has commenced. An unpleasant side effect of acceptance is a rise in hatred on the part of perpetually oppressed minorities.

Accomplishing the Goal

There are 3 perceivable options:

A) Turning back the clock. One way or another, the Arabs will destroy Israel, and the Jews will be sent back into the Diaspora. Exile will start anew not only for the Israeli refugees but for all Jews, since they will fall back down the hierarchical ladder, lose their dignity, and return to what they once were. This is the Arab's dream. We hope this will not transpire, and we must do everything (I repeat ***everything****, with no reservations) to make sure that the Arab's goal does not come to fruition.*

B) We hope for Israel to prosper in peace and for Jews in the Diaspora to continue their dignified existence. It is hard to believe that this can happen simultaneously. If Israel thrives, many of the Jewish people will immigrate to Israel, while the rest will assimilate. The purpose will be fulfilled, the Diaspora will be eliminated, and Israel will continue to exist.

C) There is a possibility that most of the Jews in the Diaspora will assimilate completely. If and when Israel is destroyed by nuclear war (and by its own hands), there will be no descent down the hierarchical ladder, and assimilation in the Diaspora will be complete. The goal will be achieved, and the Diaspora will be eradicated without Israel's existence.

Jenka asked himself many times, "What kind of a people are we?" He always reached the same answer – there is good in us and bad in us. He recalled how he'd arrived in Israel from England, had been pleasantly surprised by the widespread mobilization, and how they had managed to achieve so much with such little means. He thought that his people needed to be careful to avoid their tendency toward sibling rivalry and internal fights between Jews. He believed that the silent majority were good people but indifferent and needed to be motivated to become involved because, deep down, everyone cares. As a military man, he didn't talk about politics even after his release. But once, in a private conversation, he revealed, "I cannot be a right-wing extremist who refuses to give up any territory when our dependence on America increases. Likewise, I cannot be a left-wing extremist because we can't afford to take risks, give up territories and let the enemy front move 'closer to home.'" He believed that if and when Israel became a cohesive and strong nation internally, the two sides would reach a compromise.

*

It was 1979. Ruth returned home exhausted at lunchtime after finishing a dance class and a rehearsal. She climbed the stairs of the condominium building and saw a note in the neighbor's handwriting on the door. "Ruth. Your father has passed away. The children are with me. Go to your parent's' apartment. I'm sorry." She knew that her father sometimes suffered chest pains and had been diagnosed with heart disease. Still, the one who was seriously ill with cancer was actually her mother, who went around dressed in red clothes so that the angel of death would be confused and think that she was a young woman. Ruth couldn't imagine that someone like him could die. He was not an ordinary person who could just die.

He was like the earth, like the cliffs in the Negev desert that remain forever in their place. Ruth sat down on the steps and waited to regain her senses.

When she arrived at her parent's apartment, her mother opened the door. "You Father is lying in his room," she said quietly and went to the kitchen. Ruth entered the bedroom and found him lying on the floor. She closed the door. His assignments for the next day's work were written on the drawing table. Ruth sat down on the floor next to him. He lay on his back, his body relaxed, his brown eyes open, his gaze soft, like a toddler gazing up at his mother whispering to him that when he grows up, he'll be an adventurer and explore foreign countries, while his father stands beside her, his hands in his pockets, smiling at her lovingly, "Do you really think the boy can understand what you are saying?" She caresses the happy toddler, "Look at his big, wise eyes. He understands."

Ruth didn't remember ever seeing her father so relaxed, so at peace with himself. A dull, heavy pain started to fill her chest. She caressed his cheek again and again. She had never caressed or embraced him during his life, nor had he done so to her. She sat beside him in silence for about half an hour, maybe more. Then she got up and went to the kitchen. Her mother stood cooking quietly.

"He came home, went into the room, and fell." Ruth sat down at the small kitchen table. The silence suited them both. It was a holy kind of silence.

"How old was Father?"

"Sixty-nine years old," Shifra whispered.

"Did he say something to you that I don't know about?"

"Of course not. He died."

*

Avraham Levy opened Jenka's safe at Rafael. He found documents from Jenka's time at the British Admiralty, reports made out to Munya Mardor and Shlomo Gur, an emotional letter from Professor Bergman, poems he'd composed, and a document that revealed he'd been entangled in an illicit love affair. Avraham, who'd prided himself on knowing Jenka exceptionally well, was shocked.

In his will, he wrote, "If possible, I wish to be buried on a cliff at the south-eastern end of Shdema's northern post." His friends turned to the Minister of Defense, Ezer Weizman, but he was out of the country, and his deputy didn't know Jenka, who had always been so modest and remained far from the spotlight. So, Jenka was buried in a cemetery in Haifa at the foot of Mount Carmel. Moshe Ritterband, together with the former "Jenka's boys," didn't give up and decided to build a memorial in the place where he'd asked to be buried.

They turned to Moshe Zarhy, the architect who'd worked with Jenka back in the days of the painting studio. Zarhy designed a memorial built like a burial mound with layers upon layers of huge rectangular natural rocks, which he handpicked in the Negev. Each stone weighed five tons. The group loaded the stones onto a truck with a crane, brought them to the site, placed them one on top of the other, and drilled into the stones connecting them with a screw. On the one-year anniversary of Jenka's death, the management of Rafael and the generations of people who'd worked under him gathered in Shdema. Shifra, their children, and their grandchildren were also in attendance.

When the cover was removed from the memorial, a stainless-steel sign was revealed. Engraved upon it were the words "Colonel Evgeni (Jenka) Ratner, 1909-1979. The pioneer of defense research in Israel. He initiated, designed, and developed weapon systems to defend his homeland. A visionary, he loved his people and his country with endless devotion." In the end, it was signed, "Established by his students who followed in his path."

On the lower right-hand corner of the sign was a smaller sign in Jenka's handwriting that read: "It is desirable that the number of participants at my burial from the David Institute not exceed the required quorum of ten men by much, and preferably come to no more than two quorums of ten. I ask that the rest honor my memory with hard work like in the old days."

Chapter 20: Two Epilogues

It was 1990.

"Hello. Am I speaking to Ruth Eshel?" asked an unfamiliar voice on the phone.

"Yes," Ruth replied succinctly.

"I'm an archeology professor at the University of Haifa, and I have a letter for you from a relative in Russia."

"I no longer have family in Russia, as far as I know," answered Ruth, offhand.

"Are you Ruth, daughter of Jenka who immigrated to Israel in 1922 with his grandfather Professor Alexander Ilioff?"

"Yes, that's me," Ruth confirmed and sat down, preparing herself for a long conversation.

"I've just returned from a conference in Europe, and I have a letter from your father's cousin, Professor Pavel Borisovsky, the archaeologist. I met him at conferences in the past several times, and he ignored me... he's an esteemed Russian researcher. To my surprise, this time, he approached me, led me to a side room, and introduced himself as Jenka's cousin. He double-checked that I was from Israel, handed me a letter, and asked me to pass it on to Ruth Ratner, Jenka's eldest daughter."

"You don't say!" Ruth whispered in astonishment before

immediately carrying on in an assertive tone. "Is tomorrow convenient for you to meet?"

Ruth held the large envelope in her hands. Contrary to her custom, she opened it delicately, taking care not to rip the envelope. Inside were two letters, written in the clear calligraphic handwriting that had been taught in the era before computers and keyboards took over. There was also a big photograph. The year 1893 was written by hand on the admirably preserved black-and-white picture. The Stanislavski family materialized before her; four generations gathered in Ekaterinoslav, some sitting on chairs, others standing, children held in their parent's arms or sitting on the floor at their parent's feet. Tears of excitement welled up in Ruth's eyes as the characters from Clara's stories about her joyful years in Ekaterinoslav came to life on the page. A living testimony of a world that once was but now no longer exists.

In the center of the photo sat Ruth's great-great-great-great-grandmother and grandfather, Isaac Stanislavski, a wealthy merchant who received a badge of philanthropy from Czar Alexander II. Next to him were his son Moshe and his wife Rachel, surrounded by their children with their spouses, including Clara and Professor Ilioff beside her. In their arms, they held Daniel and Yasha, dressed in identical sailor's outfits. Anna, their eldest daughter, who would later become Jenka's mother, sat on the floor by the feet of her great-great-grandfather, a beautiful girl with a long braid. Ruth set the photograph on a table. She inhaled deeply, understanding how meaningful the picture was.

She read Borisovsky's accompanying letter over and over. He noted the names of those photographed and elaborated on their occupations and where they fit in the family tree. Most of the men were doctors and engineers. All of them sat upright but relaxed, the posture of self-respecting, educated, liberal, prosperous Russian patriots. How could anyone foresee that a few years later, the family would fall after the Bolshevik storming of the Winter Palace, which collapsed the foundations of the very society in which they lived? How could they imagine that they would be persecuted and have their vast property confiscated? How could they, in their wildest dreams, conceive that just a few short years later, the skies of Europe would be darkened by the cloud of Nazism, and that in 1941, Clara's brother Viktor, his wife, and their son would be massacred in the Babi Yar death pit near Kiev? And that grandmother Reisel, her daughter Isley, and her two granddaughters would also be thrown into the same terrible ravine, along with the thousands of dead and the wounded struggling to breathe? Ruth shut her eyes in horror. Then she examined the faces of her murdered relatives again. The rest of the family scattered throughout Russia. Some of them disappeared, and others died in the 1950s. Who could have predicted that 97 years later, the photograph would be sitting on her desk in Carmelia?

There was another letter from Professor Borisovsky in the envelope. He wrote that he only had a few months left to live. He'd led a good life full of research. He wasn't afraid to die. He had one daughter named Sofia, a curator at the Hermitage Museum in St. Petersburg. Sofia had one son, named Yosef, his only grandson, who was about to graduate high school. He explained that his grandson dreamed of one day immigrating to Israel and asked that when Yosef arrived, Ruth and her family would help him and adopt him into their hearts.

Ruth hastened to send money to Sofia so that she could buy plane tickets for her and Yosef to come to Israel. Sofia's answer wasn't long in coming. She sent Ruth a thank you note for the money and a gift of two lovely scarves. She wrote, "No, we won't come to Israel. You must understand. Yosef is my only son, and if we travel to Israel, he'll want to stay. I have an interesting job at the Hermitage and high standing in society. What will I do in Israel? Israel is flooded with Russian immigrants." Ruth's good intentions to take in Yosef wilted.

In another letter, Sofia shared that Yosef wants to be an engineer. So, Ruth wrote that he should come to Israel and study at the Technion to make his transition smoother. Then came a letter in which Sofia wrote that her father had passed away and that Yosef had been accepted to a prestigious technical university in Russia where he would study to be an engineer. This was the last letter that came from her. Ruth supposed that there was a possibility Sofia hadn't told Yosef about their correspondence at all so that she wouldn't have to deal with him pressuring her to immigrate to Israel.

***

It is 2022 at the Shdema testing site in the Negev Desert. A young man inserted a key into the rusty lock in the gate of the fence between the Shdema camp station and the cliff at the site's south-eastern end. An elderly woman stood next to him, speaking quickly. It was clear that she was excited.

"I'm glad to see that they didn't destroy the memorial. In our country, historical structures are demolished to clear lots for new real estate." The guard nodded his head in consensus.

"I remember this place when none of these buildings existed," she said. "They would set up a few tents here every time they held tests. I came with my father several times. I loved coming here. I remember that once at lunch, they served me chicken soup, and I saw a fly floating in it. Someone took the fly out, but I refused to eat the soup, or maybe, I ate it anyway. I don't remember."

"How old were you?"

"I was a girl of about ten or twelve years old then, and now I am almost eighty years old," she chuckled, surveying the extensive gravel-covered surface at the center of which stood the memorial. She continued speaking excitedly, "The area is clean. There are no wrappers, cans, or other waste you usually see at sites where Israelis like to visit."

"It's no wonder. Hardly anyone goes in there," said the young guard. "Bear with me here. Everything is rusty, the key won't turn, but I'm stubborn. I'll get it ."

"People aren't curious to go in and see? It's a spectacularly beautiful lookout point, too."

"People who come to Shdema like to take a tour around the station, and when they get to the fence, they're surprised to see a burial mound and want to go in, but the gate is locked," the young man explained.

"Why do you lock it?"

"For security reasons. Some of them ask how to get in. We explain that they need to go to the Chief Security Officer's office, get the key and then return it when they're done. Most remain content to see the memorial from afar and wonder why it was built."

"It was built in Jenka's memory."

"That's the first time I've heard the name," he said, pushing the gate open.

Despite her age, she paced towards the memorial with broad steps. Unable to hold back, she burst into tears. When she reached it, she placed her hand on one of the stones as if it were a gravestone. It crossed her mind that she never cried when her father died nor when her mother passed away. There was something freeing in the tears that erupted from deep inside her. She moved her hands over the stones and the stainless-steel plaque with the request, carved in his handwriting, "I ask that you honor my memory with hard work like in the old days." Ruth's heart ached. About his life that had been and was no more. For not hugging him, not telling him how much she loved him. Then she stood on the edge of the cliff and gazed at the expanses of desert land spread out before her, and it seemed to her that she could hear the sound of an eagle's wings.

People who visit the site say that sometimes a giant eagle glides above the memorial, flies higher up, and continues to circle the expanses below...

1927, Jenka overlooking a cliff in the Negev Desert

A map of Jenka's two major motorcycle expeditions (1933, and in 1935 marked by the dotted line), as published in *Davar* newspaper on 2.4. 1935.

1935, Sudan, Jenka carries Vefka on his shoulders

1938, Jenka instructs a pilot at the Aviron Aviation School

1946, Jenka and Ruth in Portsmouth, England

1958, Receiving the Israel Defense Prize together with Michael Shor of Military Industries. From left to right: Michael Shor, Prime Minister David Ben-Gurion, IDF Chief of Staff Lt. Gen. Haim Laskov, and Jenka

1962, David Ben-Gurion, left, visits Rafael. From left: A security officer, Defense Ministry Director-General Shimon Peres, Rafael General Manager Munya Mardor, and Jenka

1970, Jenka at "Shdema," Rafael's official testing range in the Negev Desert

1978, Jenka and Shifra on Mount Hermon

Jenka's memorial, unveiled at "Shdema" on the one-year anniversary of his death, designed by architect Moshe Zarhy

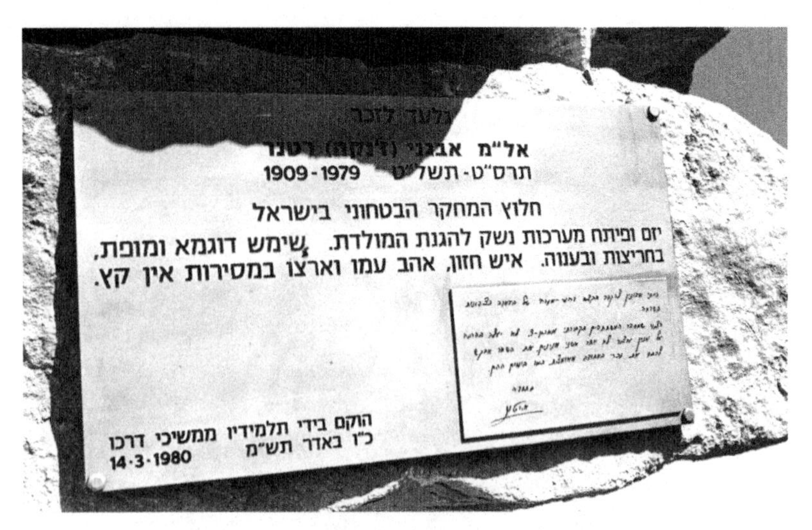

Engraving on Jenka's memorial

1979, Jenka's will and testament to the people of Rafael, in his own handwriting, on the memorial at "Shdema"

Printed in Great Britain
by Amazon